Praise for the Author

"Healy has a knack with writing scenes that are playful, with banter aplenty, but that still manage to subvert and leave you heartbroken in the same breath...a joy to read." — *Eliza Chan, Sunday Times bestselling author of Fathomfolk and Tideborn*

"Steeped in Irish folklore and mythology, Healy's tale grabs readers by the hand, guiding them on a journey filled with delicious, gut-wrenching twists and turns…an excellent read." — *Library Journal*

"The worldbuilding is fun and keeps the pages turning…Healy should win some fans with this one." — *Publisher's Weekly*

" An impressive feat of worldbuilding full of unexpected twists for fans of monstrous women." — *Kirkus Reviews*

"A sweeping romantic fantasy drenched in Irish lore and mythology…readers will delight in Healy's world of dark legends and hard-won romance." — *Shelf Awareness*

"Enchanting, complex, and romantic." — *Winter Is Coming (Fan-sided)*

Content Warnings

Dedication

For my children, so that they remember that my love for them, unlike my patience, is never-ending.

Because I love you, have loved you and will love you
— always —
to the ending of this and all worlds.

UNSEEN

CHRISTY HEALY

Table of Contents

N
W
E
S
Inis Trá Tholl
Dúnalderagh
Grianán Ailigh
NORTHERN UÍNÉILL
Ard an Rátha
Maghera
Latharna
Dubhais
Lough Neagh
ULAID
Cnoc na Loinge
Sliabh Gamh
Bréifne
AIRGIALLA
Lough Conn
CONNACHT
SOUTHERN UÍNÉILL
Mhám Toirc
Beanna Beola
Tír Sogháin
Brug na Boinne
Vale of Inagh
Tír Sogháin
LAIGIN
SEA OF EIREANN
Osraige
MUNSTER
Guagán Barra
ÉIRE

PART I

It was the eve of Samhain, the festival that heralded in the new winter season, the night sacred to all dead and dying things, when Jack, the High Prince of Éire, slipped out of his father's castle under the corpse-white light of the moon to hunt, his breath puffing soundlessly before him in the frigid autumn air.

Excerpt from 'The Snow, The Crow, & The Blood'

Chapter One
Grafadh Mór, Éire, 1082

CONOR

Between the howl of the wind outside his cottage and the terrified yelps of his dog, Conor barely heard the knock of death at his door.

Truth be told, it was a miracle that he heard it at all, a knock too soft for a true emergency. He ignored it, too busy persuading Oscar to quiet down – for the gods' sakes, it was only a bit of rain, an almost daily occurrence, as any creature born and bred in Éire should know – and then getting well and thoroughly mangled with drink.

It had been a long week, filled with far too many failures and heartaches. A lost babe, born too early, silent and blue-lipped when he'd at last delivered him into his mother's arms. A blacksmith's arm that he could not save, the infection set too deep in his blood. A springtime cough that had spread through the village, leaving old and young alike wheezing, half-wild with delirium. Now he was at last alone in his cottage on the outskirts of town, and the rain and the wind had seemed like a sign, an unmistakable omen, that he should at last crack open the seal of the bottle of rye-whiskey that had been sitting for far too long on his shelf and drink every last drop.

But Oscar was wailing, the late spring storm showing no signs of abating, and someone was here, rapping on his door. Perhaps an anxious, first-time father needing herbs to soothe his wife's aches or his newborn's wails, or a farmer with a sick ewe, or a dozen other scenarios of villagers seeking the help which usually Conor loved to give. But tonight, he wished, for once, to be left alone; to be needed by no one, free to drink himself into oblivion and forget for a night his own sorrow, his own scars. For once, he wanted to sink beneath the waves of good whiskey into mindless oblivion, all those griefs locked away in the drink-addled corners of his mind.

The knocking grew louder, more impatient, and he swore. "Give me a damn minute," he yelled, then wrapped his fingers in Oscar's wiry fur, tugging him out from underneath the table. "Come on now, love. It's just a spot of rain. You're all right." The dog buried his head into the crook of Conor's arm and whined, curled up into a quaking ball of terror. "Chin up," Conor muttered as he scratched at his quivering ears. "Could be a man-eating beast outside the door that I'll need you to be protecting me from."

Oscar whimpered, burrowing his nose further into Conor's arm, and the knock on his door turned into a strident boom, demanding acknowledgement. "It's open," Conor called, resigned to his fate. "Come in already."

He turned toward the hearth and kicked at the half-burnt logs in the fire with his boot, an explosion of sparks fizzling through the air. The door creaked behind him, letting in a gust of the cool night breeze soaked with rain, and the hair on the back of his neck prickled, not from the cold, but with a too-familiar awareness.

He spun around, his dog still clutched to his chest, to where she stood in the doorway, hood pulled low over her face. "Well," he said, because what else was there to say, after so many years of silence. "I feel a bit guilty now, yelling at Oscar for making such a fuss. I don't blame him for yowling, knowing that you were nearby."

"You have a dog now? How fitting. Mongrels and their fleas must stick together, I suppose."

It was surreal, standing here now, face to face with the object of his most sinister nightmares and darkest, most delicious fantasies combined. "What do you want?"

"Now, cabbage," she said, running a gloved finger along the door frame. "Do be kind. I'm feeling rather emotionally fragile these days."

"I doubt that very much."

Her gaze ran up and down the length of his frame, cool and assessing as ever. "You've gotten old. There's a bit of gray showing in those red curls."

She hadn't, Conor thought grimly. A pretty doe with the eyes of a serpent, a girl who had long ago been touched by the gilded hand of eternal youth — or a demon. "At least I'm honest," he said. "I look like what I really am – unlike you."

"You used to say that I looked like a wildflower blooming in the spring."

"I used to say a lot of things about you. Now I know better."

She laughed, that same silver-chimed laugh from their youth. "You won't believe me, but I really have rather missed you." She raised an eyebrow. "Have you missed me?"

He should put the dog down. He must look ridiculous, snuggling the terrier against his chest while they sniped at each other. She was regal as always, and he was covered in dog hair with dirt under his fingernails. It had always been this way, him clawing his way up the unscalable mountain of deserving her, while she lounged at its peak, laughing as he thrashed about in the mud.

A lightning-bolt of defiance shot through him, and he clutched at the snoring Oscar more tightly. "I know why you're here, Ria, and the answer is no."

She stepped forward, letting the door snick shut behind her. "Oh? What is it that you think that I want, cabbage?"

"My name is Conor," he said, and immediately felt nine years old and unconscionably stupid all over again.

Underneath the shadow of her hood, her blood-red lips curved. "Conor Eoghan Ó Ruairc, son of Cormac, the erstwhile chief of Breifne. I remember."

"If you can recite all that so easily, then you should be able to recall what I said to you the last time that we spoke."

She ran her gloved hands down the front of her fur-lined cloak, smoothing away invisible wrinkles, and it hit him.

She was nervous.

His heart thudded even harder at the revelation, because if she, of all people, was anxious about how this conversation would go, then it did not bode well for him. "I remember," she said again, her voice steady. "You told me that I would never see either of you again." Her hood slipped back, her loose locks tumbling over her shoulders. "And yet here we are."

"It's only me here." He jerked his chin toward the vacant room to the left, a half-made cot and a wooden chair piled high with unwashed clothes. "See for yourself."

"No need." She pulled off her gloves, one at a time, delicate and deliberate, and his gaze latched onto the sight of the linen bandages wrapped around her palms, stained with dried blood. "I didn't imagine you to be as much of a fool as that, to keep her here in the same house as you." She undid the silver brooch fastening the neckline of her cloak, tossing it aside, her rose-colored gown shimmering in the firelight from the hearth. So lovely, Conor thought with a pang, standing there clad in her pink silk with her porcelain skin and sleek hair, like the delicate-stemmed blossom he'd once imagined her to be. She was anything but soft then, long before she had become this obsidian-souled creature of immovable darkness.

The servant of the lord of death.

The words forced themselves into his consciousness against his will, like a midnight outlaw shoving its shoulder against a half-closed door and slamming it open, its hinges snapping from the force of the exertion.

"But she must be close by," she continued, tucking her clasped hands behind her. "I do know you, after all – no matter how much time has passed, I *know* you, and you would not let her go very far."

"You're wrong," he lied, and Oscar fidgeted in his arms at the bite in his voice. "I knew you'd come looking for her eventually, so I sent her halfway across the realm years ago. She's long gone, far out of your reach."

Her eyes narrowed, and before he could stop himself, he stepped back, toward the hearth-fire and the iron poker leaning next to it. She looked at it, then back at him, smiling. "Go on," she said. "Try it. But we both know that you don't stand a chance."

Conor crouched down to the floor and slid Oscar onto his pillow-bed by the fire, then straightened, his arms folded against his chest. "I'm not going to fight you. I know there's no point, as do you." For a brief moment, their gazes met, and his heart seized in his chest with a half-forgotten longing, that decades-old ache throbbing anew. "So get on with it. Do what it is that you came here to do, Ria, but you will not break me."

"Oh, Conor." She stepped closer, cupping his cheek in the palm of her bandaged hand, and he froze. "That is exactly what I intend to do."

He jerked away, stumbling into the stone wall behind him. Her blue eyes flared like dying stars in front of him as she snapped her fingers and spoke, rough and growling as the hungry mother bear after months of sleep in a pine-needle bed burrowed deep into the granite-cool caves of the earth, and in answer, his legs buckled underneath him, an unnatural shredding of the bones underneath his skin. Conor screamed once, collapsing onto the floor in front of the hearth, his fingers spasming as hot beads of sweat flowed down his back.

His legs, he thought dimly through the roaring in his ears. His legs were broken.

"They snapped rather easily, your bones." It was lyrical and low again, her voice, as she spoke above where he lay writhing on the floor. "Someone once told me that means you should be eating more kale."

Distantly, he heard Oscar snarl, infuriated by the sounds of his master's pain, and from the corner of his eye, he saw her turn toward his dog. "Don't –" he managed to gasp. "Don't hurt him."

"Don't worry," he heard her say. "I won't harm your friend. Even I have my standards of decency." A rustling sound, and he smelled it then, that barely-there scent of silverweed and clover as she knelt, running her fingers through his hair. "It's meant to be a healing spell, you know – it mends bones far more effectively than you do – but I tweaked it a bit." He tensed as her idle fingers played with his curls. "*He* used it on me once, to heal me, when I broke my arm. He's not all bad, you know." Conor twisted away as her nails scraped along his scalp. "Where is she, Conor? Tell me, and this all stops."

"I won't," he choked out, vision blurring and head throbbing, a mirror image to the first day that he had seen her, loved her, all those years ago. "I don't care what you do. I won't tell you."

She withdrew her hand, and he closed his eyes, bracing himself once more.

The joints of his fingers in his right hand shivered once when she spoke again, guttural and raw, then snapped, thin white bones puncturing through his calloused skin, and he screamed, high-pitched and wordless, a keening sound of agony. The hem of her rose-silk brushed across his sweat-soaked face as he convulsed, his hands and legs burning with the relentless force of a thousand fires, and dimly, he heard her pacing across the floor, prowling around him, a wildcat toying with its wounded prey right before it devoured it, still aware and alive.

"Just tell me, Conor," she said, as inevitable as the death-lord whom she served. "I want this to end as much as you do."

He doubted that. He was being ripped apart by a dozen fire-toothed beasts, their white-tipped fangs tearing into his flesh, mangling his very bones.

But he would not relent.

A shadow fell across him, and he opened his burning eyes to see her standing in front of the fire, her unnaturally youthful face drawn into cold and merciless lines. "Tell me," Riona said again, "what you've done with my daughter."

Jack had not gone far
when he looked up into
the branches of a
whitethorn tree, and saw
there a raven, black-
winged and bright-eyed,
watching him.

Excerpt from 'The Snow, The
Crow, & The Blood'

Chapter Two
The Vale of Inagh, Éire, 1073

RIONA

Riona stood before the unearthly swell of the ground before her, teetering on the edge of a precipice from which there was no return.

There were many such mounds throughout all of Éire, the sídhe-realms, buried both beneath its earth and scattered across its sea, all of them neither of this world nor apart from it, but few were quite as fearful as the one before her — the hidden kingdom of unrelenting darkness. Only a fool would enter such a place willingly, and while Riona was many things, a fool was not one of them.

But she had no choice.

If only she was wearing boots, Riona thought, rather than these soft-soled slippers, now torn and tattered from her long climb through the briars and rocks of the mountain. Not that she had known she would be making said climb when she had first slipped them on that morning.

Also, leather boots would have been a sartorial abomination if paired with her dainty blue gown. If she *were* meant to die today, she'd feel better, knowing that she would leave behind a corpse with the proper footwear.

Enough dillydallying.

Riona exhaled slowly, then with a few quick, deliberate steps, climbed atop the grassy knoll before her, staring up at the flat gray rock now looming above her. She reached out with a tentative finger, tracing the names of the scars written on her heart, each an invisible talisman to protect her against the evil soon to come, to guard her as she did what only she could do.

Da, first, then Cian and Aaden, one after another, no pause between their names, a mournful recreation of that staccato bursts of hurts from so long ago. Aisling and Sean, Killian and Maeve. Her grandmother, of course, the infamous queen of the vale of Inagh — Mamó, with the warm strength of her wrinkled hands and the gentleness in her green-gray eyes.

And Daideo.

Her breath caught as she traced the letters of that final name, the missing of her grandfather like a vise around her heart. For a moment, she forgot the menace of the hidden realm that lay before her, so poignant was the wave of grief passing through her that it seemed newborn, not the dull aching of a wound several years old.

What would he say, if he were here now? How disappointed he would be, seeing her break the final promise which she had ever made him. For a moment, in spite of everything she stood to lose, her resolution wavered.

From deep within the rock, she heard the faint purr of a velvet-lined voice, whispering her name, an unmistakable warning, and she snatched her hand away, heart shuddering in her chest.

She could not afford such weakness. Not now.

Riona removed the hunting knife from the sheath at her side. She pressed the blade against her forearm, dragging it down, a shallow wound, but enough. Once before, she had used her palm. It had taken weeks to heal, that wound, the tentative scabs ripping open every time she flexed her hand or picked up a dinner fork.

It was not the worst mistake which she had made that day, and she had learned much since then.

Riona swallowed once, gathering her courage, then pressed her arm against the looming boulder before her, her blood dripping onto the rock. Her heart shuddered in her chest at the glimmer of a few silver drops mingling among the red, glistening in the moonlight.

There it was, the proof of her birthright — the last remaining grandchild of the lost gods of Éire.

He would know she was here now, and surely, he would come.

The boulder shuddered once, then split down the middle, a yawning crevice in the center of the rock, beckoning her forth.

She forced herself to take a step, into the opening before her. An unnatural hush thundered in her ears, and the shadowy curtain of the trees disappeared behind her as she stumbled forward, hands outstretched as she groped the nothingness of ice-cold air. Then the darkness lifted, and she blinked at the trees which again surrounded her, the same as before, but frost-kissed and barren now, robbed of their spring-bright greenery. Vaguely, as though from a great distance, she felt the torn skin of her forearm knit together, a seamless restitching, as though no harm had ever come to it.

It was not at all reassuring, the unnatural healing of that wound – only further proof that she did not belong within this unearthly cluster of trees. Mortals were not meant to enter here, to witness the secrets hidden within the darkness, and she could almost hear the forest around her holding its breath, waiting to see what would happen next.

When nothing did, the thornwood around her loosed its breath in a rush of wind, its midnight shadows deepening into an otherworldly darkness, unbroken by any errant beams of moonlight. Riona clenched her jaw, venturing deeper into the watchful forest.

It *was* watching her, she thought with a shudder, whatever hidden entities lurked in the shadows and the trees alike – twisted, ageless trunks of rowan and yew and ash. She was no longer in the mortal realm, where trees were incognizant and the creatures living within them timid and shy. This was the sídhe, the home of the descendants of the Tuatha Dé Danann, her long lost ancestors, and she was at their mercy.

Riona had walked among the sun-dappled wooded glens that surrounded her vale ever since she was a babe, knew the scent of moss and cowslip as intimately as the lavender smell of her grandmother's tea – had spent her days among the oak and the pine, had lived her life in rhythm with the An Eidhneach rumbling over lichen-licked rocks. She had always been at home among the trees, wandering through the crimson-gold autumn woods as the cool rain seeped through the canopy of wood and vine and sky, and she had never once feared them.

Then again, she had never known the prescient, silent watching of trees like these, had never wandered through woods filled with such dark and ungodly threats.

A high-pitched scream pierced the gloom, reed-thin and wailing. An owl, but not the soft brown-and-gray birds that hooted sleepily behind the castle in the vale, but a midnight-black creature with a demonic voice. It scrabbled along an ice-coated branch above her, its claws clicking menacingly along the half-frozen wood, and cocked its head at an unnatural angle as she passed beneath it.

She refused to shiver. Too many eyes were upon her, whether she could see them or not.

All at once, the hum of watchfulness from the midnight forest died away, and a preternatural hush came creeping into its place, like the few tendrils of wisp-gray smoke spiraling lazily from a new-lit chimney. Riona's spine prickled, her bravado slipping away as she remembered anew how helpless, how alone she was, save for the faceless entity even now making its way toward her.

Stalking her.

A low growl rippled through the air behind her.

Riona whipped around, palms damp. It was a lynx, she tried to reassure herself over the pounding of her heart. An ordinary, run-of-the-mill lynx, and even if not — well. She was a child of the gods, after all. It was her right to be here. There was no reason for her to cower in fear.

Another growl, and the frost-laden branches creaked with an ominous force, and oh gods, it was coming from above her, from the hidden shadows of the trees, whatever unnatural beast hunted her in the darkness. She stumbled backward, head tilted back as she squinted through the gloom –

There, gleaming in the dark, two brilliant yellow eyes staring out at her from a hulking, shapeless form. Then the *thing* in the trees slinked forward along the gnarled branches of a yew tree. Riona's mouth fell open in a silent scream as she saw it.

This was no lynx, this obsidian-black, mammoth feline with the diamond-shaped head, its chest emblazoned with a gleaming white star, fangs glistening, razor-like claws digging into the tree branch, its unnatural gaze fixed on her face.

For the briefest moment, she was a child again, listening to her grandfather's stories by the hearth-fire, her arms wrapped around her knees. "Mamó was truly a beast?" She had asked, and he'd smiled.

"Sure, now," he had said, his attention flickering to where her grandmother was curled on the couch, pretending to read as she listened to their conversation, a faint shadow-smile curving over her lips. "What a fearsome thing you were, were you not, Rozlyn Ó Conchúir – both beautiful and terrible, a rival to the gods themselves."

She understood now what he had meant, as this creature snarled at her from the trees, horrific yet stunningly magnificent, vibrating with strength and unimagined grandeur.

This – this was what it meant to be descended from a god, not a few meager drops of silver blood.

Riona abandoned all pretenses of bravery and ran for her life.

She could hear it crashing through the branches behind her, ripping up the saplings by their very roots, leaping from limb to limb as its reverberating scream sent uncontrollable shudders through her. It was hunting her, just as the barn cats she had seen do to the mice in the stables, and her legs shook so badly that it was only the primal fear of death that kept her going, gown caught up in her hands as she stumbled over the twisted roots, gasping at the sound of its fangs snapping through above her. She glanced back, and those unnatural yellow eyes shimmered above her, behind her – too close, too *fast* – and then there was something hard and rough and unmovable in front of her, sending her reeling, back toward whatever awful creature hunted her in the darkness. *A tree*, she thought dully as she fell, and then there was nothing but an explosion of pain, her forearm snapping with a brutal crack as she landed on the winter-hardened earth, her crimson-silver blood spraying across the ground around her.

From far above her, the sídhe-beast leapt, improbably graceful, landing on the forest floor a stone's throw from her. It cocked its pointy-eared head and studied her, its jowls parting in what she could have sworn was a grin as it stalked toward her on those catlike paws, weaving its way through the frost-bitten leaves with deliberate, hungry steps.

Through the pain rippling in blinding waves down her broken arm, it came to her in a wild rush, a truth she could not deny.

She was going to die here.

Sweat poured down her face, the salty tang mingling with the blood and dirt in her mouth, as she clutched at her shattered arm, bracing herself for death while the monster gathered itself to rush toward her, its purr of malevolent pleasure reverberating in the air around her.

She thought of Haisley, of Conor, sending a silent apology out into the void, for all the myriad of ways that she had failed them both, waiting for the sting of death and the sweet nothingness of oblivion that followed –

"Now, Fiadh," scolded an inscrutable, whisper-soft voice behind her. "What have I told you about eating whatever trash you find lying about in the dirt?"

Riona's breath whooshed out in a stuttered rush as the demon-cat sat back on its haunches, licking at its whiskers with a pale pink tongue.

"Although I suppose she would deserve it," the voice continued, closer now. "What a fool, to believe that a few scraps of half-faded folaíocht could protect her from *you*, dear one."

Riona jerked around, peering into the gloom to catch a glimpse of her unlikely savior. Almost as if he had heard her unspoken request, the darkness suddenly dissolved around her, and the woods exploded in a bright burst of a thousand stars, shrouding the land of the dead with a luminous grace.

She gasped.

There he was, perched on a nearby rock, one velvet-clad leg crossed over the other, his booted foot swinging through the air, black-and-gold eyes glinting at her with an unfathomable expression.

"Well hello there," he said. "You've made quite the mess of your gown, haven't you? A pity. I was rather partial to that color on you." His gaze dropped to the torn fabric of her bodice. "Although I can't complain about the view."

It was asinine to antagonize such a being – especially considering she had come here specifically to win his goodwill – but two-and-twenty years of obstinacy was not a thing so easily dismissed. "Some prince you are," she managed to hiss through chattering teeth. "Shaming a lady – a *queen* – in such a way."

He smiled, slow and gentle, and yet inexplicably, at the sight of it, terror rose within her, wrapping its icy fingers around her throat. "There are no ladies here," he said. "No queens or kings – only a lord and his servants." She swallowed thickly, trembling fingers digging into the frost-covered ground beneath her, and his smile sharpened, widened. "That *is* why you have come to me at last, isn't it? After all these years."

Riona dragged herself to her feet, the pain from her broken arm coursing through her in waves, but she refused to kneel in the dirt before him, this incarnation of evil itself. She would stand tall and straight-backed, as befitted a queen, when she begged for a life far more precious than her own. "Yes," she said, as steadily as she could, watching both him and the cat-like creature prowling around her on its soft, deadly paws, unsure who posed the greater threat. "I've come, as you wanted."

That golden light flared, drowning the darkness in his gaze. "For what purpose?"

For a moment, she stood frozen, the terrible weight of the words she was about to speak numbing her tongue, seizing her throat. He seemed to recognize it, the terror that had resurged within her and dug its talons into her skin, the remembering of all that she would soon be sacrificing, and his lips curved again, an inscrutable amusement.

As though *she* amused him.

"Yes," he said, "I do intend to force you to say it."

She did not want to amuse him. She wanted – she *needed* – to astound him.

Riona threw back her head as the catlike monster yowled once from behind its master, ears pricked and teeth flashing in the starlight. "I've come to serve you," she said. "The lord of death."

Never harm a raven,
Jack's father had warned
him long ago, for they
were greatly beloved by
the most dread goddess of
the Tuatha Dé Dannan.

The Mórrígan.

*Excerpt from 'The Snow, The
Crow, & The Blood'*

Chapter Three
The Vale of Inagh, Éire, 1059

RIONA

It was nearly dawn, and Riona knew – as surely as she knew the sun would soon rise over the trees in the east, as it had every day in her six years of life – that her brother was dying.

She sat by the window, arms wrapped around her knees, staring out at the gray sky, the far-off thunder clouds threatening an early morning rain. A suitable dawn for the sleepless night before, with her mother and grandparents closeted away in her brother's room as she waited outside in the hall, her cheek pressed against the doorframe.

Sean had been sick for a long while, plagued by a stubborn, deep-chested cough that would ease for a few weeks only to come roaring back. It was worse this time, a new kind of tension vibrating in the air as her mother sat by his bed; as Mamó applied poultices and brewed teas, her fingers trembling with desperation; as her grandfather paced the halls, the lines around his silver temples more grief-worn than ever before. No one dared to say it, but she knew – the days of her brother's riding lessons and whispered bedtime stories by the fire were gone forever.

A soft snore behind her, and Riona peeked over her shoulder to where Maeve slept in her bed, listening to the sound of her untroubled breathing, a balm to the nagging fear that gripped her soul.

Sometimes, in the vague, imprecise way that children do, Riona imagined that Death itself was alive, a monstrous being who lurked in the shadows of her young and fragile life, chasing her, an immortal bully who for some inexplicable reason had set its sights on her and her alone. After all, it had been an ever-present entity in her brief life, death had – relentlessly stalking those she loved throughout her short life. First, it took her father and older brothers on some distant battlefield, perishing on the swords of faceless, far-off enemies. Then, a few months afterward, her beloved nurse-maid, Aisling – and Maeve's mother – slipping away into the night, her face drawn stiff and cold when Riona had crept to her bedside at the dawn's first light. Even now, Riona's eyes prickled with the sting of tears as the memories flowed through her, blurry and faded to monochromatic gray – her father, tapping at her small wooden sword with his steel one, laughing at her toddling attempts at spars and thrusts; Cian and Aaden, each of her tiny hands clasped in their hefty ones, swinging her between them; Aisling, who loved her as well as she loved her own daughter, with her big-bellied laugh and her hugs that always smelled of flour and basil.

Something whispered to her, in the deep parts of the night, that it was because of *her* that they had died, that her old enemy, Death, swooped in and stole them away solely because she had dared to love them, and now – now it had come for Sean, her last remaining brother.

In the clear, fancy-free light of the dawn, she shook away the idea. It was coincidence, these accidents of tragedy, pure chance that her life was so flooded with loss and grief.

And yet the fact remained. Sean – her protector, her teacher, her dearest brother – Sean was very sick.

A quiet sob escaped her.

Behind her, the door eased open, and she turned her face away, pressing her red-tinged nose against the window to hide her tears, furious with herself. Mamaí would not want to see her cry.

"It's all right," her grandfather said from the doorway "It's only me."

Riona peeked over her shoulder. He was leaning against the doorframe, looking far more haggard and gray than he had the day before. "Sean?"

Daideo sighed as he walked over to where she sat huddled on her window-seat, sinking down next to her and resting his silver head in his blue-veined hands. "You should prepare yourself, Ria. Your grandmother believes that it is only a matter of time."

Her lips trembled. "Mamaí – is she all right?"

"No, little queen." He was quiet for a moment. "I know that you and she do not always see eye to eye but be patient with your mother. She has lost so much in such a short time."

A twinge of annoyance pinged in Riona's chest, so she turned away again to stare out her window across the storm-gray skyline. "So have I," she said. "So have you, and so has Mamó. She is not the only one who —"

"I know, child. But your mother mourns in her own way, as do we all." He rubbed her shoulder, gentle and soothing. "I know it seems like there is no light to be found on the horizon, but you are young. You will learn soon enough that even the darkest days have their endings."

"Yes, and then it's the night, and everything is still dark."

Daideo shook his head. "Och, but sometimes that light is the most hopeful of all – the glow of the moon and the beauty of the stars.

Just because something is dark doesn't mean it must be feared."

"Is that what death is like? Darkness and stars?"

"I don't know, little queen. I have never died." He leaned his head back against the window. "I have heard stories, though."

"Like what?"

"Such stories are not for you, Ria, at least not now. Another time, when you're older."

She peeked up at him, his blue eyes the twin, she knew, of her own. "Please, Daideo. I want to know – what they saw, what they felt, where they go."

He did not answer, and after a beat or two, she stifled a sigh and buried her face in the crook of his arm, fighting back tears of disappointment and longing. Perhaps if she knew the truth of it all, then perhaps she could silence that nagging tug of guilt that had whispered to her for so long.

Then Daideo's arms were pulling her onto his lap, and she twisted around to see a faint smile tugging at the edge of his lips. "All right. One story." She grinned up at him, bouncing up and down in excitement, and he winced. "You have grown too big for this."

"Tell me, tell me, tell me –"

"Easy, settle down now, and listen." Riona settled her chin against his shoulder, and he smiled again, wider this time, some of the grief and exhaustion of his face easing. Her mother had always grumbled that she was undeniably her grandfather's favorite, but Riona didn't care. She was, as everyone knew, his little queen.

She loved the story – how her grandmother had wrapped her in soft linen cloths as her mother lay on the bed, eyelids drooping as she drifted away to sleep after her labor. Mamó had carried her out into the great hall where they had all gathered – her father and her uncle with his two young sons and her three older brothers, and Daideo, of course, pacing the length of the hall in his anxiousness. "It's a girl," Mamó had said. "A little princess, at long last."

As the story went, her father had dropped a perfunctory kiss on her downy head before hurrying away to his wife, and her brothers and her cousins had taken one look at her wrinkled face and promptly lost interest, but Daideo had taken her from Mamó's arms and cradled her against his chest. Mamó always swore at that very moment, Riona had opened her eyes for the very first time and stared right into his, unblinking and bright, and that was that, Mamó would say with the barest hint of a smile —that was the moment in which, after hundreds of years, she had at last lost his heart to another girl.

It was Daideo who had named her. Her mother had waved her limp hand dismissively when Mamó had asked what to call her firstborn daughter, and her father had looked toward his parents, his infant girl still cradled in Daideo's arms. "What suits her, do you think?" Her father had asked, and Daideo had touched her cheek with his finger.

"She is a queen like her grandmother," he had said. "A beautiful little queen, and no other name will do her justice."

So Riona it had been then, and even after dozens of retellings, she never tired of hearing it, how her grandfather had been and always would be her first true love.

She tugged now impatiently on his sleeve, and he smiled. "Once," he said, "a thousand years ago, when the Tuatha Dé Danann ruled the land of Éire and humans first arrived on their shores, they set about ordering the workings of the mortal and immortal realms. They divided the realm in two – the land of the living, and the lands of the sídhe, kept hidden from mortal eyes, wherein the undying beasts of the realm were bound to live. To each one of the old gods was given the charge of such a realm – to Manannán mac Lir, the god of the sea, was granted Emain Ablach, the isle of apples, and to Áine, the goddess of beauty and love, was given the charge of Tír na mBan, the island of women, and to the Mórrígan herself, Oweynagat, the cave of cats –"

"Ráth Crúachan!" Riona squealed. "Have you seen it? Have you gone *in* it?"

Daideo smiled. "Even I dared not risk the Mórrígan's displeasure by breaching its borders. She has very little tolerance for such intrusions. Besides." He tugged on her ear lobe. "It is far more dangerous than you can ever imagine, to enter the cave of cats."

"Why?"

"Because it is the home of truth itself, and that is a very scary thing indeed – knowing the truth of all things. Within the depths of that cave lies the understanding of all life and all death, the birthplace of prophecy and the foundation of the sídhe. It is not a thing that needs ever to be known by any save the one who created it."

"But *why?*"

"Listen to you," he said with affection. "Curious as a cat yourself. That's my doing, and one day it will cost you a great deal, I fear. But about this, your curiosity must remain unsatisfied. The sídhe is by nature a mysterious place, neither here nor there, you see, neither of the earth nor below it, but of everywhere at once, and that is all you need to know about it."

"But –"

"*But* it was not enough," said Daideo, tapping her nose with his finger until she reluctantly swallowed her questions and settled in to listen. "Not enough, for all that lives must die, humans and the Tuatha Dé Danann alike. So it was ordered, in those days, the balancing of life and death. The gods set aside the other-realms, dozens of deathless isles and shores of tranquility – Tír na nÓg, the fabled land of eternal youth, Tír na mBeo, the island of the souls of the ever-living gods, and of course, of Magh Meall, the evergreen meadow of endless delights, meant to house the souls of the mortals who passed on from this life. It was in this realm the gods set in place the fairy-queen Niamh to oversee that pastoral paradise far across the star-studded sea. But – and listen closely, little queen, for this is important – for every light in this world, there must be a shadow."

Riona frowned. It sounded strange, the ordering of the words, for surely, a shadow could not exist without the light, not the other way around. "I don't understand."

"Ah." Daideo waggled his finger at her. "Think of it this way – if you have never experienced the darkness, then how do you know that you are standing in the light? How can you appreciate its glow if you do not understand its worth?"

Riona shook her head, confused, but Daideo continued, smiling slightly to himself. "And so the gods created another realm, a reprieve in the journey of the soul to the paradise that awaits them in Magh Meall – the land of Tech Duinn, and within its shadowy borders they built a hall of respite for mortal souls, where they would pause on their journey before making their way across the bridge between the worlds, across the star-studded sea.

"And to the governing of this realm," he said, "they appointed Donn, the son of Mil Espaine and a powerful druid of legendary fame, crowning him the lord of death. To him it was tasked the collection of those mortal souls whose time had come to journey across the sea to the land of Magh Meall, to serve as their host before they left this world forever. And so for hundreds of years, the two worked in harmony, the Tuatha Dé Danann and Donn, the lord of death, the light and the dark, and peace reigned across the realms of mortals and immortals alike.

"There then ruled over Éire a High King, one chosen by the legendary Lia Fáil itself. Born to this High King, there was a young prince named Jack. He was bold and brave, but stubborn as a stiff-backed mule and a bit entitled, as most young princes are. One wintry day, Jack looked up into a whitethorn tree and saw a crow, the biggest he'd ever seen. He drew his bow and shot it down into the snow, the black of its feathers and the red of its blood a striking contrast to the purity of the fresh-fallen snow.

"Never had the young lad seen anything so beautiful as those colors, the dark and the light swirling together. He returned home in haste to his father's castle to announce that he was leaving to seek his bride, and that only the girl who possessed such beauty as what he had seen in the snow would be worthy enough to be his queen – a girl with black hair and blood-red lips and pure white skin."

"Like me," Riona interrupted excitedly. "She must have looked like me."

A shadow flickered across Daideo's face, a flash of worry, of fear, but then it was gone, his features smooth and smiling again as he pressed his finger against her lips, and she snapped her mouth closed, motioning for him to go on.

"Like you," he agreed. "And so away he went, determined to bring back the bride of his dreams, no matter the cost.

"Long and far he traveled, winning as his own many magical

treasures from the monsters he battled along the way – a cloak of impenetrable darkness, that granted its wearer the power to move unperceived through the mortal and immortal realms alike, and a purse of plenty, that never ran dry of gold and silver coins, no matter how often its master chose to dip into it his hand, and most magnificent of all, a sword forged from pure star-light. The claíomh solais, it was called, the bright sword of Nuada, the grandfather of the gods himself, for whosoever wielded its might could not be overcome by any other living being, human or divine. Jack journeyed far and wide, seeking the bride of his dreams, until at last he came to a great castle that housed such a princess – hair as black as a raven's wing, skin as white as new-fallen snow, and lips as red as fresh-drawn blood. She was a rare beauty, and kings and princes and lords came from miles around to woo her hand.

"But alas," Daideo said, pulling Riona closer to his side. "Her heart had already been claimed by the lord of the dead, the ruler of Tech Duinn, who had looked upon her beauty and had desired it for his own. He cast his spells upon the young girl's heart, winning her love as his own, and thus each of the suitors who pleaded for her hand were turned away by the princess. But Jack would not be dismissed, determined as he was to win the hand of the lady of death. He presented himself before the princess and demanded that he be given a chance to claim her in marriage. She agreed but warned him there would be a heavy cost to pay, should he fail.

"And fail, she meant him to do, for she had devised three impossible tasks for the young prince Jack. 'For your first task,' the princess said, 'you shall pluck this golden comb from my head tonight, from the place I reside, neither of the earth or below it. If you triumph, tomorrow morn I will assign your next task. Should you fail, then your suit shall have ended and you shall pay the price you have promised.'

'Lady,' said Jack. 'I shall not fail.'

'Foolish boy,' she said. 'Of course you shall.' She straightened the gold comb that kept her black locks pinned on the top of her head, then in a whirl of skirts, she vanished through the doorway, leaving Jack standing in the hall, mind whirling. 'She must be mine,' he thought. 'But what shall I do? How shall I ever find such a spot, neither of this earth nor below it?'"

"The sídhe," Riona broke in, unable to suppress her eagerness. "It must be the realm of the sídhe, mustn't it, Daideo?"

"For the Dagda's sake, let me tell my story. You are as impatient as your grandmother ever was." He tugged on her ear, and she snuggled in closer, wrapping her arms around his waist as he continued. "Poor Jack was quite befuddled," her grandfather continued, "but determined still, and so he sat down there on the steps of the castle, his chin perched on his fist, as he thought and thought about the best way to steal away the golden comb from her raven–wing hair.

"He sat there still when, at the stroke of midnight, the princess slipped down the castle steps and disappeared among the trees. Jack pulled on his cloak of darkness and followed her until she stopped before a swelling in the ground, surrounded by a ring of whitethorn trees. She laid her hand against a boulder, and the rock splintered down the middle. Jack watched as the princess disappeared within the gaping hole, and with a deep breath, hurried after her."

"But how? If he was mortal born, how did Jack enter the world of the sídhe?"

"The cloak of darkness," said Daideo, "was god-made, crafted by the hands of Goibiu himself, and it granted its wearer the ability to travel between worlds."

"Well, what about the princess? She didn't have a cloak like that."

"You are too sharp for your own good." He tickled her ribs, and she giggled, squirming away from him. "The princess," he said, still smiling, "had the blood of the Tuatha Dé Danann – the shining silver folaíocht – running through her veins for these were the days when mortals and the gods moved together freely, as friends, as companions, and as lovers."

"Like you and Mamó, when you were once a god and she was just a girl."

"Yes, but that's a bit of a sore topic with your grandmother, don't you know. I'd appreciate you not reminding her of my past sins."

"I'd love to marry a god," Riona declared. "I could eat cake all the time for every meal and no one would dare to tell me to do otherwise. Mamó is a fool."

"By all means," Daideo said. "Feel free to express that opinion to her whenever you like, so long as I am not around. Now hush, or the next time Eabha gives you an extra helping of cauliflower at supper, I won't be helping you eat it."

Riona clapped her hands over her mouth again, and Daideo winked as he resumed his tale. "He followed her until there appeared a man with golden-fire eyes, his arms outstretched, smiling at the beautiful princess – Donn himself, the dark druid, the lord of the dead, the ruler of Tech Duinn, and the king of the sídhe.

"The princess greeted her lord with a kiss, and Jack continued to follow, pulling the cloak of darkness tighter around him. Just before the lady and her lord disappeared into the trees, he gathered his courage and reached up to snatch the golden comb from her hair. Jack fled, back through the opening in the rock and into the world of mortals, down the mountain to the castle of the princess, the golden comb clutched between his fingers.

"He presented it the next morning, and she frowned. 'You will not succeed this time,' she said, 'for from my finger this ring must you take.' On her hand glinted a silver band with a star-bright diamond. 'If you fail to take from me this ring,' she said, 'you shall pay the price you have promised.'

"Again, Jack waited until night fell, and again he followed the princess as she ventured into the other-realm, hidden under his cloak of darkness. Again, the lord of death met his lady, and she slipped her hand into his own as they wandered away. Jack followed, until the lady yawned and the lord led her to a bed made of soft evergreen branches and lily-white flowers. Down laid the princess to sleep, with Donn, the lord of death, slumbering at her side. Jack crept up to her where she lay and slid the ring from her finger, then again fled, back to the castle nestled at the base of the mountain.

"The silver ring was waiting for the princess the next morning in the hall. 'The gods smile on you,' she said. 'But you will find that their favor will grant you only so much luck, for tomorrow, you must bring to me the lips which I shall kiss tonight, or you will surely pay a terrible price.'

"And so that night, he watched as the princess kissed the lips of the lord of death himself, and again he waited until they drifted into dreams on their bed of evergreen leaves. He drew the sword of light from his satchel as he crept forward, and then in a single stroke, he cut off the lips of Donn of death from his sleeping face.

"The lord of death's golden eyes flew open, and he screamed in pain, his ruined face a terrible sight to behold, and Jack sprinted for the splintered stone at the entrance of Tech Duinn, the still-bleeding lips clasped in his hands.

"He showed his prize to the princess the next morning, and she had no choice but to do as she had sworn and married him that same day. Yet Jack knew too well the true depths of the spells cast by Donn, and so he waited until his bride fell asleep in their bed, then stood over her, a slip of a whitethorn branch in his hand, and squeezed out its sap over her chest, cleansing her of the grasp which the lord of death held over her heart. As the last drops of the whitethorn juice dissolved on her snow-white skin, she awoke. She looked at Jack, and she smiled up at him with her blood-red lips.

'My love,' she said. 'My husband,' and Jack wept with joy to see his bride restored unto the light, made whole once more, freed from the enchantments of the lord of death. From that day on, the dread king of Tech Duinn lost its hold on the heart of the princess, and she became a sweet-natured and loving wife to Jack for the rest of their days, for the young prince had defeated Death."

Riona was silent for a moment, a nibble of doubt tugging at her. "Truly?"

He peered down at her. "Whatever do you mean?"

"Truly, they lived happily ever after?"

"Of course," he said, arching his eyebrows at her. "There are such things in this world, you know."

"I suppose. But he stole the princess away from Donn and ruined his face. Wouldn't he – the lord of death, I mean – be very angry?"

"Perhaps," said Daideo lightly. "But what could he do? The creatures of the sídhe are kept locked away in their other-realms by the confinement spells of the Tuatha Dé Danann, and none can escape."

"But –"

Across the room, Maeve stirred, yawning as she sat up and stretched, blinking sleepily at where Riona and her grandfather sat huddled together by the window. "Good morning," she mumbled. "Ria – Daideo. How is Sean? Is he better?"

An icy wave crashed down around Riona, as the heartache that had been eased by her grandfather's story came thundering back, throbbing with renewed grief. She pressed her cheek against Daideo's sleeve, eyes stinging with tears, and barely heard Daideo's quiet murmur to Maeve, her answering sob.

Daideo's arm shifted, and through her tears, she saw it, perched on the windowsill outside – a raven, glossy and still with preternatural black eyes, boring into her own.

She squeezed her eyes shut, smothering her sobs against her grandfather's chest.

Three days later, they stood together again, herself and Daideo and Mamó and her mother and Maeve. They huddled close, grouped around the black-clad funeral bier of her last remaining brother – Sean, his wood-carver's hands folded across his chest – and Riona watched dry-eyed as her mother screamed into the damp brown earth and Daideo wept silent tears and Mamó's shoulders shook as she hugged Maeve close.

Too many times, death had struck her family's hall. That uneasy feeling, that it was because of *her*, that she was the inescapable center of all these deaths, turned her stomach sour. Riona dug her nails into the palm of her hand, relishing the bite of pain as the jagged edge of her fingernail broke through her skin, watching the orange-and-red flames consume what was left of her brother.

She looked down at her hand, at the bead of crimson blood spooling in the middle of her palm.

There, a tiny silver drop gleamed, a single star in a crimson-dark sky.

It made sense, of course. She was, after all, the descendant of the gods, like that long ago princess in Daideo's story, and that silver drop was her birthright, the sign that the folaíocht of the lost magic of the Tuatha Dé Danann still lived on in her.

Riona reached down and wiped the small smear of red-and-silver blood on the skirt of her black gown. What good were the gods and their long-dead magic while her brother burned in front of her?

The looming black clouds cracked once, an ear-splintering sound, and the rain poured down, cold and unforgiving, the fire of her brother's bier sizzling underneath the lash of the storm. For a moment, it shrouded them in a hazy gray fog, the familiar features of these few remaining beloveds growing blurry and distant in the smoke rising from the fire– Mamó and Daideo and Maeve, and her mother too. Riona's heart seized in her chest as she imagined them drifting away in the wind, across the star-studded sea, and herself left alone to grieve their loss.

Daideo gripped her hand in his own, pulling her away from the dying flames of her brother's bier, back toward the warmth of the castle, and Riona knew that this was enough – these precious few beloveds were risk enough to her fragile heart.

She could not afford to love anyone else that the lord of death might steal away from her, ever again.

But Jack was the High Prince of all Éire, and he feared no queen, living nor dead. So he drew his bow and arrows, and he shot the raven through its unblinking eye.

And down the raven fell.

Excerpt from 'The Snow, The Crow, & The Blood'

Chapter Four
Neither of the Earth Nor Under It, Not Then Nor Now

RIONA

I've come to serve you. The lord of death.

Riona's words echoed in the air, and something hungry and wicked flickered in his unnaturally golden eyes in response. "Is that so?"

She nodded once, not trusting herself to speak.

"Well then," he murmured, standing in a swift, fluid rush, and she bit back a gasp at her first real sight of him, illuminated by the glow of a thousand silver stars.

He was so beautiful, this immortal master of death.

It was the only thought she could muster, sprawled out in the dirt before him with her shattered arm clutched to her side. Not only his features, clean-cut and straight-edged as they were, the classical line of his nose, the narrow jaw and high-boned cheeks, but those eyes – they were otherworldly and strange, impossible from which to look away. Depthless black, laced with whorls of bright golden sparks, swirling with knowledge, the kind that whispered of the earth's first waking, a long, slow yawn that breathed life into the primordial dawn, the rays of sunlight unfurling with wary caution, as an infant's fingers reaching for its mother's face for the first time. Riona could see it in his gaze, that initial dawning, how it must have felt, the shape and weight of the world as it lifted its infantile head and blinked at the myriad of lives which it had awakened.

He raised a finger, a silent command of some kind, because immediately, the catlike monster prowled away, disappearing into the shadows. Riona eyed the snowy tree line around her nervously, half-expecting to see it appear above her, yellow eyes gleaming with hunger, and the lord of death smiled again. "Pay no mind to Fiadh," he said. "She's merely disappointed in you – as am I. We expected you years ago, you know." He shrugged before she could answer. "No matter," he said, as though it were irrelevant, the terror he had inspired, the horror with which he had threatened her, to bring her here at last. "All is well. You're here now."

Fury swelled within her, a hatred more intense than anything she'd ever before known, this immortal, heartless being who had no understanding of what it was to love and to lose. "Only because you left me no choice, you *monster*."

"Monster, you say? Perhaps I am," he said with a careless gesture. "But I do think your anger is a bit misplaced. After all, it's the natural end to mortal life, is it not – death? All that lives must die, no matter how much you might wish otherwise."

Riona was moving before he had finished speaking, blinded by rage, her good hand clutching her grandfather's knife, her blade flashing in a silver arc toward his chest –

Something cool and wet slid down her arm as she brought down the wooden hilt of the now–bladeless knife onto his chest with an anticlimactic thud. She shrieked, stumbling backwards, the useless stub of wood tumbling onto the leaves of the forest floor, then and stared at her arm, dripping with gray-silver water that shimmered in the starlight.

She looked back up to find him smiling down at her with cool amusement. "Silly child," he said. "I cannot be so easily killed, not with iron nor steel at least. Try harder next time."

"Monster," she spat at him again, and he did not flinch at the flecks of her spittle on his cheek, but only continued to smile, unnaturally calm.

"If you are quite finished trying to kill me," he said, black-and-gold eyes glinting as he reached for her, "perhaps we can see to your arm. It looks quite painful."

"Don't you *dare* touch me."

"Why not? I mean you no harm."

"You've already harmed me."

"I don't think that's fair. You have no one to blame but your own foolishness for the current state of your arm." His teeth flashed in the starlight. "I was watching, you know. I've always been watching you, a stóirín."

At the sound of the endearment, the hair along her arms prickled, not from the cold, but from revulsion and fear. "I am no one's treasure," she said, as fiercely as she could, "and I will not remain here to be insulted and demeaned by the likes of you." She turned, ready to flee in earnest, when something leaped down from the trees before her – the same black-furred creature from before, purring as its tail lashing behind it.

Riona froze immediately.

"See?" The lord of death made a soft tsking sound. "Now you've hurt Fiadh's feelings. She's a tender-hearted creature, despite her rather ferocious appearance, and it pains her to see you so hostile." He hovered beyond her shoulder, his breath cool on the nape of her neck. "Now then. Let me heal your arm."

The sharp stab of pain in her arm had dulled to a distant throb, and she glanced down at it, her knees half-buckling at the sight of the white shard of bone poking through her skin. "I –"

Before her, the cat-monster licked its lips, ears pricked forward as it watched her with an unblinking stare. Waiting for something, a kind of yearning in its posture, a wordless longing in its slitted eyes.

"Poor child." His voice was soothing, soft as velvet-lined bed-clothes and goose-feather pillows. "To have suffered so much, so young, so many hurts that can never be healed, I know – but this one can. Our bodies are so much more resilient than our hearts." He paused. "After all, I would again remind you, that you are here because you chose to be. You knew what you would find here in my woods – what I am. So come now. Show me your arm."

He was right. She *had* come to him, fully cognizant of what she was sacrificing, to what she was agreeing, and there was no rational excuse for her reluctance to embrace it, to accept the tentative offer of familiarity which he extended to her now. It would consume her soon enough anyway, the evil that was so inherent in the air of this place, that sizzled at the tips of his fingers.

Slowly, slowly, she turned back to face him, cradling her shattered arm against her body, a silent acquiescence.

His eyes flashed with golden fire. He bent his dark head and let his fingers drift over her injured arm as he whispered, his silken-soft voice suddenly growling and guttural. She jumped as the bones in her arm shifted, an answering snap in response to his words, then looked down to see the shards of jagged bone retracting underneath her new-healed skin with only the faintest trace of a scar.

"There now," he said in his usual voice, so close to her that their breaths mingled in the night air. "That was not so terrible, was it? We can be – well. Not friends, I suppose. Lord and servant cannot ever truly be friends, but we can manage to be friendly, at the very least."

"No." She clenched her fists, her arm tingling with a renewed strength, whole as it was. "How many loved ones have I lost because of you? How many of them have you stolen away, all so that you could get my attention? And now you demand civility from me?" She inhaled shakily. "*Never.*"

"Yes, we have already covered this rather wearisome ground, if you remember." He folded his arms. "I wanted you, you were reluctant, so I gave you a nudge in the right direction. Several nudges, in fact, but here you are, at long last, so now we come to a discussion of terms. You are here of your own free accord –"

"It was *not*, you threatened–"

"Of your own free accord," he repeated, raising a finger. "So let's get to it, shall we? We both know what you want from me, don't we," and for a moment, his gentle smile turned sharp, cruelly knowing.

She tried to speak, the sudden hard lump in her throat immovable, as though if she spoke the words allowed, brought them into being, it would become inevitable, this thing that she most feared, that terrified her down to the depths of her soul, the one beloved that she could never endure to lose.

"I suppose that will suffice," he said in answer to her wordless appeal. "Very well. I will grant your request. Do as I ask, and I shall leave your beloved alone, yes? I'm not really a fiend, you know, no matter how many times you might accuse me of it."

Relief flooded through her, but she forced herself to continue.

"Then what *do* you want from me?"

"Your service, of course, the terms of which we shall discuss in a moment."

"For how long?"

His fingers drummed on his forearm as he studied her, the only sign of his impatience. "Well, that depends entirely on you."

"What do you mean?"

"I require certain things of you," he said. "Nothing too taxing – just a few simple tasks. Three in number. Once those are complete, then you are free, and we shall part as lord and servant no longer, but – dare I say it – as friends."

"Once again – *never*. What kind of tasks?"

"We'll get to that. In time."

Again, that inscrutable flicker of amusement tugging at the corner of his lips. She straightened her shoulders. "We'll get to it now."

"It wouldn't make sense to you now, I'm afraid. You'll need the proper training first."

"Training? For what?"

"You're a very curious little creature, did you know that?" He shook his head with something like regret. "I am sorry, a stóirín. But you will have to learn to trust me for any of this to work, and the beginning of that trust starts now." His eyes met hers, an unblinking burn. "I will teach you, then set you loose to do what it is that I have asked of you to do, and then – then I give you my word that you and your beloved both will be free of me. Forever."

Riona sat down, fingers gripping the rock beneath her. "I can't – can't possibly –" Her voice trailed away as she imagined it, years of servitude, of fighting and clawing to keep whatever bits of her soul she could as he tried to scrape away every last drop of it for his own, years of darkness and monsters and unimaginable evil threading its way through every secret corner of her heart.

But there was no other choice. It would have to be enough – even if it cost her everything to win it.

"Three tasks," she whispered.

"Three tasks," he repeated, wheedling and slow. "That is all that I ask of you. Such a simple thing, for such a *dear* prize."

Still, she hesitated. Riona swallowed thickly. "The other girls," she said. "The girls like me, black-haired and red-lipped, whom you called here in the past, before the sídhe-realms again became sealed away from the mortal world. I want to know – what happened to them?"

"Nothing terrible. They arrived, reluctant and heart-sick, much as are you, but in the end, they all realized that I was not the same devil which they had been taught to fear."

"I already know that too," Riona said as steadily as she could. "I know who you really are."

His smile sharpened. "Good," he said. "That makes things easier. But it won't matter. I shall win you over in the end, as I did all the others."

"You will never win me."

He shrugged. "They all say that, when they first arrive here in my realm." Riona flinched, her stomach churning at the idea of all those other lost girls who had been dragged into this place of darkness and despair, all of them black of hair and red of lip, like herself – and she, who had walked through his door wide-eyed and willing. "But it never lasts too long."

Riona jutted her chin in the air. "It will with me. I know better than most what you are."

"Do you." It was not a question, that hummed note of bitter amusement. "I suppose your dear departed grandfather told you all about it, how I was condemned to this gloomy existence, an eternity spent in the shadows." For a brief moment, his eyes burned obsidian black, a depthless well of fury and hatred. Then it was gone, his expression smoothing as he turned to run his finger along the trunk of a yew tree. "Well. Regardless of what little bit of truth he might have told you mixed in with all his lies, I suppose that only time will tell which one of us is right, won't it?" He smiled again, feather-soft and gentle, then turned away to stroke the purring head of his monstrous cat. "Take a few moments to compose yourself, and then we shall begin. After all," he glanced back over his shoulder, eyes glinting with an undeniably malevolent light, "you haven't much time to waste, have you? Or rather – your *beloved* doesn't."

Riona's head snapped back as though he'd slapped her. "Gods," she breathed, hands shaking. "You really are a heartless monster, aren't you."

"So you keep saying," he said, scratching at the beast's ears as it purred in contentment. "But it's hardly a suitable way for you to address your master."

"I can think of other things to call you that I'm sure you'd like much less."

"I'm sure you could, as I am also sure that I have heard far worse," he said with a shrug. "But, as you know, I am called many things – some call me Donn Duimche, some Finnevara or Crom Cruach. Some even name me a god, a child of the Tuatha Dé Danann – did you know?"

"Bilé," she said. "God of death. Yes, I have heard that too."

His brows raised. "But you know better, little queen."

"Don't call me that."

"But it is your name, is it not? *Riona.*" She shivered again and he stepped closer, the faint scent of moss and river-water wafting over her. "However, as you wish. I shall strike this bargain with you – you will not call me by the name which I have long forsaken, and I will not address you by the title which *you* are to leave behind forever."

"Not forever. Three tasks, and then I am done with you *and* this horrid place."

"We shall see." The lord of death let his golden-fire gaze wander up and down her person, not lasciviously or lustfully, but with an intent curiosity. "Are we agreed, then? You stay here, with me, in the land of the dead, to serve me, and complete my tasks. You will have clothes, and food, and rest as you may need it, and none shall harm you, and in return, I – I shall keep the one you love most safe. Yes?"

For only the briefest moment, Riona hesitated.

If you leave here tonight, you will never see either of us again.

He'd meant it, Riona knew that much was true. She had known him for almost her entire life, after all – had loved him for almost as long. She knew him at his best and at his worst, knew his nervous quirks and his sheepish smiles and the sadness in his bright gray eyes; knew every curve of his face, every line of his body as intimately as her own, his voice and his laugh and all the little truths of him, inside and out, better than she knew herself.

She knew that Conor Ó Ruairc never, ever told a lie.

But it couldn't be helped. There was no other way, even if it broke what was left of her already shattered heart into thousands of irreparable glass shards.

Riona inhaled, slow and shaky, then spoke, her voice dull and flat as a death-knell.

"We are agreed."

It was a strangely compelling sight for the prince— the midnight black of the raven's feathers against the pure white of the snow, the dark red blood that pooled around it.

Excerpt from 'The Snow, The Crow, & The Blood'

Chapter Five
The Vale of Inagh, Éire, 1062

RIONA

After a little while, Riona forgot the story her grandfather had told her – about the crow lying dead in the snow and the handsome young prince who saved the beautiful princess from the evil lord of death – and for a few years, life went on as normal in the vale.

Until one day, he arrived – Conor Ó Ruairc.

And Riona, usually so assured and opinionated about every other aspect of life, could not at all decide what to make of him.

She and Maeve would whisper about him, how funny his face was – absurdly freckled, with shaggy red hair that tumbled across his forehead – and about how clumsy he was, always tripping over a tree root or falling head over heels down the stairs, or stuttering over his words, even the simplest of sentences. He was an odd boy, and it was far easier to laugh at him from a distance than to like him up close.

So she stayed away, even when his gaze followed her as she would skip down the lengths of the great hall, waving hello to the soldiers and the villagers who wound their way through the castle. She ignored how he would watch her at supper as she laughed with Maeve, tossing grapes and bits of bread in one another's mouths, how he would wait in a nearby stall whenever she brushed her mare. He kept his head down as he did his chores, avoiding her direct gaze, and yet she would catch him stealing glances her way as he laid down fresh straw for the horses.

His cheeks would flush whenever their eyes met in such moments, and he would inevitably trip over an overturned bucket or the ledge of a stair, careening backward as his arms flailed in the air before landing on his back, his elbows akimbo and his hair mussed.

She would bite the inside of her cheek till it bled, trying not to laugh.

He was shy, this boy, and sweet-tempered too, with a simple kindness to him. Once she came upon him, freeing the mice from the traps in the kitchen, shooing them out the side door, glancing over his shoulder nervously lest Eabha should come and box his ears. Her grandmother, too, was very fond of him – his fascination with her beloved flowering herbs, their names and the hidden secrets of their juices and their stems.

"He's a good lad," Mamó had reproved her and Maeve once as they sat by the hearth-fire, crowing with laughter about how earlier that morning, he had tripped over his own two boots and went sprawling headfirst into the water basin in the stables.

"He's a cabbage, Mamó," Riona had managed to sputter as she giggled with Maeve. "A complete and utter cabbage."

Mamó stood, running her hand down the length of her silver-gray braid. "The world would be a much better place," she said over her shoulder as she moved out the door of the solar, "if there were more cabbages, as you say, with good hearts, and less gossips with unkind tongues."

Riona snapped her mouth shut at once, and Maeve reddened, for even though Mamó had never once raised her voice to anyone that Riona could remember, it was a fearful thing, to be even mildly chastised by the queen.

She didn't change her mind, though, about the boy, not even when Maeve plopped down beside her the next afternoon. Riona was busy wrangling with her embroidery, muttering curses she had sworn not to admit that she had learned from her grandfather. "So I talked to him," Maeve said without preamble as she peered at Riona's half-finished hoop, her nose wrinkling at the sloppy stitching. "He seems nice enough."

"For a donkey," Riona grumbled.

"Watch it." Maeve leaned over and took the abused bit of embroidery from Riona's hands, bending over it as she unraveled the tangled mess. "Your grandmother is rather fond of him. I'd be kind to him if I were you, or she'll have you peeling garlic cloves from now until solstice."

"That's supposed to be a running stitch. Mamaí said."

"I know," said Maeve dryly. "That's why I'm confused as to why you were using a back stitch."

"What's the difference?"

"I swear, Ria, do you ever pay attention in lessons?"

"I do not. That's what I have you for, Mae."

Maeve grinned, the pink tip of her tongue poking out of the corner of her mouth as she repaired Riona's sloppy work. "Anyway. He's a nice boy. A bit clumsy, sure, but he's a beast with a camán. He scored on Darragh with a single shot. Even *you* can't hit the ball that hard, Ria. He must be very strong."

"Wait, when did you play iomáint?"

Maeve licked at the end of the thread. "While you were in your geography lesson."

"I hate geography."

"You hate all your lessons."

"Yes, but I especially loathe geography."

"Our future queen should be able to read a map, Ria."

Riona scowled, her fingers drumming against her knee. "I can't believe you played iomáint without me. And with the cabbage, no less."

"You need to stop calling him that, don't you know."

"Not likely," Riona sniffed, and Maeve rolled her eyes, then held up the embroidery hoop.

"There. See that? That's a backstitch."

"I don't see a difference."

"They are fairly similar," Maeve admitted. "But with the backstitch, it leaves a cleaner line, not so many spaces in the threading."

"Fascinating. I'll give you half of my apple cake at supper if you finish it for me."

"You'll give me *all* your cake, and then sure I will."

"Right." Riona hopped to her feet, rubbing her hands together in satisfaction. "I'm off then. I'm going for a ride."

"Remember what Mamó told you," Maeve said as she bent over the embroidery hoop, brow furrowing in concentration.

"You'll need to be more specific."

"Ria!"

"She tells me lots of things." Riona blinked innocently. "How am I to remember every single one?"

Maeve rolled her eyes. "You need to be careful out there, Ria. Mamó says the trees are restless."

Of course they are, Riona thought, rooted indelibly in the ground as they were, spending a hundred years in the same spot, never moving, never existing outside of the tiny patch of ground from which they sprung. If they were restless, it was with good reason.

She said nothing of this to Maeve – clearheaded, practical-minded Maeve – but merely blew her a kiss as she skipped out the door. "See you at supper, Mae."

"Apple cake!"

"Every last crumb," Riona called back over her shoulder, then she was down the hall and out the door, jogging for the stable, her every step dancing with impatience. Because she was, of course, intent upon venturing into the forbidden mountains today, an irrepressible urging tugging deep within her, an inexplicable longing to ride among its barren rocks and silent pines and breathe deep the cold mountain air, to feel the bite of its wind on her face. She wasn't sure what pulled her toward it, but it was always present, invisible fingers curling in an undeniable summons, this longing for the mountains and the unknowable things that prowled within them.

Her grandmother sensed it, Riona knew – knew that it worried her. Mamó was always warning her to stay away, but with every passing day, it grew stronger, this need to escape, to be free and unfettered among the silent stones and watchful trees of the mountains, and she could no longer resist it.

She was no tree, earthbound and rooted to a single spot, an unavoidable fate. She was a seed in the wind, or better yet, a falling star careening its way across the night sky, hurtling toward some unknown and new destiny, full of promise and bursting with life.

She swung herself into the saddle, Darcy dancing underneath her in response to her mistress' impatience, and then they were off, galloping through the vale, up the hills and through thickets, faster and faster, until they loomed before her, the stone-kissed ridges of the mountains, singing her home.

Disaster struck not long after.

She was urging Darcy up the mountainside when the mare reared, snorting in displeasure. "Come on," Riona coaxed. "Just for a minute. Don't be chicken-livered."

Darcy's nostrils flared, tossing her head in consternation as she trotted forward. Riona bounced in the saddle as the shadows deepened and the trees grew denser, the branches crisscrossing so that only the barest glints of the sun peeked through. Darcy whinnied once, a final plea to turn back, but Riona nudged her forward with her heels, and away they went.

It was as gorgeous as she'd imagined. She studied the rain-weathered gray of the rocks, the twists of the vines, the faint wisps of fog that bled their way down from the sky. The hills of the vale were nothing compared to this, the majesty and power of the mountains. It felt like the quietude place in the world, the pristine peaks, the gentle rustling of a brook tumbling over the rocks and roots of the trees, the wind that whistled its way down the stony slopes and through the loose strands of her hair.

A few clatters of rock up ahead, and she yanked on the reins as out from the trees stalked an elk – a male, with heavy-hanging antlers and broad shoulders, reaching up to nibble at the newly-green leaves. His stare met hers, brilliant and wild, then its gaze flickered away, bending its head to rub his antlers against the trunk, lowing softly to himself.

Riona suppressed a squeal of delight. An elk, and a kingly one at that, a creature not seen in the vale for years.

She barely had time to wonder what other marvels she might find hidden away in the mountains when another rumbling caught her ear, and she turned in the saddle to find a second set of black eyes staring into her own. A female this time, and she reached for the reins to pull Darcy away – even she had enough sense to know that it was calf season, and that a sure way to incur the wrath of a mother was to cross her young – when the cow's ears flattened against her head, hooves shifting and head lowering, ready to charge.

"Shite," Riona hissed as the bull elk raised his head and looked from one to another – the cow elk preparing to charge, Darcy dancing nervously with Riona lying low on his back – and he bellowed once, shaking his many-pronged antlers, then burst forward in an explosion of speed.

Darcy whirled away as Riona dug her heels into the mare's side – "go, go, go" – but her hooves skidded on the moss-covered rock, and Riona dropped the reins to clutch at her black mane as the horse tumbled forward, crashing through the underbrush. She managed to twist one foot free from the stirrup before Darcy collapsed on her side, Riona's leg caught underneath the mare, and Riona bit back a scream as her knee twisted in an unnatural wave of pain.

The bull bellowed again, his antlers swishing and snapping through the bushes as he trampled about, goring the trees furiously, blind with rage. Darcy squealed, the whites of her eyes wheeling in her head, then clambered to her feet. Riona struggled to follow, but her knee collapsed underneath her, and she watched in horror as her black mare reared once, then galloped away, disappearing into the trees.

The elk fell silent, turn away back into the depths of the mountain from whence he had came, his cow swishing her tail in satisfaction at his side. Riona flopped on her back, arm flung across her face, chest heaving.

She couldn't walk.

Her horse was gone.

No one knew where she was.

She was deep within the forbidden peaks of the Mhám Toirc, with night fast approaching, and the Bealtaine fires had not been lit. Superstition, she told herself. It was only superstition anyway, that last thing. Daideo had himself said that the sídhe-monsters could not free themselves from the confinement spells placed by the Tuatha Dé Danann, so she was safe enough.

But still, panic surged within her.

She sat up, wiping away the sweat from her brow as she forced herself to draw deep, calming breaths.

Daideo. He would guess where she had gone, or Maeve. They would come for her, Mamó and Daideo, as soon as Darcy returned riderless to the vale. They would be angry, sure, and she would no doubt be on garlic duty for the rest of her days, but she would be home, and all would be fine.

Thunder rumbled in the distance, beyond the snow-dusted peaks, and she whimpered in response.

Daideo would come, she thought, as she dragged herself underneath an evergreen tree, curling up into a tight ball, her knee screaming in pain. Daideo would be here soon.

Any minute now, Daideo would come.

Night fell, and Daideo did not come, nor Mamó, nor Maeve – only the rain, relentless and sharp, soaking her to the skin with its icy touch. Riona rocked back and forth underneath the tree, teeth chattering, and looked down at her arms wrapped around her knee. Even through the gloom, she could see the faintest tinge of blue around the tips of her fingers.

Oh gods, she was so cold.

The sky lit up, white-hot and bright, a streak of lightning sizzling through the clouds. An ear-splitting crack followed, and she squeezed her eyes shut against the ominous growl of the storm that would soon kill her. She could have sworn it was calling her name, taunting her, right before it drowned her in a deluge of unforgiving rain.

"Riona."

Damn this mountain. How dare it mock her, right before it killed her?

"Riona!"

She shook her head. That was no mountain – that sounded like –

And there he was, his red curls plastered to his forehead, reaching for her with one hand, pushing aside the evergreen branches with the other.

"Riona," he said a third time, and she blinked at him in confusion, the cabbage-boy, because it did not seem real that he could be here.

"Riona, let's go."

"Where's Daideo?"

"He's looking for you, Ria, like everyone else. Now come on, I'll take you home."

He grabbed her elbow, dragging her forward, and she shrieked, pain slicing through her knee. He dropped her arm and staggered back, his hands raised. "I'm sorry, I'm sorry, I'm just trying to help, I didn't mean –"

"I hurt my leg, you muppet," she snapped. "I can't walk."

"That's okay, I have a horse –" He turned, his hands bracketing his brow to keep the rain out of his vision. "Somewhere, I have a horse."

Riona thudded her head against the tree and groaned. "You can't be serious."

"I left him right there!"

"Well, he's not there now, is he?"

He clutched two fistfuls of wet red hair. "I was in a bit of a hurry. I guess…. I guess I must not have tied him up very well."

"How clever of you."

"Well, where's your horse, Riona? I don't see her standing near-by, waiting to carry us home."

"I was attacked," she said, as primly as she could, though her lips chattered wildly and she could feel the mud, caked on her face. "By an elk."

"An elk wouldn't attack you. It's not their season to mate."

"Oh well, in that case – how silly of me. Perhaps it was a hare. It's easy to confuse the two, after all. Floppy ears, antlers – they're all the same."

"Oh my gods," Conor groaned, then crawled underneath the

tree, close to her where she still shivered. "If you're going to argue with me, then you could at least keep me warm while you do it."

"You should be keeping *me* warm. I'm your future queen."

He shot a sideways glance at her, an expression which on anyone else she would have sworn was a smirk. "You might not be, depending on how this night goes. You look like a corpse."

"You are *such* a cabbage."

His shoulder bumped against hers "Maybe," he said. "But like it or not, we're trapped together now, at least until morning. Might as well get comfortable."

Riona huffed, then reluctantly snuggled in closer to him, catching a faint whiff of sweat and rainwater and, strangely, her favorite fruit. "You smell like apples."

"I was helping Eabha make cider earlier." He looked down at his hands, and she could see the flush in his cheeks even through the darkness. "I spilled some on myself, so that's probably it."

"Oh, I'd love some cider right now. I'm so thirsty."

"Stick your head out and open your mouth, then. Plenty of water to be found."

"You're being very unsympathetic. I'm a damsel in distress, you know. Be nice."

He merely rested his head on the tree behind them. Riona pursed her lips, an odd twinge of dissatisfaction, of something like shame, rumbling in her chest.

"How'd you find me?"

"Maeve. She thought you might have gone here but was worried you'd get in trouble. So I told her that I'd come look for you."

The twinge grew into a full-fledged stab of embarrassment. "Oh."

For a long while, the only sound was the roll of the thunder and the crash of the rain. It was oddly peaceful, now that she was no longer alone, afraid and cold in the dark. Her knee still ached, and her teeth still chattered and her belly grumbled, but it was rather lovely, listening to the rain under the velvet-black canopy of the night.

"Conor."

He stiffened, and she realized suddenly that it was the first time that she had ever spoken his name.

"Thank you," she said, "for coming to find me."

A beat or two, then he edged closer, his arm wrapping around her shivering shoulders, pulling her into his chest. "You're welcome," he said, and she pressed her cheek against the faint thrum of his heartbeat, inhaling the lingering remnants of the smell of fresh apple.

She wasn't sure that she would ever again be able to eat her favorite cake, without thinking of this moment in the rain and the trees, without thinking of him.

They stayed like that all night, whispering back and forth, sharing their warmth with one another until at last the rain slowed and the sun crept out, a tentative pink-and-gray dawn. They stumbled out from underneath the tree, Conor's arm wrapped around her waist as she limped along, then she looked up at the sound of Conor's groan. "What's wrong?"

"Look."

There by the swollen banks of the mountain stream stood a roan horse, tail swishing as it nibbled at the leafy underbrush.

"Your horse, I presume?"

"More of an ass than a horse," Conor grumbled, and Riona

laughed once, a strained sound.

"Horse or ass," she said, "I don't care, so long as it gets me home."

It was a long ride through the rising mists, down the steep incline of the mountain, through the woodland hills toward the stone-gray castle nestled in the heart of the vale. Riona clung to Conor's shoulders on the back of his roan gelding, her knee twinging at each jostle along the way.

Then they were there, bursting through the trees in front of her home, and Daideo was sprinting across the yard, shouting her name, while Mamó came running from the stables, her silver braid whipping behind her.

And there was her mother, standing at the top of the stairs, lips pressed together in an unforgiving line, arms folded across her chest as she watched Conor ease Riona down to the ground on her uninjured leg.

She was immediately awash in a sea of arms, Mamó and Daideo and Maeve, too, crying and snot-nosed, as she hugged her close. "Ria," Maeve sobbed. "Ria."

"I'm all right," she managed to say. "I'm all right. I just tweaked it."

Mamó was the first to pull back, her face white. "Riona," she whispered. "Oh sweetheart, you don't know."

Riona looked at each of them – Maeve, with her hands over her mouth, and Daideo, his shoulders a little more bent, a little more broken than they had been before, and her mother, with stiff, white lips and hands clenched at her sides. "What happened?"

Mamó reached out, running her shaking fingers through Riona's bedraggled hair. "Killian," she whispered, and Riona's heart cracked again along too-familiar lines. Uncail Killian, who fed her sweetmeats at solstice when she was a little girl, who played ponies with her, riding her about on his back through the halls – Daideo and Mamó's last son, the new-crowned king of Connacht, the kingdom that her father and her brothers had died to reclaim.

"Oh, Mamó –"

"A fever, they wrote," Daideo said, his hand against Mamó's back. "It was very sudden, from what we can tell."

Mamó turned away, her face spasming with grief, and Maeve rushed forward, slipping her arm underneath Riona's shoulders. "Lean on me, Ria," she said as Daideo and Mamó moved away, murmuring to one another, fingers entwining. "Let's go inside."

"Wait." Riona reached out and snagged the sleeve of Conor's doublet where he stood nearby, watching her warily. "Did you know? When you came to find me – did you know, about my uncle?" He only stared back at her, and Riona's hands clenched into fists. "Why wouldn't you tell me?"

Conor shifted on his feet, running his hand through his hair. "I didn't want to upset you," he mumbled, and his gray eyes shone so honest and full of concern that Riona suddenly wanted to cry.

"You *cabbage*," she spat at him instead, and even as Maeve squawked in protest, she spun away, ignoring the bright hot flare of pain in her knee and staggered away toward the castle.

Another death, she thought as she stumbled her way inside, past her silent, critical-eyed mother, down the hall to Mamó's solar. She suddenly remembered the sensation of hearing her name whispered in the cold howl of the wind last night, how it had called to her from deep within the depths of the mountain itself.

It's happening again, she thought as she sank, exhausted, heart-broken, into a chair by the hearth. Something was stealing away the ones she loved, demanding that she pay attention, that she acknowledge its presence and its power.

Something – or perhaps, someone.

A face flashed before
Jack, a vision of
loveliness — a girl, with
hair as black as the dead
raven's wing, her skin as
white as the new-fallen
snow, lips as red as the
blood seeping towards
him.

Excerpt from 'The Snow, The Crow,
& The Blood'

Chapter Six

Neither of the Earth Nor Under It, Not Then Nor Now

RIONA

"**Y**es," Riona said, "we are agreed."

The lord of death stared at her for a long moment, then he rubbed his hands together, satisfied. "Excellent," he said. "Now then, I shall need another drop of your blood."

"Why?"

"Because our bargain must be sealed, and blood is the only coin accepted here."

Riona watched him warily for a moment, but he remained where he was, hands clasped behind his back, and at last, she extended her hand toward him, palm up. "Such snow-white skin," he murmured, an all but inaudible whisper as he threaded his fingers through hers. "Let me see," he said, then his voice again deepened to an unfathomable pitch, a string of garbled words pouring forth. The air shimmered, and a slate-gray piece of flint appeared in the air, hovering above their joined hands. He plucked it from the air, and so quickly that she could barely see, he slit the tip of his finger, and Riona watched the crimson blood shimmer against the marble of his skin.

"So you truly *are* mortal," she whispered, but he ignored her, his golden gaze fixed on her bare arm, still encircled by his fingers.

"Now," he said, and pressed her fingers until they bent backward. She bit back a scream as the flint cut above her wrist. For the second time that day, her blood welled up, dark red and silver, and he flipped her arm over so that it dripped down onto the icy earth. The drops of silver-crimson sank into the ground, and a faint tendril of black smoke arose from the spot from which they had disappeared.

The wound remained, a gaping scar of scarlet against the pale skin of her arm.

"Now," he said once again, and her horrified gaze jerked up to his, golden-black and glimmering with some unnamed emotion. "You belong to me, belong *here* – as you were always meant to be, as all the others did not. They were but practice, a kind of training of my own that needed to be completed before you arrived in my realm. You – you will be greater than they, a stóirín. You are the one for whom I have waited for so very long."

She jerked her hand away, clutching at the scar on her wrist. "I will *never* belong to you."

"Don't be so hasty, a stóirín." Something grasping and hungry roughened the velvety edges of his voice, and Riona took an instinctive step back from where he stood. "Soon you might be begging to stay here forever."

"That will never happen, and you know that. You know that I would go home tomorrow if you'd let me."

He smiled again, cunning and sharp as a serpent's tooth. "To-morrow," he said. "A year, ten years, forever – there's no difference here in the sídhe, as you will soon find."

An unnatural shiver crept up her spine. "What does that mean?"

"Come now. You're no fool. I know that you've heard the stories of the sídhe." Riona's stomach twisted at the sight of his expression, so smooth and calm, yet so smug. "Here, time passes differently than in the mortal realm." He paused. "I would have thought that ever so wise grandfather of yours would have warned you of that."

Riona opened her mouth to let loose a string of curses, then stopped. Because he had warned her, hadn't he? *Neither above the earth nor below it,* Daideo had said, years ago. *Not then, nor now.*

A niggle of doubt slipped through her. What else had she forgotten from his stories, what else had she ignored when she had run away in the moonlight to hand over her soul to the black-hearted creature in front of her? She had done exactly what Daideo had made her promise never to do, had acted like a naive lamb searching for the stream, only to ask directions from a winter-hungry wolf.

"So you *do* remember?" The wolf in question asked, and Riona sank down onto the ground, fingers twisting in her lap.

"Yes. I had forgotten, but now –" She swallowed. "How does it work? How do I know how much time has passed?"

"Oh, well. You can't." He clasped his hands behind his back as he strolled toward her. "It is ever-changing. Sometimes a mortal may spend an hour here and return to find a year has passed. At other times, you could spend a month and go back to discover that it has been a single night in the mortal realm." He shrugged. "Time is unnecessary here, where there are no beginnings and no endings."

"But there must still be a way to track the passing of days –" Her voice fell away as he cocked his head, studying her, and she thought of a bird, sleek and black-feathered, with watchful, silent eyes. "I don't understand any of this." Riona rested her forehead against her fists, elbows on her knees. "I don't – I can't do this."

The frostbitten leaves cracked and rustled as he settled down at her side, his legs stretched out in front of him. "You will learn. The sídhe does not play by any determined set of rules, and it answers to no one. You never know what tricks it may have up its sleeve – like this one."

A sudden crash thundered behind her. Riona whirled around to see a familiar pair of glowing yellow eyes in a pitch-black feline face stared into her own, its tail thrashing across the ground. "Oh my *gods*, that thing is *terrifying*."

He glanced over his shoulder, unconcerned. "Fiadh? Not at all. She's merely bored, and you're new."

"What is she?"

"A cat-sìth, born centuries before mortals ever came to Éire. Her kind's ferocity was so well-loved by the gods that they once appointed them as the guardians of their most precious treasures — until they vanished." He yawned. "Good riddance, I say, but Fiadh appears to miss them. She usually resides in another sídhe-realm, one of the few not under my command, but she is a cat, after all, and roams quite a bit."

The creature – Fiadh – mewled once, as if in confirmation, then latched its great yellow eyes on Riona, who stared back warily.

"There are many such creatures roaming about my domain, you will find." The lord of death studied the black-furred monster, a smile tugging at the corner of his lips. "I've actually grown rather fond of her."

Riona shivered as the cat-sìth stretched out its neck, sniffing at the end of her braid. "Is she – will she try to eat me?"

"Possibly." Riona shot him a glance as the cat bared its teeth at her, then sat back on its sleek black haunches, lifting its paw to its mouth to groom itself. The lord of death merely smiled. "But if it eases your fear, it's unlikely. She prefers a higher quality of meats –

kerry cattle, or a Gaillimh lamb. Oh, and stoats."

Riona frowned, irrationally offended at not being considered a worthy enough meal for this monster. "*Stoats* are higher quality than I?"

"Fiadh says that they are actually quite succulent."

The cat-sìth paused in its grooming ritual to shoot Riona a glance from its slitted yellow eyes. Perhaps it was the shock of it all, but she felt a sudden rush of appreciation for its lithe feline form, the fluid grace radiating from its relaxed posture.

"Can I pet it?" Riona asked impulsively, her fingers itching suddenly to feel the sleekness of its fur, the ripple of the muscle beneath its skin.

"If you like, but I will not be held responsible for the mess she makes of your hand. She is hardly a housecat."

Riona stood and edged closer to the cat-sìth. Tentatively, she stretched out a hand, waggling her fingers. "Hello, Fifi."

The lord of death wrinkled his nose. "Her name is *Fiadh*."

"It's a nickname. To show her that we can be friends."

"Fiadh," he said dryly, "is pure sinew and solid muscle, a stone-hearted killer. She does not have *friends*."

"What are you then?"

"Her master." His golden eyes flickered. "As I am yours."

Riona ignored the pang his words evoked, concentrating instead on how Fiadh flexed appreciatively underneath her fingers. "She's actually not so bad."

She looked up to see the lord of death staring at her with a satisfied expression. "There now. You see? You are not afraid anymore."

She wasn't – her fear drowned out by the waterfall of curiosity in this horrifying, magnificent creature now purring beneath her hand. "Of you, or Fifi?"

"Both. Either. And for the sídhe's sake, do not call the cat-sìth, one of the most fearsome creatures to ever exist in Éire, *Fifi*, or I will risk the gastrointestinal calamity that will inevitably ensue and let her make a meal of your arm."

"I don't believe she particularly wants to eat my arm at the moment. I think she likes me."

"So it seems." He huffed, a soft chuckling sound, then stood in one seamless, fluid motion. Reluctantly, Riona marveled at his grace, as light-footed as the feline snuggled into her side. Not like Conor, clumsy and stumbling–

Her breath caught, a viscid band of iron wrapping itself around her heart.

Conor. How frightened he must be, how angry he must be with her – and she might *never* see him again, never –

"A stóirín."

The lord of death was watching her intently – too intently. "Come along," he said with a touch of distaste, as though he knew where her thoughts had gone. "I have many things to show you, and –" That same smile, clever and gentle, curved along his lips. "– Such *little* time in which to do it."

"If that was a joke, it wasn't very funny."

"You shall have to learn to appreciate, soon enough, both the allure of my realm *and* my jokes." Riona glanced around at the silence that lingered among the ice-kissed trees, the snow-dusted leaves, the fog that swirled all around her. "Come along," he said again. "There is no rest to be found here in this place of darkness. You will certainly learn *that*, and soon." He beckoned to her as he began to move away. "It's time to start your training."

Riona scrambled to her feet to hurry after him as he strolled away, his hands clasped behind his back. "Don't you think it's time you should tell me what this mysterious training is for, exactly?"

"I would have thought that was obvious." He glanced over his shoulder, one eyebrow arched. "To learn the workings of death, of course," he said, and her heart plummeted into her stomach.

Suddenly, she was afraid again.

"I can't do any magic," she said a little while later, as they stood shoulder to shoulder by a black-watered river that ambled its way through the trees, the faint glow of the star-lit sky refracting off the dark sheen of its surface. "The last of the magic in Éire died with my grandmother."

There will always be magic within the land of Éire, her grandfather's voice whispered in her ear, and she shook the memory away, a lump rising in her throat. "I have a few drops of folaíocht in my blood," she continued, "but it's useless."

"Not useless." He leaned forward to peer into the black-water waves as churned below. "It brought you here, did it not?"

"Like I said," Riona said dryly. "Useless." She crossed her arms. "What are you looking at?"

He beckoned with his finger, his gaze still locked on the river below. "Come and see."

Riona dropped to one knee on the riverbank, squinting into the dark water – not black, she realized, but a deep, fathomless blue.

She caught a flash of something pale and frowned at her lord. "Is that –"

"Look closer."

She squinted, trying to make out the shape of the thing floating beneath the dark blue waves. "It's a man."

"Amergin was his name, one of the most powerful druids ever to settle in Éire."

A flash of recognition, a memory of the last story that her grandfather had ever told her. "One of seven brothers," she said. "He sailed to Éire to avenge his fallen kin."

"Even so." His mouth tightened. "You see how futile mortal ambitions are, Riona? For all his dreams of vengeance, of domination, here he lies beneath a half-frozen river, doomed to spend an eternity in shadow."

"You were not much better," Riona said, before she could think better of it, then bit down hard on her lip.

He whipped his head around, his eyes exploding into an inferno of golden fire, and still on the ground, she jerked backward, but as quickly as it had come, it was gone, the flames dying away, his features placid once more. "And see how I pay my debt, here in the shadow-lands. But Amergin – well, he made the unforgivable mistake of fighting against the gods themselves, spilling their silver blood all over the white sand beaches, before dying on the edge of his own brother's sword." He paused. "So they were punished, the sons of Mil Espaine, condemned to wander throughout the dark other-realms, an eternity spent seeking the rest that will forever be denied to them."

Riona shivered. It was one thing to listen to Daideo's stories, safe under the warmth of his arm as the hearth-fire crackled nearby, and quite another to stand here under the star-strewn sky of Tech Duinn and look upon the half-frozen face of those stories. "He looks to be sleeping now."

"He is not, I assure you." The lord of death raised his chin. "Amergin," he called. "Sit up. I have need of you."

Deep beneath the dark blue river-water, a pair of soulless black eyes opened, boring through the waves and into her own. Riona gasped. "He can see me."

"And can hear you as well, so watch your words." He crouched down on the riverbank and dipped his fingers into the water. "Sit up, I said. Come and meet my newest pet."

Riona stiffened, but the pale face shimmered underneath the waves, rising closer and closer to the surface, until the tip of his nose broke through the surface, followed by his shaven head with its hollow black eyes. "Ah," he said in a water-logged voice. "You have found another one, I see." His eyes never once blinked, boring into hers with unnerving intensity. "She is very like the others."

"I do have very particular tastes," the lord of death agreed, and Riona's fingers dug into the frozen mud of the riverbank. "This one is special, though. I have been watching her for a very long time." He jerked his chin toward her. "Hold out your hand and let him have a sniff of you."

Riona reflexively hid her hands in the folds of her skirt, her skin crawling at the thought of this eerie creature smelling her, his nose twitching like a hound hunting down a hapless rabbit crouched in the tall grass of the lowlands. "Why?"

"I am your lord now." He crouched down and gently took her clenched fist in his cool hands, tapping at the soft flesh of her wrist with his finger. "No other explanation is necessary." He laughed, humorless and low. "That curiosity of yours will be a problem, a stóirín." Then he tugged her arm over the water, toward where the druid sat, watching intently.

Amergin's nostrils flared, then his thin lips parted in a hiss. "She has the folaíocht."

"A few drops, at least." The lord of death looked at the druid, and for a moment, Riona's stomach churned at the sight of the two not-quite-mortal-but-not-quite-divine beings, communicating with one another in a wordless exchange that she knew could bode nothing good for her. "It should be enough."

"Indeed." Amergin's hollowed-out gaze returned to her face. "What shall I teach her?"

Her lord stood, wiping his fingers on the soft velvet of his breeches. "Everything, Amergin," he said, turning to amble away into the darkness of his woods. "Teach her everything."

Fate, Jack thought. A sign from the gods that this girl and this girl alone, the twin to the visage of death itself, should be his queen.

He would have her, no matter who or what might stand in his way.

Chapter Seven
The Vale of Inagh, Éire, 1062

RIONA

Her mother was leaving.

Riona stood in the courtyard, shivering in the early spring breeze and trying not to show the resentment boiling beneath the surface of her seemingly indifferent features.

Because she *was* angry that her mother was leaving – leaving the vale, leaving their home.

Leaving her.

It had been chaos, those first few days after the news of Uncail Killian's death. Mamó and Daideo had wept for their lost son, their last boy, so soon after they had grieved their first, Riona's father, fallen so far away on a field of battle. It had been Killian's idea to reclaim the lands and castle in Soghain from the southern clans who had seized it years before. Their birthright, he'd claimed, the rightful lands of them and their descendants, Mamó's ancestral home. Mamó had shaken her head, her lips pressed together. "I have no need for it," she had simply said, and Riona had watched wide-eyed from where she crouched by her father's knee by the fire, a mere child of three, as Daideo had rested his hand on the back of Mamó's stiff shoulder.

But Killian would not be put off, determined as he was to win this bit of glory for his sons' sakes, half-grown boys of eight and ten, and so they had gone, Killian and his boys, with her father and her twin brothers, strapping lads of seventeen with their swords at their sides, a legion of soldiers clad in leather and steel behind them, riding off to war.

They had won, of course, but at a too-terrible price.

And now Killian was gone too, and the lands and throne for which her brothers and her father had bled out and died stood shaky and untenable, in the untried hands of a mere boy, with enemies circling all around.

Yesterday, Mamó and Daideo had joined her at the breakfast table, where she sat with her head propped up on her hand, poking listlessly at her raisin porridge, grown cold and congealed in its bowl. She had looked up as they settled down on the bench across from her. "Has something happened?"

"Yes," Daideo said quietly. "Something has." He stole a glance at Mamó, who nodded once, and looked back at Riona, steady and calm. "Someone must go to Soghain, to bring additional forces as a show of force and support, and to be with the boys."

"Your cousins –" Mamó's voice broke over the words. "Your cousins need a regent, until they have come of age. Eamon is fifteen – he only needs a few years of help before he's fit to rule."

Riona reached across the table to grip Mamó's arm. "You can't go," she said, her voice rising with urgency. "Either of you. You can't leave me."

Daideo stood, moving away from Mamó and around the edge of the table, pulling Riona close into his side. "Hush now," he said. "Your grandmother and I are going nowhere. The vale is our home, as it has always been, and Soghain holds too many memories for us, very few of them pleasant. We'll stay here, with you."

The tension in her chest eased a little, and she relaxed against her grandfather's reassuring shoulder. "Then who?"

And so it was that she learned that her mother had volunteered, eager and willing to walk away from their life in the vale.

To walk away, it seemed, from her.

Riona was no fool. She knew that there was an unspoken tension between her and her mother, a razor-sharp wire of resentment and disdain – an often mutual one, it must be admitted. It was there in the sidelong glances her mother would give her at supper, when Riona's voice rose loud and laughing, her gesturing boisterous, as she would chatter with Maeve, or in the dismissive wrinkle of her nose when Riona would be caught daydreaming at her lessons, staring out the window toward the fog-mottled line of mountain ridges in the distance. It was nothing like she used to look at Riona's brothers, so warm and affectionate, with tender strokes of her fingers through the red-brown hair. Mamaí's fingers only touched her hair when she brushed it – a few abrupt, sharp lashes of the comb, then braided it with curt, painful tugs, tight and uncomfortable at the roots near her scalp. "It'll have to do," Mamaí would say with that ever-present wrinkle of her nose, then the comb would clatter as she strode away without a backward glance.

Perhaps, Riona used to wonder, it was because she was born so much later than her brothers, and Mamaí was older, too tired to chase a sturdy-legged toddler, especially one born with such an endless amount of mischief in her heart. But it remained, that cool, dismissive contempt, even as she grew older, desperate to win her mother's approval with gifts of fresh-picked flowers and ripe berries plucked from the bushes in the vale. Mamaí would frown, poking at Riona's proffers of love.

"Did you finish your lessons first, before you went off gallivanting in the woods?" She'd ask, brushing the drooping petals aside, and Riona's shoulders would slump in response.

"No, Mamaí," she would admit, and her mother would point a finger in the direction of the windowless room where Riona did her lessons each day, no word of thanks or flicker of affection in her disapproving features.

So Riona knew, deep within her heart, that it was because she was a girl, an unnecessary daughter after so many strong sons, the only survivor of her mother's womb, the child she had least wanted left living when all the others had died. It was an insurmountable divide, but somehow, despite her resentment and hidden hurt, Riona could not stop herself from trying to win something, anything resembling affection or approval from her mother's unyielding lips, could not prevent herself from believing, hoping, that somewhere, no matter how deep it was buried, her mother loved her.

As she stood in the morning air and watched her mother straighten her skirt without even a trace of emotion on her face, that fragile flower of hope withered a little more in her heart, fading closer and closer to nothing but a shrunken brown stem and shriveled black petals.

"Riona," her mother said, nodding once in her direction, her gaze already drifting toward the carriage that waited at the castle steps, surrounded by armed soldiers already astride their dancing horses. "Be a good girl and do your lessons."

"Yes, Mamaí," Riona answered, her gaze fixed on the ground, because there was nothing else to say to a mother who wanted nothing more from her than unthinking compliance and for her to exist solely in the shadowed corners of her life.

"When I return," her mother said as she climbed into the carriage, speaking through the open door, "we will begin discussing a suitable marriage for you. A prince, one from the northern realms, would be a good match."

Riona's heart stuttered. "I'm only ten," she managed to say, and her mother huffed.

"I know that, Riona," she said, rife with irritation. "But it is never too soon to be planning ahead to secure our future."

"But I'm to be queen of the vale – I don't *need* to marry."

"Yes, you shall be queen of the vale. But once you are, you'll need strong allies and an army to command, and marriage is the only way to secure that." She pulled off her gloves, one after the other, quick, cross movements. "I won't be questioned about this."

Riona clasped her sweaty palms behind her back. "Mamó won't allow you to marry me off if I don't wish it," she said, barely audible, and her mother's lips twisted.

"Your grandmother," she said, "will not be around forever. You will have to stop hiding behind her skirts and be your own woman, to do what is necessary for the good of your people – and yourself." Her nose wrinkled. "I will not be the mother of a fool, Riona. It's time you learned that sense is far more valuable than sentiment."

With that, she leaned forward and the carriage door shut sharply, and Riona was left standing in the cool morning air, watching the silhouette of her mother nod toward the driver, and with a snap of the reins, the carriage rolled away, a cloud of dust rising in its wake, a line of soldiers following close behind on their snorting mounts.

Riona had slipped away as soon as the dust settled in the distance, hiding her trembling hands beneath the soft fur of her cloak, disappearing into the woodlands that surrounded the vale. She knew that if she went to Mamó or Daideo or Maeve, they would comfort her, with reassuring hugs and affectionate squeezes. Yet it felt selfish somehow, to be so needy, while Mamó and Daideo grieved their lost son, and while Maeve still fell asleep some nights weeping for her lost mother as Riona stroked her back, murmuring until she at last drifted away into turbulent dreams. So she sank down onto the grassy bank of the river, arms wrapped around her shins.

Perhaps her mother was right about that much. Perhaps it was best to keep her own heartache hidden away, to try and soothe this roar of anger and resentment and hurt alone, with only the hum of the water and the rustle of the trees to ease this rawness in her soul.

Perhaps it was best to trust in no one and nothing but herself.

It wasn't long though before she heard a twig snapping behind her, and she closed her eyes for a moment, steadying herself, preparing to be the carefree, merry-hearted, sharp-tongued girl that she was determined to be. "Maeve?" She kept her eyes closed as the soft creep of footsteps approached. "Daideo?"

A throat cleared behind her. "It's me."

Riona's eyes flew open, and she twisted around in the grass, frowning. The cabbage-boy – Conor. "What are you doing here?"

He stood a little ways behind her, hands shoved in his pockets. "I saw you come in here, and I thought – I wanted to check on you."

"I'm fine," she said, a bit more sharply than she intended, and he flinched.

"Right," he said. "Sorry. I was just…I wanted –" He fumbled over his words as poorly as he stumbled over his own two feet, clumsy and stuttering, and Riona tried to ignore the answering pang of guilt at the pink spreading over his cheeks. "I wanted to say hello," he finished lamely, backing away, the flush of his cheeks deepening all over his freckled features.

"You can stay."

The words blurted out before she could think better of it, and he paused in his retreat, eying her warily. "Are you sure? Because –"

"I said you could stay, didn't I? Stop questioning it."

"You also said that you were fine," he said, creeping forward a few tentative steps. "And sometimes when a girl says she's fine, she's anything but."

Riona's lips curved unwillingly. "It's not just girls who do that, you know."

"Oh, I know." He sank down beside her, gaze fixed on the flowing river before them. "I do it all the time too."

Riona glanced at him, watching as his fingers plucked absently at the blades of grass. "And what are you not fine about, when you say that you are?"

He peeked over at her, and Riona's breath caught for a moment. She had never seen his eyes this close before, under the brightness of the sun. They were beautiful, wide and clear and gray as the moonlight glinting off the smooth silver stones in the river. "Lots of things. But mostly, I say it to my father."

"I can see why you would," Riona said, thinking of the stern-eyed soldier of her grandmother's sept. "Why did Killian –" She swallowed. "Why did the king send him here instead of staying in Soghain?"

Conor shrugged. "I don't know."

"Liar."

The tips of his ear turned red. "I'm not lying."

"You are. I can tell. You just don't want to say it." Riona scooted a little closer. "It's fine if you don't want to talk about it though."

He shot her a sidelong glance, lips pursed. "Now who's the liar?"

"All right, I want to know, desperately. I love a good gossip." She poked him in the shoulder. "Listen. You tell me what you are not fine about, and then I'll tell you mine."

He seemed to consider this as he stared at the plucked blades of grass in his hands, turning them over and over in his fingers. "All right," he said at last. "My father *asked* to be sent here, with me, to get me away from my mother." Riona watched the muscles in his throat jump as he swallowed. "He says that she is – he says that she was making me weak and soft, because I was more interested in flowers and herbs instead of training as a soldier with the other boys."

"Was she?"

"No." His fingers tore the thin green blade of grass in two, his head drooped low. "She barely knew any more about them than I did. I don't know why he blamed her."

Riona fought against the sudden urge to reach out, to run her fingers through his tangled red curls. "Where is she now? Your mother?"

"Back in Soghain. I begged her to come with us, but she stayed. Da told her to, so she did." His lips trembled. "But…I think she was glad to stay. To be rid of him. He is very stern, my father, not kind or merry, and she is – or she used to be. I remember her laughing more, when I was younger." He shook his head and Riona watched his damp eyelashes flutter. "She hasn't laughed in a long time. I wonder if she is laughing now that we – that *he* is gone."

"Do you suppose she misses you?"

Conor was silent for a long time, his fingers tearing at the blades of grass. "No," he said so quietly that she could barely hear him over the thrum of the river before them. "I think she is too busy being glad to be rid of him to miss me very much."

A hot knife of sympathy sliced through her, invisible spools of hurt pouring out of her still-throbbing wound and intermingling with his own. "My mother hates me," she blurted out, and his head swiveled around to stare at her, gray eyes still swimming with unshed tears. "She hates that I lived when my brothers died. She never even wanted another child, much less a daughter, and so she can't stand that I survived when they did not."

"I'm sure that she doesn't hate you."

"She does." Riona picked up a stone and tossed it into the river. "Trust me. The last thing she said before she rode away this morning was how she was already planning on marrying me off to some northern prince once she returns." Fresh waves of resentment swelled within her, and she shook her head, furious. "I'm sure it's because then I'd be his problem and not hers."

For a moment, the only sound was the rush of the water and the twitter of the birds in the trees around them. "Do you want to marry a prince?" Conor asked, in a strange voice.

Riona scoffed. "Of course not. I intend to be the queen of the vale all on my own, like my grandmother is, like my father intended me to be – and I shall too, whether she likes it or not." She shot a glance at his freckled face. "You really are a cabbage, you know that?"

He ignored this. "Would you marry him, though, this prince, if you could still be queen of the vale?"

"Maybe." Riona shrugged. "I suppose that I will need a more fearsome army, once I inherit the throne from Mamó. A prince could give that to me. Besides, it's what princesses do. I've always known that. We marry princes so that we can give birth to more princes." She tilted her head back to study the green-and-gold canopy above her, the barest hints of the new spring buds waving in the cool breeze. "I'm not sure that I ever want to have children though."

"Why not?"

Because I would love them too much, she thought. *And then I would lose them, just as I lose everything that I love.* "I don't like babies," she lied. "They're very needy. I don't like being needed."

"I suppose." Conor shifted in the grass next to her, leaning back on his elbows. "My father insists that I will be a great warrior someday," he said after a while, his pale face awash in sunlight. "Like he is, and my grandfather before me. But I'd rather be a healer. It fascinates me – how the death of one living thing, a plant or a flower or an herb, can give new life to something else. How cyclical the natural world is, the roots of one thing feeding and soothing another, renewal and revival, over and over again." He flushed, and she realized that she liked it, that swift spread of pink across the brown-red dapples of freckles on his skin. "That sounds silly."

"It doesn't." She raised her eyebrow at him and smiled. "That's the first time that I've heard you speak without sounding like a stuttering donkey."

"That's the first time I've ever seen you smile at me," he said, and this time, it was her turn to flush.

"That's not true."

"It is. You smile all the time at others – at Maeve and your grandparents and Eabha in the kitchen and Isleen and Noah in the stables – but never once at me." He hesitated. "I thought it was because you didn't like me."

Riona's palms tingled, itchy and hot. "I like you," she said, and it sounded oddly timid, her whispered admission, not at all like her usual self, bold and defiant and free of any fear.

He turned toward her, searching her face. "You could marry me," he said. "When we're old enough. You could stay here and be queen of the vale forever. I wouldn't care if we never had a son."

"You're not a prince. Mamaí says that I must marry a prince."

"I'm a bit of a prince, in a way." He tugged on his ear. "My father was a chief of Breifne when he was a boy. His uncle took his throne, though, and the people supported him instead of my father, because Da was just a child, so his mother fled and took him to Connacht. He talks about it all the time, my father."

"Is that why he wants you to be a warrior, so that you can take back your lands when you're grown?"

"Maybe." Conor shook his head. "But I am a prince, in a way, so –" His voice trailed away.

She gave in to that itch in her fingers and patted his head, his red curls soft and springy underneath her hand. "Not enough of one, cabbage. But it was sweet of you to offer." She climbed to her feet, brushing the grass and the dirt from the back of her skirt. "We should go back. I need to be with Mamó and Daideo."

He reached up and wrapped his fingers around her elbow before she could walk away. "Ria," he said. "Your mother loves you. I know she does."

Her lips flattened. "How could you possibly know that? You barely even know me."

"I know," he insisted. "I know because I can't imagine how anyone could not help but love you. I –"

"No." It was like drowning in a cauldron of fresh-melted caramel, sweet and thick and honey-warm, but suffocating, fighting for a breath that could never be drawn. "No," she said again, jerking her arm away from the cool slide of his fingers. "I don't want that. I don't want *you*."

"I only meant –"

"Don't ever say that to me again." She wheeled away from him, stalking into the trees, and did not look back even when he called out her name.

Stay away, she told herself savagely as she stormed through the woods, the branches lashing at her face, leaving thin red welts on her skin. Stay away from Conor Ó Ruairc, because otherwise, she knew, he would be the ruining of her.

Jack leapt atop his waiting horse, leaving the raven there dead in the snow, ready to travel the realm in search of his destined bride.

Chapter Eight
Neither of the Earth Nor Under It, Not Then Nor Now

RIONA

Amergin, the cruel bastard, was ruining her life.

What was left of it, at least.

Despite the unrelenting cold of Tech Duinn, sweat broke out on Riona's forehead as she clenched her fists so tightly that her nails dug into her palms, muttering the unfamiliar words Amergin had taught her as she tried to keep the monsters she had called into existence with her newfound magic alive.

The irony of the situation was not lost upon her.

Riona had to admit, though – these boars, while savage and wild, *were* beautiful, with their ivory-toned tusks protruding from their snouts, huge and red-skinned and rippling with muscle. They thundered around Riona, tossing their heads and snarling as she stood, still as a stone, her eyes half-shut in concentration as she breathed forth the incantation.

This was what Amergin had found that she excelled at – creation-magic, the act of forming something new from the bare minerals of the earth. Amergin had started with herbology, a cruel, cunning smile ghosting at the corners of his mouth, as though he had known the ache in her heart as she had sat, tight-lipped and white-faced, as he walked her through the various uses of the many wild herbs of the forests, remembering another life, other would-be teachers, who had tried to impart this same knowledge on her while she had huffed and ignored them and taken for granted their quiet affection and endless patience. It had been a relief when Amergin had moved on to the study of ancient runes and incantations, staring at inscriptions engraved in pale gray slabs of stone until her eyes burned with exhaustion and unshed tears.

It had felt like years, an interminable stretch of time, but when she had asked her lord, during one of his rare appearances, how much time had passed in the mortal world, he had merely smiled. "Three months," he'd said. "Don't tell me that you have tired of me already? Not after I've been such an *accommodating* host," and his golden eyes flashed meaningfully.

Threateningly.

She'd said nothing, but later, when Amergin had at last begrudgingly allowed her to lie down to rest among the frost-covered leaves, shivering under the meager warmth of her cloak, she had laid awake for far too long, trying to imagine the myriad of changes that even the few short weeks that she lost during the full stretch of time here in the realm of Tech Duinn had ushered onto the stage of her past life.

After runes and incantation came this next phase of her training – creation-magic. "To understand the workings of death, Amergin had informed her coldly, "you must learn its opposite – the workings of life, and that is the most coveted, unattainable aspect of druidecht. Which means," he had continued, with his ever-present contempt, "I have no expectation that you will have any measure of success."

Yet here she was, surrounded by the thundering of wild sídhe-beasts into which she alone had brought to life, the tenuous thread of their continued existence wobbling on the feeble strength of her wavering concentration.

She had chosen red sandstone for these, her fiery-eyed boars, had spent what seemed like weeks crafting and shaping and coaxing them into existence, and now –

"Kill them," Amergin said from where he stood, shoulder-deep, in the frigid dark waters of the otherworldly river.

Riona's lips flattened in a strained, white line, and she shook her head wordlessly.

"You created them," the druid said. "You brought them into being." He paused, a deliberate delay, as much of a silent threat as any that the lord of death himself had employed against her – and just as effective. "Now," Amergin said, cold and flat, "kill them."

A shudder ran through her, and something hatched in her chest, a dark-eyed thing of unknowable depths, black-feathered and caw-ing, scratching and scrabbling its way up its throat toward the faint light of freedom. The curse broke from her, in a voice that was not hers, guttural and harsh and rattling, a tomblike melody, and for one wild moment, she could almost see it, this hideously corvid creature with its beady, bright eyes and fiery talons, scalding her voice for all of eternity, so that the only song she ever again would sing would be a herald of death.

One of the boars squealed, a wild, agonized keening, stumbling to its knees in the midst of the ring, but the others thundered on, indifferent and still half-mad with feral rage, crushing and trampling their squealing brother beneath their wide, sharp-tipped hooves. Riona forced herself to remain frozen in the middle of the circle of wild beasts, her face impassive, even as the sound of the boar's dying screams echoed in her ears.

"Enough," Amergin said, and something cracked through the trees, the very air splitting and ripping into a thousand invisible shreds, and the boars vanished into a dozen piles of crushed red sandstone, lifeless heaps of crimson-colored dust on the icy forest floor. The severing of her incantation tore through her like the lash of braided leather whip across her cheekbone, and her knees buckled as she collapsed against a frost-kissed boulder, her chest heaving, shuddering in and out in a violent, ragged rhythm.

"Again," Amergin said. "Do it again, and do it right this time."

The icy slickness of the rock stung against her forehead, sticky with sweat as it was, and she swallowed. "I can't. I need to rest –"

"You did rest," Amergin said, the dark river water sloshing around him as he rose up higher from the waves wherein he was eternally encamped. "That is all the rest which you and I will find ever here, brief and unsatisfying. Now do it again."

"I *can't.*"

The cool breeze stilled in the trees, the whitethorn wood sucking in an uneasy breath as though it too waited to see what punishment would be doled out for such defiance, such disobedience, and Riona braced herself against the rock for the inevitable lash of his displeasure.

"Now now, Amergin." Her shoulders sagged at the sound of that velvet-dark voice just behind her. "Look at what you've done to my poor pet. She's quite pale."

"I thought you liked them this way, your mortal girls, with corpselike skin," the druid answered, and even though the lord of death merely smiled, gentle and soft, Riona flinched.

"*Snow*-white. Not corpselike," he said, his boots crunching through the leaves as he strolled closer. "I am the lord of death, not of dead bodies. I do have my limits."

"You're not the lord of anything when it comes to me," Riona managed to say, and he laughed again.

"Of course I am, a stóirín," he said, and she shivered at the light touch of his fingers on her shoulder as he played with the ends of her hair. They felt, she thought with a shudder, how the kiss of death itself might feel. "We are hardly equals, you and I — although perhaps, we might be, if you continue in this manner." He withdrew his hand, and Riona turned to face him, bracing her back against the rock. He eyed her appraisingly. "You're doing quite well."

"She could do better," Amergin said from the river, and the lord of death waved his hand at the druid, his black-golden gaze never leaving Riona's face. A slight rippling sound, a quiet splash, and Riona knew that Amergin had retreated back beneath the waves, never sleeping, staring up through the dark midnight blue of the waters at the star-dappled sky above him, waiting until his master deigned to call him forth again.

Riona waited until the waters closed over his head, then relaxed against the boulder. "He is far scarier than you," she said, and he smiled again, a little sharper, a little more wicked.

"Only because I haven't shown you the true depths of my character."

Best not to tempt him to do so. "Why are you called the dark druid," she asked instead, "when he is the more powerful one?"

He laughed at that. "Don't be such a fool. He may have been the more powerful druid in your world, but this is my kingdom here among the sídhe, and his skill is nothing compared to mine."

"Then why aren't you the one teaching me?"

Again, that gentle, terrible smile. "Are you missing me so much, then?" He did not wait for an answer, tugging at something in the pocket of his cloak. "Here. I brought you a treat, as a reward for all your labors." He tossed it to her, and she caught it in both hands, her fingers running over the smooth red skin of a ripe apple. "Now follow me. I have more to show you."

She hurried after him, biting into the crisp flesh of the fruit. "Where are we going?" She asked as she chewed. "Will it take long?"

"An hour or two, perhaps a day, perhaps a year – who is to say? We do not concern ourselves with the passing of time in the sídhe."

"Well, time is still passing in *my* world," she grumbled. "And I would like to go home and see how much I have lost."

"Eleven months," he said, toying with his sleeve as he strode ahead, and Riona walked face first into a tree. "That's how much time has passed you by in the mortal realm."

"But you said – only a few days ago, you said *three* months –"

"Was it a few days? How would you know, without the rise and fall of the sun to help you track the passage of what you mortals call time? Yet another foolish lie that humans tell themselves to give their lives some sort of permanence, of meaning." He continued to stroll through the trees, but Riona remained rooted to the ground, barely registering his taunting words.

Eleven months. Almost a full year, gone, lost forever.

"Come along," the lord of death said over his shoulder, and Riona swallowed down her tears, her grief, before tossing aside the rest of her apple as she followed him deeper into the sídhe.

She had lost much more than her appetite.

There were no trees here in this flat stretch of land to which the lord of death had led her – no bushes or brambles or even rocks to mar the pristine smoothness of the landscape, covered in a sparkling cloak of fresh powder snow. It was eerie, far more unnerving than the loom of the thick-trunked trees with their ever-watching stares and their endless shadows. At least one knew to fear their darkness, that something monstrous no doubt lurked within their depths, but this ominous gleam of pure white caused the skin on the back of her neck to crawl in fear.

"What is this place?"

He slipped his hands behind his back and rocked on his heels. "The home of the fetch," he said. "A shapeless, shadowless beast, with no corporeal form or essence until it finds that on which it wants to feed."

Riona swallowed. "What does it eat?"

"Souls," he said, his gaze wandering across the unmarred snow. "It eats souls, a stóirín."

She edged closer to him, her throat tight. "I don't understand. Why am I here?"

"This what I have brought you here for – to learn the workings of death, is it not? The fetch is one of my most loyal familiars. He has harvested so many souls for us over the centuries, and in return, all that he asks is for the occasional treat, which I of course would give him." Her lord's glance slid to hers, watchful and waiting. "He prefers young boys," he said with an expectant air, even though his voice remained as calm and passionless as always. "Between eight and thirteen years of age. Their souls have a very distinctive flavor, he says, although he has not tasted them in a long time, not since the Tuatha Dé Danann returned and locked him away here in the other-realm. He used to enjoy them, though, the souls of those fresh-faced boys, very much."

She could almost see them, wide-eyed and pale-faced before this most terrible specter of death, a smattering of freckles across the stub noses, a gash of blood across their foreheads –

"I don't want to hear this." Riona spun on her heel and staggered away, the stab of pain in her chest so intense that her very bones were a mere breath away from caving in around her heart, crushing it underneath the weight of her grief. "I don't want to hear any of this – I can't do this, I can't. I want to go home –"

"Riona."

"No." She was running now, tripping over her long skirt, gulping in deep, shuddering lungfuls of the midnight air. "I can't, I can't do this, I'm going home –"

"Then go." Suddenly, he was in front of her, his black-golden eyes bright and burning in his narrow face. "Go, and our bargain is forfeited, and I shall have no choice but to take what is mine by right before you so much as cross the threshold of the sídhe."

She stopped at that, the snow and the ice covering the forest floor seeping in through her slippers. It was always so cold here, as though she were already dead and the warmth of her blood had long ago frozen into silver-encased ice that sledged its way through her veins.

"I thought so." He stepped closer, and she ducked her head away from the intensity of that golden-fire gaze. "This is what Amergin meant, when he told you to do better. You are weak, your heart too soft and too fragile to endure the truths of our craft. We are the purveyors of death, it is true, but that does not make us evil. All things that live must die, a stóirín. It is our responsibility to see that necessity through."

"I don't want young boys to die," she whispered, and it was all she could see, that pale freckled face she had once known, marred by a deep crimson gash.

You look like a wildflower.

"I don't want anyone to die," she amended through the lump in her throat, and the lord's fierce golden eyes grew slightly softer.

"You are still thinking like a mortal," he said. "Like a mortal who only sees the limited nature of your world. I once thought the same, you know, when I was young, as you are now." He waved his hand at the ice-touched trees, the star-kissed sky, the gray shadows that wound their way across the frost-covered earth. "I know better now, Riona – and you too must learn better. There are hundreds of worlds whose gates will open to you beyond this one, once you have passed through the veil between life and death. You are all so attached to these –" He reached out and tapped the end of her nose. "These frail, corruptible bodies of yours. So was I, until I realized the truth of it. They are merely cages, made of skin and muscle and bone that keep the most beauteous part of you ensnared within its wall. Set it free, and it will fly, soaring through the night sky on an endless wind of winter, as it was always meant to do."

Riona swallowed. "Free," she repeated, and he nodded, almost eagerly, his face shining with a fanatical light.

"I am no harbinger of doom, Riona. I simply give to humans

what you all seek – freedom." He sighed. "It's a question of *balance*, a stóirín. Your world is filled with such balances. Why should the world of the dead and the unseen be any different?"

Balance. She remembered now – hemlock and moths and a green-and-brown mountainside, the wind in her hair and a pair of clever, mud-stained hands and a soon-to-be awakened monster from the depths of the earth.

She cleared her throat. "You might be right."

"Of course I am. I'm enormously clever, you know."

"Humble too." She folded her arms across her chest. "The fetch. How does it factor into all this?"

He jerked his head, and she fell into stride beside him, making their way back through the trees to that eerie snow-powdered plateau of land. "The fetch," he said, "is an odd sídhe-beast. While most of the other – monsters, as you mortals call them – of my realm obey the commands of their master without question, as is the right of the lord of death, the fetch is a more self-governing creature. It is the one, in a sense, who chooses the rightful lord of death for the rest of the sídhe. Only to he whom the fetch deems worthy does it choose to bend its will, and its example influences all the other denizens of the realm."

"And it obeys you – the lord of death."

"Without question." He shot her a sideways glance. "The fetch is a mystical creature, without flesh nor blood of its own, and thus, in order to steal the soul that resides within a mortal body, it must assume a physical shape. It mimics, then, the body of the soul it intends to steal."

Riona remembered a story from her childhood – an old legend, one that sounded too fantastical for even a child to believe. "A double," she said. "The person who is about to die sees the double of themselves."

"Exactly. It is the only corporeal form that a fetch can take. It cannot, therefore, be controlled or coerced, like all other physical entities can, and thus the key to its obedience lies in earning its compliance through merit. All my pets can kill and maim, but only the fetch can destroy a soul, immortal thing that it is. The other sídhe-beasts recognize that the fetch is the most powerful of them all, and they will follow where it leads."

"But they cannot leave the confines of the sídhe." Riona frowned. "Isn't that true? The Tuatha Dé Danann set a confinement spell in place to keep them here. They cannot leave."

"Conditionally. They cannot leave of their own accord." He wagged a finger at her with a suddenly cruel smile. "Until one with the power to do so calls them forth and sets them loose upon the mortal world."

The bean-sí.

Blindly, Riona reached out to grasp a nearby branch with white-knuckled fingers, her knees weak, that white-hot burn of grief and guilt rising to an almost unbearable pitch. "So if I had not gone to the mountains that day –"

His answer was a mere shrug of his shoulders, and that burning flame wrapped its sharp-clawed fingers around her heart, slashing at old scars for new hurts.

The lord of death continued, unperturbed by the blow he had landed. "I am not a collector, you understand," he said, surveying the ice-white blanket of snow in front of them. "I am a sunderer. I separate the mortal from the undying, set free the intangible prisoner contained within those cages of flesh and bone and blood of yours, but I have no desire to keep them here, in this place. I do not wish to surround myself with such depressing reminders of my true nature, as you can imagine."

"Can you leave?" She managed to ask through the inferno of regret and guilt burning in her chest. "The sídhe? Can you leave, or are you bound here too?"

"Why would I ever *want* to leave? Here I am the lord of all things, but out there, I am nothing, just like the rest of men."

"That's not an answer."

He laughed again, soft and low. "So now you see – I am no monster, no fiend, as you called me. I simply set the mortals free from their earthly prisons," he said, and Riona frowned at the evasion of her question. "I am the lord of death itself and its familiars, no more." His gaze locked onto hers, steady and knowing. "I am the balance that this world must have, or it ceases to be. Do you understand?"

They stood just outside that flat stretch of snow, and Riona could not tear her gaze away from the pure white powder glistening in the starlight, her heart still throbbing anew with that too-familiar pain. "Why are you telling me all this? Why bring me here?"

"You are here to learn the workings of death," he said again. "This is what death's face looks like." He raised a crooked finger in the air, and a pair of silent footsteps appeared in the snow, meandering toward her.

She opened her mouth to scream, then stopped, because there she was, standing in front of herself, black hair tousled and tangled as it fell loose of its braid. Slowly, she raised her right hand, and the other-Riona did as well, in perfect, precise unison, so she dropped her hand and simply stared.

She had not realized how different she now looked.

At first glance, she looked the same, youthful and curvy, with her pixie chin and porcelain-smooth skin. But the shadows there, dimming the bright blue of her eyes, the hungry, tense lines of her mouth – surely she had never looked so haunted as her other-self now did where it stood, watching her, in the snow, like a long-lost goddess, who had once tasted the delights of the land of eternal youth, only to have them wrenched from her blood-red lips and sent sprawling through the abyss, stumbling and shrieking her way to everlasting doom.

The fractured reflection bowed once, so swift that Riona wondered for one wild moment if she was imagining it, that strangely deferential motion, and then it was gone, this other-her, the only sign that it ever had stood before her the faint imprint of two small slippers there in the snow.

"There now," the lord of death said from over her shoulder. "That wasn't so bad now, was it?"

"The fetch took my shape! Will I – am I going to die?"

He scoffed. "Of course not – quite the opposite, in fact, if all goes well. It only wanted a look at you." He paused. "I rather think it liked you."

"How could you possibly know that? It said nothing."

"You are alive, are you not? It must have liked you."

"So you did think that there was a chance that it might kill me."

"There is always a chance," he said, eyes gleaming. "But I was fairly certain that it would not."

"How comforting."

The lord of death smiled. "It is, rather – at least, a comfort to me. Confirmation, of sorts, that I chose rightly." He moved away from that deadly silent stretch of white snow. After a moment, Riona followed him, glancing over her shoulder for a final look at the dwelling-place of the fetch.

The footprints had vanished, the snow as pure and untouched as when they first arrived, but she could sense it there, hovering just above the ground, watching her still, as hungrily, as greedily, as Fiadh once had, when she had first arrived here in the sídhe.

She shook her head impatiently as she hurried after the lord. "Wait," she called, and he paused, turning back to look at her inquiringly, one dark eyebrow arched. "If you can command the fetch, does that mean that you can also command the other monsters of the sídhe?"

"Of course." He shrugged. "They might need a bit of persuading at first, especially the ones who live in sídhe-realms other than mine own, but they tend to fall in line soon enough."

"How are you any different from the cailleachs? You are a druid of the dark arts, who uses the same incantations, the same spells."

"Hardly." He eyed her for a moment in silence, and Riona fought the urge to squirm underneath the weight of his gaze. "You are a very curious little creature, aren't you? A pity – this would all be much easier if you weren't." Her brow furrowed, but before she could object, he sighed and leaned against a tree, crossing his booted ankles as he settled in to explain. "Éire has long been home to the four great arts – the art of knowledge, which we call fis; the art of prophecy, known as fáitsine –and that one, you should know, only the Phantom Queen herself exercises successfully; the skill in magic, called amainsecht; and druidecht, the talent which I, your lord and master, wields so well." Riona harrumphed, and he smiled, his expression warm with something very akin to humor.

"The cailleachs, immortal beings that they are, practice amainsecht, a craft which they have practiced and honed to perfection over their many centuries of life, speaking their spells into being with that inborn touch of magic that they possess in their souls. The gods also possessed the art of amainsecht, but a hundredfold, compared to the cailleachs, so much so that they merely had to think their will and it came into being, such was the depth of their mastery over the art."

"Like Daideo," Riona broke in. "He was once a god."

"Indeed, and see what little good it did him, his precious divinity." Riona opened her mouth to argue hotly, but he waved his hand and continued. "Amainsecht is the only one that is a *born* gifting, you see. The others, druidecht included, must be learned, taught and studied, forced to be bent to the will of their would-be masters. It is earned, the prowess over these arts, not given. And thus must you earn it as well."

Riona pondered this for a moment. "You keep calling it an 'art'. Once before, as well, you called it a craft."

"So it is." He tilted his head back, and she studied his face for a moment, so mesmerizingly and unexpectedly beautiful, illuminated in the soft white glow of the distant stars. "That is also why I brought you here, to this particular place. I feel that you lack the motivation necessary to devote yourself to mastering this craft that Amergin and I would teach you."

She shifted on her feet, a sudden rush of nerves creeping like spiders over her skin. "I am trying."

"Not enough," he murmured, his gaze wandering over her shoulder into the trees behind her. "Amergin was right about that much."

There was an itch at the back of her neck, a nagging voice of worry, of concern, of rising, frantic urgency. "I don't understand," she said as steadily as she could. "What's happening?"

"You lack motivation," he said again. "I have brought you here to give you some." He nodded his head to whatever he watched in the trees behind her. "I have given you the chance to pay back an old debt – an éraic which you have left unsettled for too long." The hairs on her arm stood on end, and she stared at him, refusing to turn, to see what undead horror lurked behind her.

"You owe a blood-price," he said, backing away into the shadows of the whitethorn wood, his arms folded across his chest. "Pay it now, and with it, you will prove to Amergin what I already know – that I was not wrong about you, that you are strong enough, ruthless enough, to do the biddings of death itself, however unpleasant it may be."

"No," she said, a note of desperation thinning her voice. "No, please – I want to go home."

"This *is* your home now." He snapped his fingers at the lurking presence behind her. "Or it will be, once you prove yourself worthy of it." His eyes glowed, the golden fire in their depths burning fiercer than she had ever before seen. "Go on," he whispered. "Take your vengeance. I know that you want to."

A branch snapped behind her, the leaves rustling as something approached, dragging its cloak across the earth as it glided toward her.

A dark gray cloak, a sheaf of bone-white hair and eyes like embers in a dying hearth-fire.

"For Maeve." Her lord had vanished into the trees, but his whispering voice was there, everywhere, flooding through her senses as soft as the rain on a straw-thatched roof. "For Maeve, kill the bean-sí."

Jack stopped by the riverbank to wash the raven's blood from his hands. He splashed the icy water on his face and paused, staring at his own reflection – dark-haired and black-eyed – shimmering up at him in the half-frozen river.

His smile was sharp as the blade of a well-honed knife, cruel and smug, as though to mock the remnants of the raven's blood floating away downstream.

Excerpt from 'The Snow, The Crow, & The Blood'

Chapter Nine
The Vale of Inagh, Éire, 1068

RIONA

The worst day of Riona's life was also the day that she at last realized that it was a hopeless endeavor – not loving Conor Ó Ruairc.

It did not start out that way, of course – no early morning epiphany as she laid in her bed, watching the rose-golden glimmers of the rising sun, no lightning-strike of foreboding, of realization that spilt through the sky. Instead, it began as most days did, Riona sitting at the round wooden table in the kitchen with Maeve as her friend mashed the potatoes and folded in the cheese for a breakfast of potato pancakes, and Riona mocked Conor's latest efforts at swordplay while he trained in the courtyard with his father.

"You should have seen him." Riona swiped at the frothy top layer of the cream pitcher. "Flailing around like a fish out of water. He could barely take two steps without falling over his feet, Mae, and his visor kept clanging down in the midst of his sparring, all the way over his nose."

"I'm sure it wasn't that bad."

"I assure you, it was that bad." Riona picked up a wide circular platter from the table, examining a chip in the glaze as she spoke. "If the enemies of the vale had seen him, they'd attack within the fortnight armed with nothing more than a couple of pitchforks and half a dozen donkeys, and Conor would still manage to doom us all."

"*Riona.*"

The platter slipped from her hands, shattering into dozens of blue ceramic pieces on the stone floor of the kitchen, and Riona looked up into the flashing green-gray eyes of the queen of the vale standing in the doorway. She had never understood how grown men and women could tremble in fear at the sight of her soft-spoken grandmother, with her fine-boned face and ever-gentle hands.

She understood it now.

"Riona," Mamó said again. "How could you speak about Conor in such a way?"

Something churned in her gut, and she hunched her shoulders, willing herself to slink away and disappear into the shadows, like a greasy-skinned rat caught rummaging in the slop-heat in the middle of the night. "I'm sorry…I didn't –"

"Didn't know that I was here?" Mamó's expression was terrible to behold, and for a moment, Riona could see it there in the lines of her face, what a sight she must have been in the days before the magic of the gods ran dry in her veins. "That is no excuse, Riona. I did not raise you to speak with such malice about those who are your friends." Mamó drew herself up to her full height. "You will apologize to Conor."

"But Mamó, he didn't even hear me –"

"You will apologize to Conor," Mamó said, the pitch of her voice low and smooth as always, yet Riona could swear that the very stones of the castle shuddered a little at the note of steel threading through her voice. "You will apologize, and as a sign of good faith, you will take him into the woods and help him gather the herbs I've been needing, as I've asked him to do, and you will do so with a smile on your face without speaking a single unkind word, or you shall be spending the next fortnight in this very room doing nothing more than scaping pots and scrubbing floors while Eabha takes a well-deserved holiday. Is that quite clear?"

Riona swallowed. "Yes, Mamó."

"Good." Her grandmother's eyes flashed a final time, then she turned and stalked out of the kitchen, and Riona laid her head down on the wooden table and exhaled shakily.

"Gods," she whispered. "I've lost years off my life. *Years*, Mae."

"You really should apologize."

"Mamó just told me to, didn't she? Of course I will."

"You should do it anyway, regardless of Mamó. You are rather mean to him, you know, an awful lot." Maeve elbowed her in the ribs, and Riona cringed. "I don't understand it, Ria – he's so sweet, and he adores you, don't you know, like one of Mamó's hounds with their hambones."

"It's for his own good." Riona sat up and smoothed back the loose tendrils of black hair from her hot face, still burning from the force of her grandmother's censure. "He carries a torch for me and I rather suspect he thinks that it's mutual, which is delusional."

"Is it?" Maeve looked over from her bowl, her forearms covered in mashed potato and cheese. "I've seen how you look at him too, Ria. Protest all you want, but I can tell that you fancy him."

"I have no intention of ever debasing myself enough to kiss the likes of Conor Ó Ruairc."

Maeve hummed. "Perhaps I will then," she said with a sly glance in Riona's direction. "He's grown rather tall these past few months and I'd imagine he'll fill out quite nicely soon enough. He won't be nearly as homely then."

A poisonous hiss slid through her belly as she imagined it – Maeve and Conor, hand in hand as they walked through the halls, her dark head resting against his shoulder, those clear gray eyes smiling down at her. "Go right ahead," she said airily. "Such dull children the two of you shall have. I can almost see them now – the most boring, stick-in-the-mud brats ever born in Éire."

She jumped in her seat when Maeve shoved away from the table, the bowl of mashed potatoes clattering harshly against the wood. "How dare you, Riona."

"Mae, I didn't mean –"

"Why, Ria? Why must you always be this way? You can call Conor a cabbage all you like, but you – you are such a complete and utter *wagon* to everyone around you."

She reared back, stung. "Mae."

"I'm not boring, Ria." Maeve put her floury hands on her hips, bottom lip trembling. "Just because I like my lessons, and embroidery, and reading by the fire instead of gallivanting through the woods on a half-feral horse, and because I follow the rules that Mamó and Daideo put in place to keep me safe and sound and so I don't wind up breaking my leg or my knee or my wrist –"

"I only twisted my knee, and it was but a slight sprain to my wrist that other time."

"It'll be your neck that's broken one of these days." Maeve scrubbed at her face, bits of potato and cheese sticking to her cheeks. "You are wild, Ria, and I love that about you, how bold and brave you are, but we are not all like you. There is nothing wrong with liking quiet, simple things and being a quiet, simple girl who doesn't cause the people she loves to spend their days and their nights wound up with worry over whether she will one day never come back home."

Riona's stomach roiled, and she fought the rising surge of nausea in her throat. "Maeve – I don't think you are boring."

"You just said that you did."

"Mae, I love you." Riona stretched out her trembling hands. "I didn't mean that. I am a wagon, you're right, because I should have never said something so cruel, so untrue. You are my sister, my heart-sister, remember? I love you most, in the whole world."

Maeve stared at her for a long moment, then her shoulders sagged and she stepped forward, burrowing her face into Riona's shoulder. "I'm so afraid," she whispered into Riona's neck. "I'm so afraid that you are going to get yourself killed, Ria."

Riona wrapped her arms around Maeve. "I won't, Mae," she whispered back. "I'm so sorry. I didn't know – I didn't realize how worried you were."

"Well." Maeve pulled back and wiped her cheeks. "Perhaps I am being a bit overdramatic, but I needed to make an impression."

"It was well done."

They both laughed shakily, then Riona stepped away, glancing toward the door. "I should go and apologize to Conor."

"Be kinder to him, Ria." Maeve returned to the table and fussed with the bowl, sliding it closer to her before adding a few pinches of salt to the batter. "We aren't children anymore, to be laughing at others like that. We know better than that now, and Conor – he's a sweet boyo. Clumsy and a bit awkward, sure, but he has a good heart. You should be gentler with him."

"I will. I will be better, for you," Riona promised, then lingered for a moment in the doorway, fingers picking at the loose shavings of wood in the frame. "Maeve?"

Maeve looked up and raised an eyebrow inquisitively.

"You don't *actually* fancy Conor, do you?"

Maeve rolled her eyes and smiled. "Now who's the cabbage, Ria."

Riona grinned and ducked her head. "I mean, if you really wanted him, then –"

"Ria, you idiot." Maeve flicked a shred of cheese at her face. "He wouldn't have me even if I did. He only has eyes for you."

She found him where he always was, whenever he managed to escape his father's stern, overbearing eye – in the woods, elbows deep in the dirt and the flowering herbs and the leaves of the underbrush. She watched him for a moment from a distance, his lips moving as he mumbled to himself, his quick fingers plucking stems and leaves and petals. It was the only thing he did elegantly, this lanky-limbed, klutz, with his copper-red curls and freckled nose. Anywhere else, he was a stumbling, stuttering mess of a boy, but here among the peaceful quiet of the trees and the flowers and the birds, he was a man, steady and sure-handed, and a strange new pulse of awareness thudded within her as she watched him moving from tree to tree, bush to bush, with such practiced ease.

A simple, quiet boy, who liked simple, quiet things. Like Maeve.

Riona swallowed the lump in her throat, then stepped forward. "Conor."

His head jerked around, and he stood up too quickly, tripping over his discarded satchel that lay on the ground. "Hello, Ria," he said from where he lay sprawled on his back in the mud by the riverbank, and she bent over, her hands on her knees, and laughed so hard that her sides ached. He laughed too, one arm flung across his face, his shoulders shaking.

"I really am a cabbage," he said at last, and that set her off anew with fresh peals of laughter, and he grinned sheepishly before he pushed up on his elbow, wiping his sweaty brow with his forearm. "You startled me. I thought I was alone."

Her smile faded a little. "Do you want me to go?"

"No." He sat up quickly, wiping his hands on his breeches as he climbed to his feet. "Is everything all right?"

"Yes." Riona bit her lip. "No. I don't know. Listen, Conor, I wanted to tell you –" She stopped, overcome with uncharacteristic shyness, and he squinted in the sunlight as he studied her. His expression flickered once, and he jerked his head once in an unspoken nod of acceptance, like he somehow knew what she had come to say and how deeply she dreaded having to say to it, that never-acknowledged understanding that always existed between them flaring to life once more.

"Your grandmother sent me out here," he said, cutting off whatever poor excuse for an apology she had been about to fumble her way through. "She needs meadowsweet, and some willow bark. She says that your grandfather's knees have been hurting him a good bit these past few days, and those will help to ease the pain."

Riona shifted on her feet. "All right."

"I'm not having much luck though," Conor said, surveying the trees surrounding the riverbank. "I might need to go a bit further, toward the mountains, but don't you know, I'm not sure, exactly, where I'll be going." He raised his eyebrows at her. "Could use a guide."

She didn't know much about her grandmother's art, despite Mamó's best efforts to teach her. She could barely tell a dandelion from a buttercup, but she was fairly certain that the tree branches which hung over the river, their feathery leaves sweeping against the surface of the water, were those of a willow tree, and the fluffy white blooms dancing in the breeze a mere three feet from his boots were meadowsweet flowers.

Their eyes met, and her heartbeat sped up, a fierce, odd pounding.

"Well," she said. "Anything for Daideo."

He smiled, a bright burst of sunlight on a gray autumn afternoon, and then they were running for the stables, their elbows bumping and brushing as they hurried along. Riona flew through the doors, arrowing her way toward Darcy's stall, strapping on the saddle and sliding on the bridle and reins with impatient fingers. She swung up into the saddle as Conor fumbled with the straps beneath his roan's belly. "Hurry it up, cabbage," she called. "I haven't got all day."

"Missing your singing lessons, are you? That's a pity, sure."

She grinned, and at last he was ready, pulling himself up into the saddle and threading the reins through his fingers. "After you, princess."

Then they were off, Darcy's black mane streaming in the wind, galloping side by side toward the distant stony ridges of the Mhám Toirc, and Riona could not remember the last time that she had been quite so happy.

So free.

"Right," Conor said. "That's wild hemlock, don't you know. Quite poisonous, so if you could put that down –"

"But it's beautiful." Riona raised the plant in her gloved hand to peer at it. "Look at how feathery its leaves are, and those purple splotches on the stem are quite lovely."

"Yes," Conor said with infinite patience. "Very pretty. Also very deadly, so let's leave it be, all right?"

Riona tossed it down on the rocks. "You are very bossy today. You made me put that other one back too, the one with the gorgeous violet petals."

"That was wolfsbane. Also extremely poisonous."

"Why is everything that is the most lovely also the most evil?"

"They're not evil." Conor bent over to run his fingers along the spiny green leaves of a plant she could no more identify than she could be expected to dance a jig on the ice-coated walls of the castle balustrade. "They all have their uses in nature, these beauties, but they have to be treated with respect, with caution. They belong here in the wilds of the forest and the trees. Us, not so much."

"What purpose does the hemlock serve then?"

"Lots of uses." Conor squatted, hands clasped in front of him as he stared into the trees. "It sounds a bit harsh, but it acts as a balance for some of the wee beasties in the forest. Most of the animals know not to eat it, but there's always a few who do so anyway, and –" He shrugged. "It's a part of life, the never-ending cycle. Some live, and some die."

"I didn't expect such morbidity from you, cabbage."

He laughed. "Here then. This is a bit brighter. There is a type of moth that feeds on the buds and the leaves of the hemlock. That's the only bit of foliage it will eat, and it doesn't harm them at all. So without the hemlock's presence in the world, the entire species would die out and cease to exist."

"And? It's a moth. There are dozens more like it."

"Och no." Conor pushed to his feet, his gloved hand running through his hair. "It's a chain, Ria. That particular moth ensures the existence of some other living thing, and that guarantees the existence of something else, and so on and so forth. If you eliminate even one rung on the ladder, the whole system collapses into chaos."

"Are you trying to tell me that the fate of all of humanity depends on the survival of a couple of plants and a handful of bugs?"

"In a word, yes. That's what I'm trying to tell you."

"How depressing."

He grinned. "Come now, Ria. This can't come as a surprise to you. It's your grandmother's art. Does anything about her be striking you as warm and cuddly?"

She grinned back, and for a little while, an easy silence fell between them as they combed through the brush, plucking sweet-scented blooms and soft green leaves. "Tell me a story," Riona said after a little while, as they both clambered down the side of the mountain toward a clear-watered stream.

"A story? What for?"

"Because I've been digging in the dirt like a dog for hours now, cabbage, and I'm bored and want to hear a story, that's why."

"It's a punishment," he said. "It's not supposed to be fun, you know." She made a face, and he grinned again. "You tell me one.

As part of your apology."

"Fine." She sniffed, then considered for a moment as they plopped down by the stream, the tips of their boots skimming the surface of the water. "So you see, there was a prince named Jack, the son of the High King of Éire, and one day he shot a bird, a raven or a crow or something, and it fell into the snow, and he decided that it was rather pretty, the black and the red and the white, and so he decided that he wanted to find a wife who looked a bit like that – black hair and red lips and white skin. So one day –"

"I've heard this one before," Conor interjected. "Jack steals the princess away from the lord of death and then marries her."

"Supposedly." Conor looked at her curiously, and she shrugged, remembering that vague dissatisfaction at the end of the story, the neatly-tied bow on the top. "I just remember thinking that it was too easy for him, doing all that by himself – slaying giants and wielding the weapons of the gods. Also, it's far pretty of an ending for that kind of a tale. Think about it – he defied the lord of *death*. I can't imagine any soul who defies the lord of death, much less cuts off part of his face, would be allowed to live out his days in peace. But," she said, "I was very young when Daideo told me, and my brother was dying. I suppose I was inclined to be morbid when hearing it."

Conor clambered to his feet, offering a hand to help her up. "Perhaps," he said. "But folklore and legends are often a mixture between fact and fiction, lies and truth. It's just a matter of which version sounds better in the telling of it."

Riona pursed her lips, but before she could answer, she saw it, lying just below them on the boulder-strewn mountain side – an ever-so-slight swelling in the ground, a perfect circular curving in the earth, surrounded by a band of fat-trunked whitethorn trees. She reached out and gripped Conor's sleeve in both her hands as she scrambled to her feet. "Conor." She jerked her chin toward the swell in the earth. "Look. It's a sídhe."

Conor inhaled sharply. "Are you sure?"

"Yes." Riona stepped closer, her heart racing. "See the trees – whitethorns, in a perfect circle — and the swelling in the ground? It's a sídhe. A fairy-ring, the entrance to the other-realm."

Conor grabbed her hand, tugging her back toward where they had tied up their horses by the mountain stream. "We should get out of here, Ria. No good comes from wandering too close to such things."

"Wait." Riona shook free of him, pulse thrumming in her veins. Something began to sing in her veins, a warbling, seductive croon, a song of desire and longing, wild and untamable. She crept closer, tugging at the fingertips of her glove with her teeth, intermingling with a whispered remembrance of her grandfather's stories of the old gods and the power that churned within their veins. Her veins. "I want to try something."

"Riona –"

"It's *fine*, Conor." Stories of islands filled with wild, free women, of sun-kissed shores of undying merriment, of isles sweet and prosperous with fat red apples. Which one would she see, Riona wondered, if she slipped inside its secret borders? What wonders, what delights waited for her beyond these unseen walls? Suddenly, all Daideo and Mamó's warnings, their cautionary tales about the manner of monsters lurking within the sídhe-realms, did not seem so dire, so scary, in comparison to the imagining of what wonders might also await her, if she dared to breach their borders.

She paused outside the ring of whitethorn trees, craving it, that hum of darkness, the call of unimagined sights begging to be seen. Slowly, she reached down and withdrew the small hunting knife she wore in her belt.

"Riona." Conor's voice was shrill and urgent. "Riona, get away from there."

"No," she said. "I want to see – I want to see what I can do."

She pressed the sharp tip of her blade into the palm of her hand and watched as a faint line of crimson welled up, and there, mingling among the dark red drops of blood, there it was – a single shimmering bead of bright silver folaíocht.

Riona's breath caught in her throat, and she flipped her hand over, letting the silver drop of blood fall to the earth below her, sizzling as it soaked into the black soil beneath.

There was a long, slow groan that reverberated through the stones of the mountain itself, and then a shadow moved deep within the trees, a slight, gray-cloaked figure materializing in their midst, ambling its way toward them.

"Riona –"

She backed away, fumbling as she slid the knife back into its sheath at her side, and jumped when Conor grabbed her by the elbows, pulling her toward him. "Ria, what the hell did you do?"

The gray-cloaked figure halted just inside the circling line of whitethorn trees, tilting its head as it studied them with hooded eyes. It was petite and skeletal, with a silent, otherworldly presence, something rancid and foul emanating from its floating presence.

"Ria," Conor said again, his voice shaking. "What is that, Ria?"

The creature lifted its hands, its sleeves falling back to reveal bony fingers as it pushed back its hood, and Riona sucked in a horrified breath, clutching at Conor's shoulders.

This – this was no wonder, no creature that had ever walked the plains of delight.

Red eyes, she realized, terrified. Red eyes in an emaciated face, bone-white hair streaming down across her skeletal shoulders. "Run," she gasped. "Conor, *run*."

Conor did not need to be told twice, and he turned, his clammy fingers wrapped around her wrist as they fled, sprinting toward their horses, but it was too late, for behind them, it rose, the caoine – an unearthly, high-pitched wail, ear-splitting and bone-wrenching, an eternal keening for what is lost that can never again be found.

Riona sobbed as she threw herself into the saddle, gasping as she dug her heels into Darcy's side. She could hear Conor's roan behind her, snorting and whinnying as he thundered after her, their hooves clattering against the loose stones along the narrow mountain path, and behind them, still that unnatural voice wailed, singing its song of everlasting lament.

They galloped down the mountain, until at last they reached the slow roll of the hills that led into the vale, and Riona yanked on the reins, slipping from the saddle into the grass, her hands fisting in her hair as she sank to her knees. Conor tumbled off his horse onto the ground next to her, his arm encircling her shaking shoulders. "Ria – what happened? What was that?"

"Oh gods," she whispered. "Oh gods, Conor. What have I done? What have I done?"

"Ria." He grabbed her by the elbows and pulled her around to stare at her, his face white and drawn. "Talk to me. What was that thing?"

"A bean-sí," Riona said dully. "A fairy-woman of death."

Conor's fingers went limp on her arms. "Ria –"

"Conor." She covered her face with her shaking hands. "Conor, someone I love will die."

"Ria, it's just a myth, a legend, it's not true –"

She laughed once, brittle and harsh. "My grandmother used to turn into a black-winged beast, cabbage, and my grandfather was once a prince of the undying gods. There are no myths in Éire, only true things that happened so long ago in the past that no one remembers how very real they once were." She kneaded her forehead with the heel of her palm. "A family member," she said. "The wail of the bean-sí heralds the death of a family member. My mother –" Riona lurched to her feet. "I need to send word to my mother. I need to be home, I need to see Daideo, and Mamó –"

"Easy, Ria." Conor pressed his palms to her cheeks, wiping at the stream of hot tears with his thumbs. "Let's go home," he said, brushing his lips across her forehead. "They'll be fine, Mamó and your grandfather, and your mother too. It's just an old story, Ria. It isn't real. You'll see."

Riona nodded, the lump of dread in her throat grown too thick and troubled for words, and she pulled away in silence, pulling herself up into the saddle for the long ride home.

They were fine – Mamó and Daideo. Her mother too, far away in the high-walled castle of Soghain, writing back a terse message a few days after Riona sent her urgent, worry-filled missive by a fast-paced courier as soon as she arrived home in the vale that night.

But it was too late, because twelve hours after Riona awoke the bean-sí with the silver beads of godlike blood that ran in her veins, the sister of her heart died in her arms under the early morning sky, gasping for a breath that she could not take, her body racked with convulsions and foaming at the mouth, stung on the neck by a yellow-banded wasp. Mamó cried as she pressed a frantically made paste of lavender and honey to the side of her throat while Riona sobbed, her too-scarred heart shredding anew as she watched her sister's eyes roll back into her skull and her body go limp where she lay strewn across her lap, and the once-steady throb of her heart fall silent forever in her chest.

Riona keeled over, her face pressed against Maeve's distended, swollen throat and screamed for the passing of the one soul that she had never thought she would lose.

But then --

'Hullo,' said a voice from behind
him. 'What business, boyo?'

Jack whirled around in the saddle,
and his gaze lit on a small,
hunched-shoulder creature, a bright
red cap perched on his odd head.

The fear-dearg, he realized. The
mischief-maker fairy.

Chapter Ten
Neither of the Earth Nor Under It, Not Then Nor Now

RIONA

Deep within the shadows of the sídhe, Riona stared at the gray-hooded figure before her, this damnable thief of simple, quiet souls.

The bean-sí. It was here, standing before her – and she had the power to do whatever she wanted to it, if she so chose.

She had wanted to watch it burn for so long, this demon-woman with her keening and her soul-stealing wails, and this whole damnable other-world with it, filled with sorrows and unrelenting darkness. She ached to see it, consumed by the very thing it most feared, writhing in pain at her feet as she looked into its red-ember eyes and whispered the name of her sister, so that as it melted away into nothing more than ash and bone it would know who had condemned it, the one who would spit on it cinder-ridden grave after it was gone.

For the first time, she wanted it, craved it – to be the bringer of death.

Let it burn, this demon of the sídhe, she thought. Let it scream in the undying throes of agony and pain, and then be gone forever from the face of the earth, consumed by the fire of her rage and her everlasting grief.

For Maeve, she would watch it burn.

The unnatural harbinger of doom within her awoke, raucous and cawing, humming hungrily in her throat, and for the first time, staring at the cloaked figure before her, Riona set it free without hesitation, without restraint, that dark, dreadful power within her, shrieking for fresh-spilled blood and unending death.

There was no sun in the perpetual night of the sídhe, only the pale white glow of the moon and the stars, but she was the student of death, and if she wished to see something burn, then by the gods, it would burn.

Riona lifted her arms high above her head as the bean-sí backed away, its dark hood slipping back over its skeletal shoulders, face drawn with something that might have been fear. The bean-sí shrieked once, and Riona let her arms drop to her sides in a savage motion, .. letting the beady-eyed creature within her usurp her voice with its hoarse scream.

Far above the gray-trunked trees, the impenetrable blackness of the ever-night sky exploded in a brilliant bursting of white-golden light that tore its way through the star-studded sky – curving, luminous claws of sunlight, arrowing their way hungrily toward the tiny gray shadow crouched on the half-frozen forest floor. The bean-sí's scream turned frantic and shrill, and Riona concentrated all her strength, her will onto those shooting bursts of sunlit-flame, driving them deep into the bean-sí's fast-beating heart.

The sun-fire roared once, swallowing the keening, agonized screams of the bean-sí as it tore into its mottled gray flesh, snarling and savaging its luminous white teeth against the thin face of the sídhe-demon, until her wails faded away into a dying whimper. Riona raised her hands, and the flames of the sun settled, flickering lower and lower toward the earth, purring in obedience to her commands, until nothing remained of their white-hot glory but a few tendrils of pale gray smoke, meandering its way through the once-more nighttime air.

Riona looked at where the bean-sí once stood, where now only a few charred white bones and a shred of a tattered gray cloak remained.

That years-old hurt that had truly never ceased throbbing in her chest, in the place where the memory of her heart-sister still lived, quiet and simple and ever-kind, sighed, a long exhalation of satisfied revenge.

"Well." She heard the rustle of leaves behind her and turned to see the lord of death wandering toward her, that same terrifying smile curving along his lips. "I must say, that was a *decided* improvement."

"Motivation," she said, reaching up to smooth back her hair from her face with a surprisingly steady hand. "I believe that I have found it."

His golden-fire eyes gleamed, as bright and as brilliant as the sun-flames she had called down from underneath the cover of the eternal night sky moments ago. "Indeed you have."

They took their time making their way back to the banks of the dark-watered river, ambling through the gray-trunked trees of the whitethorn wood, listening to the screech of the owls and the stealthy prowling of the sídhe-beasts that lurked among the ice-coated branches. It might have been an hour, Riona thought dreamily. It might have been years. It no longer felt odd, this aimless drifting, an endless stretch of existence in a world where time did not exist. She tilted her head back to let the cool breeze caress her skin, studying the distant gleam of the stars against the velvet night-sky.

"I find that I do not miss it any longer," she said after a moment. "The warmth of the sun."

Her lord glanced down at her. "Why should you? It's a vulgar thing, the sunlight. There's no mystery to it. It lacks all subtlety, all the nuance that hidden depths lend to a thing." His lips quirked. "It does not suit you– the daytime. I have known for a long while, that you were a creature made for the dark."

A rustling in the bushes stopped Riona from answering. She turned her head and there was a familiar pair of glowing yellow eyes, gleaming from the shadows. "Fifi," she said, and the cat-sìth sprang forward, tail lashing, a low purr rumbling from her throat as it butted its sleek dark head against Riona's hand. "I've missed you. Where have you been?"

"I told you." He moved closer to where she stood, stroking the sleek black spine of the cat. "Tech Duinn is not her home. She comes and she goes as the wind in the trees, ambling through the portals between the various realms of the sídhe."

"Can you? Travel between them."

"Some of them. It depends on which gods allowed for my visitations when they cast their spells. Each realm was prized by certain gods, and not all of them were fond of me, in their time." He watched as Riona scratched behind the cat's pointed ears, his eyebrows raised. "Well," he said. "You are further along your way to becoming a proper servant of death than I thought, if Fiadh comes to heel for you without so much as a glance at me, her true master."

"You see?" Riona stroked her hand down the smooth fur that rippled along the cat's spine. "We *are* friends."

"Apparently." He beckoned with his finger, and with unthinking obedience, she hurried her steps so that she walked by his side, her arms brushing against his as they halted by the side of the dark-watered river. "You have done well enough with the incantations, and thus Amergin's time with you draws to a close." He kicked a rock into the churning waters below. "Come on out now."

Amergin's head broke through the waves, his hollowed-out gaze fixed on Riona. "Did she kill it?"

The lord of death shot her a sideways smile. "She did indeed."

"Good." Amergin folded his arms across his chest. "A pity though. I rather liked it better than this one." He jerked his chin toward where Riona stood, and she scowled. "Tell her now."

Riona frowned, looking at the lord who leaned against a boulder, ankles crossed. "Tell me what?"

"Amergin grows impatient," he said. "But he is premature. One small victory over a bean-sí does not mean that you are now a master of druidecht. You are not ready yet to complete the tasks I have in mind for you."

"We have waited long enough," Amergin snarled from the river, but her lord merely pointed a finger in his direction.

"It is not sufficient," he said, and Riona took an involuntary step back at the venom that slithered into his voice, so at odds with the velvet-softness she had come to expect from him. "She has killed," he said, more gently. "As you asked that she do, and now that will be all, Amergin."

Amergin stared at him, his jaw tight with fury, then begrudgingly, the druid once more sank beneath the dark waves.

Riona swallowed. "You mentioned the tasks, as you said when I first came to you. Will you tell me now, what you have brought me here to do?"

"Soon, and it is not what you will do *here* that matters. You asked if I am free to travel between the realms of the sídhe, and I told you – to some, yes. But it is what I intend for you to find out in the realms where I cannot go, that is so important." He shoved away from the rock, pacing along the banks of the river, his hands clasped behind his back. "Ignore Amergin. We have only just begun. You are almost at an end with his tutelage, so now your training with me begins."

"What is it that you want me to learn?"

He held out his hand toward her in response, and after a moment's hesitation, she slipped her fingers into his. He smiled again, spinning her hand around so that her palm faced up toward the midnight sky. "Now," he said. "You learn how to use that which Amergin and I do not, nor cannot, possess – thanks to that silver-coated blood of yours." In his free hand, a sliver of a slate-gray piece of flint again appeared, and again, in a single, swift motion, he slashed at the vein that throbbed just above her wrist. Riona bit her lip to keep from crying out as dark red blood welled, tinged with a few drops of silver folaíocht.

"Beautiful." The lord of death dipped the tip of his finger into her blood. "'Aithníonn ciaróg, ciaróg eile.' Do you know what that means, Riona?"

"Like calls to like," she whispered, watching the swirl of his finger across her bloodstained skin, and he nodded once.

"Like calls to like, indeed. One of the oldest incantations carved into stone by the first druids born to Éire so many centuries ago. You asked what it is that I have brought you here as my servant to do, the tasks which you must complete so that you may be free of me, so listen well to what I say. There are certain treasures, things that are most precious to me, that I have lost — centuries ago, when first I arrived here in the realm of Tech Duinn — that I would call my own again. These treasures are god-made, fashioned in the smithy of the Tuatha Dé Danann themselves, and alas, they are hidden to me, because I am not one of their kin. But you —" He lifted his finger, a single drop of folaíocht shimmering in the starlight. "You are, a stóirín."

Riona stared at it, oddly breathless. "'A stóirín,'" she repeated. "That's what you called me, when I first arrived here. Your little treasure." She looked up at him, his golden eyes and smiling face. "That's what you want from me? To find these treasures for you?"

"I want you to find them," he said, "*and* bring them back to me, here in Tech Duinn. That is your task. Then, and only then, will our bargain be complete." He wiped his palm on the hem of his doublet before he moved to stand behind her. "Do you understand?"

"Yes," she whispered, that shimmering drop of silver on the tip of her finger still glinting in the moonlight.

"Good." His hands slid onto the tops of her shoulders, easing her forward a few steps. "We will begin preparing you now."

Riona blinked in confusion. "Preparing? How?"

He smiled, as soft and gentle and terrible as ever, and it occurred to Riona that death might be much like the night itself, dark and full of mysterious, sure, but soothing somehow, of warm limbs lying wrapped around one another after the long absence of the day, of whispered secrets and muted smiles beneath linen sheets, a place of respite and quiet slumberings. "Tell me, Riona," he said. "Did your grandfather ever tell you stories of the legendary hero, Cúchulainn?"

'I am seeking a wife,' Jack said to the fairy, 'a girl with deathlike beauty, hair like the blackest raven, skin as smooth and white as new-fallen snow, and lips as red as blood.'

'I know such a girl,' said the fear-dearg. 'The princess of Connacht, a rare beauty indeed. I can take you to her, but be warned – she is the promised bride of Death himself.'

'No longer,' Jack said. 'For you shall bring me to her, and I will claim her as my own.'

Excerpt from 'The Snow, The Crow, & The Blood'

Chapter Eleven
The Vale of Inagh, 1068

RIONA

Riona could not sleep.

For months now, ever since she had watched Maeve die in her arms, she had dreaded the nightfall as never before – the way that the shadows crept into the castle, darkening its familiar halls with its cool whispering touch. She avoided the long, slow climb up the stairs to her room with a fierce, almost feral intensity. Playing fidchell with her grandparents, loitering in the kitchen as Eabha prepared the morning meal, staying up late into the night as she read by the low-burning fire in the solar. Anything to avoid lying on her back in her childhood bed, staring at the wood beams crisscrossing across the ceiling with nothing but the sound of her breathing, in and out, to reinforce the terrible truth that she could not bring herself to accept.

Her heart-sister was gone, and she was never coming back.

It was this thought that had stolen away her sleep and wrecked her dreaming. She had never before slept alone in the darkness of her little room, not since she was a babe of a few hours old, when the requested nursemaid from the village had arrived, a sleeping infant strapped to her chest. "I'll love her like she were mine own," Aisling had said to Mamó, and to prove it, had placed her own babe down next to where Riona dozed in her basket, the two girls snuggled together for warmth, their tiny fingers brushing against one another's cheeks. "See now," Aisling had said, "they could be sisters," and as though the lost gods had heard her words and granted this one small benediction on the sleeping girls, they had been, in all but name, for every hour of every day since.

Until now.

Riona sat up in her bed, the sheets tangled and twisted from her restless squirming. It was no use, she decided. She would never be able to sleep here, staring into the midnight darkness, knowing that the little bed that used to lie just across from hers was no longer there. Even though Mamó had tried to cover its absence with brightly painted clay pots of blues and yellows and greens, blossoming with sweet-scented herbs and white-petaled plants, it was a hateful thing, that gaping wound which would never fully heal.

She had killed Maeve, she and that gods-damned drop of silver-tinted blood in her veins, and she could not endure it, could never bear the loneliness of such a loss, let alone the suffocating press of guilt that weighed on her heart.

Riona flung her legs over the side of her bed and stood, dressing with trembling hands, fighting the fresh surge of nausea that rose in her throat. She needed to leave, to be free of these silent, judgmental stone walls that used to echo with the sound of her heart-sister's laughter. She needed the clean rush of air on her skin, the roar of the river thundering beneath her, the rolling majesty of the stony-ridge mountains. She would go mad, if she had to stay another night in this place that used to be home, that now only housed the fast-fading shadows of memories of a brighter, better time.

She slipped into the stables and saddled Darcy in the dark, her movements swift and sure, and then she was pulling herself onto the mare's sleek back and galloping away into the trees, the sound of the night-wind like a cleansing song in her ears, a promise of, if not absolution, at least a few brief hours of mindless freedom.

Darcy's steps slowed to a halt by the grass-green riverbank, and Riona slid down to lean against the bendy trunk of a young fir tree, her arms wrapped around her knees, watching the river thunder by below, this life-giving force of nature. It soothed her, this crash of its white-water waves against the rocks, the sound of the salmon leaping and splashing in the currents, the murmur of the owls that watched her from the branches against the cloudy night sky.

She rather liked it, she decided, the darkness of the night. There was no expectation here in the dark, to be anything other than silent and still, to let herself feel all the things she was compelled to keep hidden in the bright light of the daytime.

"Riona."

She swore. "Cabbage," she said through gritted teeth. "What are you doing here?"

There was a brief pause. "You ask me that every time," he said at last. "You should know the answer by now."

"I don't need to be checked up on, Conor."

"I know." There was a single hesitant step from behind her, then nothing. "I saw you out my window, running down the steps. I was worried about you." He crept forward a few more paces, his hands clutching at the satchel strapped across his shoulders. "You should be sleeping, Ria."

She rested her forehead against the backs of her hands, suddenly weary, as though his words had reminded her of all the many lost hours of slumbering she had endured over the past few months.

"I can't," she said listlessly. "I can't sleep anymore, Conor. When I close my eyes, all I see is her."

His hand slid down her back, wrapping its way around her waist, as he sank down into the grass next to her. "I know. I dream of her too." He swallowed. "I miss her, same as you. You're not alone in this."

It's not the same, she ached to say. *You're not the one who killed her.*

Because Maeve's death, she knew, deep in her heart of hearts, was her own fault. If she hadn't been so selfish, so stubborn, if she hadn't yielded to that gods-damned hum of curiosity, then Maeve would still be alive. It's what she saw every time she tried to close her eyes and sleep – Maeve, standing there in the kitchen, staring at with those somber, disappointed eyes.

Conor – sweet and innocent and so blessedly good-hearted – could never understand.

She cleared her throat. "I know," she lied. "But I can't sleep there, Conor. Not in the room where she once lived." Her voice thickened. "I've never slept alone before. She was always there, next to me. It was the lullaby that I learned to fall asleep to, her breathing, and now it's gone, and I'm – drifting, like I'm lost at sea."

After a moment of silence, he pulled his arm away from her waist, leaning back on his elbows in the grass, and she tried to ignore the pang that flashed through her at the loss of its warmth, soothing and heavy, against her back. "I brought you something," he said, reaching into his satchel. "I thought you might be hungry. You barely touched your plate of colcannon at dinner."

"Eabha puts extra kale in mine, and not enough butter. She claims it's good for me."

"It is good for you, and you should eat it, but nevertheless." He slid a loosely wrapped scrap of white linen toward her. "Eat that instead, just this once."

She unfolded it. "Spiced apples. I love apples."

"I know." He smiled hesitantly at her, then looked at the ground, his hands clasped on his knees. "They make me think of you."

"*You* smelled like apples, that night in the rain on the mountainside."

"That was because I spilled the cider on myself, I told you that, but you – you always smell like cinnamon, and clover. It makes me think of that –" He jerked his chin toward the baked treat in her hand as she nibbled at the slice.

"Oh." She swallowed. "It's from the mishmash Mamó lines the inside of my clothes with. She says it's a warding against evil, silverweed and clover." Riona shrugged half-heartedly. "It seems a bit silly, but there's no arguing with Mamó."

"I don't know about evil, but it's excellent if you catch a cold."

The distant cousin to a laugh bubbled up in her throat. "I suppose that explains it. I don't fall ill very often." She paused. "I do break a lot of bones though, twists and sprains and fractures. I don't suppose you know an herb to help with that."

"Sure now." He smiled again, wider this time. "Kale."

The laugh broke forth, a tired clap of a sound. "Fair enough." She popped the last slice of apple into her mouth and swallowed, wiping at her lips with her sleeve.

"What would help you sleep?" He asked presently. "A cup of tea? Some fresh-cut lavender?"

Maeve. Maeve, alive and well, laughing and saying, 'See, no harm done, just a silly legend, that old story of the bean-sí and its deathly wail' – that would help her sleep. "Nothing," she said instead. "I'm not asking for a solution, cabbage. Sometimes I simply want to talk about what's bothering me, not that I need it to be fixed."

"I understand that. But you should also sleep a bit. You look very ghostly here in the moonlight. You're exhausted, Ria, it's plain to see, so what can I do?"

"Nothing," she said again. "There's nothing."

Conor hmmed. "You never finished your story," he said presently. "On the mountain. You promised to tell me one, and I know Daideo keeps all his most interesting stories for you." He shrugged. "He doesn't like me much, your grandfather, so he never spins his yarns when I'm in the room."

"He does too like you."

He shot her an amused glance. "Sure. Come on – tell me one of his stories, Ria. I've always been curious – your grandfather, the used–to–be god. I bet he has some good ones."

"He does." For the first time in months, Riona's lips twitched with the need to smile, however so slightly. "All right, I suppose I do owe you one, from when –" Her voice caught, and Conor reached out, running his fingers up and down the back of her hand, reassuring and gentle. She cleared her throat. "But I can't tell them as well as he can, so a bit of patience, if you please."

"Always." Conor plopped down on his back in the grass, his arms folded behind his head, looking up at the faint glimmer of the stars hidden behind the dark gray clouds, and after a moment, Riona followed suit, snuggling a little closer to him than was necessary. She was cold, she told herself, even though it was late summer and rather warm even under the shade from the trees and the midnight sky.

"Once upon a time," she said, and Conor chuckled to himself.

"What?"

"Nothing," he said. "It's a very predictable start, that's all. I expected better than that from you."

"Hush, or my grandfather will hear about the time you followed me into the barn and tried to kiss me."

"I never did any such thing –"

"He won't care, so you best not mock me." Conor's mouth snapped shut, and Riona settled deeper into the grass. "Once upon a time, when the great hero Cuchulainn was a boy, he wasn't named Cuchulainn at all, but Setanta, and one day he and the other boys played a game where they all tried to tear off one another's cloaks –"

She stopped as he laughed, his head tipped back toward the starlit sky, eyes closed. "Sorry, Ria," he said. "But I've heard this one too. Cuchulainn steals all the other boys' cloaks, but none can steal his, then he knocks all the other boys down without ever losing his feet, then he wins at iomaínt, and then the dog comes, and –"

"All right, all right, you know the story." Riona huffed. ""You tell one then, if you're so picky. You're better at it than me anyway."

"I can't believe you'd admit to that," he said with a smile. "That I'm better at something than you," and she poked him in the ribs with the tip of her sharp finger in response before nestling in closer to his side.

He talked then, low and soothing in that ambling, clumsy way of his, a tale of Fionn mac Cumhaill, the legendary ruler of the Fianna, the great warrior-tribe of the eastern realm, and his defeat of the demon-beast named Aillén the Burner, with his enchanted songs and infernal wind. "He was a fire-breathing beast," said Conor, "like an oilliphéist, but worse, who enchanted his victims with the power of his song before he burned them alive, a fairy-monster who craved above all else the treasures of men and gods alike, hoarding them away high upon the cliffs of Éire in his nests of charred limbs and wilted leaves. He wreaked havoc on those early tribes of Éire, greedy for their blood and their gold, and it seemed that they were all doomed to perish beneath the magic of his scream and the fire of his tongue."

"I knew you'd be a good story-teller," said Riona, looking up at him, and even in the darkness, she could see the flush that darkened his cheek. "How'd Fionn defeat him?"

"How do you know that he did?"

"It's a story," said Riona. "One of your choosing. Of course it has a happy ending. But most stories don't – at least the true ones."

"That is a very depressing thought, Ria."

"That's how my thoughts tend to go, these days." She shrugged. "Now you know why I can't sleep."

He pulled her head back down to rest against him and continued, telling her how the brave warrior Fionn mac Cumhaill came to Cnoc na Teamhrach to brave the wrath of the incendiary sídhe-beast, how he breathed in the poison of his legendary spear, Birgha, so that it might stave off the sleeping-spell of the monster's song, half-killing himself to save himself. "That's how the hero conquered him," Conor said, his voice for once free of stutters and stumbles, here underneath the quiet of the moonlight, "the dread fire-beast of the sídhe. Because sometimes, the cure is in the poison." Riona listened, her head leaning against his shoulder, letting the rumble of his voice flow through her like a mountain stream tumbling down the sleek gray stones of a crystal-clear waterfall, and the last thing she remembered before she drifted off to sleep was Conor, deepening his voice to a guttural pitch as he mimicked the speech of one of the greatest warriors ever to walk the earth of Éire.

She awoke in the sunshine of the early dawn, her head pillowed on the top of Conor's chest, one of his arms slung across her shoulders, the other tossed languidly over his face. She studied him for a moment, his mouth ajar as he slept, his face placid and smooth, his freckles warm and red-brown in the light of the morning sun.

She was no fool, to believe that he had been the sole solution to her sleeplessness, that it was because of him that she had at last been able to rest, or even that she was somehow fixed now, that her grief and her guilt would no longer haunt her in the dark hours of the night, and yet – it was nice, having him here when she at last succumbed to her exhaustion in the clean, crisp breeze that wafted over the churning waters of the river.

Riona poked him in the shoulder. "Conor, wake up."

His eyes flew open, gray and clear and beautiful. "Ria," he mumbled, rubbing at his face. "We fell asleep."

"I guess you'll find out after all," she said, "what my grandfather will do to you for kissing his best girl."

He dropped his hands, startled. "But I didn't kiss you."

"Will *he* believe that, seeing us stumbling in from the woods at the first light of dawn?"

He looked so horrified, that it was stronger this time, that half-forgotten urge to smile. "You have to tell him, Riona – tell him that I didn't – that we didn't –"

"I can't do that, you cabbage."

"Why not?"

"Because," she said, "we did."

Then she leaned forward and pressed her lips to his, and oh, it was sweeter, softer, than anything she could have imagined, the taste of his mouth, and he made a strangled noise in the back of his throat. His hands slid up her arms to cup her face, his thumbs running over her cheeks, and he pressed himself closer, deeper, angling his head to nip at her lips –

Their teeth clashed against one another, and she jerked back, wincing. "I'm sorry," he gasped, his eyes brighter than any stars that she had ever seen before. "I've never done that before. I'm so sorry, I don't quite know what to do."

"You'll have to practice more, I suppose," she said, and then wrapped her arms around his neck, pulling him in, and their lips met again, fierce and wild and sweet, nipping at one another with a hunger born of innocent impatience. They sat there on the riverbank for a long time, while the forest came to life around them, the birds chirping and the river roaring and the bees humming among the trees. They practiced and rehearsed and trained one another's lips in the fine-tuned art of kissing, murmuring in approval and whispering instructions, testing and trying the secret likes of the other, exploring the tender, sensitive spots in each other's lips and throats and the hollows just below their ears, until they were deliciously proficient, adept and skillful performers enacting a scene they might have rehearsed a thousand times, cocooned in one another's arms in an embrace as effortless as breathing.

Conor was the first to pull back, cheeks flushed and lips swollen, his dark red curls a tangled, tousled mess from the tug of her hungry fingers. "I should get you home," he whispered, and she pressed her lips against the side of his neck.

"All right," she whispered back, then let him pull her to her feet, his fingers wrapped around her own. She hesitated when he tugged her toward where their horses waited, tied to a nearby tree, their noses buried in the grass as they munched. "Conor. Meet here again, tonight?"

His chest heaved once, even as he shook his head. "You need to rest," he said. "In your own bed. Besides –" He chewed on his lip. "You deserve better than this, Ria, being tumbled in the leaves by the side of the river."

"Oh cabbage." She reached up and patted his cheek. "You sweet thing. Even I know that what we just did does not by any means count as a proper tumbling."

He flushed scarlet. "That's not what I meant."

"Listen to me, Conor." She put her hands on her hips. "I decide what I deserve. Not you, nor Daideo, nor my mother, and I decide that I like your kisses, very much, and I should like more of them. So." She ran the tip of her finger down the contours of his chest toward the slim tapering of his waist, and his gaze blurred as she swirled her finger in slow circles over his stomach. "Will you meet me here tonight again or not?"

He kissed her then, deep and hungry and not at all clumsy. "Yes," he breathed into her mouth. "Every night you want."

"Good," she said, slipping her hand into his as she pulled him toward the horses. "Because I'll be wanting all of them from here on out."

"Forever," he said, looking up at her as she swung up into the saddle, gathering the reins in her hands. "You can have all my nights, forever, Ria, if you like."

She smiled at him then, brief and feeble and wan, but a smile nonetheless, then kicked her heels into Darcy's side and thundered away, leaving him standing alone underneath the sun-dappled trees, watching her go.

Maeve would approve, she thought, her chest tight, if she knew that Riona were dangerously close to admitting that she might be in love with Conor Ó Ruairc.

'To claim her,' the fear-dearg told Jack, 'you will need help. You cannot do such a thing alone.'

'I am the High Prince of Éire,' said Jack. 'There is nothing denied me that I desire.'

'You will need help,' the fairy repeated. 'Divine magic, full of ancient power.' He bowed his head. 'A purse, a cloak, and a sword.'

Chapter Twelve
Neither of the Earth Nor Under It, Not Then Nor Now

RIONA

"Tell me, Riona," the lord of death said to Riona as they stood shoulder to shoulder at the doorway to his realm, the great white rock that divided the land of the living from the shadow-world of monsters and long-doomed men. "When your grandfather told you stories of Cúchulainn, did he ever mention his famed spear, the Gáe-Bolg?"

The distant echo of a memory chimed from deep within her. "Yes," she said slowly. "Daideo told me – it first belonged to Scáthach, the great female warrior, and then once she had shown him its secrets and he had mastered its ways, she gifted it to Cúchulainn." She hesitated. "He killed his son with that spear."

"Along with many others," her lord said dryly. "It is quite fearsome, this weapon, and stained with the blood of so many thousands of lives. It was fashioned from the bones of a dread sídhe–beast, a monster of the seas, called the Curruid. It bears, then, the mark of the gods, and you, child of the gods that you are, should thus be able to find it for me." His gaze fell to her bare forearms, now scarred a dozen times over with still-healing marks, cuts made with dull–bladed knives and the jagged edges of stones. Reflexively, she folded her arms across her chest, hiding them from him, and his gaze snapped back up to her face, calm and smooth as ever. "Now then, a stóirín," the lord of death said, "for this part of your training, I would like you to find for me the famed spear of Cúchulainn. Prove to me that all your training hasn't been for naught, that you are worthy of the mantle which I will soon ask of you to wear, and you shall be one step closer to your freedom from me."

"And this shall count as one of my three tasks?"

He smiled, no softness or gentility, only pure amusement. "So eager to leave me, are you?" He held up a hand, cutting off her retort. "But no. This is not a task – it is merely a test that you must, make no mistake, pass, or you will prove useless to me."

"And if I am? Useless to you – then what?"

His golden-fire eyes met hers, and she forced herself not to shudder at the sight of such unfathomable brilliance, dancing and sparking within their depths. "I think we both know the answer to that."

A shiver ran down Riona's spine. "I will find the Gáe-Bolg," she said quietly, "and I will bring it to you."

"I have no doubt that you shall do just that," he said. "And as a sign of my goodwill – and because I've grown so fond of you during our non-time together – I will not send you out alone on this first quest of yours." He turned, clicking his tongue softly, and out from the shadows of the trees bounded the cat-sìth, yellow eyes glowing and tail lashing. "Take Fiadh."

Riona frowned. "But she's a sídhe-beast," she said.

"Is she indeed? How odd. I hadn't noticed."

"I meant," said Riona dryly, "that according to you, she cannot leave the sídhe. The confinement spells keep her here, don't they?"

He smiled again, his gaze flickering back down to her scarred forearms, hidden away in the folds of her gown. "I can think of someone who could set her free."

Ember-red eyes and a gray cloak and a long, lethal wail echoing along the rocks and the ridges of the springtime mountains. "No," she said. "Last time –"

"Last time," he interrupted, "you were not a servant of death, but a scared little girl. Are you still, Riona? Because Fiadh will obey you without hesitation, if you so choose – if you can summon the strength to command her."

Fiadh sidled up to her, butting her sleek head against her thigh, her purr echoing hollowly through the snow-frosted wood, and Riona's hand drifted down to rest between her ears, scratching gently. The tightness in her chest eased a bit at the affection shining up at her out of those unnatural yellow eyes. "I can," she whispered.

"Excellent." The lord clapped his hands together. "Listen carefully now. Once you are back in the world of mortals, cast your revelation spell, and then the two of you shall go on your quest together and bring to me the Gáe-Bolg and *only* the Gáe-Bolg."

"I understand." She scowled up at him. "Is it venomous? One of Cúchulainn's spears was, if I remember correctly."

"I haven't the slightest idea, but by all means," the lord of death interrupted, wandering away toward the trees with an impatient gesture. "Feel free to play with it a bit once you've found it and see for yourself."

"I have no intention of dying for some ridiculous whim of yours."

"You wound me. Would I ever risk *you*, my most prized possession?"

"You brought me face-to-face with the fetch, crossed your fingers, and hoped for the best."

He laughed, low and soft, as he slipped back into the trees, his face shrouded in the ever-present wisps of dark gray fog, so that only his eyes, bright and burning, were visible in the shadows. "Hurry home," he said. "I shall be missing you terribly, you know."

"You'll hardly even notice I'm gone," she said. "You won't have the time."

She thought she saw a flicker of a smile, a flash of teeth, at her feeble attempt at a joke, glinting in the darkness before he turned away. Then he was gone, and Riona was left shivering, not from the cool icy wind that slithered across her skin, but from the inscrutable promise of his words, that somehow, no matter how gentle, still sounded like a threat.

It was simple enough, freeing Fiadh from the confines of the sídhe. There had been a strange rightness to it, an innate knowing of what to say and how to speak, when she pressed her bloody forearm against the slate-gray rock before her. Just as before, it split in two easily enough, with a sleepy groan, and Riona hesitated only for a moment before she beckoned to Fiadh, her palm resting on her furry spine as she guided her into the void, and then they were free, blinking in the sunlight, surrounded by the call of the birds and the distant gurgle of a summertime brook.

She let out a long breath, a half-sobbed whoosh of relief, and then immediately drew in another, cleansing and deep, savoring the smell of the flowers and the trees, so many green growing things

– life once more blooming all around her. Fiadh prowled forward a few cautious steps, tail twitching, her nose sniffing the air. Riona tapped her sleek skull with her index finger, and those yellow eyes swiveled around to stare at her reproachfully. "Sorry," she said. "But listen – you will harm no one within the mortal realm, do you understand? No one."

Fiadh clicked her teeth together, whiskers twitching, and Riona stroked her hand along the length of her spine. "Go explore," she said. "But stay close. I need to cast the spell."

The cat-sìth bounded off, looking for all the world like a kitten who has happened upon a stray piece of twine, an unexpected plaything, and Riona allowed herself a small smile before she sank to her knees in the grass, trying to remember Amergin's many lessons on incantations and runes. She leaned forward and began to draw, hesitantly at first, then quicker, more assuredly, as the memory grew strong within her, a natural kind of rhythm to the runes and the symbols that she sketched into the dirt.

This – this was Éire, she thought, as even the trees themselves around her seemed to bend forward, craning their necks to peek at her work, anxious to see what was being brought back into their world after so many centuries of lying dormant and lost in the shadow-lands of the sídhe. This was Éire, and there would always be magic here.

She leaned back on her heels, fingers near-black with mud, and closed her eyes, steadying herself, before she unwrapped the makeshift bandage from her still-bleeding forearm and let a few crimson-silver drops puddle onto the ground amid her sketchings.

"Taispeán," she whispered, the command crawling off her tongue like some scaly-bellied beast, testing the air with its tongue before it belched forth its fire.

Then she was drowning in a sea of endless blue waves, churning and crashing against a white-sand shore, her tongue soaked with the briny tang of ocean water, and just beyond its beach, she could make out a deep shadowy forest of low-hanging yew trees. Her nostrils flooded with the sweet scent of apples, ripe and red and bursting with divine flavor, and her ears rang from the sound of a melodious trumpeting – *oh, oh, oh*, it called, over and over again – a song of sadness and yearning for something long lost that could never again be found.

As quickly as it had come, it was gone, and her senses were dull again, bland and empty and devoid of feeling. Riona blinked, her gaze dropping down to the runes she had drawn in the dirt.

They were gone, and in their place, the vague shadow of a map, her destination marked with a round, leafy symbol.

An apple, she thought, remembering again the sweet scent that had overwhelmed her during the song of the spell.

"Where are you?" She whispered, bending closer. "Where are you, where do I need to go to find you –"

The markings drawn into the earth shivered a little at the sound of her request, as though aching to answer, to reveal to her the mysteries bound into its soil, but then they grew still and unmoving again, the secrets locked away, unreadable as ever.

Riona hissed between her teeth. Damn it. She could not fail this test.

Something soft and wet nudged against the bare skin of her neck, and she gasped before she realized – Fiadh, her glowing yellow eyes narrowed into serpentine slits as she studied her, clearly curious about the source of Riona's distress. "It didn't work," she said through the lump in her throat. "The spell. I can't find it."

The cat huffed, her breath warm and exasperated against Riona's skin, then gripped her hand lightly between her teeth, tugging at Riona, her tail whipping with impatience, and Riona gasped.

Fiadh would know where the spear was hidden. She had once been its keeper, the cat-sìth who had served as the guardian of the gods, to whom they entrusted their most prized possessions all those centuries ago.

And the lord of death had insisted that Riona bring her along.

A twinge of uncertainty, of doubt, had rippled through her – not of Fiadh's abilities, but of the lord of death and his secrets and his mysteries and the hunger she sometimes saw in his gaze when he looked at her. *A test*, he had said, but not, it seemed, of her ability to cast an effective revelation spell.

A test, perhaps, that had more to do with this black-eared creature before her than with any of the magical arts which he and Amergin had so painstakingly instructed her in for so long now.

She had fallen into something a lot like trust with him, lulled into by his soft voice and gentle smile, so unthreatening when compared to the menace that was Amergin and his dead, soulless eyes, but perhaps – perhaps that was what she had been meant to see.

Perhaps he had lied about other things too.

The lord of death is the master of sweet-sounding lies, she remembered, and shivered as the memory of her grandfather's voice crept through her.

Fear, iron-cold and heavy, suddenly gripped her heart, and she patted Fiadh again on the head, moving down the overgrown path that curved its way down the mountainside. "Good girl," she said again. "First we find that spear and then – then we find our answers."

For a day and a night, she followed the silent shadow of the cat-sìth, avoiding the well-trodden roads and smattering of villages along the way, keeping to the shadows of the forests and the thickets, eating half-ripe berries and fresh-caught fish from the streams for food. Riona slept during the daylight hours, half-hidden among the underbrush while Fiadh stood guard, crouched far above her in the thick lush leaves of the summer-green trees, gnawing on the bones of whatever poor woodland creature she had caught as her meal that day.

And tried her best not to think about how close she might be to home — to the vale, and its familiar, green-leafed trees and the warm, welcoming scent of the turf-fires burning in the hearths and the soft, downy pillows of her bed.

How close she might be to Conor, with his gentle healer hands and clear gray eyes — and close to Haisley, too.

Whenever the temptation to return home grew too great, however, Fiadh was there, her yellow eyes narrowed and watchful, a low, insistent purr rumbling in her throat, reminding Riona that such a reunion was not hers to seek.

Now, at last, the cat-sìth came to a halt, apparently having arrived at her mysterious destination, and Riona eyed the small mouth of the cave before them, shrouded in tendrils of light gray fog, surrounded by half-a-dozen slim-trunked whitethorn trees. "I don't think this is right," she said over her shoulder. "In the vision after the spell, I distinctly saw an island."

From far above her, perched on her haunches atop an overhanging boulder, Fiadh grumbled, protracting her claws to scratch at the rock petulantly. "Yowl at me all you want," she said. "I saw what I saw, though – apples and yew trees and great white swans floating upon the waves of the sea. I don't know why you led me here."

Wherever here was. Riona had no idea, having placed all her faith, her trust, in the sharp-eared creature before her.

The cat-sìth grunted, then leapt down to land on the hard-packed earth next to her, nipping at her calf impatiently. "Ow," she yelped, swatting at the cat's spiked ears. "Very well, I'll go in and look around, but either you're wrong or I did an even poorer job of casting that spell than I thought." Fiadh purred softly, a wordless approval, rubbing her sleek side against Riona's hip before loping away, apparently mollified, toward the ring of whitethorn trees that awaited them. Riona let out her breath in a long whoosh, then straightened her shoulders before following, approaching yet another strange sídhe-realm.

But this time, she did not know who – or what – awaited her within its borders.

There was a strange lightening in the air around her as she approached the mouth of the cave, a lifting of some invisible weight, and she heard rather than felt a warm puff of air brush across her face. The cut on her arm had scabbed over during their long journey here, another scar to mar her once-smooth skin, so she reached for the small knife she kept sheathed at her waist, gritting her teeth at the now-familiar pinch of the dull blade slicing into her flesh. Her blood welled up in answer, and for a moment, her breath stuttered in her throat, because it was pure crimson, dark and wet and unyieldingly red, until at last a silver shimmer peeked through. Riona pressed her forearm against the rough rock of the cave's door, her brow beading with sweat as the previously gentle warmth turned oppressive, sweltering, a humid, hot surge of air thundering across her skin. She swallowed, suddenly nostalgic for the cool night breeze of Tech Duinn, the splash of the frigid river-water on her flushed cheeks.

Then the air shivered in front of her, parted somehow, and she knew that it had worked. She stepped through, a sudden blast of dry heat washing over her skin, and she turned, already blinking back the drops of sweat leaking down her forehead into her eyes, motioning for Fiadh to follow.

The cat-sìth was nowhere to be seen.

"The gods damn it," she hissed, the back of her gown growing damp and slick with sweat. "I swear, Fiadh," she said into the empty grove where the sídhe-cat had prowled only a moment ago. "If you're wrong about this –" She wiped at her brow with her sleeve, torn and hot and not a little bit afraid at the thought of braving whatever horrors awaited her without Fiadh by her side, then sighed once, turning away to venture deeper into the sídhe.

There was no sun to be seen in the dark gray sky, but the heat was overwhelming, oppressive and heavy on her skin. Every breath she drew was leaden in her chest, dense and full like the salt licks laid out in the stables for the horses back home.

She ducked underneath the paltry shade of a brown-leafed tree and leaned her sweat-soaked back against the trunk.

Home. How she missed it. How she longed to see it again, even for a moment.

A twig snapped nearby, and she straightened, searching the gloom for the source of the sound. She relaxed at the sight of a great black stallion nosing its way across the wilted grass by the banks of a gurgling stream nearby. The horse raised its head and stared at her through the tangled strands of its tousled mane, and she froze at the sight of its luminous golden eyes.

It was not the preternatural fire of her lord's black-and-golden gaze, or Fiadh's bright serpent-yellow stare, but a brilliant honey-brown color. Something whispered in the back of her mind, a half-forgotten memory. She frowned, trying to remember, but then the horse eased forward, lifting its sleek black neck to the branches above her. It tugged once, then bent its head, a shriveled red apple held in its teeth. She looked up sharply, at the hundreds of equally withered apples dangling from the limbs above her – red and green and pale yellow – and as her gaze wandered over the drooping trees clustered along the banks of the stream, here and there, scattered among them, the glimmer of more shrunken fruits half-hidden in the sparse, dried-up leaves.

An apple orchard, just as she had seen in that brief glimpse during her ineffective revelation spell. Fiadh had been right all along. She remembered her grandfather's stories from so long ago, sitting by the hearth-fire on cold winter nights with her hands wrapped around a warm mug of cider, snuggled with Maeve under a warm knitted blanket. The other-realm of Emain Ablach, the home of the great sea-god, Manannán mac Lir, and the isle of apples.

Daideo had described it as a tropical paradise, an island in the middle of the far eastern sea, a place rich with lush green fields that led down to white-sanded beaches, bursting with greenery and lush, ripe fruits, filled with beautiful, white-feathered swans. The cursed children of Lir, she remembered, and she pushed away from the tree, her exhaustion from the oppressive heat forgotten for the moment, as she searched the banks of the feeble stream for any sign of them.

"They have long since died."

Riona whirled around, but there was only the stallion, crunching on the core of the shriveled fruit. She stared at it, heart pounding, as it thrashed its long black tail and extended its neck to nibble at another low-hanging fruit in the branches. "I —"

"You are looking for the children of Lir." It was a high-pitched, teasing voice, a boy-child who had not yet reached puberty, and Riona backed away as she realized that it was in fact the horse speaking to her. "The cailleach known as the Bright One cursed them hundreds of years ago, transforming them into those graceful birds, and Lir in his grief settled them here, in his home." The horse's shoulders moved in what she could have sworn was a shrug. "The sea-god has long been absent from these shores, and like the land he once tended, they withered away on the shores of their father's sea." Those honey-golden eyes locked on hers. "No longer is this a fruitful realm, but one of dead and dying things, and the scavengers who feed on their remains."

Riona swallowed. "What does that make you?"

His tail lashed again. "A survivor." He stretched out his nose and snuffled at the end of her braid. "I know you. You carry the blood of the gods within your veins."

"My grandfather was once a member of the Tuatha Dé Danann. I'm Riona."

"Little queen." His hooves clattered against the charred ground.

"You are aptly named. I remember them all too well, those from whom you are born."

She shifted on her feet uneasily. "Who are you?"

"Your grandmother once called me the púca."

Riona remembered now – dark hair and golden eyes, a shifter of shapes. "The mischief-maker."

"Perhaps once I was. The only mischief I make now is in pursuit of my own survival." He stamped his front hoof restlessly. "I came here, years ago, to revel for a time in this land of plenty, but then the gods vanished again from the world, leaving me locked inside the borders of this realm. It would not have been such a bad place to spend eternity, but without the sea-god's care, you see what it has become, and now the creatures who thrive are the ones who lust for the taste of death on their lips."

"And what *does* it taste like? Death?"

He eyed her silently for a long moment, his nose twitching in the humid air. "Why are you here, little queen? This is no place for a mortal."

"I am looking for something – a lost treasure, the spear of Cúchu-lainn. Gáe-Bolg." She hesitated. "Perhaps you can help me."

He laughed once, a harsh tinkling sound, dry and bitter rather than humorous. "I have fallen far from my past days of merriment and trickery, and yet even still I do not grant favors for nothing. If you wish for my aid, then you must promise me something in return for my services, and there is precious little that you can give me in this land filled with decay and despair."

Riona pondered this for a moment, thinking of Fiadh and the wonder that glowed in her eyes as she roamed about the realm of Éire for the first time in hundreds of years, the joy in her gait as she loped along, the peace that had seemed to settle over her sleek black shoulders as she basked in the light of the sun. "I can get you out," she said at last. "I can set you free of your confinement here."

His ears pricked. "How?"

"I have the blood of the gods." She held out her hand, still stained with dried red-and-silver blood. "You said so yourself. I can use it to break the confinement spell placed on you and lead you into the land of Tech Duinn."

He laughed, dry and hollow as the land surrounding him. "I think not, little queen. I will not trade one hellscape for another." His tail lashed. "There is only one place where I am truly free."

An oily pool of nausea swirled in the pit of her stomach. "What do you mean?"

"I think you know." He moved restlessly in place, hooves thudding against the sun-scorched earth. "If you would have my help, then you must return me, back to the home in which I was born a thousand years ago – the true land of Éire."

Riona chewed on her lip, the intensity of his gaze causing her stomach to twist, her throat closing up as she remembered, the keening wail of the bean-sí.

Maeve convulsing in her arms as her eyes rolled back into her skull, her chest shuddering one final time before falling horribly, terribly still.

Fiadh was a monster, true, but she was her monster, loyal and obedient to her. This creature of mischief and mayhem though –

As though he could read her thoughts, he stepped closer. "I am no monster." The horse nudged her shoulder with his soft nose, nickering reassuringly, even as his tail lashed impatiently behind him. "I wish to go home, you see. I want nothing more but to see the roll of the vibrant green hills, to feel the cool mist of the rain on my cheeks, to hear the night-song of the owls and the howl of the wolf under the moon."

It was a reverberation of that own ever-present ache in her heart, that had throbbed so furiously only a few moments ago, that something twisted, painful and deep inside her. "Help me to find what I seek," she said at last, "and perhaps – perhaps I will bring you home."

He shook his mane, a blurred swirl of black, and Riona blinked to see a small, dark-haired boy with honey-gold eyes standing in front of her. "First, a question. Why is it that you seek such a weapon, little queen?"

"It is not for myself," she said. "It is for another, and he didn't tell me why."

The boy's mouth tightened. "The lord of death has sent you."

"Yes." Riona twisted her fingers together. "How did you know?"

The púca turned on his heel, beckoning over his shoulder with his pale fingers. "I can smell it on you – the scent of druidecht. He is the only one who would dare to train you in such arts, so long lost to mortals. Use it if you must, but it is the silver in your veins that will save you. Remember that above all else."

"What does it smell like?" Riona asked. "Druidecht?"

"So many questions. You are far too curious for your own good."

"You are not the first person to tell me that. What *does* it smell like?"

"River water and moss, and moon-spice." He glanced at her. "Mortal-made magic, so that they might face creatures far more powerful than they and survive. It no longer has a need in your world, confined to the sídhe as we have been for so long."

"And I am letting you loose again," Riona said, stomach twisting. She thought of Fiadh, vanished from the grove, the supernatural speed of her pounce, the curve of her fangs and her claws, the feral light in her gaze. "And they have nothing – no way to defend themselves."

The púca paused, his honey-warm eyes softening a bit. "I will do them no true harm," he said. "I will overturn their milk pails and pull at their hair on soft summer nights, but no more." He jerked his chin toward the gentle slope before them, shrouded in wilted green-brown grass and the dense collection of twisted, gnarled trunk of looming yew trees atop its peak. "Unlike what waits for you beyond."

"What is in there?"

"The spear of Cúchulainn, of course – and its current master." He glanced at her, his jaw set. "The Ellén Trechend."

A flicker of a memory stirred – tales of an incendiary, three-headed beast. "A treasure-hoarder, like Aillen the Burner. But I thought it dwelt at Rath Crúachan, in the cave of cats."

"Once, yes – but it made its way here years ago, skulking the shadows of the craggy rocks by the ocean cliffs, and grew to unnatural size and strength in the absence of the sea-god. But –" He shrugged. "The power of Lir lingers still, in this place, his appointed home, and any conjuring you use to invoke the salt-water of the sea will be amplified a thousandfold. Do you understand?"

"Yes," she said, licking at her lips. "Call upon the sea, use water spells – I understand."

"Good, because it is the strength of the sea which you must harness if you wish to defeat him." His nose wrinkled. "Remember, above all else, the power that you and you alone possess, in all the realm, both mortal and immoral alike – the blood of the gods themselves, and with it, their dominion over nature and its creatures."

"Even you?" Riona asked, her curiosity piqued even as she shivered in the face of what was almost certainly her encroaching demise.

"Even me," he said. "The beast keeps its treasures hidden within its nest. I will draw it out for you, so that you may enter and find the Gáe-Bolg, but do not linger, and take nothing but the Gáe-Bolg, do you understand?" She nodded, tight-lipped. "Then stop up your ears, with leaves, with blades of grass, with anything you can find. If you hear his song, you will die far faster than I can save you."

"What about you?"

He bared his teeth in a grin. "His warbling has no effect on me, little queen. I am no weak-minded mortal as are you."

She huffed, but crouched down, snagging up a handful of half-dried leaves and rolling them into tight wads, plugging her ears as securely as she could. She glanced at the púca, who raised his dark brows and spoke, but all she could hear was a muffled garbling. She nodded once, and he beckoned again with his finger as he crept up the wilted hillside, toward the ominous copse of yew trees at its peak. Riona swallowed once, then followed, racking her brain to remember the incantations Amergin had forced her to recite, over and over again, for the gods only know how many weeks and months, years even, perhaps, in the timelessness of the sídhe by the dark-watered river.

River water. It made sense, that the púca could smell it on her, the musty aroma of that dark water and the black moss that grew along its rocks.

Moon-spice, though – that bittersweet scent of silverweed and clover. She remembered Mamó's hands, tucking her homemade mishmash among the lining of her drawers where she kept her gowns, smoothing them down among the folds of the fabric. "A warding against evil," she had said with that ghost of a smile that so often lingered on her lips, and Riona felt a little steadier, a little stronger, knowing that it still hovered around her, her grandmother's protection and love.

The ground grew blacker as they climbed the gentle slope of the hill, not the rich, loamy texture of the earth that she knew, but brittle and charred, scorched from the fire of whatever creature lurked within the cluster of yew trees ahead. Her slipper kicked against something hard, and she stumbled forward, glancing down to see a bleached-out skull, lupine and elongated in shape, its bony jaw forever frozen in a terrified snarl.

The god of the sea, she reminded herself as her gaze wandered across the blackened earth, the soot-coated rocks as they approached the tree line. Fight fire with water, with the impenetrable depths of the sea.

Then the púca was gone, disappearing among the shadows of the trees, and she paused underneath a gnarled yew tree, her breaths fast and ragged in the humid oppressiveness of the air, as she slid one of the makeshift plugs from her right ear, listening intently. It was far hotter here, even under the shade of the tree, the very ground itself smoking under the weight of the monster which lurked nearby.

From deep within the copse of yew trees, a hoarse, reverberating rasp slithered through the air, a smoke-choked wheezing of a sound, followed by a crescendo of maddened, furious hisses. The idle warm breeze that played along the ends of her hair swelled to a roaring gust of white-hot air. Riona threw her arms over her face, crouching at the base of the yew tree, trying not to scream as unrelenting squalls of blistering smoke rolled past her, shrouding the wilted hillside in a dark cloud of white-gray smoke. Then the earth trembled once, as though some enormous thing within the trees had launched itself into the sky, shoving itself off the ground with unnatural force, and she knew it was time.

Far above her, a falcon screamed, and Riona shoved the plug deep down into her ear and ran into the shadowy forest of yew trees.

It was a furnace filled with intangible flames, a thick, pervasive layer of smoke heavy in the air, and her lungs burned as she sprinted through the woods, clambering over fallen trees and stumbling over gnarled roots as she searched for anything resembling a nest. A shadow passed overheard, far above the charred limbs, reflected there on the ground – a massive, winged shape with three long-necked, gangly heads.

She kept her gaze locked on the ground, scanning the trees as she ran, heart thudding, lungs screaming with pain, until –

"Oh my gods."

Riona bent over, hands on her knees, half-sobbing. There it was, an enormous nest made of yew trunks and thick-limbed branches, nestled high above on a ledge of a smoke-blackened stone cliff.

She would never be able to scale the side of the cliff. It was a sheer wall, no crevices or cracks which she could use to climb, no narrow paths etched into the stone that she could thread her way through to reach the nest. She was trapped, out of options and nearly out of time.

What would he do, the lord of death, what price would he exact from her, if she returned to him empty-handed?

She knew, all too well, that it would not be her own blood that he would shed.

A fresh wave of terror, far more crushing than anything that this beast could ever inspire, rolled through her.

The shadow swooped overhead again, drenching her in darkness, and even through the deadened noise of the makeshift plugs, she could hear the faint reverberation of its raspy call, and her hands clenched into fists at her sides.

If she couldn't climb it, there was only one other way to gain access to its nest.

Slowly, she reached up and loosened the makeshift plug in her ear, and that hoarse, rasping call swelled to an almost unbearable pitch. She exhaled once, licking nervously at the sweat beading on her upper lip, then closed her eyes in concentration.

The savage, black-feathered creature that lurked within her stirred, its insatiable hunger roaring to life, and Riona's voice grew guttural and hoarse as she chanted her incantation. From far away, a thunderous crash echoed, the impatient lash of distant waves against the rock-studded shore.

The shadow above her paused, hovering in the air, hissing in confusion.

She repeated the spell, harsher and more urgent, over and over, and all the while the corvid harbinger of death clawed its way up her throat, cawing ravenously and clicking its talons at the thought of power, of freedom. The great winged shadow above her shrieked, and she watched the faint outline of three heads swivel in her direction. Slowly, she looked up at what soared above her.

A massive, three-headed beast with copper-red feathers and wicked, jagged talons. Its necks were skinny and bald, dull gray skin that bled into three black, beaked heads, its curved mouths razor-sharp and glistening, tongues lolling out the sides. Even as she watched, the middle head hissed, its red-rimmed eyes narrowing in its smoke-black face, then it coughed once, hacking and raw.

A fiery column of orange-and-red flame burst from its center mouth, and she flung herself behind a large charred boulder, hands over her head, while fire erupted all around her, licking its way across the seared dirt of the forest, climbing up the scorched trunks of the trees. She screamed, the heat from the white-hot flames searing the exposed flesh on her arms and face, tears dripping down her already-blistering cheeks.

The raven-like creature within her managed to caw out her spell a final time through the swell of the smoke and the fire all around her, and this time, in answer, a thunderous crash again echoed through the air.

Riona looked up, squinting through the smoke and scalded air, and watched the clouds above shudder once, then erupt in an explosion of water and wind.

From far above the sheer cliff above her, an answering boom shuddered, and a tidal wave of blue-green water surged over the rocks above, crashing down the fire-riddled land beneath. The Ellén Trechend screeched as the water from the skies poured down around it, drenching its feathered wings, and it toppled through the air, its heads swiveling frantically as it flapped at the salt-water sodden air, crashing into the ground a few feet away.

Riona drew her knife from her belt with shaking fingers, slashing at her arm, then stumbled forward, blinking away the salt-water spray from the summoned ocean waves, a cooling balm against the scorched surface of her skin, and threw herself on the thrashing middle neck of the Ellén Trechend. She pressed her blood-soaked arm to the beast's throat, right at the place where its pulse pounded erratically, wildly in its skeletal neck. "I am the child of the gods," she gasped, her voice raw and rasping from the merciless talons of the black-feathered, beady-eyed entity clawing furiously within her throat. "Give me what is mine, or I will drown you in a sea of storms."

The Ellén Trechend hissed, as the sea-waters which she had summoned continued to rain down upon them, from the cloud-drenched skies and over the tops of the cliffs above them, shrieking in protest, and she pressed harder on its neck, watching that thin trail of red-and-silver blood slide down its neck. "Give me what is mine," she said again, "and I will spare your life and leave you to rule this wasteland as your own for all eternity."

The sídhe-beast screamed, flailing its sodden, too-heavy wings against the drowning earth, its talons ripping and tearing up the roots and the rocks of the sea-swept forest floor while its other two heads whipped about, snapping its razor-sharp beaks at Riona where she clutched flat against its middle neck, digging her fingers into its flaky skin. Without warning, it stilled, and for a moment, the only sound was the thrum of the sea-rain as it thundered down from the sky, churning over the tops of the cliffs, surging all around them in white foamy waves around the roots of the trees.

Too late, she remembered her discarded ear plugs, the bits of leaves and grass tossed aside in her mad dash for the nest.

"Little queen!" From far away, she heard the púca bellow in alarm. "Cover your ears!"

Then she was floating, adrift on the gentle, warbling sound of the sweetest song she had ever heard, wordless and serene, a lullaby of the tenderest element, and her arms grew limp and her eyelids drooped, slipping of the side of the beast's rain-soaked neck to collapse into the churning salt-waves that still churned over the once-charred earth.

It was dark and quiet under the waves, dreamless and peaceful, and it was almost as though she were outside of herself, watching with clinical, cool detachment, as the water filled her nose and lungs, dragging her down to the soft silt mud to rest, lulled to eternal sleep by the faint echoes of the beast's song and the hum of the waves. It reminded her of something, she thought dreamily, as the darkness closed around her. Another time, another place, sitting by a riverbank listening to the soothing sound of churning waters, a familiar gentle voice telling her an old tale of another, similar sídhe-beast and his songs and his reign of fire –

Deep below the water, Riona's mouth flew open in a silent, gargled scream of remembrance.

Conor's story, on the banks of the river, so long ago.

Fionn mac Cumhaill. Aillén the Burner. The poisoned blade.

She needed an antidote, a distraction, just like Fionn.

She shook herself free of the lingering sleepiness, the effects of the beast's enchanted song, grasping at the knife strapped to her side. She fumbled it free of its sheath, kicking weakly at the surging water around her, keeping her head below the waves to block out the song still warbling through the air above her. No poison to be released from within it, sure, but it was sharp enough to pierce the skin, as she knew all too well, and that would have to do.

Riona broke through the surface of the water, and just as the enchanted notes swirled around her, she buried the dull-edged blade of the knife deep into her thigh.

She screamed, the agony in her leg clearing the cobwebs in

her mind, still addled from the unbearable sweetness of the Ellén Trechend's song. She grabbed the slick sides of the beast's neck, digging her nails into the soft give of its flesh as she dragged herself atop its still flailing head. It threw back its trio of heads and sang with renewed urgency, and Riona gritted her teeth as she gripped the knife more firmly in her shaking hand and plunged it once more into the soft flesh of her thigh.

Her vision blurred in an explosion of black-and-red dots as the agony of the twin bites of her blade roared through her, and she leaned over and vomited into the churning waves beneath. She spat once, gagging on the acrid taste of bile and blood, then wrenched the blade out of her thigh and drove it into the thrashing center neck of the Ellén Trechend. "Give me what is mine," she snarled, her voice raw and burning from the salt-water waves and the bile still surging in her throat, and the sídhe-beast hissed, its poisonous melody vanishing as it flailed in agony among the churning sea-waters. "Give it to me, or I will cut every last throat you have."

Underneath her quivering legs, the beast trembled with fury, its muscles bunching as it gathered itself to attack, and Riona braced herself, wrapping her arms tight around its blood-soaked neck, half-blinded and dizzy from the savage pain in her thigh. The Ellén Trechend coughed in quick succession, its wounded neck sagging, then launched itself out of the water and onto the sheer side of the rocky cliff, digging its talons into the smooth sand-stone side, climbing and scrabbling its way toward the nest high above the salt-water waves below. Its wings drooped uselessly, soaked and heavy with the weight of the sea-water, and it screeched in pain as it dragged its body up the side of the cliff, Riona still clinging to its slick, injured neck. She watched as it extended its two good necks and latched onto the boulders that jutted out from either side of the nest with its beaks, lunging forward until it crashed into the thick-branched walls of its den high above the world.

Riona slid limply to the dry-leafed floor of the beast's burrow, her breathing ragged, her forehead pressed against her knees as she tried to staunch the thick blood oozing from the gashes in her thigh. The beast hissed once, and she jerked her head up to see it staring at her, its expression rife with hatred. It turned, and launched itself from the top of the cliff, wet, useless wings and half-severed head and all, screaming as it went, fumbling its way across the sky in a wrathful, clumsy flight until it disappeared into the horizon.

Riona sobbed once, scrambling backwards, glancing around the nest, half-delirious with pain and exhaustion, and her mouth fell open.

Fiadh, once the most trusted guardian of the Tuatha Dé Danann, had not failed her.

She had led Riona straight to the entire treasure trove of the gone gods themselves.

Jack sat atop his horse, staring at
the castle before him.

'This is the home of a giant,' said
the fear-dearg. 'He who commands
the purse of plenty. You must have
it, to win your bride. Go and
knock.'

So Jack did, and with a deafening
roar, the wooden door splintered
from top to bottom, and a single
great green eye peered out at Jack.

Excerpt from 'The Snow, The Crow, &
The Blood'

Chapter Thirteen
The Vale of Inagh, Éire, 1070

RIONA

Her mother had returned to the vale, looking very much the same as she always had – dark hair, pale lips, disapproving eyes.

Riona was too tired, too heart-sore to care.

It had been coming for some time, Mamó's steps growing slower and shakier over the long, cold months of the past winter, her hands trembling as she would rest them against the wall while she climbed the steps in the castle, her breaths laborious and hard. Riona could tell that Daideo knew it too, following her about the castle like her blue-eyed shadow, and Mamó, who had always been so independent, so aloof, so self-contained, was now never left alone.

It was, Riona tried to remind herself as they gathered around Mamó's bed on that fateful evening in early spring, the nighttime breeze wafting in the scents of honeysuckle and thyme through the window, the natural ending to all life, this kind of passing. Not the senseless scream of a fifteen-year-old girl gasping away all the promised potential of the still-budding years of her girlhood, or a young man, emaciated and weak-chested, conceding forever the dream of the man he might have been, or a soldier, black-bearded and tall, sinking to his knees on a blood-soaked field of battle, an evergreen sapling brutally cut down in the midst of summer.

She watched the slight rise and fall of Mamó's chest grow slower, shallower. Her grief was not for her gentle-handed grandmother, as she had surely earned her rest on the plains of delight in the other-realm of Magh Meall, having cared tirelessly for so many with her quiet strength and never-failing patience, mixing poultices and setting bones and healing hurts that no one but she had the skill to set right. Riona mourned, not for Mamó, but for herself, for the yawning void that her absence would leave behind, and through a veiled sheen of tears, she looked to where Daideo sat by her grandmother's bedside, his fingers entwined with Mamó's, his face calm as he watched his wife take her final breaths.

Wheresoever Mamó went, Riona knew, Daideo would not be far to follow.

And Riona did not think she could endure it.

Mamó slipped away in the hours just before the dawn. Riona cried, her forehead resting on the side of the bed by Mamó's still-warm hand, then stumbled to her feet and wrapped her arms around Daideo's shoulders.

"I'm so sorry, Daideo," she whispered. "So very sorry."

He patted her on the hand, his gaze never leaving Mamó's face. "Go along now, little queen. I need to be alone with my brèagha."

And so Riona had staggered away, wiping at the hot wet tears that would not stop flowing down her grief-ravaged face, until she tripped over something long and solid stretched out beneath her. She caught herself against the back of a chair, then twisted around to see Conor sitting on the floor, his long legs sprawled out in front of him, his copper-curled head tipped back against the stone wall. "Conor – what are you doing?"

There was no response, and Riona peered down at him in the dim light of the corridor, its torches having burned away over the course of the long, hard night. His eyes were closed, his nose was red, and there were wet streaks of tears, the twin to her own, lining his freckled face.

"Conor," she whispered, and sank to her knees next to him, gathering him in her arms. "Oh cabbage, I know how much you loved her."

He said nothing, but clung to her waist, burrowing his head into her shoulder as he cried, a fresh wave of pain pooled in her stomach. Poor Conor. He had never before known this pain, this soul-searing helplessness, this storm of grief, to lose forever one so beloved.

Not like her. She had tasted the rusted-iron flavor of grief too many times to count in her nineteen years, so much so that sometimes she wondered if she would ever be able to wash away the bitter taste of it.

Then Conor let out a deep sob, his shoulders shaking uncontrollably, and Riona banished her resentment, her bitterness, and cradled him against her, soothing him with quiet, wordless murmurs, united in their shared grief.

He sat back at last, wiping at his red-rimmed eyes, and Riona fought the urge to pull him back in, to revel in the warmth of his closeness, to let his sadness intertwine with her own, twin tiers of ivy winding their separate ways along the same trellis in an overgrown garden of loss and grief. "Sorry." Conor wiped at his nose with the back of his sleeve. "I don't mean to blubber –"

"Don't." Riona pointed her finger. "That's your father talking. You are allowed to cry, you know. There's no shame in that."

The tips of his ears flushed pink. "I know." He swallowed. "I just – I didn't get to say goodbye."

On impulse, Riona leaned forward and caught hold of his wrist. "Come on," she said. "Let's go." She stood up, pulling him to his feet and tugging him after her, down the corridor and up the narrow stone stairs that led to her room. She pushed open the door and went to tug him inside, but he braced his hand against the doorframe, hesitating. "Ria. I shouldn't be in here."

"It's fine." She tugged at his wrist. "Eahba's sure to have left some apple cake for me. I thought we might share it."

"You want to eat cake right now?"

"What else is there to do? Mamó is gone. My sadness won't bring her back." That sharp lump of pain in her chest twisted savagely. "Cake seems like as good an answer as any."

He wavered for a moment longer, searching her face. "All right," he said. "Let's have some cake."

Riona settled on the end of the bed cross-legged, the small tin plate balanced in her lap, and after a moment, Conor sank down on the opposite end, his hands placed primly on his knees, his boot jiggling up and down as he watched her cut the slice in two with her knife. "There's some whiskey in a jug under the bed," she said, peeking up at him through her lashes. "I nicked it a while back from Daideo's study."

"You stole your grandfather's whiskey?"

"Is that a problem?" She didn't wait for an answer but jerked her chin in his direction. "Grab it, will you?"

He hesitated, then bent down and fumbled underneath her bed before sitting back up, a squat brown jug clutched in his hand. "Do you have a goblet?"

"No. We'll have to share it." She scooped up a forkful of cake. "Go on. Take a swig."

Conor stared at her for a long moment, then raised the jar to his lips and drank, his throat working as he swallowed. He coughed once, then handed it over to her, his eyes watering. "Gods," he managed, and she smiled.

"It's not for cabbages, that's for sure, Daideo's liquor." She pushed the half-empty plate toward him before taking a deep swig for herself. "Eat. You'll need it."

They sat for a long time in silence, passing the jug back and forth to one another in a wordless exchange, as the sun crept higher and higher into the midmorning sky, until at last, Riona waggled the empty jar in front of him. "Gone, every last drop. Well done, us."

"I'm not sure it's anything to celebrate. I feel quite…odd."

"But in a good way, yes?"

"Too soon to tell." He tipped back against the headrest of her bed. "What d'you suppose it's like?" He asked drowsily after a few moments. "Magh Meall?"

Riona cleared her throat, tossing the empty jug into the ashy hearth by her bed, ignoring the resulting crash as it shattered against the stones. "I don't know. Peaceful, I suppose. Beautiful." She paused. "Boring, I would imagine."

He opened one hazy gray eye to peer at her. The cider had clearly affected him, and she almost giggled, then it struck her. "Conor," she said. "You have had liquor before, haven't you?"

"Yup. Loads."

"Liar."

He grinned, his gray eyes mere slits in his freckled face. "Fooled you for a minute, didn't I, though?"

"Not really. You've a terrible face for lying." She edged closer to him, the sheets rustling underneath her. "You'll probably have quite the headache in a few hours."

"Maybe, but you were right. I do feel good right now."

"I'm sure." She reached out and ran her fingers through his copper curls. "You have the nicest hair."

He reached up, wrapping his fingers around hers, and pressed his lips to the soft skin of her wrist. "Ria," he said, his lips tracing their way up the underside of her arm, and something hot and wild unfurled within her. "You can't say things like that to me."

"You're fluthered, Conor," she said, her eyes fluttering shut as his lips meandered their way up her arm, pushing the loose sleeve of her gown aside so that he could trace the curve of her bicep with the tip of his tongue. "I know that you don't want to. At least, not like this."

"I do though," he said, shifting closer, his lips leaving her skin only long enough to latch on the swell of her collarbone just beneath the neckline of her gown. "I have been dreaming about nothing else since you kissed me by the river."

"You wouldn't even come into my room an hour ago."

"I didn't say that I should be doing this," he whispered, venturing further north to press hungry kisses up and down the side of her throat, and she bit back a moan at the faint scrape of his teeth along her neck. "Only that I wanted to." He froze. "Do *you* want me to?"

"My poor, sweet cabbage." Her fingers tiptoed down his chest, sliding toward his belt, and his face drew tight at the soft brush of her hand against him. "Why do you suppose I brought you here? Although I didn't mean to get you drunk first, I swear."

"I'm not fluthered," he said, bending his head to resume his lips' perusal of her skin. "I told you – I feel *good*."

She almost laughed as he shifted on top of her, pressing her down against the soft sheets of the bed. "That's what being drunk feels like."

He raised his head, flushed cheeks and swollen lips, and settled down on top of her, and she slid her hands underneath his shirt, caressing the boyish lines of his chest. "That's how I always feel, when I'm with you."

"Conor," she whispered, then his lips were on hers, urgent and fierce, and she wrapped her arms around his neck, lost in the heady warmth of his kiss and his touch, and for a long while after, all the terrible truths of life seemed far away and distant indeed.

She woke up, hours later, clad in her wrinkled, much-abused shift, nestled against the bare, smooth skin of Conor's chest. She ran her fingers down his belly, playing with the soft tufts of dark hair that grew along his stomach, but he did not so much as stir, one arm flung across his eyes, breathing slow and steady as he slept. She pressed a kiss against his freckled shoulder, then eased away, fumbling for her discarded gown at the foot of the bed. Riona dressed quickly, combing her fingers through her tangled hair, then took one last look at Conor, sprawled out on his back in her bed.

She slipped out the door, braiding her hair with practiced ease as she descended the stairs.

A twinge of guilt pulled at her heart. It was not how Conor would have intended it to go, their first time together. She knew it had been inevitable, ever since that day by the river, when she'd first felt the firm press of his lips to hers, the caress of his fingers against her skin, but she had hesitated, unwilling to cede this final boundary-line of her heart to him. He had never once questioned it, never once tried to push for more than the long, lingering kisses that they had stolen in dimly lit corridors, or tangled in each other's arms in the fresh hay of the stable-stalls, or pressed up against the bookshelf in the solar, his hands on her hips and her fingers buried in his hair. He had always appeared content with whatever she had deigned to give, but they had both known that this was inescapable, this clumsy culmination of their hot-blooded, youthful love.

But it was not, she was sure, how Conor had planned – not only the liquor and Conor's cider-induced good-feeling – but their shared grief acting as a driving force in the urgency of their kisses, the slide and shove of their bodies a fiery outlet for their deep-seated sadness, the groans of passion a release of all the heartache that festered inside their individual souls.

Conor, she knew, would have preferred love-making by candle-light on a bed strewn with wild cherry blossoms and the taste of sweet white wedding-wine on their lips. A shining silver ring on each of their entwining hands.

It would never happen, that last imagining. She knew what her mother still intended for her, the path that she was born to walk, and there was no room for Conor by her side on such a narrow, bleak road.

Surely he must realize that, deep down.

She hurried down the castle steps, pulling her cloak tight around her, the mid-afternoon growing ominous and dark above her. She had not felt so alone, wrapped in Conor's arms, drowning in the warm oblivion of his kisses, his caresses, but now it came rushing back to her – Mamó, still and cold in the bed upstairs, and Daideo –

Riona halted in her tracks.

As though she had summoned him, there he was, sitting on the gray-stone bench nestled among the line of fir and birch trees that grew around her grandmother's vale, alone and still, his head tilted back to stare up at the darkening sky.

She stepped closer, and even though she knew he must hear her, her keen, clever Daideo didn't move, his gaze never leaving the coming storm that gathered far above the trees.

He looked so tired, so frail, her strong-armed, bright-eyed grandfather. He had always been so full of life, like he had drunk from the stream of eternal youth despite the lines of his face and the gray of his hair, a little boy bursting with laughter living inside an old man's body. He had never seemed old to her, not until now, his shoulders drooping and his features inexpressibly weary.

"Daideo." Riona sank down next to him, pressing her hand into his.

His fingers curled around her own. "It was her time. She could not have stayed here with me, even if she wanted to." He closed his eyes for a moment, and Riona could see the unimaginable weight of the years he had lived for so many centuries bearing down around him. "But it won't be for very long."

Riona's heart seized in her chest. "Daideo," she said, shrill with panic. "Don't say that. You're so sad, I know. I know you are, but you mustn't say that. I need you, Daideo. I need you here."

His lips flickered in something that might have once been a smile. "I'm sorry, little queen." His blue eyes grew blurry and distant. "But she waits for me, you know, just beyond the sea. She'll be wanting to see our boys, Killian and your da, but she won't go without me. I can't bear to keep her waiting long." He squeezed her fingers. "You know how impatient she gets. Even in death, I fear her wrath."

"Don't," Riona said through the unbearable tightness in her throat. "Don't tease."

"Ah, it's what I do." He sighed, and her heart splintered to see him so weathered. "You'll be all right, Riona. You have been treated so unkindly by the whims of fate, it is true, but it has made you strong – and fierce too. There is nothing so terrible that this life could devise for you that you could not conquer."

"But I'll be alone," she whispered, and Daideo turned his face toward her.

"Not alone," he said. "Never alone. It is not so great a distance as you think, between us and the land beyond the star-studded sea. Even now, we are surrounded by the sídhe, the darkness and the light, living side by side – you simply cannot see them. Magh Meall, it is not another realm at all, little queen, but the more perfect realization of this one – a place free from sickness and war and old age." He smiled down at her, gentle and sad. "Free from grief."

They sat in silence for a long time, hand in hand, her fingers wrapped around his blue-veined wrist, savoring the faint thrum of his pulse underneath his skin. "I know that you lied to me," she said presently, and his silver brows shot up as he looked over at her. "That story you told me, before Sean died, about the prince named

Jack who defeated death."

"The *lord* of death," he corrected. "No one ever defeats death itself. And what makes you think I lied to you?"

"Please, Daideo. I know that I was a child then." She leaned her head against his shoulder. "But I'm not a little girl anymore, though, and I would like to know how it ended."

"Och." He reached up and rubbed his hand across his jaw. "It's not a pretty story, Riona."

"Are any of them?"

He shook his head. "You are so cynical, so determined to keep your heart so closely guarded – too much so. One day I hope that you learn that without the risks that come with seeking it, you can never taste true happiness."

"Perhaps. But for now, I'd like to know what truly happened to the prince of Éire."

Daideo bent his gray head, a silent concurrence. "Jack was a foolish, arrogant boy, little queen – one who dared to claim the hand of the mistress of death, to steal her away from her lord, and he paid the ultimate price for it, with both body and soul, all those years ago." He shifted on the bench, wincing as the bite of the frost-kissed breeze whipped across their ears. Riona shivered once, snuggling in closer to the soothing warmth of her grandfather's once-tall form.

"The lord of death," she said. "Will you tell me his story?"

"Why so many questions?"

"Because." She rested her cheek against his arm. "I have walked with him all my life, Daideo, his presence overshadowing me every day since I was a child." Her grandfather tensed at her side, and she pressed her hand to the top of his. "I would like to know what kind of monster it is that watches me from the hidden realm of the sídhe."

Daideo was silent for a long moment. "Very well." He hesitated. "But you must promise me something first, a vow that you must never break, no matter what happens. Do you understand?"

A shiver that had nothing to do with the rising wind snaked down her spine. "What do you want me to promise?"

He turned his head to stare at her, his expression grave. "Do not," he said, "ever go into the sídhe to seek him out."

"Why would I?"

Daideo's expression did not flicker. "Promise me."

Her fingers clutched at the smooth stone bench beneath them. "I don't understand."

"This is important, Riona." The wind howled once, a mournful, low sound, and a few drops of rain pelted their faces, but still Daideo did not move, his blue eyes searching hers with an urgent intensity. "The lord of death is the master of sweet-sounding lies, an endless well of hollow promises and false dreams. Too many souls – many very like you, so bold and brave and full of that particular kind of arrogance that only the youthful can have – have been drawn in by the siren song of his promised rewards, dooming themselves for all eternity, enslaved to his will." He touched her cheek, wiping away the droplets of rain. "Your grandmother worried for you greatly, Riona. She believed that you were drawn to the mountains, to the darkness that lives there. I laughed it off for too long. My little queen, I would say, she is far too clever, too wise to fall for the false promise of such lies, but now –" He shook his head. "Now, as I stand on the threshold of those other-worlds I knew so well in my youth, and as I imagine you left behind in this one, I find that I fear it as well." He rested his forehead against hers. "Promise me, Riona, that you will never go into his realm."

Riona shuddered. "I promise," she whispered, and her grandfather's chest heaved once before he pulled away, pressing a kiss to the top of her hand.

He sighed, tilting his face toward the black-and-gray sky as the rain continued to fall in a steady wave. "Legend has it," he said at last, "that the lord of death was once a man, mortal as any other. He lived in a land far beyond the sea that borders the eastern realms, he and his six brothers. His father was a greedy man, a bloodthirsty chief who lusted for war, until one day he sailed for the shores of Éire, determined to conquer her for his own. But in those days, so many hundreds of years ago, the land of Éire was no place for mortals. It was a realm of only magic, home to the immortals, the Tuatha Dé Danann and their brethren, those creatures that seem like monsters to anyone not a god themself, the light and the dark swirling together in this rain-shrouded isle of ours. So when this foreign chief approached these shores in his great wooden ships of war, he was met with the full might of the Tuatha Dé Danann, who crushed his army before ever it touched the land and slew him where he stood on the bough of his ship, spilling his blood into the sea, to wash up onto the white sands of the beaches of Ulaid with the spit of the white-tipped surf.

"A lone surviving ship of his army escaped the wrath of the Tuatha Dé Danann and returned home, bearing news of his chief's death to his seven sons. And so Donn and his brothers – Amergin, the dread druid-priest, and Heremon, and three other warriors of fearsome strength and skilled – raised an army of their own, determined to avenge their father's death. They arrived in Éire, these foolish mortal men, landing at Cnoc na Teamhrach, and Donn leapt over the side of his boat, his boots sinking into the wet sand and the churning white-foamed surf. He surveyed the looming cliffs, the mist-gray rain that fell across the land, breathed in the salt air of the sea, and was overcome with greed, with lust for the beauty and majesty of this land, burning with a desire to rule it as his own.

"It was not long before he came face to face with the earth-mother herself, Ériu, one of the primal sisters three. She had ventured forth from her burrows deep within the rocks to see for herself the wealth of ships that were docked on her shores. She crept close to Donn where he stood, braced against the salt-kissed rocks, staring up into the cloudy sky. She had never before seen anything like him, this steely-eyed, broad-shouldered man, and deep within her moss-soft heart, the wellspring of all creation, she felt a surge of love for this new, mysterious creature who walked on her shores. 'Boy,' she said in her river-smooth voice, and he whirled around to face her, his hand resting on the hilt of his sword. 'What is that you wish? Love me, and I will grant it.'

"Donn surveyed her with disdain, her green-and-brown skin, her wrinkled hands and leafy tresses. She was nothing like the mortal women he had known, this tree-like woman with the weight of all ages in her eyes. 'What are you?' he sneered, and her nut-brown teeth glistened as she smiled. 'I am she who promises you the victory you seek,' she said. 'Make me your wife, and the gift of my gratitude shall be my dowry.' Donn dug the toe of his boot into the mud at his feet, kicking it into her face as he spat on the ground. 'You tree-born hag,' he scoffed. 'What need have I for your blessings? I have my own gods for that, and a wife as well, in the land of my birth, far more beautiful than you, white of skin and black of hair with blood-red lips, and she will bear for me an army of sons who will crush this land of yours with the iron of their fists.'

"Ériu was hurt, a terrible wound to her soft heart, and she straightened her bent and twisted limbs to their full height, her leaf-green eyes flowing wet with tears. 'Boy,' she said. 'I vow to you now, that you shall never have the rule of Éire.'

"The next day, the battle began to rage, and Donn took to the sea in his iron-bowed ship to fight with the god of the sea himself, hand to hand, sword to sword, when Ériu rose up from her bed in the earth and raised the very rocks of the sea against him. The storm-clouds churned and the wind howled, and there arose a storm of rage and ruination the likes of which would never again be seen in the land of Éire, and when at last the sea settled and the winds slept and the rocks returned to their homes on the ocean floor, Donn was nowhere to be found, drowned underneath the weight and press of a thousand angry waves.

"And so," said Daideo, "Donn indeed became the first mortal man to ever walk upon the land of Éire – and the first there to die."

Riona said nothing but shivered a little from the lash of the cool evening rain.

"The battle eased," said Daideo, "the beaches of Ulaid stained red and silver with the blood of the gods and monsters and mortals alike, and a truce was met. The gods admired the bravery and resilience of these fierce mortal soldiers, and allowed them to settle in the land, to farm and care for it as their own, to raise sons and daughters of Éire who knew nothing of immortality, but only the brief, simple life of a mortal existence. And thus a new realm was born, one belonging to the men and women of Éire, branching off into the four kingdoms – Ulaid and Leinster and Munster and Connacht, with the northern isles belonging to the gods and the monsters alone.

"But –" Daideo looked down at Riona, his blue eyes darker than she had ever before seen him, and her fingers tightened around his.

"I know," she said. "I remember this part. For every light –"

"There must be a shadow." He nodded once. "Another realm also needed to be born, for the gods looked around and saw a sight never before seen in the land of Éire – a swarm of thousands upon thousands of undead souls, wandering gray-shadowed and bleak across the bloodstained fields of battle. No mortal had ever before died under their purview, you see, and it became necessary to establish an ordering for their new-found subjects, a new other-world in which for them to reside, away from the concerns of the living and the realm of the gods. Ériu looked upon them, these thousands of weeping, lost souls, and saw in their shadowy selves something gentle and weak and childlike, and her heart again stirred within her at the sight of them, these motherless souls, searching for home. She knew that the unfettered rule of the gods and their kin had passed, for there were new creatures now in the land of Éire, fragile and frail and in need of so much care, and she took it upon herself to see it through, the caring of these mortal souls."

"But she was not their mother," Riona objected. "Why should she care about them?"

Daideo shook his head. "One does not have to shed blood and tears to become a mother, and Ériu was no different. Like all mothers, she needed no other reason to love," he said, "than existence."

Riona said nothing, but something venomous and resentful swirled in her belly. Not all mothers, she thought. Not hers, who hated her so much, for no other reason, it seemed, than existence.

"The earth-mother stretched out her ancient hand," Daideo continued, oblivious to the storm raging within Riona's heart, "far across the star-studded sea, and cleft the waters in twain with a single stroke. Across its waters, she fashioned a bridge, made from the bones of her body and the blood of her heart, a passageway granted to these newfound children of hers, so that they might find peace in a realm built only for them, and then sank down, down into the sea, forever. And thus," said Daideo, reverent and soft, "the plains of Magh Meall were born, and upon its throne was established Niamh, the fairy-queen, to watch over the blessedness of its inhabitants who found their way across the bridge formed by the sacrifice of the earth-mother's heart, granting them eternal youth and happiness there in the promised land of light."

Riona frowned. "A bridge," she said. "That leads to Magh Meall?" Her da's face, blurry and distant, flickered in front of her, and with it the fast-fading memory of Cian and Aden and Sean, those long-lost brothers of hers. Aisling, her nursemaid, Maeve's mother, and her half-forgotten big-bellied laugh. Maeve herself, her heart's sister. Mamó. "Where is it? How do I cross it?"

"Och," he said softly. "You cannot."

"But –"

"It is not that kind of bridge, little queen."

"I don't understand."

"One day," he said, so quietly she could barely hear him. "You will."

A long silence stretched between them, Riona frowning in confusion, until Daideo roused himself from his reverie and continued his story. "But," he said. "Even after the sacrifice of the earth-mother, the wrath of another goddess was not yet soothed against those who had wronged the land that she loved. As she surveyed the pools of silver of her slain sisters and brothers, her blood-bound kin, she recalled the injury dealt to her clan by the doomed druid, and so she called upon her powers as the dread goddess of war and ruin, of fate, the whispering of death itself, for vengeance."

"The Mórrígan. Your mother."

Daideo bowed his head in acknowledgment. "The Mórrígan, one of the primal sisters three, swore to avenge the slight paid to the all-powerful gods of Éire, to her now-lost sister. She condemned the dead soul of Donn and all his brothers to an existence spent in eternal service to her will, forbidding them to enter the realm of Magh Meall and taste the delights of eternal joy. For Donn in particular, the Mórrígan confined him to an otherworld of hi sown, and named it Tech Duinn, the realm of mourning, to which all mortal souls must first travel before winging their way to plains of delight far across the sea – Donn would be its king. 'You wished to rule,' she said to his half-frozen soul which she had fished out from where it had sunk to the bottom of the sea. 'Rule this, then, a kingdom of empty grief for that which is lost and can never again be found. Never shall you again so much as touch the land of Éire, but instead shall watch it flourish and thrive in front of your eyes for the rest of eternity while you languish away here, the lord of lost souls. You wished to collect for yourself the secret treasures of my people, but now you shall collect only dust, until I choose to free you from the darkness of the eternal night.'

"And so," Daideo said, his voice growing soft and low as he stared into the distance, toward the dim light of the window high upon the wall of the castle, the room where Mamó lay, so quiet and so still. "It was through the powers of the Mórrígan, those dread arts about which none dared to speak, immortal and mortal souls alike, that Donn was reborn from the waves of the sea, to become the lord of death, the collector of lost souls as they shed their mortal bodies at the end of their days. He ruled Tech Duinn, growing in might and power as he practiced his arts within the unbroken silence of the sídhe, and the monsters of the world – one by one, they flocked to him and his dark powers. They swore allegiance to the lord of death, becoming his faithful servants, one and all, until at last he grew to rule over all the other-realms, the uncontested king of the sídhe."

Daideo grew quiet, and Riona shifted on the stone bench next to him. "But Tech Duinn is so far away," she said. "A barren rock in the far eastern sea. Why would I need to promise to never go into the Mhám Toirc to see him?"

"The lands of the sídhe," he said, absently, as though he were already so far away from her, winging his way across the sea in search of his lost bride, "are neither on the earth nor under it, uninhibited by space or time – do you not remember, little queen? It is an easy thing, to travel between them, wandering from realm to realm."

"But they are still there now, aren't they?" Riona asked. "The lord of death and his monsters. They are still trapped in the sídhe?"

"Now, yes. But when the Tuatha Dé Danann fell to the witch Fúamnach," Daideo said, looking away from the castle and down at his hands, clasped together between his knees, "the confinement spells placed on the sídhe loosened, allowing them to roam about the world of mortals, wreaking havoc on whatever poor souls crossed their paths, unchecked and unrestrained. The lord of death no longer felt compelled to curtail their appetites, and thus their thirst for blood ran amok throughout the land, and the people of Éire suffered from their wrath. When your grandmother awakened the gods, they re-invoked those spells, securing the safety and peace of the world of mortals from the worst of the ferocity of those beasts in the other-realms, forcing him to leash their wildness, and they have not been seen since in the realm of Éire." Daideo sighed once. "But I find that I am too tired for more. I am sorry, Riona. I think that I must go inside now, to be with my brèagha."

Her eyes burned at the finality in his voice, a tired resignation. "All right," she whispered, and linked her arm underneath his own, helping him to his feet. Daideo peered down at her, and his weary face softened into a smile. "My best girl," he said. "My little queen." He leaned down to press a kiss to the top of her rain-soaked head. "If you wish to know the full story of Jack, that doomed prince, and his unhappy fate," he said, "look in the solar, if you feel so inclined. The brown book, leather-bound, with the silver threading. It's there, if you choose to read it." He straightened and slowly made his way through the rain toward the castle, his arm shaking beneath her own. "But I would not recommend it. There are happier tales to read in your grandmother's and mine collection. I would suggest those instead, to carry you through these sad days ahead."

She said nothing, matching her steps to his slow ones, up the broad stairs into the front doors of the castle and down the halls, into the great room where the fire burned low. Daideo withdrew his arm from Riona's, patting her gently on the hand, his gaze fixed on his wife, her face so clear and lovely that she might be sleeping, a deep dreamlike slumbering from which there is no wakening. "Remember," he said. "Never alone."

She nodded, unable to speak, then a flutter outside the window caught her eye.

"Go along now, little queen," Daideo said. "I'll see you in the morning."

But Riona remained frozen in the doorway, staring.

There, outside the window, its bright black eyes staring into hers, perched the raven.

The morning came, the new-rinsed sky bright blue and free of clouds, and yet Daideo slept on next to his wife, their fingers entwined, their breaths forever stilled. Riona stood at the foot of their bed, dry-eyed and tight-chested, watching as Isleen drew the white sheet over their peaceful faces.

She was the queen of the vale, and that final benediction from her grandfather weighed heavy and hollow in her chest, for she had never felt so utterly alone.

The giant leaned down, massive hand closing tight around Jack's ribs, blood-stained teeth drawing closer and closer to the screaming prince -

Then, a gurgling sound, and a surge of something hot and metallic-tasting splashed across Jack's face. He saw a dark crimson hole torn through that horrid green eye, then watched as the giant tumbled forward past him to collapse lifeless on the hillside below.

Excerpt from 'The Snow, The Crow, & The Blood'

Chapter Fourteen
Neither of the Earth Nor Under It, Not Then Nor Now

RIONA

High in the Ellén Trechend's nest, Riona understood now what the púca had meant when he warned her not to disturb any of the treasures but for the spear. She found herself surrounded by a wealth of beauteous objects, glistening while the water still thundered down from the sky all around them – a club, inlaid with silver, twice as tall as any man, resting against the gray slab cliff wall; a brown-leather purse, washed-out and tattered at the seams, the blue-and-silver emblem with three yellow boars faded by years of sweltering in the fiery heat; an ivory statue of a long-forgotten goddess, her head tipped back, hands outstretched, bedazzled with an infinite number of bright winking jewels; a gray-skinned bag, marked with finely-drawn etchings of shoves of wheat and loaves of a bread and a oak-handled scythe – the insignia of Lugh, she realized, the great god of the harvest, and this – this must be his legendary crane bag.

And there, in the corner of the nest, nestled among heaps upon heaps of gleaming silver coins, a spear with a bronze tip, crafted from the thick branch of rowan tree, welded together with strands of pure gold.

The legendary Gáe-Bolg — the spear of Cúchulainn.

She shivered once, then she crawled forward, biting down on the inside of her cheek to keep from screaming as the gashes in her thigh began to burn with unbearable intensity, intent on claiming the spear and then finding some way, any way, out of this hellhole, when something prickled along the back of her spine, a silent whisper, demanding to be seen, to be found.

She looked down, the side of her hand brushing against the brown leather purse, lying innocuously there among the piles of gold and silver coins, as though someone had rifled through its contents and then tossed it aside, a worthless bit of rubbish compared to the dazzling array of treasures which surrounded it.

Far from worthless, that unearthly whisper sounded in her ear, soft yet insistent. Something far more priceless than gold and jewels and half-forgotten weapons of wood and stone, base metals and tree flesh, that will rot and rust as the rain and the snow and the heat of the sun and the slow, inexorable roll of the centuries beat down upon their temporal forms.

This though, that voice murmured. This will never die.

Her trembling fingers closed around the purse, and she felt it – a shift in the air, a sigh of rightness that brushed cool, soothing fingers across her blistered cheeks – and on a deep impulse born from some unknowable, primal urging, she reached her hand inside the purse and wished to be healed.

It was like running her fingers through the soft powder of the winter's first snow in the early morning dawn, crisp and light and cold, the purest sensation of peace that she had ever known. The chilled balm spread up her arm and across her scorched skin, down through her still-churning belly, and over the deep, gushing wounds in her thigh.

Riona opened her eyes, impossibly strong, as immovable and powerful as the snow-touched peaks of the Mhám Toirc, watching as the world below unfurled with new life, observing as it lived and it died and was born again, over and over throughout the endless stretch of years, while she remained, imperious and all-seeing, more eternal than the dawn.

This. This was what it felt to be a god.

An unwelcome memory threaded through her, the velvet-soft sound of her lord's voice whispering in her ear. Take nothing, he had said, but the spear.

Riona considered for a moment, feeling the worn leather of the purse, then without hesitation, slipped it into her pocket.

He was wrong, she decided. The purse had called to her, beckoned her from its place of ignominy among so many bright and shiny things. It belonged to her, and she would never let it go.

She spun on her heel, letting the tip of the spear drag along the dirt and bones of the vulture's nest, letting her fingers trace the raised outline of the boar-headed crest through the dirty fabric of her gown, and went down into the darkness without another thought.

"So you have ignored my warning," the púca said later, once more a dark-haired boy with honey-brown eyes, as he led her back through the withered wasteland of the sídhe. "You have taken something which would be best left hidden."

"How did you know?"

His eyes gleamed. "Do you even know what it is, that you have so foolishly laid claim to?"

Riona's fingers curled over the lump in her pocket where the purse lay hidden. "Of course I do. I know my fairy-tales."

"Then you should know that the coire ansic is a dangerous thing."

She frowned. "I did not find the coire ansic," she said. "I found a purse, one with a crest of three boars and a backdrop of silver and blue. I recognize it, from an old story my grandfather once told me, about – the high prince and a magical glowing sword and a cloak and –"

"The purse of plenty," he finished. "Yes. Also known as the coire ansic, from which none who dip their hand within its depths is left unsatisfied."

"No, that's Dagda's cauldron. I know about that – Daideo, my grandfather, told me that as well. This is something different."

"The purse and the cauldron are the same," the púca said curtly as they tramped through the ankle-deep water that lingered even though the rains had ceased, the sweltering humidity returned a thousandfold to the once-thriving apple orchard. "Long ago, the Dagda fashioned the un-dry cauldron from the earth of Éire, welded it together from the stones and the mud, and the magic that ran through the land granted it limitless power, a wellspring of wishes that left no one who sought out its magic unfulfilled."

"Food and drink." Riona nodded as she hurried after the púca, falling into step beside him, the spear tip dragging in the dirt behind her. "Dagda would eat his oatmeal from it with his giant ladle."

"Not only food and drink. If that was what its suppliant sought, it would be given, but it possessed far more magic than that." The púca glanced up at her, his face dark with shadows. "Riches, gold and silver and copper coins. Beauty, or healing, or the gift of song." He paused. "Even, so it was rumored, the power of rebirth."

Riona stopped in her tracks, the hot sweat pooling along her spine turning cold. "Rebirth?"

"An unnatural, twisted magic." The púca's lips coiled in distaste as they resumed their walk underneath the shade of the browning apple trees, and Riona's stomach rolled at the pungent smell of rotting fruit in the humid air. "All mortal things were meant to die. It is their natural ending, and to avert such an act, to twist it, pervert it – nothing good comes from such magic. Remember that."

Riona's fingers drifted down again to feel the soft corners of the purse, tucked into her pocket. "Still," she said, to herself rather than to the creature by her side. "What power – to bring back that which is lost, from beyond the star-studded sea. I wonder –"

"Do not wonder." The púca cut her off sharply. "You do not understand its power – you cannot control it. No mortal can." He glanced at her again, and his face softened at the sight of her tight lips, the stubborn set of her jaw. "I would have thought you would have learned that," he said, very quietly, "given the fate of the one who last tried to do so."

"Jack," Riona murmured, and the púca nodded once.

She followed him in silence, until they came to a stop at a looming gray ash tree. "Are you quite certain this is it?" She asked, and he rubbed his hands together, dancing a little on the toes of his booted feet. "The way to your home?"

"I have cursed this tree more times than I care to count, for denying me passage. I am sure." He pointed toward the west. "You will find the entrance to your own realm there. Do you remember the cave by which you entered?" She nodded. "Very well." He paused. "You could come with me, back into the land of the living once more, and not return to him, this master whom you have chosen to serve." His gaze latched onto hers, searching and soft, but Riona shook her head.

"I must," she whispered through the lump in her throat. "I would pay too high a price if I did not."

"A pity. You would have a knack for mischief-making, I think."

She almost smiled at that. "Thank you," she said instead. "For helping me. Without you, I –"

He waved his hand. "We made a bargain. It was hardly a gesture of sentimentality. I do not indulge in such things often."

"Well. Regardless of why you helped me, I thank you. I hope that you find peace and plenty of harmless mischief to be made in the land of Éire."

"If it is anything like I remember," he said, "there will be much of both for me to find." He reached out a small hand, his fingers brushing against the trunk of the tree, then jerked back, and Riona's eyes widened to see a white-hot burn scalded onto the back of his hand. "You see?" He waggled his fingers. "I am bound still. Now – now keep your vow to me," he said. "I have helped you, saved you when you otherwise would have died. So set me free once more in the lands of Éire."

Riona stepped forward and closed her eyes, imagining that silver shimmer that ran even now through her veins, then removed the rust-stained blade from her side and drew it across the soft flesh of her forearm. Before the blood had time to bloom over the shredded skin, the air shimmered before them, and the tree shuddered as the silver drops of blood soaked into its bark, its trunk cracking wide, revealing a yawning gap in its center, a dimly lit passageway that threaded its way through the ephemeral air between the mortal realm and the land of the sídhe. The púca leapt forward, and after a moment, she followed, catching a glimpse of the dark gray twilight sky blanketing the slumbering mortal world.

"I don't understand," she said, frowning, taking in the soft clouds, the muted light of the moon behind its foggy coverlet. "Last time, it was so hard, but this time, I barely had to think it and here we are."

His gaze fell pointedly again to the treasure hidden within her dress, and she flushed. He smiled, then lifted his face up to the sky, inhaling that petrichor-rich scent of the earth and the sky and home. "Be careful," he said, eyes closed, face upturned. "The lord of death does nothing by accident, and to teach you, the last remaining child of the gods left in this world, the lost arts of druidecht can bode no good for the rest of us." He jerked his chin in the direction of the brown-leather purse hidden underneath the curve of her hand. "Do what you like with the spear of Cúchulainn. It holds little value to any who do not possess the knowledge of how to wield it, which your lord does not."

"He will not be my lord for long – not once I have paid my debt to him." But her gaze fell to her bare arms, the undeniable evidence that she had obeyed his commands, dozens and dozens of times. She stared at the scars crisscrossing over her skin, as though she were seeing them for the first time, as though she could see the throb of her silver-tinted blood pulsing through her veins just beneath the skin. She remembered the hunger in her lord's expression as he traced the swell of her blood with the tip of his fingers, the intense need that sharpened the lines of his features.

"Whatever you do," the púca continued, beginning to wander away from her, hands clasped behind his back. "Do not give him that purse. Take it, hide it away in the other-realm of mortals, in some far-off, well-hidden corner of the sídhe. Cast it into the star-studded sea to rest for all eternity – I care not. But if you were wise, you would never entrust even the smallest bit of the power of the gods into the care of the lord of death." The púca's features softened with something like pity, then he turned away, stepping into the yawning doorway. "Goodbye, little queen. Live well and die happy – if you can."

He disappeared, and she retreated down the passageway, the ash-gray trunk of the tree closing behind her in a swift, sudden motion, and Riona was left alone in the sweltering heat of the charred forest, surrounded by the too-sweet scent of half-rotted fruit in the realm of dead and dying things.

Fiadh was waiting for her, dozing in the moonlight, stretched out on the grassy knoll above the cave, and greeted her with the kind of lazy exuberance that only a cat can truly master. She had nuzzled at her legs and then nipped at her calf, a greeting and a reproach all in one. "Ow," said Riona, swatting at her with the shaft of the spear. "Is this going to be a regular thing between us now? Because I have enough scars without the bite of your teeth on me, don't you know."

The cat-sìth yowled, then loped away, impatient to be gone. Riona followed, resigned to another long march across the land until they reached the silhouetted slopes of the Mhám Toirc mountains.

She paused outside the entrance, the spear hoisted in one hand, the leather purse gripped the other, and, the púca's warning words still ringing in her ears, made a choice. A stone's throw away from the great gray boulder that marked the doorway into Tech Duinn, she buried the purse in a shallow grave, then covered it with the rocks and evergreen limbs she found lying loose on the ground around it, an innocuous cairn for such a creation of infinite, immortal power.

She would enter the sídhe with only the spear she had been sent to find, because the purse – the purse was hers, and she would not share it with him, this lord of death who commanded her as idly as he commanded the monsters beneath his purvey. She would have this one treasure, this one prize, that was hers and hers alone.

A wise decision, she soon discovered, for he snatched her prize from her hands as soon as she appeared before him.

"Well, well." The lord of death held the spear of Cúchulainn up in the starlight, balancing it in the palm of her hand. "What a clever girl you have proven yourself to be, a stóirín. I asked for the Gáe-Bolg, and you have delivered it to me." He eyed her, his black-and-gold gaze bright with curiosity. "How did you manage it, all by yourself?"

"I am a servant of the mighty lord of death, and a child born with the blood-magic of the gods." Riona said primly, tugging at the hem of the sleeves of her gown. "I hardly needed a sidekick."

Some instinct whispered to her not to speak of the púca, of the bargain they had made or the warnings that he had given her. The púca was first and foremost a creature of the sídhe, and the lord of death was its king, and Riona knew beyond a shadow of a doubt that if so compelled, her newfound friend would have no choice but to reveal what else she stole, high up in the nest of the Ellen Trechend.

"You were gone for so long," her lord said as he ran his finger along the sharp tip of the spear. "I half-thought some nasty beastie was having a bit of fun with you before it killed you at last."

"Yet here I am, alive and well."

"So I see, and you can't imagine how relieved I am. I would have lost a rather large wager to Amergin otherwise."

"Amergin thought I would be killed?"

"It was the first true moment of glee that I have seen from him in two hundred years. He was positively giddy at the idea of it." Her lord let the spear fall to the ice-crusted earth with a clatter. "He despises you, you know."

"The feeling is mutual." She paused. "Are you just going to leave that there?"

"I have no use for it."

"So you had me risk my life for nothing?"

"Not at all. Now I know that I can rely on you, to do what it is that I require you to do."

"How nice for you," she said. "Might I now be included in the secret of what that is?"

"Soon – but not yet," he said, turning to wander away, waving his fingers in her direction in a silent summons to follow. Riona gritted her teeth, but obeyed, fists clenched at her side, but before she could take a step, a low rumbling erupted underneath the frost-covered ground, and the lord of death sighed. "Duty calls, I'm afraid," he said, and snapped his fingers.

An echoing sigh filled the air, and Riona shivered as a sudden breath of ice-cold wind rushed through her and took shape on the ground before them, an ephemeral mass of shadowy arms and legs wrapped tight around one another. "Well," he said. "Here is a lesson in death for you, somewhat ahead of schedule. Look, and see your own future in all its sorry glory."

The shadowy figure unwound itself until it lay sprawled in the dirt, silent and unnaturally still. Riona took a hesitant step forward. "What is that?"

"It's a soul, of course. A mortal soul that must be given passage to Magh Meall, and so it has arrived here, in my realm, the land of the forever dead, before I send it along its way across the star-studded sea to the east." He nudged the motionless shape on the ground at their feet with the toe of his boot, and Riona watched in fascination as it passed right through the gray-shadowed shape.

A shudder passed down her spine. "Why does it look like that?"

"It lacks a corporeal form, until the fairy-queen Niamh bestows one upon it." He nudged it again, toying with it almost, like a cruel-eyed boy prods at a mouse caught quivering in a trap, and Riona watched, stomach twisting, as his boot again cleaved the shadowy substance of the soul in twain.

She stared at the soul on the ground, faceless and bleak. "What happens to them, once they are there? In Magh Meall?"

Her lord smiled, that beautiful, too-gentle smile. "How would I know? You know my story. You know that I am forbidden ever to breach its borders, confined to the darkness as I am."

She swallowed. "Do you – do you regret it? What you did, that caused you to be locked away here?"

"How could I? Look at me. The lord and master of death itself. It is what I have always wanted – power and might beyond that of any other mortal man." He looked back down at the soul at his feet, his lips pursed. "Would you like to see it, the power that I command?"

Without waiting for a response, he again snapped his fingers, and the soul shrieked, a wordless scream of agony, as it splintered into ghostly tendrils of smoke and ash.

"Stop," Riona cried, grabbing at his arm, digging her nails into his shirtsleeve. "Stop, you are hurting it –" She broke off, staring at the shadow beneath her, because for a moment, something like a face appeared within the swirling storm of its dark gray fumes. Riona inhaled sharply.

"I know him."

The screaming stopped, and the soul shivered once, resuming its tightly wound shape of tremulous air. The lord of death quirked his eyebrow. "You mean you knew him. After all, he's dead."

"Yes," she said softly. "I knew him." She crouched next to the insubstantial cloud of gray air, letting her fingers glide through the swirling mist of his soul. "He was a cobbler in the village by the vale. I don't remember his name."

"It doesn't matter." Her lord watched her, a lynx crouched among the underbrush of the mountain, stalking the deer drinking from a stream choked with dead leaves. "His name, that is. All that he once was now is lost. What he will now become – that is far more intriguing."

"Why was he screaming like that?" She asked, unable to pull her hand away from the preternaturally cold mist that swirled all around the shadowy shape of what were once his limbs and his torso – his face, she thought with a shudder.

"Because it hurts," he said, and even without looking up at him, she could feel him watching her, hungry and expectant. "He has been set free of his prison, his feeble mortal form, and it is agony for him, to again be so locked away."

Her hand cleaved through the ethereal gray matter, her fingertips brushing against the half-frozen dirt below. "I – I remember he had a brother. He was younger, frail and thin, a sickly boy. He died though, when I was a girl." She glanced up. "Do you remember him? The younger brother?"

The lord of death nodded. "Oh yes, I remember all of them. Thousands upon thousands of souls." He kicked a clump of icy slush toward the shuddering gray-shadowed soul on the ground before him. "A testament to my cleverness, you should know. They mostly look like this, fuzzy-featured and vague – and yet I remember them still."

Riona could not tear her eyes away from the cobbler's soul. He had been such a force of a man, she remembered, red-cheeked and jovial and bursting with life. What a terrible thing, she thought with a shiver, to be reduced to this, a gray-shadowed thing scratching in the dirt, indistinguishable from any other wispy remnant of a mortal life that made its way into this icy land. "What will happen to him?"

"I shall have one of my familiars escort him to the far side of my realm and send him on his way." He jerked his chin toward the soul on the ground. "The dobhar-chú can take him. It's been growing a bit restless, lurking about in the river with only Amergin for company." He snapped his fingers, and from deep below the earth, a sinister hissed reverberated in response, and the soul on the ground let out a high-pitched keening sound. The lord of death turned away, half-yawning, beckoning to Riona as he wandered away. "Come along," he said over his shoulder. "Our duty is done."

She took one last look at the shadow sprawled in the starlight and shivered, then hurried after her lord, wringing her hands. "It seems cruel," she said. "Surely there are other ways, kinder ways, to send him across the star-studded sea. Why do you torture him with that monster?"

"The dobhar-chú is no monster. He is simply doing what nature intended him to do." He smiled, gentle and slow. "Never fear, a stóirín. Your erstwhile friend shall arrive at the plains of unending delight soon enough, and whatever indignities he suffers at the claws of my dobhar-chú will soon be a half-remembered dream."

"It seems cruel," she said again. "They deserve better than this."

"A bit hypocritical of you, I must say. What about my poor friend, the bean-sí? Wouldn't you say what you did to her was rather – what was the word – 'cruel'?"

"No," Riona snarled. "That was *just*. She killed Maeve – sixteen years old, barely begun to live, a good person, the best person, and that monster *killed* her."

He smiled, not at all soft, but wicked and sharp, an adder rising up from the grass to strike at the unsuspecting songbird warbling in its nest. "Only because you let her." Riona whimpered, an involuntary sound, and the lord of death's smile widened. "You must lose that bit of softness that still lingers in your heart, a stóirín," he said. "Or you will not succeed in the next part of your training."

"What must I do?"

"What a master of death must always do." His eyebrows arched. Riona suddenly found it hard to breathe, an invisible, merciless vise clamped around her lungs. "You mean –"

"Yes," said the lord of death mildly. "Now I'll be needing you to steal a soul for me."

'Well done, boyo,' said the fear-dearg, bloodied knife in hand. 'You make an excellent bait. Here.' The fairy tossed Jack a worn leather purse, with a faded sigil embossed on its side — three boars' head stacked one upon another. 'Your prize.'

'The purse of plenty,' said Jack.

'Yes,' the fear-dearg said. 'Made by the Dagda, it is never known to leave its master unsatisfied, no matter the asking. To possess the purse is to hold in one's hands undying power.'

Jack stood, the purse in his hands, and felt, for the first time, like a god.

Excerpt from 'The Snow, The Crow, & The Blood'

Chapter Fifteen
The Vale of Inagh, Éire, 1070

RIONA

Riona made it almost a full fortnight after Daideo followed Mamó into the realm of Magh Meall before she went hunting for the true story of the young prince of Éire and his black-haired bride.

It had been a long two weeks, to be sure, filled with mourning feasts and funeral fires and dignitaries from half of the realm come to pay their respects to the last of the old gods and their unfathomable power. Her cousins, Eamon, the young king of Connacht, and his brother Shay, had come as well, standing dark-eyed and solemn by her side, the new-crowned queen of the vale, in her gown of silver-black and a crown of lilac and clover atop of her loose flowing hair.

Her eyes had sought out Conor's in the throng that clustered in her grandmother's hall – her hall, she realized with a pang – as they roared out her name, their feet pounding on the cold stone floors, fists raised in celebration, but it was Conor who held her gaze, steady and calm in a sea of unfamiliar faces. They were the ones who grieved. They were the ones who felt more than the mere trappings of sorrow, she and him, in this crowd of celebrants who had come seeking the gratification of their idle curiosity and several nights of riotous feasting.

Either that, or to win the hand of a queen as their bride.

Riona had never dreamed that there could be so many princes belonging to a single country. They had all lined up to kiss her hand and voice their congratulations and condolences in the same, mellifluous breath. They had flashed her their dazzling, toothy smiles, cool and assessing as they looked her up and down, the tall and the short, the dark and the fair, each one almost indistinguishable from the next as they eyed her with matching expressions of insincere interest.

Not one of them saw her. Not like Conor did, with his clear gray eyes and healer's heart.

All the while, her mother stood just behind her, her fingers wrapped around Riona's elbow in an iron-tight grasp, smiling broader and broader with each pretty-faced prince who bent over her outstretched hand.

Gods, she missed them.

But at long last, the castle grew quiet and peaceful again, the sudden influx of guests and courtiers riding away into the mountain paths of the Beanna Beola, and it was only her again, her and Conor, alone once more.

And so it was that two weeks after she lost Mamó and Daideo, Riona slipped into the dark quiet of the solar and lit the squat, half-melted candles that were cluttered about the room to peruse her grandmother's shelves of leather-bound books. It was an indulgence, she knew, these hundreds of thick-backed tomes, collected from all corners of the realm for so many years. They had both loved stories, her grandfather to tell them and her grandmother to read them, so it soothed that relentless ache in Riona's heart a little, to be so surrounded by them now, these faded scrawls of ink on well-worn pages, the last remaining scrap of them she had left to hold in her hands.

She ran her finger across the leather spines that were nestled along the bookshelves, squinting to see the embossed titles, until she paused at a thin tome, brown leather and silver binding. *Tales of Loegaire,* it spelled out in faint, faded letters, and her heart beat a little faster as she pulled it from the shelf, settling her grandmother's chair by the fire, the candle flickering on the table by her side.

She opened it up, inhaling the smell of rosemary leaves her grandmother had placed within the pages, smiling faintly as she lost herself in the soothing lull of the silent scrawl of words and the musty scent of half-faded ink and the soft swish of turning papers, and for a moment, they were there again, sitting in that small, familiar room, her Mamó and her Daideo, keeping her company as she read late into the night.

Then her fingers stilled, tracing the black-tipped letters scrawled on the top of a new page.

Her pulse thudded erratic and loud in her ears, and Riona swallowed once before she hunkered down closer to the low-burning fire, and began to read.

Much later, Riona slammed the book shut, her heart thundering her chest.

Black hair, red lips, white skin. The Mórrígan and the raven and the lord of death.

And the princess who served him.

The words roared through her, and she threw the leather-bound book across the room, the cream-colored leaves fluttering as it skidded across the floor, coming to rest by the red-brick walls of the hearth.

This was why, then. This was why so many of her beloveds had been snatched away from her, a sick, twisted love song to her, the call of the darkness, summoning her own. He wanted her, the lord of death.

The only thing that Riona could not fathom – and was not sure that she wanted to know –was what he would do with her once he had her.

'Now you must win the cloak of darkness,'
said the fear-dearg to Jack. 'Crafted by the
gods, it renders its wearer unseen to the
mortal eye, and provides passage into the
sidhe. It is kept in a castle three days' ride
to the west, by the brother of this giant. A
two-headed creature, far more ferocious.'

'Unnatural beasts,' Jack said.

'Some would say such creatures provide
balance,' said the fairy. 'The dark and the
light.'

'Those people,' Jack said, 'are fools.'

Excerpt from 'The Snow, The Crow, & The Blood'

Chapter Sixteen

Neither of the Earth Nor Under It, Not Then Nor Now

RIONA

"The first thing you need to understand," the lord of death said, "is that we are not thieves. We are not stealing lives. We are but harvesters who tend their crops and recognize when they are ripe, ready to fall beneath the blade of our scythe."

Riona nodded, not quite trusting herself to speak.

She was going to *kill* someone.

Not a crimson-eyed monster from the sídhe this time, or a three-headed, venom-fanged beast, but another person, a mortal like herself, someone with hopes and dreams, someone who loved and was loved in return.

"It's a simple matter." He leaned forward and brushed a loose strand of hair away from her face, and Riona jumped at the glide of his cool fingertips against her skin. "We wait and we watch, and when nature so determines, we harvest the souls of those who have been separated from their bodies by the ill-will of fortune or the workings of nature, the determining of the earth-mother, or at the hands of another. Sailors who drown at the whim of the sea, soldiers who fall on the field of battle – a sick child, perhaps."

Riona ignored the faint smile that accompanied this last pronouncement. "How is it decided?" She asked, level and dispassionate. "Who decides, when it is a person's allotted time?"

"I just told you. Fortune. Nature herself. Other, less conscientious mortals." He sniffed. "You are distracted. Was it something I said, perhaps?"

"And it's settled then? When fortune speaks – whatever that means – a person is doomed to die, and you pull their souls from their bodies like a dutiful little boy and send them along to Magh Meall, is that it?"

"Not distracted," he said. "But quite angry, I see. The remark about the child, was it?"

"Just answer the question."

"It's not my fault, you know, the wayward manner in which the gods first ordered the workings of your world. You needn't blame me."

She clenched her trembling hands into fists at her sides. "Sean," she said as calmly as she could. "My brother. That was nature – fortune, whatever you wish to call it – and not you, then, after all?"

"Ah." Her lord held up a finger. "That's why our preservation of life and death and the precarious balance that must be maintained between them is so very important, don't you know. I am the lord of death, after all. Your brother was sickly for a long time, sure now, but he would have lived – painfully, it is true, but lingered on, feeble and frail – had I not chosen to relieve him of his suffering prematurely."

Riona's vision blurred. "So you did kill him."

"It's a harsh word – 'kill.'" She felt him shift away from her, as if sensing the rage that threatened to boil over from deep within her. "He was not well, your brother. Do you remember him, how pale and weak and wan he was, how his chest rattled when he coughed, the bloodshot eyes, the thin pallor of his once-full cheeks? It was a mercy, what I did, calling him home. His harvest had come."

"And my father?" She asked, something dark and depthless and terrible roaring within her, aching to be set free on the creature before her. "My other brothers, cut down on that battlefield so long ago? Was that a mercy?"

"I did not bring war to your family, Riona," he said, steady and low as ever. "They rode to it of their own free wills, and death, as you know, is an all-too-natural end to war."

"You could have let them live – wounded, crippled, bed-ridden, whatever condition. You could have let them live. It was not their time."

"It was, and it is hardly my fault that they were not swifter, stronger. If they had been –" He shrugged. "Then they would still be alive, and you would not be here, most like. But so go the workings of fate, you know – your father slipped in a puddle of mud and fell beneath an enemy sword, and your brothers were too distracted, too distraught by the loss of him to put up much of a fight after that." He paused while Riona seethed, lips trembling, hands shaking. "Their harvest had come, so I took them."

"You heartless *bastard*."

"I see that we are back to name-calling. What would you like me to say? That I am sorry? I'm not, you know. I had been waiting for you for such a long, long time – the girl born with the blood of the gods in her veins, and your father, your brothers – their lives gave me the chance to command your attention, to force you to face the truth that so few mortals do."

"And what truth is that?"

"This truth." He placed his palms flat against his chest. "That I am not a monster, but your *savior*. Humans choose instead to ignore this truth, to wander in the shadows of ignorance for all their days, ignoring this most fundamental truth about their natures – all that lives must die, Riona. Fathers, brothers, grandparents, nursemaids, sisters – even children."

"Do not *dare* –"

"You needed to know death," he interrupted, swift and urgent, "to understand it, to be able to look upon its face and call it friend, intimate and well-known as the back of your hand, and so you have, every day of your life. A cruel necessity, I admit, but a necessity nonetheless." His expression darkened, a rising anger to match her own swirling in the depths of his golden-fire eyes. "Now. There is far more at stake here than you can possibly imagine, and you would be wise not to challenge me further."

Riona gritted her teeth together, her fury boiling within her. She thought of that long ago night, standing before the moss-covered boulder that led into his realm, tracing the names of so many lost souls into the rough shale of the rock – a talisman, she had thought, a steadying reminder that she had once loved and was loved in return.

They had died, all of them, because of *her*.

He was silent for a moment, his nostrils flaring as he watched her, then he turned away. "I am not the monster you all believe me to be," he said again. "I am not a murderer. Now you though – well. You loved your little friend, Maeve, did you not? And how did she die again?" His voice fell to a low hum, slow and cunning, a golden-skinned snake shifting through the dead autumn leaves. "Killed by a bean-sí, that should have been safely locked away in its home in the other-realm, had not someone – who could that have been, to behave so foolishly, so recklessly – had not *someone* set it free against the laws of gods and men." Riona's lips lifted into a snarl. "You see your hypocrisy? You blame me for keeping the order in the world, for balancing scales between life and death, because it causes you pain, gives you grief, but you are no different. You had power too, very like mine, and you chose to use it without thinking, to play with it as though it were a toy, and all that followed as a result was *your* doing. Not mine."

"You truly are evil."

His smile flashed, wicked and cruel and achingly beautiful. "If so, then I am *the* evil, the king of all the evils that exist in our world, and don't you ever forget it." He folded his arms across his chest, breaking her hot stare to look away into the ice-laden trees. "Now. Will there be any further complaints? Because I have quite a lot to teach you, if you don't mind."

Riona closed her prickling eyes. She had chosen this, she reminded herself. She knew what he was, what he had done, and yet she had agreed, of her own volition, to surrender herself to his service. It was imperative that she not forget the reason for which she had paid such a price, that she not let the unhealed hurts from the past scar the way for new, unnavigable avenues of immeasurable pain. "We harvest souls," she said at last. "In accordance with nature, a balancing between life and death."

"Indeed." He appeared somewhat mollified by her apparent acquiescence. "This is the next step in your training, Riona, and it is imperative that you be able to put aside your soft-hearted sympathies and do so as well."

Riona dropped her gaze to the ground, trying to ease the rising surge of panic in her chest. "Please," she begged, softer than she'd ever before spoken to him. "Please. I don't want to."

Her whispered plea was met with silence, but she kept her gaze downcast. She heard the crunch of his boots against the snow-capped leaves, and then his fingers were pressed underneath her chin, tilting her face up to his. His expression was surprisingly gentle, almost tender. "I know, a stóirín," he said. "Neither did I, my first time, yet it is necessary, to keep the checks and balances of power between these two worlds in place." His hand slid up to cup her cheek, and her pulse quickened. "I shall make it easy for you, this first time. Would you like to know who I have chosen for you?"

Riona froze, her breath lodged, thick with dread, in her chest. "Please –"

He pulled his hand away from her face, crouching down with fluid ease, his palm flat against the half-frozen earth. He murmured something, guttural and low, and Riona watched as a thin, crystal-smooth layer of ice spread from underneath his fingers, a round orb of gleaming white frost. Shadows swirled across the surface of the ice – within it, Riona realized with a start, the shadows were taking shape inside the ice – and she watched a familiar face materialize in the smooth, reflective surface, pale and steely-eyed with a jaw of iron.

She staggered backwards. "No."

"You don't like him. You never have. You despised him – a cruel, hardhearted man, that is what you once called him, do you remember?"

"He doesn't deserve to die."

"All living things deserve to die, Riona." She flinched at the sound of her name on his lips. "It is their just end, their natural conclusion."

"No."

"His harvest has come, Riona."

"I won't do it."

"You will." Her lord stood up, brushing his hands against his doublet, and even though the ice beneath them vanished, Riona could still see the flash of steel-gray eyes in that shimmering orb before her, that hard-set line of a dark-bearded chin. "Or you can consider our previous bargain null and void. You have done very well so far. You have come a long way, but you still have far to go before we are finished, you and I, and this – this is the next step."

Riona stared at the damp earth below. She had never thought that they had looked similar before, Conor and his father, but she could see it now, the faint resemblance in the soft boyish curves she remembered in his face and the unforgiving lines of the man's high-cut cheekbones she had just seen reflected in the glass-smooth surface of the ice before her.

She wondered if Conor would look the same in a few years. She wondered, suddenly, her heart clenching anew, if he already looked like that now. She had no idea how much time she had lost, wandering here in this dreamlike existence of shadows and spells.

"Perhaps," her lord said, as though he could hear the whisper of her thoughts spoken aloud, "you would like me to choose someone else, someone else whose harvest *should* be ripening, even now – had not you bargained with me otherwise."

The threat was there, unmistakable and clear.

"No." Riona swallowed, steadying herself. "No," she said again. "I'll do it."

"Good girl." She looked at him then, his beautiful, terrifying smile. "Then first things first." He clicked his tongue, and from the frost-kissed branches above came the rustling of wings, two bright black eyes blinking down at them through the glistening branches. "You'll be needing a raven."

"The spell is useless without this beauty," the lord of death explained. He reached out to stroke the glossy black head of the raven that perched on his forearm. "The raven is the most ancient familiar of death, and the only who can enter and exit the lands of the sídhe without being hindered by the confinement spells of the gods. Never forget that."

"Why?" Riona asked. "Why ravens?"

His face shuttered. "Your ancestor, of course. She who appointed me here all those years ago."

Riona shivered, remembering.

The Mórrígan, the goddess of war and fate, the Phantom Queen.

Something in his expression forbade her from questioning him further, so she bit her tongue and held out her arm, allowing the raven to settle onto her wrist. "Remember the words of the spell," her lord said, clasping his hands behind his back as he stepped away. "Do exactly as I have told you, and nothing more."

"I understand."

"Nothing more, Riona. Do not trifle with the workings of death." He paused, studying her, his eyes roving over her tense face. "His harvest has come," he said again, more gently. "This is his natural end."

She nodded through the sudden lump in her throat, and then he was gone, disappearing into the trees, and she was alone, the raven blinking up at her from where it sat perched on her wrist. Riona waited for a moment, staring at the invisible boundary line that divided the world of the sídhe from the land of the living, then at the bright-eyed raven perched. "Go," she said, and it ruffled its inky feathers once before it shot into the star-dappled sky, winging its way through the barren trees of the sídhe.

Riona followed its path, the watching eyes of the hidden creatures of the sídhe boring into her as she tramped through the leaves dusted with snow. They knew. They knew what she was going to do, and they would be here, waiting for her return.

Above her, the raven squawked once, a hoarse cry, shaking her from her reverie, and she straightened her shoulders and stepped forward. It was almost unconscious now, the quick cut to her arm, the sprinkled drops of blood all along the ground, and then she was moving unhindered through the line of slim-trunked whitethorn trees. A cool mist rain greeted her, falling from a gray, overcast sky, but she could see the pale rays of the sun blanketed beneath the dense, murky clouds. She lifted her hand and touched a pale green bud that danced in the breeze, soft and dewy with raindrops.

Spring, she realized. It was springtime here in the land of mortals — early spring at that, judging by the sight of the leaves still curled tightly in their buds, the chill that lingered in the air. She had almost forgotten such a thing existed, locked away in the realm of eternal winter and starry skies, things like blue-petaled blossoms and the pink-and-orange glow of a sunrise and the sounds of life beginning anew across the yawning world.

It would be Haisley's birthday soon.

For the first time in a long time, she allowed herself to wonder how old her daughter had grown, while she had been locked away, unageing and sad, in the shadow-lands of the sídhe.

The raven screeched again, this time in a strident warning, and Riona strode forward viciously, slashing her way through the underbrush toward the narrow, overgrown path that led down from the mountains to the rolling hills of the vale, all the way to the doorstep of her grandmother's castle.

She found that she was suddenly in the mood for a bit of soul-stealing.

The vale was exactly as she had left it – the gray stone walls of the castle shrouded with dark green ivy, smoke drifting across the gray cloudy sky from its many chimneys, the courtyard bustling with life, soldiers and horses and villagers alike. Riona stood hidden in the shadows of the surrounding trees and watched as they hurried by, hoods pulled up over their heads against the steady rainfall, chattering to one another as they passed. She left her own hood down, letting the rain drench her, chilling her down to her very bones, as she studied each of them, dispassionate and indifferent.

So here she was now, crouching in the shadows of the woods, waiting to steal away the soul of the man who might have been her father-in-law.

And almost as though she had summoned him, he appeared. She recognized that swinging, purpose-filled walk, the broad stretch of his shoulders underneath his dark gray doublet, the way he pushed his way past anyone who happened to stand in his path.

Cormac Ó Ruairc.

The raven on her shoulder crooned softly, and without taking her eyes off the broad-shouldered captain, she reached up and plucked a single glossy feather from the bird's proffered wing. She balanced it in the palm of her hand, breathing softly on it so that it fluttered against her skin. She opened her mouth to speak the words, the bitter-tasting incantation that her lord had so painstakingly coached her through, but just before the raucous, black-winged monstrosity inside her could loose itself from deep in her belly, she watched as Cormac turned his head and smiled – smiled, the severe, steely-eyed captain who had been so unrelentingly harsh and unforgiving toward his own sweet-natured son for so many years – at a red-haired girl who scampered past him, her curls damp with rain, her face bright with laughter.

Riona's chest splintered.

It was not Haisley, she knew that, even as she bent over, dry heaving and sick, her hands braced on her knees. Haisley had green eyes, a freckled snub nose – Riona could still see her daughter's little face, clear and shining in her memory, and that sweet-faced child had not been her own.

But it could have been, in another, kinder life, and Cormac had smiled at her, this girl who was not his granddaughter – smiled fondly, affectionately, a softening of his severe features, and Riona found herself wondering if he might have ever smiled at Haisley in such a way, if she might have slipped her small hand in his and skipped along by his side, if she had ever grinned up at him and called him 'daideo.'

She could not do this. This was not who she was, a thief of life, a harvester of souls. She could never do such a thing — to rob someone of their life, natural ending or not. She could not snuff out their hopes and their dreams with a few muttered words and a feather plucked from a midnight-black wing –

The raven on her shoulder squawked, low and threatening, and she could almost see a pair of bright green eyes and copper-colored curls and a toothy smile, growing white and still and unmoving before her.

She could not fail this test, no matter the cost.

No matter if it would be the ruining of her, once and for all.

That clicking, corvid creature within her rose up of its own accord, beady-eyed and cawing in hoarse triumph, and the guttural roll of the incantation rolled off her tongue. The raven's feather in the palm of her hand shivered once, and a shadow moved behind her, and then raven squawked again, its wings spread wide –

A torrent of screams broke forth as Cormac stumbled to his knees, his hands clutched to his chest, his face white and strained. A passing soldier grabbed him by the shoulder, bracing him as he slid boneless to the ground, and a matronly woman knelt in the mud beside him, pressing the side of her face to his heart.

"Cormac," Riona gasped, then froze.

Something cold and fog-like encircled her ankles, a cat made of shadow and mist arching its spine against her legs, and she looked down to see a faceless gray shape collapse on the ground before her, a huddled mass of ethereal legs and arms and the shadowy remnants of an iron-like jaw.

The soul of her would-be father-in-law had come to heel for the servant of death.

She handed it over to her lord when she returned to the sídhe, her fingers stiff and cold from the shadowy weight of the soul she had clutched in her shaking hands. She kept her eyes fixed on the ground below, unwilling to meet his gaze and see whatever judgment awaited her.

"Amergin said that you would be too weak," she heard that velvet-smooth voice say. "'She'll never be able to see it through,' he said, but I defended you, boasted about your strength." She shivered as she felt his fingers brush hers, gently prying the shadow-soul from her white-knuckled grip. "I am very disappointed in you, a stóirín, to be made such a fool of."

"I did it, didn't I?" She asked listlessly, half-frozen arms hanging by her sides.

"Be honest, Riona," he said. "We both know how perilously close to failure you came."

She kept her gaze locked on the frost-covered ground beneath her feet. "I did what you asked."

There was a moment of silence, and then his cool fingers wrapped around her elbow, tugging her toward him. "So you did," he said, his voice brushing against her ear, soothing and soft. "You did very well, you know, for your first try. You'll do better next time. It gets much easier, the more you practice."

"I have to do that – again?"

"There are so many souls," he half-whispered, his chin nestling against the top of her head. "So many souls waiting for you to set them free. It is all that any of us truly want in this life, you know – to be free."

Riona closed her eyes, letting her forehead drop against his chest.

Conor, she thought. Poor Conor, would he hear of it, would someone send him word, would he somehow know, sense somehow, that she had been there, hovering nearby, had shredded his father's soul from his body?

"Still," the lord of death said. "It's been four years, you know. I would have thought you'd be further along by now."

For a moment, Riona forgot how to breathe. It couldn't be.

"Four years I've had her," he mused, more to the stars that burned so coldly so far above them than to her. "Four years I've trained her, and she can't even yet steal a soul properly." He laughed once, rueful and dry. "Amergin will be throwing this in my face for *centuries.*"

Four years. Riona jerked her arm free of his grasp, stumbling backwards, staring at him. "Wait. You said – earlier you said that I was gone for a long time, when I was in Emain Ablach, the isle of apples. You said a long time – how long?"

There was a flicker of something like sympathy, passing over the marble-cold beauty of his face, and then it was gone. "A little over two years."

Her knees went weak, and she sank down into the damp black soil of the forest floor, pressing the heels of her hands against her face, blinking back the hot surge of tears.

Six years old now. Her baby, her green-eyed girl, of the chubby, dimpled knees and the lisping voice and the bow-legged, toddling steps, was a baby no more.

And she had missed all of it.

Three days later, Jack stood above the lifeless, two-headed giant, his handsome face disfigured with blood, holding aloft the treasures of the gods — the purse of plenty, and now the cloak of darkness, an airy, cream-colored thing. He wrapped it around his shoulders and sighed. 'It is as though I am wearing the wind.'

'It was crafted from a rain cloud,' said the fear-dearg, 'and - '

'Och, I do not care,' said Jack. 'Now take me to my sword.'

Excerpt from 'The Snow, The Crow, & The Blood'

Chapter Seventeen
The Vale of Inagh, Éire, 1071

RIONA

The midafternoon sun was unbearably bright, and far too hot, streaming in through the glistening glass pane of her window. Riona considered getting up to draw the curtain in a feeble attempt to block out the relentless, overpowering light, but she was so tired, her very bones aching with an inexplicable weariness, and her pillow was soft and cool, the sheets silky and smooth against her skin.

She would just have to endure it, this unrelenting pounding of the sun against her half-closed eyelids, because the allure of a long, self-indulgent nap on this unseasonably warm afternoon was far too appealing and summoning up the energy even to wobble across the room to draw the curtain seemed unthinkable.

It had been an unusually tiring morning, she supposed, sitting in council for the village aldermen, listening to interminable recitation of a myriad of issues concerning the upcoming harvests – petty feuds about border lines to mitigate and needless complaints about the division of labor to negotiate and anxieties about poor yields from the expected potato crops to dispel. Diplomacy had never been a strong suit of Riona's but this morning, her temper was particularly strained, the urge to snap and snarl far more compelling than she could ever remember it being. Not for the first time, she wondered how Mamó had managed it for so many years, with such infinite patience and unfailing gentleness.

Not for the first time, she wondered if she would ever be able to fill those shoes that Mamó had left for her, if she would ever be able to do the memory of her the justice it deserved.

For now, though, she was tucked away in the soothing quiet of her room, with only the sound of the curtains rustling in the soft breeze. She felt like she could sleep for weeks here in her bed, snuggled among the pillows and blankets, utterly and blissfully alone.

It lasted a few brief minutes, but even as her eyelids drooped, heavy and thick with sleep, there was a soft rap on her door. "Ria?"

She groaned. "Go away."

The bottom of the door scraped against the stone floor anyway, and she huffed through her nose. Only one person she knew would ignore that order and come lumbering into her room with such hurried, ungainly steps. "What's the matter?" Conor asked, the door snicking shut behind him.

"Nothing." She lay curled on her side, eyes half-open. "I'm only tired."

"Oh." The mattress creaked as he sat down on the edge of the bed, and her eyes fluttered shut as his fingers rubbed the small of her back in slow, soothing circles. "You looked so pale, and disappeared so quickly after lunch. I thought that bit of a cold you'd had a few weeks back might have come back."

She shook her head, sighing a little at the warm press of his fingers into her skin, settling deeper into the coolness of her pillow. Conor bent over, brushing her hair away from her face with his free hand. "Ria. Talk to me. Are you sick?"

A flash of irritation cycled through her. "No, cabbage," she grumbled. "I told you – I'm tired. I only wanted a bit of a nap, and for the gods' sakes, some peace and quiet."

"A nap in the middle of the afternoon?"

"It's not unheard of, Conor."

"For most people, sure, but it is for you. You're the most restless soul I've ever known."

"Well, I don't know what it is you're wanting me to tell you." She pushed herself up, wincing as his arm brushed against her chest. "I was wanting a rest, and –"

"Are you hurt?" She blinked at him in confusion, and he gestured toward her chest, his face flushing slightly. "You flinched, just now, when – well, when I –"

Two nights ago, the boy had slept wrapped around her body, not a stitch of clothing between them, and now could not bring himself to mention her fully clothed breasts. Riona wasn't sure if she were amused or irritated. "I'm a little sore, that's all. Only in my chest. I don't know, perhaps you were a bit rough the other night –"

"Ria."

She looked up, frowning at his shaky tone. "What?"

"Ria," he said again, in that same shaky voice. "When is the last time you bled?"

Riona froze. "Oh." Her fingers fluttered to her mouth, her mind whirling. "Oh my gods, it's been at least two months. *Conor*."

Conor bent over, his elbows on his knees, and clutched at his head. "Ria. You're with child, Ria."

She shot to her feet, hands trembling, stomach churning. "But I take my herbs, every morning, Conor, without fail. Every morning, I take my herbs."

He peered at her through his fingers for a moment, then dropped his hands to hang loosely between his knees. "A few weeks ago, when you were sick," he said slowly. "Did Isleen give you willow bark?"

"I don't know. It was some sort of tea." She paused, trying to remember. "It had a bitter aftertaste, like wintergreen."

"That's it then." He laughed humorlessly, hoarsely. "Willow bark lessens the strength of your woman's herb, Ria." Conor scrubbed his hands across his face. "I didn't think of it. I assumed Isleen wouldn't give it to you. I thought she knew, about us. I thought everyone knew."

"They will now." Riona sat down heavily on the edge of the bed, her legs suddenly uneasy and weak.

A child. She was carrying a child, their child, Conor's and hers, and she was utterly terrified. If there was anything in this world that she knew she was not prepared to be, it was a mother. She was meant to be, she knew, but as the wife of a prince as well as the queen of the vale. Perhaps one day, many years from now, then she would be ready to bear the strong-armed sons which were expected of her, when she had a king by her side to help her rule, with nursemaids and governesses and a veritable horde of ladies-in-waiting to take the child off her hands, to give it the nurturing that she knew she was wholly unqualified to give.

That time was not now, when she was only a girl herself, a fledging queen with barely a year's worth of a rule to her name, and a freckle-faced, clumsy-footed, decidedly non-princely boy for the father.

Her mother would be so furious. So disapproving.

"Cabbage," she whispered. "I'm really scared."

He said nothing, but his hand slid wordlessly toward hers, the scrape of the callouses on the tips of his fingers steadying her some-how, grounding her with the rock-solid warmth of his presence. "We'll be all right, Ria," he said at last, and his voice was firmer now, deeper somehow, and Riona hated herself for it, but she leaned into his shoulder and, just for a few brief moments, let him be strong enough for the both of them.

She leaned on him for a little while longer, while she told her mother.

He'd offered to leave, to let her do it alone, but she'd shook her head soundlessly. So it was then that her clammy palm was pressed tight against his, her fingers gripping his clever ones, as she stood before her mother in the great hall of her grandparents' castle and told her the truth.

Her mother stared at her for a long moment. "Are you sure?"

Riona nodded, her throat too tight and swollen to speak.

Her mother's fingers drummed on the arm of her chair. "You are the queen of the vale now, Riona," she said at last, deliberate and biting. "Such mistakes are unacceptable."

Conor tensed at her side. "I beg your pardon," he said, an unchar-acteristic note of steel underlining his voice. "But Ria and I –"

"There is no *Ria* and you," she interrupted. "I should have nipped this infatuation in the bud years ago. What am I meant to tell the young lords with whom I have been corresponding for months now, Riona, trying to arrange a suitable match for your hand? Do you suppose that any of them will have you, even with your title, now that you have so disgraced yourself?"

"She is *not* disgraced," Conor said hotly, and Riona squeezed his fingers once before easing her hand free of his.

"Mamaí." She cringed a little to hear the meekness, the apology in her voice, and she knew that Conor could hear it too because he stiffened at her side, his hands clenching into fists. "I am sorry, Mamaí. It was not – it was not planned, and I –"

"We will tell no one." Her mother ignored her stammers, rising swiftly from her chair, pacing back and forth with her hands clasped behind her back. "You will wear loose dresses – you are certainly round enough as it is that it shouldn't be too difficult a thing to conceal – and then when it becomes too advanced for you to hide it properly, you will keep to your room. We will say you have an illness, a worrisome cough and a fever, something. Only Isleen will attend you, until the – child – arrives, and then we will send it away, to the village, to be raised there. No one shall know."

"No."

Riona swiveled to stare at Conor. His jaw was set, a faint twitch of the vein his throat the only sign of his agitation. "You will not lock her away," Conor said. "You will not treat her like she is a shameful thing, and you most certainly have no say over what happens to my child."

Her mother's face blazed. "You are the child here, you foolish boy," she snapped. "What will your father say of this, when he returns to the vale?"

"I don't care." Conor tilted his chin, those clear gray eyes hot and defiant. "I love Ria. I always have, and I mean to marry her."

"Conor," Riona said softly, but he shook his head fiercely, his gaze locked on her mother's.

"My daughter," she said, her nose wrinkling, "will marry a prince. She will secure this family's future as the one of the most powerful in the realm. Her cousin rules in Soghain, and she will rule a great kingdom in the north one day, by the side of a king, not a half-grown boy with dirt under his nails."

Conor flushed at that, a rush of pink up his freckled cheeks. "I can be worthy," he said flatly, but Riona could hear it, that note of uncertainty in his voice. "I will be a soldier, like my father and grandfather before me."

"Oh Conor," she said again, because gods no, she knew that it would kill him, to sell his soul in this way, trading in a lifetime of healing hurts and mending bones for one spent breaking them, coming home to her arms smelling of blood and steel instead of dandelion and bilberry juices.

He refused to look at her. "If that's what you want from me," he said, meeting her mother's furious gaze unflinchingly, "then that is what I shall do. I don't care what happens to me. But Riona and the child – they stay."

She barely heard her mother's irritated protests, Conor's sharp-tongued rejoinders, over the roaring in her ears, the sound of both their lives being swept away on the white-churning waters of this inescapable river of ruin.

This baby would destroy everything, she thought. Not Conor after all, but this child, this *thing* growing inside her – it would be the ruining of her.

'There.' The fear-dearg pointed. 'Within there, lies the sword of starlight, Nuada's blade, whose wielder will never taste death.'

Jack studied the cave before him, surrounded by a dozen high mounds dotting the frost-kissed plain before them, an ominous place of reverential shadows. A prescient chill that had nothing to do with the thick wintry fog slipped down Jack's spine. 'What is this place?'

'This,' said the fairy, 'is Ráth Crúachan. The home of the Mórrigan.'

Excerpt from 'The Snow, The Crow, & The Blood'

Chapter Eighteen
Neither of the Earth Nor Under It, Not Then Nor Now

"**S**he is ready."

Riona looked up sharply from where she knelt on the frost-covered ground, drawing ancient runes and signs into the half-frozen earth. Nearby in the dark-watered river, Amergin watched her, his lips curled.

"I agree." Her lord pushed away from the tree where he leaned, studying her markings in the earth with pursed lips. "She has surpassed what you have taught her, Amergin, for all your grumblings."

Amergin merely grunted. "Took her long enough."

"Hush." Her lord winked down at Riona, who smothered the sudden urge to smile up at him, his obvious pride in her accomplishments warming her even through the ever-present chill in the midnight air. "Do not malign my most prized pet."

Fiadh yowled once from where she lay sprawled on her side next to Riona, her tail thrashing lazily in the fallen leaves, and Riona reached out to stroke her behind her pointed ears. "I think you hurt Fifi's feelings."

"When *Fiadh* brings me the god-forged treasures that I seek," her lord said drily, "then she may once again resume the title of my favorite pet, but for now, that title belongs to you and you alone, a stóirín."

It shouldn't warm her, this small show of seeming affection, but Riona couldn't seem to stop herself from smiling. And why should she, after all? He and Fiadh were the only friends she had left in this world.

Everyone else she had once loved had long since forgotten her.

Which was for the best, both for her own sake and theirs. They might both be old and gray by now – Conor and Haisley – and there was nothing she could do to gain back those lost years with them. She wasn't even sure if she would, if she could. Perhaps they had both now lived long and happy lives, free from the grief and the pain she no doubt would have brought them.

It's the all she had ever wanted for her child – a simple, peaceful life.

After all, she had sacrificed her own for it.

Fiadh rolled onto her back and batted at Riona's loose-hanging braid with her enormous paw, mewling softly, and Riona obediently scratched at her thick-furred belly. "I'm afraid that I cannot return the compliment. Fiadh is by far my favorite."

"I can hardly even bring myself to be offended." He watched them for a moment, his golden-fire eyes amused. "But perhaps that is only because you have not yet made the acquaintance of her many siblings. They are equally as charming – well, some of them. I personally cannot abide the slúagh. Such nasty, foul-tempered birds, with their rotting teeth and molting feathers." He paused. "Would you like to see them?"

"The slúag? Not particularly."

"Not only them. I mean the others as well – hundreds of them, all trapped here in the shadow-lands, all longing to be free." His smile curved along his finely-cut cheekbones, and for some inexplicable reason, despite the carelessness of his tone, she felt a shiver of anticipation, of fear, trickle down her spine. "As are you."

Riona swallowed, her fingers tightening on the silky strands of the cat-sìth's fur. Underneath her suddenly tense fingers, Fiadh grumbled once, a strangely reassuring sound. "Will they try and harm me?" She asked, remembering the hiss of the Ellén Trechend, the ember-red eyes of the bean-sí.

"They *will* harm you,," he said calmly, "if given the chance."

"This is hardly a convincing argument that I should meet them."

He shrugged. "So do not give them that chance. You defeated the Ellén Trechend, did you not?"

"Barely."

"Well," he said, "remember too that you are untested and untried in the workings of death no longer. How many souls have you stolen for me now, a stóirín?"

"Dozens," she whispered, and he smiled, broader this time, prowling closer to where she stood.

"Dozens and dozens," he echoed, tugging idly on a loose strand of her hair. "You have reclaimed the spear of Cúchulainn himself, have mastered the lost arts of druidecht, have won the heart of the dread cat-sìth." His fingers brushed her cheek as he tucked the wayward lock of hair behind her ear. "I hardly think you need fear anything in this or any world– do you?"

There was something hypnotic about the velvet-soft drawl of his voice so close to her ear, something soothing about the feel of his cool fingertips against the flush of her skin. "No," she said. "I am not afraid."

"Of course you are not." He slipped around to stand behind her, his hands resting on her elbows as he spoke, low and soft, into her ear. "You and they are the same, you know. Just like you, they, too, are denied access to their homeland, the rich, rolling hills and the green grasslands and the gray stone mountains. They are condemned to shadow and sorrow, and for what? Because mortals see them as monsters?" He clucked his tongue sadly, mournfully. "Yet this was not how it was meant to be, you see. Éire was their home after all, the wild, mystical land which they were born to rule. It is the mortals who do not belong here, who sailed here on the ships of wood and of war, who tried to tame the wild, free land – they who have disrupted the natural ordering of the world, not my poor pets, whom they have named the monsters of the sídhe."

"I –"

Her eyelashes fluttered closed. His voice was low and soothing like the roll of the river in springtime, the salmon leaping in the water as they wound their way through its waves toward the deep clear blue loch in the vale.

His fingers tightened on her shoulders, a silent urging. "Look and see for yourself," he murmured. "Look there."

Fiadh shifted under her hands, prowling away from her side, and when Riona opened her eyes they appeared, creeping into the clearing before her, the unholy creatures of the sídhe.

They were terrible, a motley assortment of creatures of unimaginable ferocity and strength, some with fangs and some with scales, some that slid across the earth on their bellies and some that soared through the air on giant batlike wings, some formed from hard, rippling muscle beneath leather-tight skin and others as wraithlike and intangible as the air itself.

They were all perversely, unfathomably beautiful.

There was a gaunt, emaciated figure, with skin like ash, limpid and bland as new-curdled whey, limping its way through the trees, dragging its skeletal fingers along the ice-slick branches as it went. "The fear-gortach," the lord of death murmured into her ear, his breath tickling her hair as he leaned over her shoulder, following her gaze. "Look at him, the skinny beast. He used to warn the earth of encroaching famine, a herald before disaster, and now look at the poor lad, locked away in this wood of eternal winter." He nodded toward the shape of a silver-blue horse, with a fluid, ice-kissed tail and glistening mane, pacing restlessly by an empty, leaf-filled streambed. "See the Enbarr, the child of both the sea and the land. He once swam across the waves of the dark sea as gracefully as he galloped through the high grass of the lowlands, swifter than the wind, and now he is bound here, confined to this tiny prison, this small swell in the ground."

"Why?"

"None who sat astride him could be defeated in battle, such was his speed and his indomitable strength, and so wars were fought for the right to his silver reins, brother against brother, father against son, until at last the Tuatha Dé Danann banished him forever from the world of the living. He is a sídhe-beast, after all, so he must be evil, a twisted, hideous creature, mustn't he, a stóirín?"

"He is beautiful," she whispered, and his lips curved into a smile against the back of her neck.

"So he is." He nudged her with the tip of his nose, and she looked across the wooded copse of trees. "And what of him? The red-capped little man you see there, perched on the rocks? Not the prettiest of my pets, by no means, but such a clever, cunning boy."

She noted the dark crimson cap pulled low over his eyes, his gnarled, dirty hands, his squat, wide frame, the whip-thin, rat-like tail protruding from beneath the tattered hem of his grease-stained jacket. "What is he?"

"Your grandfather did not tell you about him, then? My fear-dearg. He is a cunning creature, sure." His velvety voice deepened to something akin to a growl. "But that cunning has caused him a fair bit of trouble." He jerked his chin toward the stooped-shoulder figure in front of them. "He is a vicious little thing, pitiless and cruel. He does not have the *wisdom* –" his voice sharpened, lethal and savage "– to know when to restrain his penchant for meddling in others' affairs, and thus owes me a debt that he can never repay because of it."

A faint bell of recognition echoed in the smoke-addled corners of Riona's memory, sitting by the fire in her grandmother's solar with so much grief in her heart, reading the story of spilled blood in the snow and the bold young prince wielding the weapons of the gods – the purse of plenty and the sword of light and the cloak of darkness. "Yes," she said quietly. "I remember."

The lord of death made an indecipherable sound under his breath. "Perhaps you should consider then, the great harm this devil has done to other mortals, just like you." He paused. "You could avenge them, you know. All the innocent, unsuspecting victims of his malice. Imagine them – widows weeping for their lost husbands, sisters grieving new-dead brothers. Mothers, screaming as they clutch the still-warm bodies of their blank-eyed children to their splintered chests."

The beady-eyed creature within her raised its head at that, clicking its talons and crooning stridently – hungrily.

"Go on." The lord of death continued to lean his shoulder against the tree, ankles crossed, while Amergin watched silently from the dark-watered river with hollow, hungry intent. "Pass judgment on him, this miserable little rat. What justice do you think he deserves – what justice can you give him?"

Riona looked at the squat, dirty-bearded figure, his red-capped head dropped low, shoulders sagging with defeat, and hesitated. "Nothing." She licked her lips. "I don't – it's not my place, to judge him. I don't know anything about him." Even she could hear the uncertainty, the doubt in her own voice. "As far as I know, he has done nothing wrong."

"Hasn't he?" The softness of his voice transformed into a serpentine hiss, his tongue lashing against the edges of his sharp white teeth. "Have you considered that *you* would not be here at all, were it not for his mischief all those centuries ago, his devilry? Remember the story, a stóirín." He pushed away from the tree to prowl in tight, predatory circles around her. "The story of crows and quests and the deep red stain of blood in the winter snow, which you read in your dead grandmother's solar. I had been watching you for so long, a porcelain-pale reflection in the dark river water. Imagine my shock, my delight, to see you curled up by the fire, your feet tucked underneath you like a child's, reading all about me, learning about *me*, as I had spent years learning about you."

"The snow," she said slowly. "I remember the crow, lying dead in the snow – and the red-capped man."

"He cost me everything, didn't he – and so, in a way, he has cost you too. You would not have grieved the loss of so many beloveds that I never otherwise would have called home far too soon were it not for him."

"The princess," Riona said faintly, dull and listless, and behind her, her lord's teeth snapped together in a hungry, merciless bite. "He helped to steal the princess who served death."

"So he did," her lord said from the shadows of the ash-colored trees. "Now show me –" His words slithered over her skin like a wide-bellied serpent, twisting and entwining its way into her very heart. "Show me that you understand what it means to be the servant of death – to pass your judgment, to show no mercy, to forgive no one the debt which they all must pay, to right each wrong with the ultimate, most final price." From amid the churning river-waves, Amergin grunted once in wordless agreement, and the lord of death drifted further back into the trees. "What if I told you of all that you have missed, all the time that you have lost, the years of your mortal life that you have wasted here in the sídhe of death with me?"

Years.

Just like that, all the sweet, consoling lies she'd told herself, to soothe away the pain of her heartbreak and all her losses, vanished, leaving nothing but a cold, brittle emptiness in their place.

Her baby girl — lost to her, forever.

"She turned nine today, you know." As though he could hear the horrified scream of her thoughts, his smile twisted about his lips, an ugly thing now, its fragile, cold beauty erased, a leer of scornful triumph. "She ate strips of roasted lamb and potatoes, and a fresh-baked apple cake for dessert, surrounded by a hoard of chattering, bright-eyed children."

The hollowed-out place that had once been her human heart splintered in two.

"She clapped her hands," he continued in that venomous, slippery-skinned voice, no trace of gentleness. "She squealed with joy when it was brought out of the kitchen, in the hands of the woman she now calls 'mamaí,' and she never once thought of you."

Riona's breath shuttered in and out, ragged and harsh. Haisley. Her little girl — lost to her, forever.

"*He* was there too, your red-headed farm boy, smiling as he watched her squeal over the gift he'd bought for her in the village. He has not lost her, as you have, while you have been here, shrouded in the darkness of the eternal night, fighting off monsters and shedding your blood in defense of your child. What has he done, but take her from you, turn her against the fast-fading memory of you, to replace you with another who could never love her as you have – you, who sold your very soul for her sake?"

A whimper escaped her lips before she could stop it, and the raven-like harbinger of doom deep within her cawed again, more insistently this time, its sharp-tipped talons digging deep into her throat, hungry and restless and wild, aching to strike at something, anything, to distract her from this all-consuming pain, a thousand knife-points buried in her heart, and suddenly, she was desperate with anger — desperate to do *anything* rather than to sit quiet and grieve.

Her green-eyed daughter with her sun-bright smile. She would never see her again.

"She has forgotten you," the lord of death whispered in her ear, and her shattered gaze fell upon where the red-capped fairy still stood, head hanging, waiting. "She has replaced you – *you*, her own mother. They both have, these feeble-hearted mortals for whom you have sold your soul, and so soon – a mere handful of years, and it is as though you never even existed, were never even real."

Conor. He had forgotten her, too — had let Haisley forget her own mother, the mother who had given her life and all her love, the mother who had sacrificed every last part of herself for him and their child's sakes.

The gods damn Conor Ó Ruairc for this. The gods *damn* him for this.

Her vision blurred as a sudden spurt of rage gushed through her, that savage, black-winged creature screeching to be set free, to open its beak and scream out its ruination on the cold-hearted mercilessness that was her world. "And who is to blame for all this, a stóirín?" His fingers slid under Riona's chin, fixing his blazing golden eyes on hers. "Pass your judgment," he whispered, fierce and hungry. "Take your vengeance, Riona, no matter the cost."

He stepped away, and Riona stared at the fear-dearg, with his dark crimson cap and his muddy fingernails.

For a moment, she forgot who he was, this fairy-man, and saw instead only a swath of tangled copper curls and root-stained hands.

Conor, with his red hair and his love of all things green and growing.

Conor, who had betrayed her.

The corvid creature within her broke loose, raw and savage and screaming for death, and she raised her hands and let loose a string of curses at the copper-haired being before her.

The boulder on which the fear-dearg sat splintered, and the fairy-man tumbled into the crevice, squealing once before Riona raised her hands and brought them together in a thunderous clap. The two halves of the boulder shuddered, then crashed together, crushing the fear-dearg between them, then broke apart, only to smash together again, over and over, as Riona snarled, caught in the throes of her unearthly rage, until at last she dropped her hands, and the rocks crashed together one last time, the ragged edges of the splintered boulder welding together in a seamless line.

The only remaining sign of the fear-dearg was the flecks of blood on the gray-stoned boulder, and a tattered shred of his dark crimson cap fluttering to the ground in the sudden silence that followed the cacophony of bone-crushing sound.

From the river, Amergin barked once, a cruel, mirthless laugh. "At last," he said in that flat, toneless voice, rife with contempt. "I was beginning to think –"

Riona turned toward him, her teeth bared in a snarl, and flicked her wrist in his direction, and from far above, there came a high-pitched screaming. The moon-lit sky darkened even further as a dozen, gray-feathered bodies swooped in from the shadows of the trees, their half-rotted faces of bone and decaying flesh barely visible against the dark waters of the river. Amergin's head jerked back, his pale mouth falling open in shock, as the slúag descended on him in full force, ripping and slashing and tearing at his skin, shrieking with hungry glee as they devoured him alive.

The molting gray feathers that had swirled so wildly through the air in the fury of their attack slowed, coming to rest on the churning dark waters of the rivers, floating idly away in the rapids, as the sídhe-birds settled down on the waves to feed on what remained of Amergin and his magic.

Riona exhaled once, reveling in the thin tendrils of smoke rising from the river-water, then turned around to look at her lord, steeling herself for his wrath.

He was grinning, a smile of sheer delight, of pride. "There," he said, soft and sensuous as cool silk sheets bathed in candlelight.

"Now you truly are my good and faithful servant."

"You are not angry?" Riona asked later as they wandered through the moonlit woods, Fiadh loping ahead, her paws moving silently through the frost-touched leaves. "About Amergin?"

"Why would I be?"

Remember the story, a stóirín, Riona heard the voice of her lord whisper, and shrugged. "You seemed to value his wisdom."

"Wisdom?" The lord snorted. "Hardly. He was merely a burden that I inherited, as *you* well know." A sly glance in her direction. "I grew bored of him an age ago."

Riona reached up to run her fingers across an ice-covered branch, savoring the way it glistened in the starlight. "He was cruel, and heartless, and he deserved to suffer." She hesitated. "I was not sure what he was – or rather, what he now was." Another uncertain pause as she glanced cautiously, surreptitiously, in his direction. "If he could even be killed. I thought he might be invincible, an immortal being."

"Ah." Amusement tugged at the corners of her lord's mouth. "You were wondering if you could as easily kill me, were you?" She tensed, but he merely waved his hand and continued to stroll by her side, wholly unconcerned. "It is true, that Amergin and I were both mortal once, but a debt was owed by both of us. Him, for the shedding of the blood of the gods on that long ago battlefield, and I

– well, you also know too well why it is that *I* am fated to roam the realm of eternal night." He moved his shoulders in a restless motion. "So here I am, neither mortal nor immortal, really – neither living nor dead, simply existing, interminably."

"So," Riona said slowly, "I *could* kill you then, if I wanted to."

Another sly smile. "I am still the king of the sídhe, a stóirín, and all that lives in its domains. You would not find that my pets would obey you so easily if you tried to turn them against *me*." He glanced at her, eyes glowing. "But by all means, feel free to try and see how well that turns out."

She smiled back at his gleaming golden-fire gaze. "Fiadh could likely be persuaded to help me in that endeavor."

Ahead of them, the cat-sìth paused at the sound of her name, glancing back over her sleek shoulder, her ears perked. Her lord shook his head ruefully. "Such a fickle heart for such a beautiful beast, my Fiadh. To think that she almost ate you, once upon a time." He paused. "And speaking of time –" She tensed suddenly at the coaxing edge that crept into his voice. "The moment has come for you to complete your three tasks." His fingers toyed with the end of her braid, tucking it over her shoulder with a gentle stroke. "To return to me the lost treasures of the Tuatha Dé Danann."

Riona halted. "That's why you told me to remember the story," she said. "Is that what you're wanting from me? To find for you the cloak of darkness, the sword of light – and the purse of plenty." She turned to face him, eyes narrowed. "You did all of this, to bring me here so that I could fetch a few trophies for you?"

"They are hardly trophies, Riona. The purse of plenty, which answers any desire its master makes –"

Rebirth, she heard the voice of the púca echo from deep within her memory. *Nothing good comes from such magic, little queen.*

" – the cloak of darkness, which grants its wearer the gift of shadow itself –"

The ability to travel between worlds, Daideo's voice murmured in her ear. *To part the veil between the shadows and the sunlight.*

"–and the sword of starlight, whose master will never know death."

The god-slayer sword, said Conor in the moonlight, over the steady rush of the river, *from which every blow, however slight, proved lethal to its victim – gods, giants, and mortals alike.*

Her heart began pounding so loud that she was sure her lord must hear it, but a surreptitious glance at his face saw him as calm and serene as ever.

He is lying, she thought. He is lying to me.

The lord of death is the master of sweet-sounding lies, of hollow promises and false dreams.

She remembered the sound of her lord's voice, his chin nestled on the top of her head, his hands soothing, coaxing her, in slow, steady strokes up and down her arms, whispering in her trembling ear. "It is all that any of us truly want in this life," he had said, "to be free," and that – that might have been the truest thing he had ever spoken to her, this lie that had been meant to placate, to pacify her.

He wants, she realized, to be free, to be reborn again, to reclaim the life which he had lost so foolishly, so arrogantly all those centuries ago, to take up his sword of light and to claim the throne on which he had never been allowed to sit.

The lord of death wanted to leave the sídhe, and he needed her to do it – to set him free.

And if she didn't, she thought, horror flooding through her, he would without a doubt kill her daughter, and there would be nothing she could do to stop him.

'Ráth Crúachan,' Jack said slowly. 'I have heard many stories of its secrets.'

'A terrible place,' said the fear-dearg. 'The most feared sídhe in all Éire. It is the doorway carved by the Morrígan herself, when the world was first divided into the lands of mortals and the lands of the sídhes. From its mouth was belched forth Aillén, the fire-breathing fairy of deadly song, and the cat-sìth. Here the Phantom Queen created the fetch, the spectral shadow of Death itself, to restore the balance between the living and the dead.'

Excerpt from 'The Snow, The Crow, & The Blood'

Chapter Nineteen
The Vale of Inagh, Éire, 1073

RIONA

It was well past twilight by the time Riona stumbled up the stairs to their room, rubbing wearily at her gritty eyes with the back of her hand. Another interminably long day, filled with council meetings and negotiations and mediation, smiling false smiles through grid-locked teeth, praying for even the smallest glimpse of freedom in these stone walls, once so beloved, now growing more and more prison-like with each passing day.

She really hated being queen.

Mamó had always made it look so effortless, the day-to-day ruling that she had done with such fluid grace, but for whatever reason, it did not come quite so naturally to Riona. She remembered suddenly as she paused at the top of the stairs her father's almost-forgotten voice from so many years ago, tugging on the end of her braid. "You're a wild thing, Ria," he'd said smiling after he'd caught her wandering in the woods hours before the sunrise. "There's no taming you."

She wondered now if that had been a prophecy or a curse.

She shook herself free of such gloomy thoughts, and quietly pushed open the door to their room, pausing for a moment in the doorway, watching as Conor sat sprawled in the chair by the small wooden cot in the corner, rubbing his calloused hand over the tiny back of their daughter in gentle, soothing circles.

He glanced up, and a smile flickered across his tired face. "You only just missed her."

"She's asleep early," Riona said softly as she slipped inside, easing the door closed behind her. "That's the third night in the row."

"I know." Conor stood slowly, wincing a little, and that now-familiar pang cut through her, to see the toll that the long, brutal hours of training continued to take on him. Tender-hearted Conor, with his clever, healer's hands, that now only knew the unforgiving weight of iron and steel instead of the soft press of the dirt and the leaves against his fingertips.

For her, for them, he had given it all up, and she could not soothe away the heavy weight of the guilt that she felt because of it.

"She's growing, maybe," Conor said, coming over to Riona to press a light kiss to her cheek. "She's due for a spurt."

"Sure." Riona leaned her forehead against his shoulder for a moment. "You look tired, Conor."

"A hard day." He reached up to run his fingers through the loose strands of her hair. "New boys from one of the southern villages to train. They're a bit soft."

She smiled into his undershirt. "Are they now? That's ironic, coming from you."

"I'm hard enough, when I need to be."

"If I didn't know better, I'd say that Conor Ó Ruairc might be making a dirty joke."

"I wasn't, though now that I listen to it myself, it did sound a bit like that."

She laughed, then pulled away to walk over where their daughter slept on her back, one arm thrown across her face. So like her father, Riona mused as she watched her. Sweet-natured and gentle, just as he was. It was difficult, most days, to see anything of herself in this tiny person that they had created together.

She did have Mamó's eyes, though. Little green-eyed Haisley, with her father's copper curls. How she loved this little light of hers, that shined so bright even on the darkest of days.

Her heart tugged in her chest, and she leaned down to press a kiss to the top of her daughter's curly head, then frowned, her nose wrinkling. "Conor," she said. "She's wet through her nappy."

He turned around from where he stood by the table, pouring cider into two glasses for them to drink by the fire. "Not possible. I freshened her right before I tucked her in, not more than an hour ago."

"It smells a bit ripe." Riona eased her hand down to press against the sheets. "Conor, she's soaked all the way through."

Conor strode across the room, his brow furrowing. "Impossible."

"Feel it. You must not have put it on properly."

"I did, Ria. It's hardly my first time." He frowned at the wetness of the sheets. "Damn it. I don't understand."

Riona sighed, turning resignedly toward the linen closet where the fresh sheets were kept. "Maybe she is growing," she said over her shoulder as she pawed through the stack of linens. "Or perhaps she's ready for training. Nora told me yesterday she'd wet herself through three times before lunch, so –"

"Three times?"

Riona raised her eyebrows at the sharpness in Conor's tone. "It's hardly unusual, cabbage. She's a child, not even two yet. Such things happen." He said nothing, and she glanced back to see him staring down at Haisley as she slept, his face tense. "What's wrong?"

Conor kept quiet, and she straightened, hurrying across the room to put her hand on his forearm. "Conor." His face was paler than normal, and suddenly her heart seized in her chest. "Conor, what's wrong?"

"I – nothing." He swallowed. "Something I read, long ago."

Her fingers tightened. "What did you read?"

"It's nothing."

His voice was feeble, unconvincing. "Conor. Tell me."

He stared through her, unfocused and distant. "Did Nora say anything else? About her eating, drinking water, more than usual?"

"I watched her plow through at least half a dozen pears earlier today, and Nora mentioned she'd been rather demanding about her milk. I had told Nora to cut her off after two glasses – it's a bit rich for her – but Haisley threw quite a tantrum when she ran out." Her eyes narrowed as Conor's jaw tightened. "It's nothing, cabbage. She was in the solar with me only this morning, bouncing off the walls and flitting about like a half-crazed dragonfly. I was exhausted merely watching her. The child is a whirlwind of energy – of course she gobbles down snacks and gulps her water like she hasn't touched it in days."

He closed his eyes for a brief second, then cleared his throat, looking down to where Haisley slept heavily on her cot. "Ria," he said. "I need you to do what I ask of you now. I don't – I don't quite trust myself to –"

"Conor, I swear to the gods, I will strangle you if you continue being so damn vague. What is going on?"

"Smell her breath, Ria." He avoided her gaze, keeping his tense gaze fixed on their daughter, the steady rise and fall of her chest. "Tell me what it smells like."

Riona took a step back. "Why?"

"Please, Ria. Do this for me."

She watched him for a moment longer, the tense lines of his shoulders, the nervous clench of his jaw, then crouched down beside their daughter's bed, leaning forward lightly and inhaling.

She could smell it, underneath the lingering fragrance of the lavender and mint in Haisley's evening cup of tea, in the ragged puffs of air that blew from her daughter's lips, a strange, citrus-sweet scent, pungent and wrong-smelling.

"Fruit," she said, puzzled. "It smells like fruit, but rotten somehow. Did she eat something, did she eat an apple gone bad –"

She broke off as Conor sank to the floor, his hands gripping the back of his head, rocking back and forth on his heels. "Oh gods. Oh gods."

"Conor." Riona grabbed at his arms. "Conor, what's wrong?"

He lifted his gaze to hers, broken and dull. "The blood-sickness," he whispered. "Riona – she has the blood-sickness."

They huddled together in the doorway that led to the terrace, a few feet apart, as Riona tried to calm herself, to force the wild thundering in her heart to ease. They could fix this, whatever it was. There was nothing that she and Conor could not fix.

They had become parents when they were hardly more than children themselves, unmarried and ignorant of all the ways in which their lives would be so radically upended. They had stood firm with one another, side by side, in the face of her mother's frigid scorn and disapproval, his father's shouts of anger, the whispers of everyone who came to their hall and eyed the baby in her arms and the ringless finger on her hand. They had never wavered, he and her, and they would not waver now, whatever this new obstacle that was rising on the horizon of their love.

They would not. They could not.

She shivered. "I've heard of it before," she said. "But I thought it was hardly common."

"It's not, from what I remember." Conor rubbed his hands against his biceps, staring off into the distant trees, illuminated underneath the soft light of the crescent moon. "There were stories of it in some of Mamó's books in the solar, the signs of the disease –"

"The wet nappies." Riona rubbed agitatedly at her forehead. "The smell on her breath."

"The hunger and thirst, the sleepiness too." Conor ran his hand through his curls. "I should have caught it sooner."

"There's no point to that, cabbage. What do we do *now*? That's what matters."

"I don't – I don't know, Ria."

Her nails dug into her palms. "So let's go then, go to the solar, find Mamó's books. We have to find out how to fix this, how to stop it, how to help her –"

"Ria –"

"We have to fix our daughter, Conor. We have to make her better."

"Riona." She froze at the sound of his voice, quiet and low. "Riona, there is no cure."

It couldn't be her heart, thudding so loud and so hard in her chest. It didn't seem that she could endure such pain and still live. "What do you mean, no cure?"

He shook his head. "There is no cure, Ria, for this kind of sickness."

"You have a whole damn room stuffed to the brim with herbs and poultices and the gods only know what else, Conor, and you're telling me that there is nothing in there that can help my daughter?"

"Our daughter," he said quietly. "And no, there's not." For a moment, the only sound in the room was the crackling of the fire and the shallow, steady breaths as Haisley slept in her little bed, sprawled on her back. Conor swallowed. "I don't know much about it. It's so rare, but I'll learn. I promise. I will study and I will read, and I will keep her safe."

"How, Conor?" Her voice was flat and dull. "How? You just said that you don't know of a cure."

"I don't." He ran his shaking hands through his hair. "But I told you, I'll learn. There's been enough written about it, about the best ways to manage it, to ease the symptoms, so I'm certain that there's a way. I just have to find out what it is."

"You're a soldier, Conor," Riona said, pressing her fingertips against her eyes. "You're not a healer, no matter how much you like to play-act at being one."

His expression didn't flicker. "Mamó taught me so much, that I —"

"Stop calling her Mamó," Riona snapped. "She was not your grandmother, she was *mine*."

His gaze cut away from her, toward where Haisley lay sleeping, and Riona cursed inwardly. Another lash, another soon-to-be scar on the soft contours of his heart that she had given to him. She inhaled deeply, trying desperately to steady herself, to ease the wild flares of panic blooming within her, and failing utterly.

Her daughter. Her light in the darkness. Gone.

Even as she thought it, almost as though she had summoned it to her, she heard the faint rustling of wings. She looked up sharply across the terrace, at the half-formed shadow perched among the trees, beady-eyed and black-winged, watching her.

A crow.

Something snapped in her chest.

She endured the loss of so many beloveds, stood by the fires of so many white-flamed biers, bore so many scars on the hidden skin of her heart, but this one would not be endured. This would be no scar, but an ending, the ruination of everything, the implosion of all that was good and fine and beautiful in life.

Death was coming for her daughter, stalking its way through the cedar-scented night even as she stood here a half a dozen steps from where Haisley lay, helpless to stop it, powerless to protect her.

A voice bloomed in her head, the whispered remembrance of a tale forcibly forgotten, shoved away into the back corners of her mind.

She could not stop death, perhaps, but she could become it.

That wild, dark song that had hummed just beneath her consciousness for most of her life broke free inside her, full-throated and fierce, that irresistible, intangible draw toward the gloomy depths of the stony ridges of the mountains, the velvet-voiced call of whatever dark being waited for her inside its shrouded borders. Her pulse throbbed against her skin, and she could almost see it, that thin thread of silver whistling its way through the dark crimson stream of her mortal blood.

Only the master of death could command it, and there was only one way to command *him*.

She looked up into Conor's worried face – gentle, gray-eyed Conor, who watched her with so much worry and grief etched across his freckled face.

She loved him, sure, but she loved their daughter more.

"I have to go."

He startled, his brow furrowing. "What do you mean?"

She was backing away, feeling her way blindly toward the door. "I have to go. I know how to fix this." She swallowed. "I'm sorry."

"Ria, wait –"

She turned and ran, her slippers slapping against the stones as she fled down the stairs, along the familiar, torch-lit corridors, out the front door of the castle and into the rain, sucking in heaving gasps of the cool night air.

"Ria!"

His voice was faint behind her, a fading memory of what already seemed a past life, and she burst through the stable doors, saddling Darcy with shaking hands, her teeth chattering with something far worse than cold.

So many souls he had stolen away, this lord of death, grinning at her from the hidden shadows of his dark realm, waiting for her to heed his call. She had ignored it for years, had lied to herself, deceived herself, that it was not happening, this siren's song of death that had chanted in her ear for so many years with such deep, compelling tones.

Death had walked by her side all her life, tugging on her sleeve, demanding her attention, but she had never deigned to give it to him, until now.

She barely heard Conor calling her name as he ran after her, chasing her into the stables — was all but deaf to the pleas he shouted at her as she brushed away his shaking, desperate hands; could hardly recall the answers she gave him as she saddled her horse and swung into the shadow; the undeniably truthful threat which he yelled after her nothing more than a faint and distant echo, as though he were a ghost already long lost to her – *if you leave here tonight, you will never see either of us again* – and galloped away into the night without a backward glance.

Haisley.

She forced herself to think only of her – her toothy grin, her perpetually sticky hands, the weight of her cheek on her shoulder as she carried her to bed – that sleepy-eyed face for whom Riona would watch kingdoms fall and cities burn without flinching, so long as she remained, safe and warm, tucked away from anything that might wish to harm her.

She was galloping through the woods, the wind and the rain cutting into her cheeks, her determination hardening in her heart.

If you leave here tonight, you will never see either of us again.

They haunted her far more terrifyingly than any phantom from her past, those echoing words, because Conor Ó Ruairc — her sweet-natured, honest, naive Conor — never told a lie. And yet Riona galloped on, further and further into the dark and rainy night, because if the lord of death wanted her this badly, then he could have her, a trading of lives, hers for Haisley's, an impulse as innate and effortless as the breaths that rose and fell so raggedly in her chest.

In exchange for her daughter's life, the evil that haunted her, that called to her from deep within these mountain peaks – he could have every last part of her.

'I care nothing for balance,' said Jack. 'I never mean to die. I shall conquer death when I take his bride as my own.'

'You do not know what you wish for,' said the fear-dearg. 'You know nothing of such a time, when there was only eternity to contemplate. It was as the land of Éire was always meant to be, full of magic and unrestrained power, before mortals came and sullied its glory.'

'Well, we are here now,' Jack said, 'and whatever resides in that cave has my sword, and I shall claim it as my own, no matter the cost.'

'So be it,' said the fairy. 'Let us enter.'

Excerpt from 'The Snow, The Crow, & The Blood'

Chapter Twenty

Chapter Twenty – Neither of the Earth Nor Under It, Not Then Nor Now

RIONA

"Find the sword, a stóirín," the lord of death said. "Find the sword, the purse, and the cloak. I have tried myself a thousand times, but even in their slumbering, the Tuatha Dé Danann still guard their secrets from any without their bloodline." His nostrils had flared for a moment as he studied her, and she forced herself to keep her expression placid and cool, as unreadable as his own.

"What about Fiadh?" Riona asked. "She could help me to find them."

"I doubt it," he said, a little sourly. "I have been asking it of her for years, but she remains irritatingly loyal to them, her first masters, and refuses to show me where they are hidden."

Riona bit down on the inside of her cheek, remembering the unerring confidence of Fiadh's gait, the affection and the warmth shining in her glowing yellow eyes, as she led her straight to the mouth of the cave of Emain Ablach, to the treasure trove of the gone gods – to the purse of plenty, hidden within its depths. "She was certainly no help last time," she lied, strangely reluctant to confess that she already retrieved one of his most coveted prizes, had claimed it as her own – had in fact used it, harnessed its power and felt its magic roll through her veins. She knew, instinctively, that such a confession would not be well-received. "I'll go on my own."

"Find them," he said yet again, an intense, unending refrain, as though speaking it aloud often enough would cause the treasures he so desperately sought to materialize in the air before him. "Bring them to me, and then you will be free."

"Of course," she lied once more. "It would be my honor."

He smiled, that gentle, kind smile that sent skitters of dread up and down her spine. "A stóirín," he said. "You are so much more than I had ever hoped you to be." He bent over her hand, his lips pressing against her skin, and she fought the urge to dig her nails into his flesh and tear at his eyes, his white-marbled face, so lovely and so false. "Hurry home to me."

Only a little while ago, it would have thrilled her to hear him say that to her, in that warm, honey-sweet tone that he only seemed to use when he wanted something from her. A testament, she supposed, to just how good of a deceiver he really was – or of how desperate she had become, aching for nothing more to love and be loved in return, even if from the devil himself.

No longer. She could see the whole truth of him now.

And yet, what choice did she have but to give him exactly what he wanted, considering what – who – was at stake?

She would cross that bridge when she came to it, she thought grimly. For now, the location of the treasures was her sole focus. At least she had found the purse already, by pure happenstance, and had hidden it a little ways down this very mountainside. It would be easy enough to retrieve it. The cloak though – the sword.

So Riona knelt down in the snow, staring at her scar-ridden arms, the faint dark lines glimmering in the pale morning sunlight.

So many wounds, knitting themselves back together again and again, leaving behind only the faintest silver threads as proof of her suffering and her sacrifice. How much blood had she spilled out on the unforgiving dirt of the half-frozen earth, how much of herself had she forfeited, lost forever, during these blurred-out years of living in the shadows of death?

She wondered how many more scars crisscrossed the unseen contours of her soul, all those griefs, hidden deep below the flesh and bone of her body. What an ugly, tattered thing it must be, to have been so callously shredded and haphazardly patched back together again so many times.

She brushed away the thought, clenching her jaw in determination, focusing again on the runes she had scrawled in the ice and the snow covering the forest floor.

They could be anywhere, in any number of worlds, the sword and the cloak, perhaps lost for centuries in the vast unknowability of the sídhe. No doubt the lord of death knew this, and had accounted for such a possibility. *A test*, he had said, when he had sent her out in search for the spear of Cúchulainn – and she had passed it. Surely she could do so again. She studied the runes which she had drawn so carefully in the snow, and then once more, she drew the sharp-tipped blade of her knife across her forearm.

That single silver drop glinted in the pale light of the stars, taunting her, mocking her.

"Taispeán," she said, letting the guttural growl of the corvid creature within speak for her, and let her blood drip down onto the earth. She closed her eyes as it flowed through her, a wave of images, fleeting and frenzied in nature, a swirl of color and light and sound, and then it came to her in a preternatural rush of understanding.

Cnoc Meadha. The sídhe-realm of Finevarra and his undying queen.

Riona groaned.

The cloak of darkness was hidden within the cairn of Medb, the legendary warrior-queen of Connacht, and to steal it, she would first have to outwit Finevarra himself, the cruelest of all the sídhe-lords in the realm. Riona chewed nervously on her bottom lip as she strove to remember the tales that Daideo had once told her about the trickster-lord and his cold-blooded queen, absently pressing her still-bleeding forearm against the silk of her gown to staunch the bleeding.

The lord of the harvest, she recalled, a grandmaster of fidchell and a horse-whisperer, who frequently rewarded the mortals who pleased him with bountiful crops of potatoes and barley, and the most swift-footed steeds in the realm, but not without a price. Finevarra had a taste for young girls, and would demand from the neighboring chiefs their virgin daughters to enjoy before he would bless their fields and breathe his honey-voiced songs into their stallions' ears, stealing them away from the land of mortals to serve as his concubines until they produced a son, after which he would return them, disgraced and dull-eyed, back to their father's homes, keeping the half-mortal children to raise as his own in the sídhe.

His queen, though, was rumored to be far, far worse. Riona swallowed thickly at the memory of the tales her grandfather had once told her, stories of cold-calculated seduction and wild-eyed madness and unimaginable wickedness.

The blackthorn queen of spring, the thief of hearts.

Riona stood swiftly, brushing her hands against her skirt. It was irrelevant, what manner of monster awaited her this time in this particular sídhe. She would face of whatever fresh horrors this new land might bring, and she would vanquish them, because the alternative was too terrible to bear.

She wrapped her cloak about her shoulders and as she walked, she feverishly reviewed every last detail that Mamó had ever tried to teach her about the game of fidchell.

The entrance to the sídhe-realm of Cnoc Meadha was simple and unassuming, a slight swelling in the ground at the base of the gentle-sloped grassy hill with that distinctive dappling of slim-trunked whitethorn trees clustered nearby. Riona loitered for a moment, squinting against the unfamiliar brightness of the mid-day sun, her gaze wandering across the vibrant green of the rolling hills, the endless stretch of light blue sky, the distant gathering of pale gray clouds far in the west.

It would rain that evening, a gentle, drizzling patter of droplets on the leaves of the trees and the crumbling stone walls that meandered their way across the countryside. She could see the vague outline of thatched huts and red-walled stables in the distance. A village, a full day's journey north of the borders of her family's vale.

She was not too far from home – or what had once been her home.

Riona pulled out her knife and did not even wince as she once more paid the blood-debt to enter the hidden realm of the sídhe.

The air quivered in front of her as her blood soaked into the grass-green earth at her feet, and she stepped forward through a warm wall of sunlight and surveyed this unknown sídhe-land. There was no darkness here, no star-lit sky or dark gray fog threading its way among ice-coated trees, but a realm of an explosion of red-golden colors, with rich autumn leaves and the light scent of cedarwood smoke and the distant sound of cheery, piping songs. Finnevara, she thought grimly as she made her way toward the source of the music, had no qualms about fully embracing his role as the lord of the harvest, even locked away from the land of mortals as he had been for so many years.

They were beautiful though, these autumn-touched woods, the burnished gold of the sunlight dancing across the mellow orange-and-red of the leaves with a timid grace. Riona ignored for a moment the churning in her stomach, the tension in her shoulders, tipping her head back to savor the afternoon sun on her moon-pale face, the musky-sweet scent of the leaves that fluttered softly toward the ground through the air around her. She twirled her skirt through the leaves piled on the forest floor. Balance. She had been lacking that for so long now, living underneath the sunless sky of the eternal night, in a monochromatic world covered in dark-watered ice and dusted with snow.

She ducked under a low-hanging branch and halted at the edge of the woods, looking down at the crumbling ruins of a gray-stoned castle at the bottom of the hill, half-hidden in the gently waving sheafs of tall, ripe golden wheat. Just beyond it, atop a round, blue-grassed hill, stood a cairn, an imposing pile of dark gray rocks that stood stark and commanding against the late afternoon sky.

The tomb of Medb, the first queen of Connacht.

The cloak.

She was *so* close to freedom, to securing her daughter's safety forever.

Riona gathered her skirt in her hands and hurried down the hill, her slippers crunching through the fallen leaves. The castle was in far worse shape than it had appeared from a distance, overgrown with weeds and covered in thick green moss and entangled ivy vines. She crept closer, toward what had once been a vast terrace, its granite floor cracked and hidden underneath a dense layer of dirt and dead leaves. Surrounded by a dozen thick-trunked oak trees, there sat at the center of the terrace a massive throne, its wood half-rotted and crumbling, the bronze inlay of its edges rusted and dull. Riona could see the long-faded emblem engraved on its sides – a dozen serpents, entwined through the antlers of a dying stag, their fangs sunk deep into his throat and sides, set against the backdrop of a red-and-gold tree.

Finnevara. She moved cautiously onto the broken stone floor of the courtyard. This had once been the hall of the lord of autumn, and a trickle of unease threaded its way through her belly.

She realized that the breeze that had so playfully ran its fingers through her loose strands of hair as she walked through the woods had fallen still and silent.

Something was not quite right about the abandoned hall.

The grandmaster of fidchell, she remembered grimly. The trickster-lord. This was an opening gambit, a furtive strategy to lure her into pinning her king into an inescapable corner from the first move. This quiet scene of ruin and neglect was a cleverly crafted illusion, nothing more.

She knelt down, and in the thin layer of dirt covering the cracked granite floor, she drew sigils and runes, her lips moving soundlessly as she traced the ancient signs across the deserted courtyard, straining to break whatever invisible enchantment hovered so thickly in the autumn-crisp air.

A burst of applause shattered the silence, and she jerked her head up to see an impossibly tall, black-bearded man lounging on the decomposing throne, smiling amiably at her. "Well done," he said. "I was not hopeful, when I first sensed you enter my realm. Mortals too often are hopelessly outmatched in a battle of wits, but you — you recognized my spell for what it was almost immediately." He leaned forward, resting his elbows on his crimson-clad knees, and winked. "Allow me to lend a helping hand with the rest."

He twitched his nose, and Riona blinked in wonder as the granite healed itself into one smooth, gleaming stretch of tiled floor beneath her, the piles of soggy, dead leaves evaporating into the crisp afternoon air, the crumbling walls of the castle righting themselves into sure, solid lines. All around her, dozens of figures appeared, all dressed in gauzy gowns and embroidered robes of yellow and red, longbows strapped to their backs and gleaming bronze swords by their sides, their stares fixed on where she still crouched in the middle of the terrace, surrounded by the full might of the sídhe-court of the lord of autumn.

From deep within the multicolored leaves of the oak trees surrounding the newly-restored throne, Riona could see flashes of bright green scales, slithering through the branches high above the head of their lord. The crest – those serpents devouring the antlered stag. She forced herself not to shiver.

Her attention flew back to Finnevara as he pushed to his feet, thrusting his many-ringed hands into his pockets as he rocked back and forth on his heels, surveying her with a bemused, somewhat calculating expression. "So who are you, exactly, a mortal girl who comes sneaking into my realm, reeking of druidecht and the blood of the gods smeared on her skin?"

She stood as gracefully as she could, brushing away the lingering traces of dirt from her skirt. "I am Riona," she said. "I am the grandchild of the Tuatha Dé Danann and the dread Beast of Connacht. You would be wise to hear what it is that I have come to say."

Finnevara merely tsked, eyes twinkling. "Now, now. No need for threats, veiled or otherwise. We are," he said, gesturing toward the watching members of the sídhe who stood clustered silently about the terrace, "all ears, metaphorically speaking."

Riona straightened her shoulders. "I have come to claim the lost treasure of the gods, my birthright, the cloak of darkness, which lies hidden here in your realm, buried beneath the cairn of Medb, the warrior-queen."

"So very formal, this girl." Finnevara looked delightedly around the stony faces of his court, grinning widely. "You would think that she were afraid, pretty, foolish mortal that she is, and that she were trying to conceal her fear from us with a terribly transparent veneer of bravado." His gaze perused up and down her body, slowly, lasciviously, before returning to rest mockingly on her face. "Are you afraid, girl, of what price I will ask you to pay for the famed féth fíada? Perhaps you have heard that I have little use for mortal women – save for one very particular purpose."

Her fingers twisted into her skirt. "I have." She narrowed her eyes. "Yet you will find out what it means to be afraid, if you even dare to ask it of me."

He crowed in delight, gesticulating toward his still-silent court. "Listen to the girl," he said, ambling closer to where she stood, stiff-backed and wary. "It is a good thing that she is pretty, is it not? Otherwise that tongue of hers would have to go. As it is –" He paused a few feet from her, letting his gaze linger deliberately on the swell of her breasts beneath her gown. "We shall let it stay in its place. We might find use for it in time."

Riona bared her teeth in a snarl, but before she could answer, Finnevara leaned forward, sniffing curiously at her. His brow wrinkled. "Bah," he said. "You are of no interest to me. Another has known you first. You have nothing to offer me, mortal girl."

Her fists clenched at her sides. "I challenge you," she said coolly, "to a match." She jerked her chin toward his marble-and-bronze fidchell board, gleaming in the warmth of the autumn sunlight on the cherry wood table sitting by his throne. "If I win, you will give me the cloak that I seek."

"And if I win?"

She raised her eyebrows. "That depends, I suppose. What would you like, lord of the harvest?"

He licked his lips. "A maiden," he said. "You will bring me a maiden, untouched by any hand, from the mortal lands. It has been so long since I have tasted one. I prefer them young, not yet seen seventeen winters, with auburn hair and as round and ripe as a dew-skinned apple – like you."

Riona was silent for a moment, considering, her fingers tapping lightly against her silken skirts. Could she do it? Could she stoop so low as to steal away some poor, unsuspecting girl and deliver her into this handsome and cunning monster's hands, to suffer only the gods knew what indignities and abuses?

It turned her stomach to imagine it.

And yet – and yet she *had* to win that cloak.

She nodded once, even as she shuddered in disgust and self-loathing, and the lord of autumn grinned, clapping his hands again delightedly. "Excellent," he said. "Let us play then."

Riona held up a finger. "Not so fast," she said. "Swear that once we are done and I have won our match – swear that you will give to me the cloak of darkness as I have asked."

"Yes, yes, I swear it." He rubbed his hands together impatiently. "If you win, the féth fíada is yours."

"It is not his to give."

Riona jumped at the abrupt sound of the voice behind her, crisp and tinkling as the sound of cymbals chiming together in the utter silence of a frosty spring night, then turned to face the blackthorn queen.

She was impossibly tall, a lean, willowy figure who slunk across the smooth granite floors of the hall with catlike grace. Her snow-white hair fell to the hem of her pale blue gown, swirling around her as she moved, and Riona thought wildly for a moment of Mamó, her fine-boned beauty still blooming even in the lateness of her years, because this creature was radiant, a luminescent force of unearthly beautiful, shining through her weathered features, the deep-carved lines on her face, the wrinkles on her blue-veined hands.

"Mo bhean," she murmured as she sidled closer, the ice-blue gaze of the fairy-queen roving over her with hungry curiosity.

"The féth fíada is not his to command," she said in that same frost-chimed voice, and Riona stole a glance at Finnevara, whose expression had soured at the sight of his queen. "The cloak of darkness lies buried with the bones of my mother, and I alone can breach its walls."

"You mean Medb," Riona said, and the blackthorn queen inclined her snow-white head in answer. "I understand the desire to guard the legacy she has left you, but it is urgent that I be given this cloak." She pressed her lips together briefly to stop their trembling. "So much depends – I shall lose something beyond precious to me, if it is not given to me."

Her expression did not flicker. "Your child."

"Yes." Riona straightened, eying her warily. "How did you know?"

"For what else would you brave the unknown horrors of the sídhe?"

"There could be many reasons," Riona ventured. "A lover, perhaps, or a brother or a sister, a friend –"

"Pah." The fairy-queen waved her hand dismissively. "You lost all these things, did you not? And yet only now are you here." She raised a finger as Riona opened her mouth to protest. "I did not say that no one would feel so compelled to do so, but only that *you* would not. I have looked into your heart, child of the gods, and I know its secrets."

Riona took a step back, but the fairy-queen merely clasped her wrinkled hands before her, waiting. Riona glanced nervously at the silent members of the court of the harvest-lord, at the handsome, petulant face of the lord himself, then back at the blackthorn queen.

"What will it cost me," she asked at last, "for you to give me the cloak of darkness?"

"The féth fíada is the most prized possession in this realm. To obtain it, you must grant to me that which no one else can." Her ice-blue eyes fell to Riona's hands hanging limp at her sides, at the faint dark scars etched across both of her arms, and understanding lanced through Riona like an icy spear.

"You want me to set you free," Riona said as calmly as she could. "To let you out of the sídhe."

The fairy gestured contemptuously towards her deep lines carved on her face, the wrinkles bunched so thickly at her temples. "You see what has become of me, denied so long the magic I crave to remain young throughout my immortal days. I can only find it in the world of the living, where the hearts of the poets still beat with red-hot blood, their music and their verse singing in their veins." She inhaled sharply through her nose. "I have been hungry for so long, you see."

"If you set her free –" Finnevara broke in before Riona could respond. "Then you must give me a maiden as well. Two, three perhaps. That is the price for doing business in my realm."

Riona whipped her head around to the fairy-lord, his lips trembling, the tip of his tongue licking feverishly at the corner of his mouth, and she imagined so many young girls, dragged screaming and wailing from their homes, delivered into his greedy, lustful hands. "This is the only price that I will pay to you," she said, and within her, that beady-eyed creature awoke, shrieking and cawing.

From the red-golden trees surrounding the throne of the lord of the harvest burst two dozen green-bellied, white-fanged serpents, drops of silver-black venom dripping from their open jaws. A gasp from the court as the vipers wrapped their scaly bodies around the lean, well-muscled body of the fairy-lord, sinking their fangs deep into his sun-kissed skin, and his eyes rolled back into his skull as he screamed in agony, his shoulders twisting and jerking as the sídhe-serpents struck, again and again, ravaging his handsome face with their fangs.

He was still screaming, jerking uncontrollably, fingers convulsing, when Riona turned back to the blackthorn queen, who watched her husband die with indifference. "Now," she said. "You would be wise to bargain more wisely, lest you suffer the same fate as your husband."

She merely smiled, bloodless and cold. "You are as much a fool as he was if you think that you can master me so easily," she said. "I taught the north wind its song when still it slept in its cradle, have given voice to every winter's storms and breathed life into each new spring."

"Poetry, while pretty," said Riona steadily, "is not much of a weapon. I'll take my chances."

The fairy-queen's smile widened. "And how will you unlock the cairn of my mother without me, so that you can claim your prize?" Her bone-white teeth gleamed in the sunlight. "Only my voice will send the stones of Medb's cairn tumbling to the ground." Her shoulders moved in an idle shrug. "And my price for such a liberation is that you do as I ask, and set me free."

She hesitated. The fairy-queen of hearts, Daideo had said, steals the hearts of any who dare to accept her love – and no mortal living has ever been known to refuse her touch.

Riona's own heart clenched. "I know what you do to them," she whispered. "You feast on them. All those poor boys, those doomed girls. They are but children, most of them, barely out of their youth, and you drain them of their passion, their joy, their very *lives*."

"Of their own free will they accept my love," the fairy-queen said, slinking away toward the edge of the terrace, and Riona watched as the other fairies cringed at her approach, staring at their queen with wide, terrified stares. "These children, as you call them – to me they grant their uttermost love and devotion, the gifting of eternal youth, and in exchange, I whisper to them the finest, purest notes of song ever heard by mortal ears. They live in beauty, walk with it bedazzling their eyes, strumming in their ears, for the rest of their days, and all they must do is adore me."

"They go mad," Riona said, sudden, inexplicable tears welling. "I know the legends. They are driven mad by the incessant call of your songs, the unbearable beauty of your gift. They love you, they give you their hearts and go utterly, horribly, mad, and then they die, young and wasted and wretched."

"But for while they live –" The fairy-queen hummed softly. "While they do live, they truly live, full and gorgeous, nothing like the dull, inharmonious existence that most mortals know, scratching in the dirt and picking at their fleas, fornicating and feasting and snoring, rotting away in their own filth and mindlessness, before at last they are released from their misery by the hands of your dark lord. My loves, though – they are bárds, the masters of art and song, and the words they leave behind cement their legacy, grant them the only kind of immortality that most humans can ever hope to achieve." She sighed once, rumbling with hungry satisfaction. "They come to me, willing and eager, to taste the delights that I can offer them, the inspiration that I can awaken in them, the beauty with which I can shower them, and there is no cost so high, even their very hearts themselves, that they would not pay it." Her head cocked inquiringly. "Surely, you can understand that, at least."

Haisley's face, freckled and round and brimming with life, flashed before her.

It was true. She would pay any price, to see her safe, no matter how many innocents she damned in the process.

"I will give you one day," she said, and the fairy-queen sniffed.

"You will grant me a year and a day. Art is a craft, an arduous labor of devotion, and cannot be rushed."

Riona gritted her teeth. "A fortnight."

"A year and a day." The blackthorn queen smiled. "I have far more time to bargain than you, little queen."

There was something sinister and knowing in that smile, and Riona's heart clenched.

Haisley. Something was wrong with Haisley.

Everything within her screamed at her to run, to grab the damned cloak and go, to throw it in the lord of death's face and fly to whatever corners of the realm she must to find the sword, that last treasure, and be done, to secure her daughter's life beyond a shadow of a doubt. Whatever it takes, she had sworn to herself on that long ago night as she galloped away from her childhood home, seeking a path of irrevocable darkness, whatever the cost.

Innocents would suffer, no doubt, and some would die, but, she thought grimly, as her lord himself had so often reminded her, all that lives must die, the natural ending to a mortal existence.

As long as it was not Haisley.

"A year and a day." Her voice was clipped and curt, almost a snarl, but the fairy-queen remained unmoved. "I shall free you into the mortal realm for a year and a day, and you can do as you please."

She held out her hand. "Now give me that cloak."

It was paper-thin, the lightest, airiest piece of fabric, cream-colored and brittle in her hands, as though if she twisted it too roughly it would rend itself into a thousand irreparable pieces. She would have thought something god-made would have been made of sterner stuff. Like Daideo, like Mamó.

Like her.

Because she *was* strong, a veritable fortress of iron and stone, an unmovable force bent on achieving its single, sole purpose. She had doubted before what she was capable of, if she could attain something so unattainable, but now she knew. From the moment the fairy-queen smiled, mocking and cruel, Riona knew that there was no true choice in this battle of souls she waged with the lord of death.

There was no price so high that she would not pay it.

Not even that of her own soul.

She hardly acknowledged the presence of the blackthorn queen slinking behind her through the autumn-colored woods, barely winced at the bite of the knife as she slashed blindly at her forearm, stumbling through the hidden doorway of the sídhe into the mortal realm with the fairy-queen close behind. The musty-scented air washed over her as she breathed in the early morning air. It had recently rained, just as she had thought right before she entered the realm of Cnoc Meadh. No matter how much time passed, some things never changed in Éire, and a hysterical laugh bubbled up in her throat.

"You are frightened."

She whirled to face the fairy-queen, who looked even more withered, more wrinkled in the wan light of the pink-and-gray dawn. "Yes."

"Do not be. The lord of death is not the all-powerful being you believe him to be. Immortality is a lie, little queen. Remember that there is nothing of this earth that truly lives forever, not even the gods themselves." The fairy-queen gathered her white gown in her hand, slipping away into the trees. "Thank you, child of the gods," she said over her shoulder before she disappeared into the trees.

"Do not thank me. It was a bargain, one that I was loath to make, no more."

"Nevertheless." The icy chimes of her voice drifted back even as her lithe shape was hidden from view beneath the thick branches of the evergreen trees. "I thank you."

Riona stared down at her trembling hands. She could not afford to think about who she had condemned, the bright lights of so many young lives that would be forever snuffed out because of what she had done, consumed by the insatiable greed of the thief of heart's lust for unending youth.

Haisley. That was her only focus now, her only concern, and nothing would stand between her and the wellbeing of her child.

She set out, almost sprinting through the trees, making her way back toward the stony ridges of the Mhám Toirc and the sídhe-realm of Tech Duinn. A day's journey, then she would retrieve the purse from where she had hidden it on the mountainside and deliver it and this infernal cloak to that damned lord of hers and be gone, to whatever far corners of Éire she must journey to in order to win this last treasure – Nuada's blade, the sword of starlight.

Let him do with them what he willed, so long as he kept his word to her.

It was a blur, running wildly through the woods, through the press of the noonday sun, the fading twilight hours, through the all-too-familiar chill of the star-dappled night, until at last she stumbled into the cluster of whitethorn trees nestled deep within the dark of the mountains.

She sank to her knees, the cloak carefully folded and tucked away safely into the pouch latched to her belt, and for the briefest moment, she rested her sweaty forehead against the cool boulder stone of the entrance to Tech Duinn. It soothed her, the rough caress of the rock against her flushed skin, as though, inexplicably, she had returned home.

She pushed herself upright, wiping wearily at her stinging eyes, then fumbled for the hunting knife in its sheath at her side. Only a few more cuts, she silently promised her scarred, too-tender flesh. Only a few more, and then it would end, this frantic, ceaseless blood-letting spent in the service of this lord of death and his dark desires.

Riona clenched her jaw, then sliced the sharp blade across her arm.

A surge of bright red blood welled forth, and on instinct, Riona flipped her hand and sprinkled her blood against the gray boulder.

Nothing happened.

She frowned, pulling her hand back to study the blood oozing from the wound. Red – a dark, thick gush of crimson blood, with no trace of silver to be seen. She swallowed, then gingerly held the knife between the fingers of her injured hand, fumbling slightly as she slashed at her other arm.

Still red, a steady stream of unrelenting crimson, devoid of that telling, all-important silver tinge.

Panic, raw and desperate, clawed at her throat, and she slashed wildly at her palms, digging into that tenderest bit of flesh in the middle of her hands with the sharp-tipped blade of her knife, watching with a feral-eyed fear as two thin welts of pure deep red bloomed over her white skin.

It could not be gone, this divine folaíocht that had always been there, just beneath the surface of her skin, surfacing with every childish scrape of her knee or cut of paper on her hand. It could not have vanished –

She remembered suddenly, sitting at Daideo's knee, listening to his stories of his and Mamó's adventures together. "So you are no longer a god?" She had asked, and he had shaken his gray head, a touch ruefully, sadly. "The folaíocht in my veins has long dried up," he had said quietly, stroking her hair with his still-strong hand. "I am wholly mortal now. It is a fleeting thing, if one does not have the full magic of the gods flowing within them to keep it strong."

Riona keeled over at the waist, her bloody fingers clutching at her head, her nails digging into her scalp. Too have lost so much, to have gone so far, only to fail now, so heartbreakingly close and to still fail. Intolerable, impossible to bear. She dropped her hands, her chest shuddering with the force of her panic, and tried to concentrate.

She had to find the sword, hidden somewhere within the four realms of Éire, either in the mortal lands or a sídhe-world, and only a revelation spell would reveal its secret location.

And for the revelation spell, she had to use the silver-tinted blood of the gods, and there was only one other living soul in all Éire who might have it running through her veins.

Riona shoved to her feet, weaving slightly as a dizzy wave of exhaustion swept through her. Conor. She turned and hurried down the mountain, toward the overgrown path that led to the vale, tugging scraps of semi-clean linen from her pockets as she went to wrap around her still-bleeding palms. Conor had taken her daughter somewhere, and he might no longer be in the vale, but he would not have gone far, not her simple-souled healer with his love of hearth and home and sweet-scented herbs. All she had to do was find Conor, and she would find Haisley.

She paused for a moment at the entrance to the path, pulling on a pair of gray silk gloves to cover the bloodstained bandages binding the wounds on her forearms, on her stinging palms, before beginning her descent of the mountain, her slippered steps soundless and swift down the rock-strewn trail.

She was at long last going home to her daughter, and the gods help whatever fool tried to stand in her way.

'Put on the cloak,' said the fear-dearg, 'so that you may pass into the land of the sidhe. Your journey has been painless hereto, but now — now you must pay a price that is all your own.'

'I do not care,' Jack said. 'I have gold enough.'

'Not gold,' said the fairy. 'For blood is the only coin accepted here.'

Excerpt from 'The Snow, The Crow, & The Blood'

Chapter Twenty-One
Grafadh Mór, Éire, 1082

RIONA

Riona stared down at Conor, broken and writhing in pain on the floor at her feet, but she did not — could not — relent. "Conor," she said as calmly as she could through the roaring in her head, the thudding of her shattered heart. "Tell me what you've done with my daughter."

Daughter.

The word rolled off her tongue, bitter and wrong-shaped after so many years of non-use, and she bit down on her lip to stop from screaming in frustration.

"*Our* daughter," he said, his freckled face scarred with pain, and she closed her eyes for a moment, struggling to breathe through the vise-like grip of sorrow that suddenly threatened to overwhelm her.

This was not how she had intended for this confrontation to go. It was inevitable that there would be animosity between the two of them, angry words and hostile glares born from years of resentment and hurt, but it wasn't meant to end like this, with Conor shuddering in agony on the floor, his legs bent and twisted at unnatural angles underneath him, his beautiful, clever fingers raw and shredded on the floor.

Suddenly, she could see him again, the golden-eyed lord of death, leaning against a tree, his fingers waving so carelessly at that innocent gray-shadowed soul, how it had shrieked, twisting and buckling under the influence of whatever wordless spell had been inflicted on it, and he, indifferent to its screams, merely watched, an idle yawn tugging at the corners of his lips.

Her chest turned to a solid sheet of black ice.

Conor. She was torturing *Conor*, hurting *Conor*, her sweet, gentle-natured cabbage, the father of the child for whom she had sacrificed every last shred of what was good and noble and true within her soul. She was torturing him, as indifferent to his screams as the lord of death himself was to the shrieks of the nameless souls under his domain.

Perhaps she truly had become the exact kind of monster she had once feared after all.

Riona took a sharp step backwards, clutching at her skirt in a vain attempt to still the sudden quaking of her hands. Beneath her, Conor groaned once, and his dog whined – what a hideous little thing, with his matted brown-wired hair and his lopsided face, but then again, Conor had always nursed a soft spot for finding beauty in ugly things – his wiry body vibrating with concern for his master's pain.

It was unforgivable what she was doing to him, something she had silently sworn to herself as she stood outside his door in the rain that she would not under any circumstances do. But she was just so tired, so beaten down from so many hurts, so many struggles, and then all that tamped-down desperate rage had seized control of her when she had seen him there, tall and slim-shouldered by the fire, his once open, honest face closed off and cold as he'd looked at her with such contempt. It wasn't fair, how he blamed her, how he despised her, for doing the exact same thing that he himself had sworn to do.

She had *saved* their daughter. She was alive, and it was Riona's doing that kept her so.

Riona swallowed once, then snapped her fingers as she choked out the counter-curse, her throat oddly hoarse and strange, as though her regret and her heartbreak were strangling it even as it clawed its way toward freedom. There was a slithering, rapid-fire clicking sound as his bones knitted themselves back together, the jagged shreds of his skin wrapping themselves around the new-healed bones in a faintly scarred curtain of flesh. Conor gasped once, his forehead pressed against the warped wooden boards of the floor, his limbs trembling from the sudden absence of pain.

She cleared her throat. "I'm sorry," she said, her shoulders stiff, and he laughed hoarsely, humorlessly, before he rolled over onto his back, chest heaving.

"Well, that makes it all better now."

Her fingers twitched. "You said cruel things too."

"You're right, Riona. I surely did deserve to have my bones snapped in two for having the audacity to question you."

The corvid creature shrieked with renewed outrage as her throat spasmed, aching with the sudden swell of desire to unleash the full force of her spells on him, to call forth those lovely, vicious green-skinned serpents to wrap their scaly bodies around his self-righteous, condescending chest –

She swallowed the bile that had surged up into her mouth, ready to strike and attack and take what she wanted, what she needed, by whatever means necessary. "I said I was wrong."

"Actually, you didn't." He sat up and scrubbed his still-quaking fingers through his copper-red curls. "It's probably for the best. We both know you'd be lying if you did."

"Conor." She walked over to face him, leaning against the wall across from him. He peered up at her, those gray-stone eyes of his brimming with mistrust and dislike. "Please, just tell me where Haisley is. I would never hurt her, you know that. I need her, I need to see her —"

"You need her? For what, Riona? It's been ten years, and you both seem to be doing just fine without the other."

She straightened. "So you have seen her, then."

"Of course I've seen her. Who do you suppose has been looking after her all these years? Certainly not you, as you've been off cavorting with the lord of death in the other-realm."

Riona's lips flattened. "I've been looking after her more than you think."

He laughed once, an abrupt, humorless sound. "Sure now, of course you have, Riona."

"I'm her *mother*, Conor."

He raised his hands, and the faded silver stripes of newborn scars that wound their way across his fingers glinted in the firelight. "That doesn't make you a good person, Riona."

She ignored this, pressing on with her plea. "I promised to help him with something, tasks that he needs completed – tasks that I alone can complete. If I do, she'll be safe." Conor flinched. "There is one last thing that I need to do for him to ensure that he keeps his vow, but I can't do it without her. I need her for –" She swallowed. "For a spell."

"No."

"Conor –"

"I said no, Riona. Are you completely mad? You want to involve our daughter in your dark arts? With your black-hearted lord? She's eleven years old."

"I know how old she is, Conor. I'm the one who spent thirty-two hours giving birth to her."

"You're right. The pains of childbirth trump all other parental sacrifices."

"Oh, sod off." Riona shoved away from the wall and glared down at him. "I knew you would refuse to even hear me out."

"Is that why you went straight for the torture technique? Is that what you thought to yourself as you walked up to my door? 'Conor now, he won't be particularly receptive to hearing my explanation as to why I want to endanger our daughter's well-being even more than I already have, so I probably should cut right to the breaking of his legs and the mutilating of his fingers.'"

"I was angry, Conor." Her voice snapped through the air like the last of a leather whip as they glared at one another. "Not only about what you said to me tonight, but about how you left me, how you abandoned me, ten years ago. You stole our daughter and you *left*."

"*I* left?" Conor climbed to his feet unsteadily, towering over her, hands clenched at his sides, and she tilted her head back to stare up at him. "You ran off into the mountains, Riona, saying that you –" He fell silent, and she jabbed his chest with her finger, prodding him.

"I what, Conor? Say it."

He looked away into the fire, his shoulders sagging, and her heart leapt for a moment to see a glimpse of the boy she had once loved, sweet-natured and gentle. "You didn't see yourself that night, Riona. So cold and remote and – gone." She watched the muscles in his throat jump as he swallowed. "You were gone, a glass mirror with no reflection, like he had already stolen away your soul and there was only an empty shell left, while he kept the truth of you behind with him, locked away in a place where I could never follow."

"I was scared," she whispered. "You said that Haisley would die," and he shot her a glance, his expression shuttered and reserved once more.

"You should have trusted me," he said after a moment. "You and I – we could have figured it out. Together."

She reached out tentatively to touch the back of his hand. "No, Conor. It was inevitable."

"What was? Selling your soul to evil – and for what?"

"For our *daughter*," she shot back.

"The daughter you are now asking me to help you throw to the wolves? That daughter?"

"You have no idea what you are talking about. Everything that I have done, Conor – everything – has been for her. I have sacrificed *everything* for her sake."

"And so have I," he snarled. "Yet I did not need to damn myself to do so."

They glared at one another from across the room, chests heaving and lips trembling, until at last Riona looked away, staring blindly into the fire. How had it come to this, the closeness that had once existed between them, the close-knit knowing of the other's innermost thoughts without words or touch, an ever-present harmony that hummed between them that only they could hear?

It was gone now, that voiceless song, drowned out in the thundering crash of the white-watered cataracts of their anger and their resentment and their fear, and there was no getting it back.

Riona cleared her throat. "It's a simple revelation spell," she said, quiet and low. "That's all, Conor. I need a few drops of blood from her, and I'll be gone. It's an easy enough thing, all things considered, and then I can complete the spell and give him what he wants and be free of *him* at last."

Conor folded his arms across his chest. "Why can't you use your own blood?"

She sighed, sinking down onto his couch, her hands clasped in her lap, while he continued to stand, stiff-backed and wary, by the door, his dog crouched at his feet. "It's gone," she said. "The folaíocht in my blood. It's run dry at last. There was only the merest trace of it there to start, and I have used too much of it, all these years I've been gone in the sídhe. I've tried and tried, but there's no hint of silver left." She swallowed. "I need her, Conor. She's the only one left who might have it, that last remaining shred of divinity, and without it, I can never finish the incantation."

He stared at her unblinking for a long moment. "What is it for?" He asked after a long moment. "This revelation spell – what are you trying to find?"

Riona fought the urge to twist her fingers in her skirt. "That's none of your business."

"Consider it now my business. What does he want you to find for him?"

She closed her eyes briefly, steeling herself. "He needs some-thing," she said at last. "Three things, really."

"I'm listening."

She swallowed. "Do you remember, the story of the young prince Jack and the three treasures which he took from the giants? The purse of plenty, the cloak of darkness –"

"The sword of light. I remember, but it's just a fairy-tale, Riona. A story, told to children at bedtime."

"It's not." She dug her fingers into the wood of the chair. "They were forged by the gods, and only those with the folaíocht in their blood can call to them, can find them. I need Haisley to help me locate them, and then my service to him is done, and Haisley will be safe."

"What does he want them for?"

"I don't know," she lied. "And I don't care. I just want to give them to him so Haisley can be safe, and I can be done."

"And then what? You move back in the castle, after all these years away, and take up being the queen of the vale again as though no time has passed?"

"No," Riona said sharply. "Haisley is meant to be the queen of the vale, not me."

"She doesn't even know she's a princess."

"You haven't told her?"

"No." Conor dropped his gaze to the floor, his knuckles white as they gripped the table's edge. "She doesn't even know who I am, Riona."

"What? Why not?"

His lips tightened. "It's easier, this way." He was silent for a moment. "When she is older, maybe then I'll tell her the truth, but for now, she believes me to be her uncle who comes to visit. She doesn't know." His face looked so strained, so careworn, that for a moment Riona ached to wrap her arms around his neck and pull him close against her. Then he looked up, his face hard and unforgiving, and the urge faded away as swiftly as it came. "It stays that way, Riona. She is happy where she is. I'll not see that ruined for her."

Hope bloomed in her chest. "Does this mean you'll take me to see her?"

He stared at her for a long moment. "You're sure?" He asked presently. "You are certain that if you do this – thing for him, then he'll leave Haisley alone?"

Riona licked her lips. "Yes. I'm sure."

Conor rubbed his hand across his face, sighing heavily. "Very well. We use her blood to cast your spell," he said at last. "And then you leave, and you never come back, to me, sure, but certainly never back to her. Never, Riona. No matter what."

"That's not fair."

"That's the bargain. Take it or leave it." He raised his eyebrow. "I can't imagine this being a particularly difficult choice for you. We both know that you have no intention of coming back to the vale when all this is over."

"Don't I?"

"I think," he said flatly, "you'll find whatever it is he wants you to find and then go running right back to him, regardless of whatever bargain you've made. I can see it in your eyes, Riona. You belong to him now – to death."

She bared her teeth in a snarl. "You don't know anything about me."

"You're right about that." He shoved away from the table, running his hand through his hair as he stalked towards the window. "Not anymore at least. Even an hour ago, I would have sworn that no matter how far you had fallen, no matter how much darkness you had let into your soul, you never would have harmed a hair on my head, and we both see how wrong I was." He glanced down at the faint lines of scars on his knuckles, and Riona's throat burned.

Because she had tortured Conor – *tortured* him – her freckle-faced cabbage.

"I'm sorry." Her voice was soft as the rustle of pages turning in a book on a quiet, snow-laden night. "I'm sorry, Conor. I have been living with monsters for so long – I suppose that I have become one myself."

"I wouldn't say that," he said, his back still toward her as he stared out the window. "You've always had a mean streak in you, and before you hex me again, think on it. I'm not telling you anything that you don't already know yourself. You've always been a bit callous, sometimes even cruel, towards others, even those you claimed to love."

She flinched a little at that, a half-forgotten voice suddenly echoing in her ears.

Why must you be such a wagon, Ria.

Maeve. Her sweet, kind-hearted friend, standing in that cozy warm kitchen from her girlhood, elbows buried in potatoes and cheese, her voice sharp with censure. She was still so ashamed, stricken with grief to her very core, that this was the memory that was most fresh in her mind of her long-lost heart-sister, one unbearably embittered with disapproval and anger.

Riona swallowed thickly. "I know," she said, her shoulders sagging. "I know I have. And yet – I regret nothing. I would do it all over again." She paused. "I will be cruel, I will be callous, I will become a *monster*, Conor, if that's what it takes to protect her. To save her."

He stared at her, as immovable and pitiless as a stone, and for one terrifying moment, Riona thought he would refuse, and she wasn't at all sure what she would do if he said no.

"Very well," he said at last, and Riona's heart clenched in her chest. "I will take you to see Haisley. Tomorrow," he said firmly as Riona sprang to her feet. "For tonight –" He jerked his chin to the little room in the corner. "Take the bed. I'll sleep on the floor with Oscar."

"You don't have to give me your bed, cabbage."

His face did not flicker at the murmured endearment. "Take the bed," he said flatly. "I'd rather stay here, by the door. Makes for an easier getaway in case your demon-lord decides to come calling."

Riona nodded once, ignoring the heavy lump of lead that settled in her stomach. "Thank you, Conor," she said softly. "I – it does matter to me, that you trust me again."

His gaze met hers, flint-gray and unforgiving as steel. "I don't trust you, Riona," he said, moving toward the hearth. "Make no mistake. If you do anything to harm her in any way, if a single hair on her hair is singed by whatever magic you try and muster around her, I will kill you, right where you stand." She refused to shiver as he watched her from across the room, an unmovable slab of granite and stone. "I will cut your throat and not think twice."

She turned away. "Believe me, cabbage," she said as she stalked blindly through the doorway into the small room with the narrow cot tucked into the corner. "I would love to see you try."

She shut the door with an emphatic slam, then sank down onto the edge of the bed, her knees too weak to support her any longer, buried her face into her hands, and wept for everything that she had, and everyone that she had lost.

'I am ready,' said Jack, then jumped at the sudden cacophony of squawking, urgent and hoarse-throated, that erupted all around him. He looked up into the shadowy branches of the gray-barked trees and saw them — hundreds of midnight-black crows all along the frost-licked limbs, their eyes unnaturally bright in the gloom.

And he remembered the raven, bleeding out in the snow, his arrow buried in its beady black eye.

'Good,' the fairy said. 'Now give me the cloak, and walk up to his door and let him chop off your head.'

Excerpt from 'The Snow, The Crow, & The Blood'

PART II

Chapter Twenty-Two
Grafadh Mór, Éire, 1082

CONOR

Conor knew that he would have to burn his bed as soon as he returned.

There would be no sleeping in it after this, lying on the same straw-filled mattress that Riona had slept on, smelling that faint scent of silverweed and clover on his pillow, imagining those sheets twisted between her legs as she curled up on her side, one hand tucked under her cheek, just as he had seen her do so many times before.

He stood just outside the front door of his cottage, the leather strap of his satchel clenched in his white-knuckled fist, Oscar whining uneasily at his side. "I know, love," he murmured, scratching idly at the dog's ears with his free hand. "I don't much like it either. One visit, and then she'll be gone. It'll be all right."

"For the gods' sake, cabbage." Her sing-song voice floated through the open door, and he gritted his teeth at the sound. "You might at least try to be subtle about how much you despise me. It's rather hurtful."

"More hurtful than a pair of broken legs?"

A pause. "Fair enough." He could hear rustling in the dimly lit cottage behind him, the faint sound of his cupboard doors being opened and closed. "You have nothing to eat in here."

"We need to go."

"In a moment. I'm famished. Do you have any biscuits?"

"No." Conor pinched the bridge of his nose. "Riona –"

"Yes, I heard you the first three times, and I will again, for the third time, reiterate that it is an ungodly hour in the morning, I haven't eaten a proper meal in I don't even *know* how long, and I can hardly be expected to trudge through the fog and the rain to be reunited with my only child after nearly ten years on an empty stomach. So if you wish to be rid of me, I would suggest telling me where you keep your secret stash of biscuits, because I *know* you have them."

"Bottom shelf, to the left of the oven."

He heard the door creak open, then a muffled crow of triumph. She swooped through the doorway, his tin of biscuits clasped triumphantly in her gloved hand, munching contentedly. "They're a bit dry," she said as she glided to a stop a few feet from where he stood, arms folded impatiently over his chest. "But I suppose it will have to do. Did you make these? You shouldn't skimp so much on the butter."

"They're cauliflower biscuits," he said. "No butter."

He watched with a hint of smug satisfaction as she gagged. "There's something wrong about you, Conor. What would possess you to even try such an abomination. Joke's on you, though," she continued. "I stole a couple of your raisin oatcakes and an apple while you were ranting about how much you loathe the very sight of me."

There was a tentative question hovering just beneath the surface of her teasing words, but he merely turned away, settling his satchel more securely on his shoulder. "Let's go," he said curtly. "It's a long walk."

She said nothing, but the weight of her disappointment lingered in the air as she fell into step behind him. Even Oscar, trotting by his side, looked up at him with perked ears, but he ignored them both, striding determinedly down the dusty road that led to the village of Maigh Eo. It unnerved him, how easy, how seamless it had been to fall back into their previous rhythm, their bantering and their unspoken sense of the other's innermost thoughts and longings and secrets.

It was not a road he ever intended to travel down again, one strewn with far more thorns than roses, a dozen draughts of bitterness for every sip of sweetness.

"It's about a three hour walk," he said over his shoulder, ignoring her quiet hums of pleasure as she munched on her apple. "Remember what I told you – she does not know who I am, nor that she's a princess, and it will stay that way until I decide otherwise."

"I know." He heard the soft plop as she tossed away the apple core into the trees. "You'll have to tell her eventually though. She'll be queen of the vale one day."

He grunted. "Maybe not. Your mother seems content enough to rule."

"My mother," said Riona coolly, "is not Mamó's heir. She was only ever meant to serve as regent for Haisley until she came of age."

"She has another six years until then."

"Yes, but Haisley needs to learn how to rule, Conor. She needs lessons, and –"

"I remember you objecting very vocally against those same lessons."

"I was a child. No child enjoys lessons."

"I did. Maeve did."

Even with his back to her, the tension sizzled in the air between them. "Don't talk about her."

His lips flattened. "Why not? Do you wish to forget her too, erase her from your memory, as you have erased us these past ten years, Haisley and me?"

There was no response, only a brittle, broken silence as she walked silently behind him, and a brief twinge of shame, of guilt twisted deep within his belly. "Perhaps you should tell me more about it," he said at last, gruff with a wordless apology. "What you have been doing, how you have learned all of this – this magic."

"It's not magic." Her voice was crisp, cool, and his shoulders relaxed a little to recognize it, this thick stonewall of reserve she had erected between them. It was safer this way, he told himself. Safer, and for the best. "Magic is inborn, a power that one is born with. Druidecht is a learned art, a craft that must be studied and practiced." She paused. "Through *lessons*."

He flinched at the venom in her tone. "What kind of lessons?"

"Many kinds," she said vaguely, and he glanced back to see a faraway, empty expression solidify over her features. "None of them particularly pleasant."

He looked back down at the dusty road as he walked along, his fingers tightening on the strap of his satchel. "You were in the land of the dead," he said. "I would hardly imagine any of it to have been pleasant."

"Some of it was." He peeked back again to see her head tilted back, studying the sunrise breaking across the distant horizon. "The sky – the sky was the most beautiful thing that I have ever seen. Eternally night, such a deep, pure black, bedazzled with thousands of the brightest, clearest stars, and the moon, a full, white moon that lit up the forest with a glow far more luminous and beautiful than any sun." She sighed, and he jerked his gaze away from her awestruck face. "It's strange. I miss it, that pale light. The sun seems too harsh to me now, too crass."

"Yes well, monsters do tend to prefer darkness," he said before he could stop himself, and then bit down hard on his lip.

She laughed, bell-like and humorless. "You have no idea."

He closed his eyes, inwardly cursing. "I only meant –"

"I don't care what you meant," he interrupted him, an emphatic door slammed shut in his face. "Why did you do it, anyway? Send Haisley away from the vale."

"She wasn't safe there. After we…fought, and you disappeared, I worried that you would come back for her."

"Me?" Riona asked, staring straight ahead. "Or someone else?"

Conor cleared his throat. "Try to see if from my perspective, Ria. I saw what happened, that day in the mountains – I saw you use your blood to open a portal to the sídhe, saw that thing come out of it, and a few hours later, Maeve was dead. So then you tell me that you mean to go back into that same hellscape and bargain for our daughter's life? With the lord of death, no less?"

"What choice did we have?" Her fists clenched at her side, and Conor took a few wary steps to her right. "Just sit and watch her *die?*"

"Ria –"

She whirled to face him. "It worked, didn't it? Haisley lived. You told me that she would die, that there was nothing to be done. Well, I *did* something, Conor. I saved her. Are you forgetting that? Or are you too concerned with being right that you don't even care that my choices, my actions kept our daughter alive when you could not?"

Before he could think better of it, Conor reached out to touch her elbow. "No, Ria," he said gently, softly. "Never. I am glad – unbelievably so, that Haisley is still alive. I'd say it was a miracle, except that I know the truth of why she still is. I know full well that it is your sacrifice that has kept her alive all these years."

"Then why –" Her voice cracked, and she closed her eyes for a moment. Conor tightened his grip on her arm instinctively. "Then why do you hate me so?"

Conor was quiet, studying the youthful lines of her face, the curve of her red lips, the silken sheen of her black hair. Still so lovely, so delicate-seeming, even when he knew she was anything but. "We were a team, Ria," he said at last. "We always have been, you and I. Whatever decision that needed to be made about our daughter and our future, it should have been made by the two of us, together."

"But –"

"I understand," he interrupted, slowly pulling his hand away from her arm. "I understand why you did what you did. In a moment of panic, of fear, you acted, and I understand that – but that doesn't mean I can forgive it." He paused. "At least, not yet."

She stared at him, unreadable and cold, all traces of her earlier emotion vanished. "You don't understand," she said. "It was no accident, Haisley falling ill. It had been coming for a long, long while – far longer than either of us knew. He was going to take her, Conor, one way or the other, unless I went to him." Riona turned away, rubbing fitfully at her eyes with her fingertips. "You don't understand," she said again. "It was inevitable."

Conor stiffened. "What's really going on here, Riona? What does he want with Haisley?"

Riona dropped her hands with a sigh. She looked, he realized suddenly, exhausted, despite the full night's rest she had gotten, asleep in his bed while he lay awake and restless on the uncomfortable wooden floor. The porcelain-smooth skin underneath her bluebell eyes was smudged and bruised with dark purple circles, and her cheeks were drawn and pale. "Nothing," she said. "He doesn't want anything with her. He only wants me."

"But –"

"I said it was nothing, Conor."

"Riona," he pleaded, reaching for her again, but she stepped back, away from his outstretched hand as though it were a burning brand. "You say I don't understand, and you're right – I don't. So help me. Help me understand."

She shook her head. "Let's go." She started walking, the hem of her gown swishing in the dirt, and Oscar looked up to where he still stood in the middle of the road expectantly, watching her glide away from him. He pinched at the bridge of his nose, frustrated, then jogged after her, Oscar bounding happily in front of him, tail wagging.

"Ria, please wait."

She drew up her hood over her loosely braided hair, pulling it down low over her face. "It's likely for the best," she said flatly, "if we do not talk the rest of the way."

They walked in silence, the sun slipping behind billowing dark gray clouds filled with rain in the distance, shrouding them in shadows, and Conor tried to tell himself that it was not an omen portentous of fast-approaching doom, a fate that had been galloping towards him on swift-flying hooves for over twenty years now.

Cut off his head – his *head.*

'I shall do no such thing,' Jack said, and as one, the black-winged ravens perched so silently in the barren branches of the trees whipped their heads around to stare unblinkingly in his direction.

'You wish to steal away the bride of Death,' the fear-dearg said. 'You must know it then, intimately, as a lover and a friend.'

Excerpt from 'The Snow, The Crow, & The Blood'

Chapter Twenty-Three
The Vale of Inagh, Éire, 1062

CONOR

Conor Ó Ruairc first laid eyes on the princess of the vale when he was nine years old, and either despite or because of the severe head injury – he was never sure which – he had fallen immediately and irrevocably in love with her.

To be fair, she had only moments before almost killed him, so it was possible that it wasn't so much love as his brain having been well and truly addled. And yet somehow, despite a complete lack of experience in the matter, it felt an awful lot like love to him.

Had he obeyed his father's strict orders not to go exploring the woods surrounding their new home and remained inside the castle walls as he was told to do, it would never have happened. But given the current trajectory of his recently uprooted life, Conor did not much care for his father's unceasing litany of edicts and expectations about what he should and should not do and had promptly snuck out of the solar window as soon as his father's footsteps disappeared down the corridor, and off into the woods he went.

His quasi-rebellious quest barely lasted an hour before it was brought to an abrupt and painful end.

He was squatted down at the side of the narrow, half-overgrown path that wounds it way through the shrouded, deep green thicket that grew wild and unchecked around the outskirts of the castle in the vale, hunched over a patch of tangled weeds that were just beginning to bloom. He rubbed his thumb down the thick green stalk of one of the plants, examined the white-purple blossoms of another, sniffed the deep blue, bell-shaped flowers that waved gently in the breeze, the ever-present tension in his shoulders brought on by his father's stern-faced presence easing ever so gradually.

This was where he belonged, with his hands in the dirt and smelling of goats' leaf and gorse-blossom, not wielding swords while clad in iron and leather. It was in his blood, this love of the earth and its many flowering things and the magic that could be coaxed from their roots and their petals.

He had just reached out to pluck a particularly luscious clump of devil's parsley when he heard a faint rumbling sound, and his head swiveled to peer down the shady, winding path. Before he could move, a horse, black as night and as big as a barn — or it seemed to him from where he crouched in the undergrowth — came galloping straight at him. He managed to yell once as he stumbled away in panic, but caught a glimpse of its muscular black shoulders and two front hooves rearing above him as it tried to halt its furious rush. Then a savage, stinging pain split his forehead, and everything went dark.

It was still dark when he slowly came to, a groggy, dull awakening, and blindly, he raised his shaky hand toward where his head was supposed to be, as he was no longer entirely sure that it was still in its accustomed place.

"Oh, thank the gods," he distantly heard a light, sing-song voice call out from somewhere in the blurry darkness that surrounded him. "You're not dead. Mamó would have been so upset with me, I would have been shelling garlic for *years*."

He turned his head listlessly, side to side, trying to catch a glimpse of the owner of this childlike, lilting voice, but that savage stab of pain sliced through his skull once more, and he moaned. "I can't see – I can't see, I'm blind –"

The voice huffed. "Of course you can't see, you've got your eyes shut tight, you cabbage."

Conor felt a vague sense of outrage at the utter lack of sympathy in that heartless, lovely voice, but it was a good point about his current sightlessness. However, his brain hurt and his forehead felt like someone had embedded an archer's ax all the way through his skull-bone, so perhaps a tiny show of patience, of basic human kindness was warranted, especially considering he had been the one who had been run down by the voice's clearly feral steed.

He opened his eyes to say exactly this to the mysterious owner of the voice, and instead, promptly fell in love.

It was a goddess who had tried to kill him – the most beautiful little goddess, with an impossibly pointy chin and wild blackberry hair and bluebell eyes. Her lips were as red as the ripest rosehip berries in the mid-autumn months, and her skin was as pure and smooth as his mother's treasured porcelain teacups.

"Well," the goddess said, her nose wrinkled in disdain. "Are you blind or not, little boy?"

"I'm – I'm not."

"Good." The goddess spun on her heel and stalked toward her horse, no longer quite as vicious, standing docile and quiet nearby, its snout buried in the same clump of weeds that Conor had been perusing only a few moments before. "Down, Darcy."

The horse shook out its mane, then eased down onto its front knees, and in one fluid motion, the goddess – a girl, she was just a normal girl, surely, even though he wouldn't be the least bit surprised if she suddenly sprouted wings and flew away into the cosmos from whence she came – scrambled into the saddle on its back, tucking her tiny booted feet into the stirrups at its side.

"Wait," Conor said weakly, pushing up onto his elbows. He blinked furiously as a slow, thick trickle of blood dripped down from his forehead. "What's your name?"

"Not likely that I'll tell you. I don't need my grandmother hearing about this."

"I won't tell." Conor reached up and wiped feebly at the bloody gash on his forehead. "I just want to know."

The girl stared down at him, her brow furrowed. "You're bleeding quite a lot. It's gotten worse since you sat up."

"It's not too bad," Conor said, even though his head was throbbing properly now and he wondered if he might black out again. "What's your name?"

She ignored him, scowling as she stared off into the surrounding forest from far above him on her horse. "I can't just let him die here," she grumbled to herself, and he opened his mouth to agree when she huffed again, nudging her horse forward a few ambling steps. He tried not to flinch as it eased up next to where he still sat sprawled in the dirt. "So," she said, those gorgeous eyes narrowed at him in what he could not help but notice was most certainly a deep feeling of irritation. "I will give you a ride back to your home, but only because you do look absolutely awful and if you die out here and my grandmother does somehow hear about it, my life will pretty much be over, but you aren't allowed to tell anyone what happened. If I find out you do, I will hunt you down and let my horse stomp all over your face until you can't even remember your own name, is that clear?"

"My name is Conor," he said rather stupidly, but really, the gash in his forehead was screaming now, a wild, high-pitched shriek of agony, and everything seemed a little hazy and twirly, except for her. She was crystal-clear and shining, a single glimmering star in a dark world of pain.

She pursed her lips. "Let's go then," she said, and her horse again lowered its down to its knees, snuffling gently into Conor's hair, an unspoken apology and a silent reassurance all in one.

Well, at least one of them liked him. He clambered onto the horse's broad back, wrapping his shaky fingers around the leather straps on the side of the saddle. He was unbearably dizzy now, after moving even such a short distance, so he laid the side of his temple against the top of her shoulder, breathing in slowly through his nose.

"You there." She poked his side with a sharp-tipped finger, and he jumped, jarring his cheek against her shoulder. "Where to?"

"Home."

"The gods grant me patience with dim-witted fools. I know *that*, but I don't know where you live, you cabbage."

"Oh." He tried to remember. "The castle in the vale."

The shoulder underneath his cheek stiffened. "You live in the vale? I've never seen you there before."

"Just arrived," he murmured, increasingly drowsy and light-headed as the dancing shadows of the forest swirled around him. "Sent from Soghain by the king."

"Killian sent you?"

"Well, not me," he said sleepily, smothering a yawn. "My father, but I had to go with him. My mother stayed. She didn't want to leave. It's her home, and –" His voice trailed away as his stomach rolled anew at the thought of his mother, alone and content and at peace for the first time in years.

Without him.

The girl was silent for a moment, and he slumped against her, the seductive waves of drowsiness washing over him as he drifted away, the savage pain in his skull easing and softening as his eyes drooped close –

"Wake up, cabbage." He jumped again, her finger digging into his ribcage, and she clicked her tongue at the horse. "You can't go to sleep, not after you get hit on the head like that. We'll be at the castle soon enough."

The horse lurched forward, and he abandoned the leather straps on the saddle to wrap his arms around her waist, the lurching, up-and-down motion of the horse's gait sending fresh spikes of agony racing through him. "I'm going to be sick."

"That's all right," she said over her shoulder as they sped up, the horse moving faster and faster, until the trunks of the trees and the bushes and the vines were a swirling green-and-brown blur as they whipped through the forest, the horse's hooves pounding into the earth like the steady, warning sound of fast approaching war-drums. "You're probably owed that much, after I ran you over. Although to be fair, you did jump out right in front of us. If you'd just stayed where you were, you'd have been fine."

His brain was most definitely addled, because he gripped her waist a little tighter and silently thanked the gone gods for sending him sprawling directly into her path. It was worth a blow to the head and inevitably a few stitches to have seen her standing above him, her hands on her hips, as beautiful as any wild thing that bloomed in the sun-kissed air.

It seemed important that he tell her this. "You're like a wild-flower," he said thickly. "Your eyes look like bluebells."

She laughed, a thousand tiny silver bells chiming through the crisp cold air of a winter dawn, and he shivered at the sound. "Oh, cabbage," she said, and perhaps it was the delirium from the head wound, but he thought he could hear a faint note of affection threading its way through her sing-song voice. "You're smitten with me. That's so sweet, but my mother simply won't have it. Move your head. You're getting blood all over my shirt."

He jerked back. "Sorry." He bit down on his lip to try and stop his vision from swimming as they galloped along the path. "Who's your mother?" He paused. "Actually, who are *you*?"

She glanced back over her shoulder and shot him a smile, red lips bright against her lily-white skin, her black hair swirling loose from her braid to fall about her face like a midnight halo. "I'm Riona," she said. "Princess of the vale, and one day, you silly cabbage, I will be a queen."

And even through the sharp ache in his head, the fog creeping in through his wavering consciousness, he had known it then.

She would be the death of him, this goddess-girl with bluebell eyes and a wicked smile.

'I am marrying her,' Jack said, 'not her art.'

'They are the same,' said the fairy. 'You mortals fear death so much, yet it walks beside you all your days, a companion that you can never see nor shake from your side, and you are blind to the truth of it. The only way for you to defeat death,' the fear-dearg said, 'is to become it.'

Excerpt from 'The Snow, The Crow, & The Blood'

Chapter Twenty-Four
Maigh Eo, Éire, 1082

CONOR

That old familiar sense of doom did not dissipate when Riona and Conor stood on the outskirts of the small village of Maigh Eo, blanketed as it was in a thick mantle of wispy gray fog. Riona crouched by a nearby stream, cupping her hands as she lifted the cool water to her lips, and he tried not to notice the graceful line of her neck when she bent her head. "I brought her here soon after you left," he said suddenly, and her head snapped up to stare at him. It was the first time either of them had spoken since their argument hours earlier, and he could not bring himself to look at her, staring instead down at the cluster of thatch-roofed cottages and stables of the village below. "I knew of Páidí. He'd come to the vale a few times in the past with other farmers, and I'd talked to him a bit. He was a good man. He had told me that he and his wife, they couldn't have children, and it grieved them both. So I thought – she'll be safe here, and well loved. I brought her to them, and settled her in, and then I left her."

"Why did you leave her?" He refused to look at her, but knew she still hovered there by the stream, her elbows propped up on her silk-clad knees. "Why didn't you stay with her?"

Oscar bumped his wet nose against his knee, as though sensing his master's agitation, his nerves, and Conor scratched lightly at the top of the terrier's head in a silent thanks. "I knew it'd be easy enough for you to find me, so I thought I'd settle her with poor folk you knew nothing of, far enough away you couldn't find her, but close enough that I could see her as often as I liked."

"How often was that?"

"At first, only every few months. I would come by at night, after she was asleep, and give money to Kayleigh and Páidí, to check on her, make sure she was well, but it was too hard on her to actually see me more than that. She still got confused, would call me 'da,' and –" He swallowed roughly. "It was best, to let her forget first, to allow her to only remember this new life, these new parents, and then I came more often in the daytime, to see her."

"I haven't seen her once in ten years." He flinched, but she continued without looking at him. "What does she look like now?"

There was no point in lying to her. "Like you," he said. "But with Mamó's – your grandmother's eyes."

"Is that difficult for you?" She traced the tip of her finger in the swirling water of the stream. "Seeing traces of me in her face?"

"No," he said quietly, and she peeked up at him from underneath the shadow of her gray hood. "I grieved for you, Ria, for who you had been, every day. It gave me peace, to see you there, alive and well in our daughter's smile."

"I was alive." She pushed to her feet, flicking the drops of water from her fingers. "But hardly well." She brushed past him before he could respond, gliding toward the village's edge. "Let's get this over with."

Oscar loped alongside him as he jogged to catch up with her. "I thought we'd introduce you as my apprentice," he said. "So as not to raise suspicions."

"So, 'hello, I'm your mother, the servant of death, resident of

Tech Duinn, and druidess of the dark arts' would not be an appropriate introduction?"

He shot her a glance. "No more jokes, Riona. You are my apprentice, helping me with a few visits in the village, and nothing more."

"I shall endeavor to look raptly interested in grubs and weeds."

He almost smiled at that, and then again when Oscar snuffled at the hem of Riona's skirt, causing her to stumble a little as she made her way down the grassy incline to the village below. She turned around, glaring at the dog with fiercely narrowed eyebrows, but Oscar merely huffed once and pranced by, his tail wagging unconcernedly as he trotted away. "He doesn't take well to new people," Conor said half-apologetically, and Riona sniffed.

"Honestly, I am more of a cat person these days myself."

They fell silent again as they followed Oscar into the village square, him bounding confidently along, knowing full well that a bone and a glorious reception of pats and belly rubs awaited him at the end of his journey. Conor watched as his dog burst into a full sprint, barking joyously, disappearing through a half-open doorway of a small cottage in the middle of the town. "This is it," he said.

"I gathered."

He risked a glance at her, noting how her fingers twisted in her skirt, the stiff, tense set of her jaw, her blank expression. "You're my apprentice," he reminded, and she nodded once, a curt motion. He tapped lightly on the doorframe. "Anybody home?"

"Your dog leapt up on the table and ate my barmbrack. Teach the lad some manners, will you?" A woman with sandy blonde hair lightly streaked with gray appeared in the doorway, wiping her hands on an apron, smiling broadly. "Hello, Conor."

"Kayleigh." He leaned forward and kissed her cheek. "You look lovely, as always. Sorry about Oscar."

She waved her hand. "I adore him, the rascal, and so does Haisley, as you well know. He's already run out back, searching for her, still munching on my breakfast." Her gaze slid over his shoulder. "Who's this?"

Conor cleared his throat and stepped aside, gesturing at Riona to come closer. "My new apprentice," he said. "She's, uh –"

"Fiadh," Riona said without moving. "My name is Fiadh."

"Right. Fiadh." Conor shot a tentative glance at Kayleigh, who merely stared at Riona, her usually good-natured expression unreadable. "She's giving me a bit of help on my errands in the village. I thought I might stop by, say hello to Haisley."

For a long moment, Kayleigh said nothing, her gaze locked on Riona's face, then with a visible effort, she turned toward Conor. "Of course," she said with a forced cheeriness. "She's just out back reading."

"Thank you, Kayleigh. We won't be long." He unslung the satchel from his shoulder, the coins inside tinkling gently as he handed it over. "Here. For Haisley."

"I've told you a dozen times it's not necessary, but thank you." Kayleigh took the satchel, brow furrowed. "Well," she said, her gaze wandering back to Riona. "I'll just go put this away then, and leave you to it." Without another word, she turned and disappeared inside the cottage, closing the door with a gentle snap behind her.

"She knows."

Conor rubbed anxiously at his stubbled chin. "Perhaps she suspects, but it's more likely that she's thrown off by you being here at all. I've never had an apprentice before, and she would find it odd, and –"

"She knows," Riona repeated, and Conor shivered a little at the dullness in her voice.

"Riona –"

"It doesn't matter." Riona clenched her fists at her sides. "A few drops of blood, and I will be gone, and you all can go back to your tidy lives and never think of me again."

Conor once more reached for her hand, his fingers brushing against the smooth silk of her glove, but she wrenched it away, stalking toward the side of the house. "Let's go," Riona said without looking back. "I want to see my daughter."

'I will not do it,' said Jack.

'Go home then,' said the fear-dearg. 'Marry some other girl. For it must be done. If you are not willing to taste the kiss of death on your lips, then there is no point in going further.' He held out his hand, and slowly, slowly, Jack removed the cloak of darkness and gave it to the fairy. 'Now,' the fear-dearg said. 'Decide what kind of king you shall be.'

And Jack was left alone in the snow-covered woods, with death as his only companion.

Excerpt from 'The Snow, The Crow, & The Blood'

Chapter Twenty-Five
Maigh Eo, Éire, 1082

CONOR

It had only been a week since Conor had last seen Haisley, but it still took his breath away seeing her lying on her back in the grass still damp from the morning dew, her arms folded behind her copper-colored head, Oscar already stretched out on his side next to her, tail thumping contentedly as he snuggled into her. She looked so old now, a too-tall child on the threshold of girlhood, bursting with promise and possibility.

Beside him, Riona halted. "She still has your hair," she said in an unbearably soft voice, one that somehow managed to slice right through him, despite its tenderness.

He could not bring himself to look at her, to see whatever emotions were flooding across her face, but simply strode forward to where Haisley reclined on the grass. "That doesn't look much like doing a bit of reading, a chnó coill. Slacking, are you?"

She sat up immediately, her narrow face curving into a bright, joyous smile. "Are you planning on tattling on me now, Uncail Con?"

"I'd never." He grinned, bending over to ruffle her red curls with his hand. "Hello, Haisley."

Almost twelve, he thought with a sudden pang, and too old for hugs, as she had informed him loftily a few months back. She was almost grown, and he had missed so much of it.

His spine stiffened as Haisley's gaze wandered behind him, to where Riona still stood, rooted to the ground. "Who's this?"

"This is…Fiadh." Conor risked a glance at Riona's bloodless face and gestured toward her. "My apprentice. Come and say hello."

Haisley climbed to her feet, brushing at the damp blades of grass stuck to her breeches, and Oscar huffed in annoyance at her feet. "Hello," she said, eying Riona curiously. "I'm Haisley."

Riona took a single step forward. "Hello."

"You're learning from Uncail Con? He's the best healer in the vale, don't you know. Everyone says so."

"Yes." It was too brief, too curt, and Conor narrowed his eyes at her, a wordless warning. Riona's throat bobbed as she swallowed. "So I've heard."

Haisley waited another moment, then shrugged, turning toward Conor. "Where's my present?"

"What makes you so sure I've brought you anything?" She merely quirked an eyebrow at him, and he smiled. "You're getting a bit old for this." He dug into his pocket and brought out a thin silver chain with a small green gem set in its center. "Here. I was saving this for your birthday, but as I was leaving this morning, I realized that I had nothing else for you, and didn't feel up to risking my life so early in the day by showing up empty-handed."

She rolled her eyes. "I'm not that spoiled." She held up the delicate chain in the dim light of the overcast sky. "It's lovely, Uncail Con. Thank you."

"You're welcome." He shoved his hands into his pockets, stealing another glance at where Riona stood, silent and still, a little way behind them. "So. Listen, Haisley –"

She peeked up at him as she fastened the chain behind her neck.

"Yes?"

"This isn't – well, we were wondering –"

Conor hesitated, unsure of what to say next, when Riona spoke up suddenly. "Haisley," she said. "I need you to do something for me." He wheeled around, and watched as she slowly, deliberately, tugged off her silk gray gloves, one at a time.

"It's not true." She spoke coolly, matter-of-factly, and a wild surge of alarm rushed through him. "It's not true, what your uncle has told you. I am not his apprentice." Conor stepped forward, gesticulating in a silent warning, but Riona ignored him, her steady gaze fixed on Haisley. "I am a druid, and I need something from you."

Haisley looked from Riona to him, standing between them with his hands raised and his mouth ajar, ready to protest. "Really?"

Conor lowered his hands, watching his daughter warily. "Yes. But –"

"You don't have to protect me from everything, I'm not a child anymore, Uncail Con."

You are though, he longed to say. You are, and will always be, to me, a child.

My child.

He kept silent, though, even when she glanced over to Riona, her expression bright with curiosity. "I've never met a druid before. I thought they were all long gone from Éire."

"Mostly." Riona clasped her bandaged hands behind her. "Yet here I am."

"I also thought that they were all evil, who practiced the dark arts."

Riona smiled. "Druidecht is like all other things in this world –

by itself, neither good nor bad, unless its user makes it so.”

“So you are…a good druid?”

“Mostly,” Riona said again. She smiled, cool and unhurried, and after a moment, Haisley smiled back.

“We should go for a walk.” She jerked her chin toward the cottage. “I don’t want Mamaí to hear this. She worries almost as much as Uncail Con does.”

“We’re not hiding anything from your mother,” Conor said firmly. “Go along inside and tell her the truth, Haisley. She deserves to hear that from you.” Haisley’s expression soured, her mouth turning downwards in a petulant pout, and Conor cleared his throat. “Hurry though,” he said, because he might as well nag at her about this as well while she was already annoyed with him. “It’s about to rain, and you catch cold easily.”

Surprisingly, she grinned. “You see?” Haisley turned toward Riona, half-laughing, and it was like a mirror carved from flesh-and-blood, two pairs of identical rose-red lips curving around delicate cheeks, as they smiled at one another. “He’s like a grumpy wet hen. All right. I’ll only be a moment.” She hurried inside the cottage, and Riona and Conor were left standing across from one another under the gray-clouded sky, Oscar stretched out in the grass between them, gnawing happily on a stick.

“What the hell, Riona.” Conor hissed as he edged closer to her. “We had an agreement.”

“Did I tell her any of the things that you asked me not to?” Riona reached up with her bandaged hand to brush back the loose strands of her hair from her face. “Don’t be a fool, Conor. She is certainly not one. I could tell within a moment of hearing her talk that she would not fall for whatever half-baked tale you had concocted for her about why I'd be needing a sample of her blood."

"You don't know that."

"She told you herself, didn't she – she is not a child." Riona's voice snapped like a whip through the air. "Not anymore." She looked away sharply, and Conor could see her chest heaving as she stared across the straw-thatched roofs of the nearby homes. "She has grown, a little woman in a child's body, and I have missed all of it."

It was such a close echo of his own thoughts only a few moments before that Conor's heart ached. Before he could stop himself, he reached out and touched her shoulder lightly. "I know, Ria. I know." He paused, watching a myriad of emotions swirling in her eyes. "I'm sorry."

She nodded once, then stepped away from his touch, folding her arms across her chest. "It'll be better to warn her anyway," she said, her voice steady and cool once more. "She's bound to notice the silver in her blood, if she hasn't already, and I don't want her making the same mistakes that I did, Conor. I have seen the horrors that she could unwittingly call forth. I can't risk her discovering that power on her own."

"What power?"

They both jerked around. Haisley skipped toward them, the back door of the cottage swinging shut behind her. "All is well, Uncail Con. You can rest easy." She shoved him lightly against his shoulder, and despite the worry in his heart, he smiled.

Nothing – nothing – made him as happy as this, the teasing and affection from the daughter he so loved.

Suddenly, he became hyper-aware of Riona watching them, like a thousand thin-pointed needles tickling along the exposed skin along his arms and neck. "This won't take long, though. I promise."

"All right." Haisley slipped her hand into his, swinging it as they walked toward the green-grass fields that rolled away from the village to the east, an unconscious habit of hers that she had yet to abandon, and one that Conor secretly prayed she never outgrew. "Is it magic? There is an illusionist who travels through every now and then, doing stunts and tricks, but I would love to see real magic."

"It's a sort of magic," Riona said with a faint smile, and Conor raised his eyebrows at her. Haisley, it seemed, would not be receiving the same condescending lecture about the distinction between inborn magic and the learned art of druidry. "You see, there are some spells that require certain elements in order to work properly, and I believe that you possess one of those elements that I need."

Haisley bounced by his side. "Can I talk to the animals? I bet that's it. I've always suspected – Oscar always understands what it is I am saying to him, and Da says that I have a way with the horses and the sheep. He says that they just do whatever I ask them to without a second thought."

"Perhaps you can," Riona said, and Conor bit his lip to hide his smile at her indulgent tone. "But in this case, I am talking about your blood."

"What about it?"

"Well, have you never noticed anything unique about how it looks?"

Haisley's brow furrowed. "Sometimes – sometimes it changes color."

A flicker of excitement flashed across Riona's face. "What color?"

"I've always thought that I was imagining it though. Mamaí

never could see it."

"You weren't." Riona sped up, coming to stand in front of Haisley, her bandaged hands on her hips, and Haisley and Conor stopped walking. "What color, Haisley?"

She looked up at him quickly, and he gave a small nod. "Silver," Haisley said, and Riona clenched her teeth. For a moment, she rubbed at her temples, an absent gesture, then she exhaled slowly as she crouched down in front of where Haisley stood, her hand still clasped in Conor's.

"Haisley," she said, low and urgent. "There is something that I need to find, a special magical object, that I have to locate and give to an extremely powerful lord, or else he will take something very precious away from me." She held out her bandaged hands, and slowly began to unwrap the bloodstained linen that was tied so tightly around her palms, carefully pushing up the long silk sleeves that covered her forearms. "To find them, I need to cast a certain spell, a revelation spell, that will show me exactly where in Éire it is hidden. That spell requires a sacrifice of folaíocht – the silver-tinted blood that once flowed in the veins of the lost gods of Éire."

The bandages fell to the ground, but Haisley's gaze remained fixed on Riona's tense face. "Is that what I have?"

"Yes, Haisley. Once, I had it too, but it is gone now, run dry because I used too much of it too quickly these past few years." She swallowed. "But you have not. That silver blood is still buried deep within your veins. I doubt that you would see much of it all with a tiny prick drawn from the tip of your finger, but –" She held out her hands, and Conor's mouth went dry as his gaze fell upon those once-beloved hands, those pale-skinned arms. "From a small cut across your arm, I think you would."

Conor had suspected, but none of his imaginings had prepared him for this degree of mutilation – the smooth white skin of her forearms and her palms mangled and scarred with dozens of dark, crisscrossed lines, an intricate webbing of a story whispering of lost blood and dark arts and the ransom she had paid for their daughter's life so many times over. There in the center of each palm, and just above her wrists on the inside of her forearms, he could see angry red welts from her still-healing cuts, horribly swollen and inflamed.

Through the roaring in his ears, he studied the wounds with a healer's objective eye. She should put some goldenrod, mixed with a little yarrow root on those.

Next to him, Haisley squirmed, and he jerked back, realizing that his grip on her hand had tightened to an iron-like clench.

Perhaps not so objective, after all.

He had called her a monster, this woman who had bled and suffered and half-died for Haisley's sake, and she had said nothing, but merely walked along beside him, head down and shoulders hunched.

"It won't hurt much." Riona held out her own hands toward Haisley, smiling encouragingly, and Conor forced himself not to flinch at the sight of her once-beautiful arms, so irreparably scarred, all her sacrifices and sorrows tattooed there on her skin in indelible ink for him to see. "I can't heal myself," Riona continued, her voice gentle and low. "The spell does not work that way, unfortunately." She glanced at him quickly, and he remembered – broken legs and finger-bones shredding through his skin as he writhed on the floor before she had healed the hurts that she herself had inflicted.

Then again, calling her a monster had not been *completely* unwarranted.

"But." Riona ran her fingers over the scars on her forearm, lightly tracing her fingertips over the dark raised ridges. "I can heal you with it, in a blink."

"Quick like a bunny," Haisley said, and in spite of everything, Conor's lips twitched in a smile. "That's what mamaí used to say, when I was little, when she needed to prick my finger to test my blood and I was afraid of the pinch."

Riona frowned. "Test your blood?"

"Yes. I have the blood-sickness, you see." Haisley shrugged, as though it were a matter of little importance – as though it were not the cataclysmic event that had derailed all their lives in one fell swoop. "Most people die from it, but for some reason, I survived. No one knows why, not even Uncail Con, as he's a great healer."

"I'm not," Conor said quietly. "Otherwise, I would –" He drew a deep breath. "I'm not."

"Well, mamaí says you are, and she says that you are the one who figured out how I can test my blood – I prick it with a sewing needle and sprinkle a drop or two on the connemara rock. It tells me if I'm getting sicker or not." She smiled at him. "He's even working on a cure in case I do. Become sicker, I mean."

Slowly, slowly, Riona turned to look at him, eyes wide in her too-white face, and Conor cleared his throat. "The rock changes color when the blood touches it, because of its alkaline structure. Very interesting, but really, it's not –"

"A cure?" Riona whispered, visibly trembling. "You've found a cure?"

Conor shook his head, even as Haisley looked curiously between them. "There is no cure," he said softly. "You know that. But there could be a way to treat it – to manage the illness so that it's not…fatal." His chest tightened painfully at the heartache flashing in Riona's eyes. "It's not for certain. Only a theory."

"Mamaí says that you are brilliant," Haisley said proudly. "She says that you'll be the saving of me for sure."

Riona closed her eyes, then opened them, expression shuttered and cold once more. "Your mamaí must take very good care of you," she said to Haisley, and Conor's chest tightened again. "We should get on with it," Riona continued, "so you can hurry home to her before she starts to worry for you."

Haisley nodded eagerly, and Conor laid his hand on his daughter's shoulder. "You do not have to do this if you don't want to, a chnó coill."

"It's all right." Haisley studied Riona with that bright-eyed impudence of a fearless adolescent. "I'd rather like to see it, a bit of magic. Besides." She shrugged. "I lose blood every day. It might as well be for something interesting instead of simply splashing it on a silly piece of connemara rock."

"That connemara rock keeps you healthy," Conor said, and from the corner of his eye, he saw a ghost of a grin flit across Riona's face. *Cabbage*, he could almost hear her tease, in that sing-song voice, warm and wry and affection-filled.

It was a dangerous memory.

"Well." Haisley folded her arms across her chest. "Let's get on with it then, shall we?" She said it so casually, striving, he could tell, to appear aloof and unimpressed by the promise of the power humming within her, but there was a gleam in her eyes, burning with curiosity.

She was so like her mother.

Riona studied her for a minute, that same keen glint shining in her eyes, the blue and the green. "I've never used anyone's blood other than mine own before." She knelt down, pulling at the blades off the grass around her, clearing a small patch of dark wet soil before her. "It will be interesting, to see how it affects the spell."

Haisley plopped down next to her on crisscrossed legs, rubbing her hands on her knees eagerly as she watched Riona's preparations, bright-eyed and curious, and Riona peeked up at her quickly through half-lowered lashes before ducking her head back down, focusing on the task at hand. "Will it still work?"

"Yes." Even with her head bent, Conor could see the shadow of a smile tugging at the corner of Riona's rose-red lips, and for a moment, he could see traces of her long lost grandmother in her face and in her smile, the woman that they had both so deeply loved. "I think it will."

This giant, Jack found, was far more terrible than the two previous giant -- a horse-headed monster of a beast, with razor-sharp teeth and two meaty hands atop his well-muscled body, wielding a blade that shimmered with an improbable radiance in the darkness, divine steel forged from the incandescent light of a thousand stars.

He could not take his eyes off of it, even though the giant towered over him, roaring with fury and spraying hot drops of foam-flecked spittle on his face. Jack watched its iridescent arc, a slash of bright burning silver across the midnight-dark sky.

His sword — his treasure.

Excerpt from 'The Snow, The Crow, & The Blood'

Chapter Twenty-Six
The Vale of Inagh, Éire, 1062

CONOR

Conor still remembered that first fateful day he had arrived in the vale as a broken-hearted boy of ten, the thick gray fog hanging heavy and foreboding over the stone-walled castle nestled deep within the tree-covered hills, so unlike the grand, high wall of the castle in Soghain where he had lived for so long. He struggled to stave back the tears that threatened to consume him, the memory of his mother watching him ride away with nary a sigh, amplified a hundredfold by the severe, impatient weight of his father's gloved hand on his shoulder as he had pushed Conor forward so that he could stumble his way through a greeting to the two gray-haired figures waiting at the bottom of the front steps.

He knew who they were, of course. Everyone in Éire knew them – the Beast of Connacht, Rozlyn Ó Conchúir, and her handsome husband, who used to be a god.

The latter merely watched him as he fumbled over his words, his fingers twisting nervously, wishing desperately for a cap to cover the deep red blush spreading over the tips of his ears.

The queen though – she took one look at him as he had stood beside his father that first day when they had arrived in the vale, his shoulders hunched with his hands tucked behind his back to hide his dirty fingernails, and her entire expression softened, her demeanor shifting ever so slightly from the straight-backed, cool-faced queen of the vale, once the most feared creature in all of Connacht, to a lady who crouched in front of him, reaching out to lightly pluck the leafy strands of a weed from his pocket that he had pulled from beside the stream that morning.

"Euphrasia," she said, "although often we simply call it 'eyebright.' It's very good for eye inflammations, best brewed in teas or used in a warm compress." He immediately raised it to his nose and sniffed, inhaling the slightly bitter scent, and their eyes met and just like that, a bond was formed between them, unspoken and bright.

Hours later, she bandaged the wound in his forehead after Riona's horse had run him down, and it was the steadiest thing in the world, the gentle dab of her fingers against his skin. "It's a nasty cut," she said with a slight frown. "How did this happen?"

"I tripped on a root and bashed it on a rock." Her eyebrows raised, and his cheeks grew hot yet again. "I'm a bit of a klutz. Just ask my father."

"Och." She wiped briskly at the excess ointment she'd lathered on the wound. "Only because you're still growing, little wolf. It won't be long before the rest of you catches up to those lanky legs of yours."

"Why do you call me 'little wolf'?"

"Listen to you. Don't you even know what your own name means?"

"My mother said that she named me after my grandfather. She never told me what it meant."

"Well." The queen leaned back in her chair, wiping her fingers on a damp linen cloth, her lips pursed as she studied the dressing on his forehead. "That's a shame. Names are rather important, you know. Too often they are a self-fulfilling prophecy, as though fate nudges the game-pieces a bit at the start of a match to ensure a certain ending."

"So I am meant to be a wolf?" He shifted nervously in his seat. "Honestly, I'm more of a sheep."

She smiled then, that barely-there smile he soon learned to love so well, then tousled his hair with her hand before she rose from her chair. "We'll see about that. Now run along to the kitchen and you tell Eabha that I said you've earned an oatmeal biscuit."

Conor knew that from that moment on, they were friends, he and the queen, and he found that the missing of his mother was not so terrible when she was near.

He had barely been in the vale a fortnight before she was coming by his room, rapping lightly on the doorframe. "I'm in need of feverfew," she'd say with that shadow-smile of hers, never fully formed but gently playing at the corners of her lips. "Keep me company, little wolf?" He would grab his tattered leather satchel and away they would go, with her wolfhounds trotting before them, and him trailing behind her sure strides through the trees, squatting next to her as she wiped her hands on her breeches before uprooting the correct plants with swift, practiced ease, murmuring explanations of each chosen herb.

"Thank you, my queen," he said late one evening when they returned to the castle from a long afternoon in the woods, with dirt-stained hands and cobwebs in their hair and his satchel and her basket overflowing with flowers and herbs. "For teaching me." She looked down at him, a streak of mud on her delicate-boned face, and he'd seen it then, the full force of her smile, and he'd shivered a little at the sight.

"Call me Mamó," she said. "And no need to thank me. I'm only doing for you what someone once did for me long ago." She ruffled his hair with her fingers. "You're a natural-born healer, little wolf. I expect great things from you."

It did not take long before he proved to her exactly how clumsy he was, whether through the fault of his too-lanky legs or not. Within a few days of her tending to the gash in his head, Conor found himself being led down the hall to the queen's solar again, clutching at his bleeding hand, a long, shallow cut from a rusted nail in the side of the barn door the culprit this time, and then a fortnight after that, with a gash in his chest from a sharpened sword that had somehow slipped unnoticed into the batch of dull blades during sparring practice. Mamó had frowned, shaking her silver-dark head as she rummaged through her cupboards, brow furrowed in concentration as she searched through the cluster of dark brown bottles and dried herbs. "Klutz, not so much. Cursed, more like. By the harp, child, that's a vicious-looking cut."

At first glance, they did not look much alike, Riona and her grandmother. It was subtle, the few similarities between them, and even then, only in the subtle underlying structure of their features, but Conor could see it. The same narrow angles to their faces, the same high-boned cheeks. It would be like watching the time-kissed version of Riona here in front of him now, if it was not for Riona's wide-set, thick-shaped brows, the sharp-pointed chin, and of course, the eyes. Mamó's eyes were like the evergreen trees set against the midwinter sky, when the gray wisps of fog slid in through the branches, but Riona – Riona had her grandfather's eyes, that endless dark blue that always reminded Conor of the cool water of the loch shining under the bright summer sun.

"This is thrice in as many weeks that I've stitched you up, little wolf," Mamó said as she carefully dabbed at the deep gash on his chest with a sweet-smelling poultice. He sniffed deeper, ever curious about the mysteries of her art, even through the painful throbbing of the wound, and a shadow of a smile curved along the edges of her pale lips. "Yarrow root," she told him. "And a bit of goldenrod."

He nodded once, filing the information away, then winced as even the slight movement tugged painfully at the tight edges of his stitches. "I guess I just like to dance with death," he said, then frowned as he caught a glimpse of Riona from where she hovered in the doorway.

Her face was like a sheet of splintered glass, distorted and mangled beyond repair, her expression frozen with something that spoke, impossibly, of fear.

Conor opened his mouth to ask her what was wrong, but before he could say a word, she wheeled around and disappeared through the doorway, and he was left blinking in confusion on the table in Mamó's solar, wondering if he had hallucinated the whole thing.

Riona didn't speak to him for a fortnight after that. He saw her often, skipping through the halls of the castle, her black braid swinging behind her, or galloping through the trees of the vale on that black mare of hers, raised up high in the stirrups, her cheeks bright red from the whip of the wind on her porcelain-smooth face. He knew that she noticed him too, their gazes meeting in the corridor or across the table at supper or as she flew past him atop her horse, but she would scurry away in the opposite direction or throw herself into a conversation with someone else or whip her mare's head around, nudging her to fly faster and farther, so long as she carried her far away from him.

It stung far more than he liked to admit, this avoidance of him, almost as much as it baffled him.

"Does Riona – the princess – not like me?" He ventured to ask Mamó one day as they tramped through the woods, one of her ever-present hounds snuffling through the underbrush beside them. "She won't talk to me, won't even look at me."

Mamó merely laughed, soft and low. "Give it time, little wolf. You are both children yet, and Ria has never been good at admitting what it is she feels." She leaned forward to whisper in his ear. "Just know that I approve."

Conor laid awake far longer than he liked to admit that night, pondering those words, a tiny seed of hope sprouting in his heart.

Then the fateful day came when the news arrived from Soghain – the king, Riona's uncle, had died, Mamó was heartbroken, almost wild with grief at the news of the loss of her last boy, and Riona – Riona was nowhere to be found. Maeve, teary-eyed and trembling, had cornered him in the kitchen where he had been helping Eabha make her apple-cider. "She's gone into the mountains again, I just know it," she whispered. "They'll be so worried if they find out, Conor. She's been forbidden to ride out that far. You have to go and find her. Please – go and fetch her and bring her back before they figure it out. They don't need any other troubles right now."

He had grumbled about it the whole ride up the mountain, through the icy sheets of driving rain, his teeth clattering uncontrollably as he bounced in the saddle. He still wasn't sure what it was about the sight of that lone pine tree, weaving in the wind, that had drawn him forward, but he had cantered forward as soon as he had laid eyes on it, inexplicably drawn to it, a brown-winged moth to a flickering candle flame, and slid from the saddle, calling her name through blue, shivering lips.

He stopped cursing the decision the moment she had laid her damp, musty-smelling head onto his shoulder and the rhythm of his breathing synced up with hers, a steady rise and fall of two chests and two hearts, alone in the woods except for the sound of the falling rain and the whisper of her voice in the midnight air.

It was unavoidably clear to him after that, his fate in life, an inherent truth as simple and inevitable as the blossoming of the yellow-petaled gorse and broom shrubs in the early spring.

He was destined to love the princess of the vale until his very last breath, and it was both a blessing and a curse, the knowing of this, that had never once left him with more than a few stolen moments of fleeting, all-too-brief peace from that day on.

Jack knew, in this moment that he was about to die, that he was meant for more than other men. He was born for true greatness, a kingship that surpassed all others, and when he had watched that black-winged raven die at his feet, he had seen his future written in blood in the snow before him.

The sword of starlight sliced into his neck, but he remained oddly detached from the pain, indifferent to his own demise.

And just before everything went dark, his fingers, seemingly of their own accord, slipped into his pocket and found the purse of plenty still hidden there.

Excerpt from 'The Snow, The Crow, & The Blood'

Chapter Twenty-Seven
Maigh Eo, Éire, 1082

CONOR

Reluctantly, Conor was forced to admit to himself that he found it fascinating, watching Riona's craft come to life underneath her scarred hands, drawing intricate runes and sigils into the cleared patch of earth before her. He had prepared himself to be horrified, disgusted at whatever atrocities he was about to witness, but there was an elegance to the glide of her fingertip through the mud, an archaic, primal beauty in the lines of the markings she made in the dirt that whispered of such eternal power that he could not tear his gaze away from them.

She looked different too, squatting in the grass, a streak of mud across her pale cheek, eyes narrowed in concentration. She was an artist, caught in the throes of creation, molding and crafting something glorious and fine from the nothingness of the air. Her lips moved quickly, soundlessly, as she cast her wordless incantation over the finely-drawn runes in the soil at their feet, and even the wind itself gusted around them a little faster, a little more eagerly, in anticipation of what magic she might make.

Haisley watched, mouth slightly ajar, her hand outstretched, her upturned palm waiting obediently for Riona's signal as she had been instructed, without a single tremor to be seen.

Riona looked up, and Conor could see a faint shimmer of something not of this world burning deep within her bluebell eyes, an unearthly fire crackling deep within her. He could not bring himself to speak when Riona reached out with an impossibly gentle hand to wrap her fingers around Haisley's wrist, steadying her. Her lips kept moving, fast and silent, as she carefully drew the sharp tip of her blade across the soft flesh of Haisley's forearm.

Haisley yelped once, and Conor stepped forward, shoulders stiffening instinctively, then watched as a thin line of bright red blood welled up from the gash, and shimmering in the dim, hazy light of the cloud-blanketed sun – a faint sheen of silver.

Riona flipped Haisley's hand over and let the blood from the cut above her wrist drip down into the dirt, holding it still for a few, interminable heartbeats, then slowly relaxed her grip on their daughter's wrist, her attention never leaving the markings she had drawn in the soil as she motioned wordlessly for Haisley to move away.

"It's for the best," she had explained previously, in that unusually gentle voice she used whenever she spoke to their daughter. "Best to not let you get too close to such a spell."

"But I want to see –"

"It is not," Riona interrupted, "what you would see that I fear, but what might look back through the window which we open, and see you."

Haisley had swallowed thickly at that, and Conor had shifted nervously on his feet, flexing his fingers over and over at his side. "Haisley," he had said. "Move far away when she tells you," and Haisley had nodded once, an uncharacteristic show of compliance.

Even now, she obeyed that command, backing slowly away and perching atop a half-crumbled stone wall a good distance away, craning her neck to watch as Riona bent her head low over the earth, so close that her forehead brushed against the black soil, her lips moving faster and more furiously than before. Conor watched, entranced, as she suddenly froze, her body going rigid and stiff, her expression glassy and unseeing as she stared into the depths of some other world into which he could never go.

She was a mere three feet away from him, so close that he could lean down and run his fingers through her loose black hair, but he had never felt so far away from her as he did now, watching that unnatural glaze dull the bright blue of her eyes.

Then she gasped, a hoarse, choking sound, her fingers digging into the dirt as she braced herself on her forearms, chest shuddering. "Ria – what happened?"

"Conor," she said, and it was a desperate cry, a keening wail far more terrible than that long ago scream of the bean-sí that she had awakened in the stony hills of the Mhám Toirc.

"Ria." Conor moved quickly, squatting down next to her, reaching out to touch the back of her hand. "You're as white as a ghost. What's wrong?"

"The sword," she whispered. "The sword – it's in Ráth Crúachan, in the cave of cats." Riona reached out with a trembling finger to rub away the runes she had traced into the dirt. "The most dread sídhe in all of Éire, the rumored realm of the Phantom Queen herself."

"Surely it can't be any worse than Tech Duinn," Conor said, and Riona laughed, brittle and dry.

"Oh, cabbage." Her shoulders sagged, her head drooping in what looked like defeat. "Believe me when I say it can." She hissed through her teeth. "I won't be able to enter there, won't be able to find it, unless –" Her voice trailed away, and Conor's fingers tightened on her wrist.

"Unless what?"

She looked up at him then, dull-eyed and bleak. "Unless I bring Haisley," she said, and Conor's heart turned to ice in his chest. "Unless I bring Haisley into the sídhe."

There was a searing pain, a distant thudding, and he was enveloped in a shadow far darker than anything he had ever known before, a newborn hare swaddled deep within the earth, blind and feeble, groping against the darkness with his outstretched, unseeing hands.

And then a whisper, low and cold, shivered in his ear, something guttural and indecipherable, a language not of this world —

Excerpt from 'The Snow, The Crow, & The Blood'

Chapter Twenty-Eight
Maigh Eo, Éire, 1082

CONOR

Ráth Crúachan. He had never heard those words before this day, and yet Conor had never been so terrified in his entire life.

He did not had the nerve to question Riona further after her choked revelation in the aftermath of her spell, but instead surged to his feet, that primal need to protect Haisley rushing through him. "Not here," he said curtly when Riona opened her mouth to explain further, to tell him a story of darkness and shadow and doom that he knew that he was not ready to hear. "Not here, and not now. I need to get Haisley home."

A distant rumble of thunder corroborated this, a low growl of confirmation that all of his premonitions and forebodings were at last coming to fulfillment. He turned away without another word and left her there, kneeling in the dirt, her fingers covered in mud, her face white and drawn, and hurried over to where Haisley still sat perched on the crumbling stone wall, her expression sharp with interest. "What happened?" She asked, and he merely shook his head, reaching out to wrap his trembling fingers around her wrist, tugging her back toward the little village and the safety and comfort of her adoptive parents' cottage.

This – this was exactly why he had hidden her away, had sacrificed watching his little girl grow up, had surrendered the right to be the one whom she called 'da' and who would wipe away her tears when she was sad and make her laugh with silly jokes on dreary days and tell her bedtime stories on warm summer nights. "The rain is coming," he managed to say through the lump in his throat. "Let's get you home."

"But what about the spell?"

"It's done." He forced a smile, and out of the corner of his eye, he saw Riona clamber to her feet, wiping her muddy hands on her silk skirt, trailing after them in silence. "It worked perfectly, thanks to you. All is well, and there's no need to think about it any longer."

"But –"

His grip on her arm tightened. "Haisley," he said, too quietly. "Leave this alone now."

She fell silent, but he could feel her peeking up at him on the short walk back to the cottage, glancing back and forth between him and Riona following them, her expression stony and emotionless even as the rain began to softly fall all around them.

Kayleigh was waiting for them in the doorway as they walked up the dirt path to the front door, her arms wrapped tightly around her waist. She smiled, but Conor could see it, the tension quivering at the corners of her mouth and etched in the faint lines across her brow. "Oscar's inside by the fire," she said. "Haisley, the goats are out in the back. Be a good girl, and put your cloak on and gather them up into the stable, would you? It's looking to be a nasty storm."

Haisley's lips tightened, but she merely nodded and slipped away with only a single burning glance back over her shoulder to where the three of them stood underneath the thatched stoop, Kayleigh with one hand pressed against the doorframe, he and Riona, side by side, stiff-shouldered and silent. Kayleigh waited until they heard the soft click of the back door closing, then looked straight at Riona. "I know who you are," she said through trembling lips. "I can see it, in the curves of your face, the shape of your chin. I just – I need to know –" Her voice cracked, and Conor watched her inhale deeply, steadying herself, before she continued. "If you're here to take her from us, I cannot stop you, I know this, but you must know, you must understand, we love her, so much, our girl, and I would beg you – I would beg, on my knees, that you please –"

"I'm not." Riona spoke, brittle and terse. "I am no fit mother, as I am sure you have been told."

Conor flinched, but Kayleigh visibly sagged with relief against the doorframe, her eyes fluttering shut for a moment before she looked back into Riona's expressionless gaze. "She looks so much like you," she said, and something unreadable flickered across Riona's stony face. "I should have known. There's nothing of Conor in her, except that hair," and then, impossibly, a shaky laugh, and Kayleigh clapped her hand over her mouth, horrified.

For a moment, Riona simply stared at her. Then, to Conor's astonishment, her expression softened, until she looked like a child again, that girl he had once known, sitting by the riverside, chin resting on knees, grieving all her private, hidden hurts that the cruel whims of fate had burdened her with for so many years, vulnerable and tender-hearted, that softness she kept hidden away so carefully from everyone but him. "She has my brother's mouth, his chin," she said softly, almost to herself. "My brother Sean. I'd all but forgotten him, it's been so long, but then I saw her, the way the sunlight slanted over her face and for a moment – for a moment, it was like he was here again, back from the dead." She fell silent for a moment, staring at the ground, lost in thought, then looked back up at Kayleigh, steady and serious.

"I won't be taking her from you," Riona said. "Not now, or ever. I may be her mother, but you –" Her lips quivered once. "You are her mamaí now, and I can never be." Her gaze darted away for a moment, and when she looked back, she was cold again, her expression carefully carved from unforgiving marble, a statue of flawless, unattainable beauty. "Keep her safe," she said, turning away to stalk away from the cottage door into the rain. "Keep her well."

Conor barely had time to murmur his reassurances and goodbyes to Kayleigh before he was running after Riona, whistling over his shoulder for Oscar to follow as he pulled up the hood of his cloak against the thrum of the rain on his face. "Ria, wait."

"Go say goodbye to Haisley," she said without looking back, stalking toward the trees. "I'll wait for you outside the village."

"Don't you want to –"

"No." It was an iron gate slamming shut, the lock snapping irrevocably into place, the clanging of an impassable drawbridge as it was pulled away from the shore. "I do not."

It was all too familiar, that cold dismissal, an icy shock of a heart-breaking remembrance from a past life that he had long struggled to forget.

Then the darkness shattered, an explosion
of golden light, scorching and hot. Jack
tried to scream without breath or body as
those golden fire-tipped claws tore through
him --

He woke up with a gasp, lying on the ice-
covered ground of the sidhe, alive and
whole, the quiet stillness of the midnight
air shattered by the sound of hundreds of
ravens cawing and shrieking in a
deafening chorus.

And there before him lay the shining silver
sword of Nuada himself, half-hidden in a
pool of deep, dark red blood.

His blood.

*Excerpt from 'The Snow, The Crow, & The
Blood'*

Chapter Twenty-Nine
The Vale of Inagh, Éire, 1073

CONOR

"That's it, a chnó coill." Conor waggled the biscuit in the air enticingly. "Walk to Da. Walk for a bit of biscuit."

Haisley stood on wobbly legs by the couch, her dimpled hands clutching the cushion as she eyed the biscuit speculatively through a tousled mop of tangled red curls. "Eat?"

"Yes, you can eat. Just walk to Da, and you can eat the whole biscuit, don't you know."

"You're going to give her a complex," Riona said absently from where she sat hunched over at the table, her chin propped on her fist as she read through a long missive from the chiefs of the southern region. "You shouldn't bribe her with the promise of food."

"It's one biscuit." Conor inched forward, waving the biscuit slowly back and forth as Haisley's greedy green eyes tracked it hungrily. "She's so close, Ria. She just needs the proper motivation."

"Complex," Riona repeated without looking away from the parchment, a slight frown furrowing her brow. "I would know, wouldn't I? 'Don't eat that, Riona, you're chubby enough as it is – finish your lessons and then you can have your supper, and not a moment before, it certainly won't hurt you to skip a meal or two.'" She grunted. "So again, I say – complex."

A twinge of annoyance. "Me trying to encourage Haisley to take a few steps is not the same as what your mother did to you, Riona." She said nothing, but from the corner of his eye, he saw her lips tighten, that wordless signal that he had crossed a forbidden threshold to a secret sickroom of long-festering hurts and slow-mending wounds which he was not allowed to soothe. He glanced away from Haisley, manufacturing a smile and a wink. "Besides, you know I like your curves just fine, Ria."

She hummed wordlessly, still focused on the piece of parchment in front of her, and Conor turned back toward Haisley, then let out a shout. "Ria, look!"

Haisley stood a handful of steps away from the couch, weaving back and forth uncertainly as she balanced on her sturdy legs, staring at the biscuit in his hand. "What a brave girl," he crooned. "Walk to Da, now, and it's all yours."

She eyed him suspiciously. "Eat."

"Yes, come eat. After you walk to Da." Haisley seemed to consider this, then took two wobbly steps forward. Conor grinned, then glanced back at Riona.

She was still reading.

"Ria, you're missing it." Haisley toddled forward another couple of steps, and he smiled at her, something soft and warm glowing inside his chest. "She's finally walking – look, Ria."

"Very good."

"You're not looking." Haisley stumbled forward the last three steps, and he caught her in his arms, balancing her on his knee as she grabbed happily at the biscuit in his hand. "Ria, you missed it. Put that down for a moment and watch."

She bit back a sigh, glancing up wearily. "Conor, it's been a long day, and I need to read through another half-dozen of these before the morning council meeting, so can you please let me concentrate?"

"Haisley can *walk*, Ria."

"I know." She returned to her reading, settling her chin deeper into the palm of her hand. "She walked to Eabha this morning in the kitchen."

Conor's heart sank. "This morning? Where was I?"

"You were in the courtyard with your father." Riona smothered a yawn. "Training."

Throat burning, he looked down at the top of Haisley's curly head as she munched contentedly on her biscuit. He had missed it, then, this momentous first for his little girl. "You might have told me."

"I forgot."

"You forgot that our daughter walked for the first time this morning?"

She peered at him crossly. "I don't know if you've noticed, Conor, but I am rather busy these days, being the queen of the vale and all."

He pressed a soft kiss to Haisley's temple. "I know," he said after a moment. "Too busy. You're overworked, Ria. You need help. It's too much of a burden for you to carry on your own."

"My mother helps me."

"Your mother undermines you, and belittles you, and makes you doubt yourself. She's far more hurt than help."

Riona inhaled deeply, her irritation a palpable thing. "I won't be having this argument with you again, Conor."

"I could help you." He plunked Haisley down on the rug, patting her head before he pushed to his feet, walking over to stand beside Riona where she still sat at the table, her face drawn and tired. "I could help you shoulder these worries, these concerns that weigh on you so heavily, and give you a bit of rest, if you would only –"

"We've had this discussion a dozen times now. I have no intention of marrying you, Conor." Her fingers drummed impatiently on the wood table. "You know that."

It was an old bruise that had never healed, this almost contemptuous dismissal of him. "Ria," he said as calmly as he was able. "Do you truly believe that marrying one of these princes –" His voice trailed away as he gestured to the stacks of parchment sitting next to her elbow, and her lips flattened into a thin white line.

"I won't be marrying a prince, Conor."

He ignored this. It was a thin, tired lie, one that he had heard too many times over the years. He had seen the way that they eyed her, had watched the constant influx of letters and messengers with ostentatious gifts and promises of armies and gold. He had seen the gleam in her mother's eye as Riona stood, regal and cool, her hands clasped beside her back, accepting their fawning and their proffers with a murmured word of noncommittal thanks.

She still had never once told him that she loved him, and it terrified him.

Conor licked his dry lips nervously. "Do you think that a marriage will at last win her approval, when nothing else you have done in the last twenty years has? Why do you still try so hard to please her?"

"And as I have told you a dozen times as well, this has nothing to do with my mother. I do not intend to marry anyone at all, prince or no. I am the queen of the vale, and that is enough." She refused to look at him, her jaw set in a stubborn, irritated line. "And more importantly, it would be incredibly foolish to offend them, to scorn their offers and then turn around and marry a nobody instead."

That invisible bruise throbbed anew, aching and sore to the touch. "Right," he said shortly. "You're right. It would be foolish. Better not risk it." He pushed away from the table and stalked to where Haisley sat on the rug by the hearth, happily licking the last of the biscuit crumbs from her fingertips. "Come along, a chnó coill. Time for bath."

"Conor."

He swung Haisley up in his arms, and she shrieked once, grabbing at his hair and tugging eagerly. He winced, then hoisted her up on his shoulders, her sturdy legs tucked securely over his shoulders. "Say good night to Mamaí."

"Ni-ni," Haisley sang out, and Conor kept his gaze determinedly fixed on the doorway of the solar as Riona rose from the table and came forward to stand on her tiptoes, pressing a kiss to Haisley's round cheek.

"Good night, Haisley." There was a pause, and the weight of her stare roamed across his face. "Good night, Conor."

It was a question, hesitant and faint, and as always, the resentful ache in his heart eased a little. "I'll see you upstairs," he said gruffly. "Once you've finished."

"It will be awhile."

"I'll be up." He looked at her then, her pale face, her wary appearance, tense and guarded – a wild lynx caught in a snare. He hated seeing her like this, his wildflower girl, ripped away from the whistling breeze and the thrum of the river, uprooted from the cool black soil of the mountainside and locked away in the dim shadows of these walls of wood and stone. This was not, he thought with a sudden stab of sadness, the life that either of them had been meant to lead.

He bent his head impulsively, careful not to jostle Haisley too much, and brushed his lips lightly across hers. "I love you, Ria."

She exhaled softly, leaning into him. "I'm sorry," she whispered. "I'll be better."

He pulled back and forced a smile. "It's hard now, but things will get easier, for the both of us. I promise." He bounced Haisley as he backed toward the door and their daughter squealed with laughter, pulling wildly at his hair. He grimaced even as Riona smiled. "And look at this little monster. She's well and happy because of you, because of us. Doesn't that make it all worth it?"

The ache in his heart faded away entirely when her whole face softened, a rare moment of tenderness breaking through that distant, cool-glass expression of hers. "Yes. Whatever it takes."

"We're a team, Ria, you and me and our cnó coill." He smiled again, genuine this time, encouraging and bright, then turned away to take Haisley upstairs. "We'll all be just fine. You'll see."

He didn't wait for her to answer, but when he glanced back just before jogging up the stairs, she was rooted to the spot, staring vacantly into the hearth-fire, a flower with drooping petals and wilted leaves, too long deprived of the sun, and a chill of foreboding slithered up his spine.

As though their time was running out.

Quick as a flash, Jack seized the sword from where it lay in the blood-price he had paid for it and buried it deep in the belly of the enraged giant.

The giant crashed to the ground, and Jack stood over him, panting wildly, the bloodied sword of starlight in his hand.

'Now,' he said to the watching fear-dearg. 'Take me to my bride.'

Excerpt from 'The Snow, The Crow, & The Blood'

Chapter Thirty
Maigh Eo, Éire, 1082

CONOR

Conor wrapped the memory of their daughter's laughter close around him, a shield against whatever hurts disguised as kindnesses she might throw at him now, as they stood underneath the paltry shelter of the evergreen trees, the rain lashing at their tight, worried faces as Oscar huddled at their feet. Riona rubbed her gloved hands over her upper arms fretfully. Conor fought the urge to wrap his arm around her shoulders, to pull her tight against his chest, to run his hands up and down her back in slow, soothing strokes, to shelter her, shield her from the lash of the rain and the wind and the fear that he could see gnawing at her even now.

Instead, he remained where he was, his own arms folded across his chest, trying not to panic. "Explain," he said, kneading his hands together. "Why must you do this – bring her into this place, this sídhe?"

"It's complicated, Conor." Riona rubbed wearily at her forehead. "The purse and the cloak were different. I saw them, in the spell, where they were and how to find them, but this time, with the sword, it was –" Her voice trailed away, and Conor stepped closer.

"This sword of light," he said. "The god-slayer, yes? I remember the stories about it – every blow from its blade is lethal, no matter how glancing; fatal to whomever receives it, no matter how slight." He spread his hands wide. "What good does that do him, anyway?

He's a druid, like you, isn't he?"

"Far more powerful."

"Even more reason for it to be useless to him," he said. "Why do you need a sword when you can snap your fingers and kill someone just by looking at them?"

"It's a little more complicated than that. But it is also said," Riona continued, nibbling at her thumbnail, "that its master will never die, can never be defeated, even by death itself – that's the legend, at least."

He made an impatient gesture. "But he is the *lord* of death. What does he need it for?"

"I don't know, Conor," she snapped, rubbing at her forehead. "I wasn't particularly concerned with understanding his motivations at the time. He commands, and I obey."

"What a good little servant you must have made him."

"There was," she ground out through her clenched teeth, "rather a lot at stake, if you remember."

Haisley. Conor swallowed. "Right." He sighed, his fingers reaching out to brush against hers briefly. "I'm sorry. I'm just –"

"Terrified?" Riona laughed harshly. "As am I, but lashing out at one another won't help." She fell quiet for a moment, chewing on her lip as she stared past him into the falling sheets of rain. "He will kill her, Conor, if I don't bring him this sword."

"Well, she'll certainly be killed if you take her into that damned place."

"I could just take her to the entrance, use her blood to open the doorway –"

"And that would work? Just like that?" Conor folded his arms across his chest, his eyebrow quirked. "Be honest, Ria."

Her mouth flattened. "I don't know," she admitted. "It's always been my own blood that let me pass into the sídhe. I don't know if it would allow another to enter." She huffed. "It's an éraic, a blood-debt owed that is demanded by the sídhe, and –"

"It doesn't matter. She's not going. So the sword," he said flatly. "That's what's in this cave of cats. What about the others?"

"What do you mean?"

"The other treasures," Conor said impatiently, dropping his hands and turning back to face her. "From the story. The purse of plenty, the cloak of darkness."

"Oh right. Yes well, I've already found those."

"What?"

Riona dismissed his incredulity with a wave of her hand. "I had to deal with a creature very like Aillén the Burner to get the purse – do you remember that story you told me, about Fionn and the poisoned spear and the enchanted song? It saved my life, funnily enough. Stabbed myself twice in the thigh because I remembered what you said, about Fionn Mac Cumhailll distracting himself by inhaling the poisonous fumes of the spear so that he wouldn't be seduced by the burner's song. And actually, a regular blade works just as well." Her grin faded as she took in the expression on his face, and she ducked her head down to fumble within the folds of her gown. "I found the cloak hidden in the cairn of Queen Medb. I couldn't bring it back to *him* though."

"Why not?" She didn't meet his gaze as she handed him a cream-colored cloak, woven from a strange, brittle fabric, airy and flimsy as it lay in his hands, and the realization flooded over him. "That was when you realized."

"No more silver." She forced a smile. "So I came to see you. What

I've always done, I suppose, when I'm in trouble and don't know what else to do."

"You broke my legs and fractured my fingers, Riona," he said. "It was hardly a cry for help."

But he could feel his sternness, his resentment wavering.

How frantic she must have been. Half-mad with desperation, to see the talisman of all her power siphoned away, gone.

She always had hated feeling trapped.

His attention snapped back to the present moment as she shrugged, her expression shuttered. "What can I say I never did learn to control that temper of mine."

"At the moment," he said dryly, "I'm far more concerned about why he even wants them, these treasures. Do you know?"

She stared at him for a long moment, unreadable and stone-faced. "No."

"Ria."

"I don't know, Conor. He didn't tell me, and I didn't ask." She looked away at that, fingers twisting together in front of her. "It was the policy that worked best for me, I found soon enough."

A too-familiar pang of sympathy twisted inside of him. "Ria," he said, turning the cloak over and over in his hands. "What are we going to do?"

He looked up to see her chewing on her thumbnail, watching him warily. "I might," she said, "have an idea."

A fortnight after he died and was born again, Jack sat atop his horse, staring at the castle of Tír Soghain in the distance.

'There resides your bride,' the fear-dearg said. 'There alone you shall find her, for there is more magic hidden in the earth of Connacht than all of Eire combined.'

'I shall offer her father a bride-price the likes of which the world has never seen,' said Jack.

'Och,' the fairy said. 'It is not her father you must pay.'

Excerpt from 'The Snow, The Crow, & The Blood'

Chapter Thirty-One
Maigh Eo, Éire, 1082

CONOR

Nearly ten years since he had last seen her, but Conor still knew nothing good could come of that particular look on Riona's face, speculative and sly. "I have never liked your ideas," he said, folding his arms across his chest, and a faint grin curved along her rose-red lips.

"Now cabbage," she said with a return to her former lightness, that sing-song voice that breezed so softly along his skin, his arm hairs prickling at its teasing touch. "When have I ever steered you wrong?"

"When I was eleven, and you said that the blood pudding that had been left out all night in the kitchen instead of being put away in the ice box would be safe to eat, and I spent the next two days vomiting up my guts in the pig-trough as a result."

"How was I to know? I genuinely thought it would be fine."

"I should have known better when you had nary a bite of the stuff."

"Other than that," Riona said with great dignity. "Name one time."

"When we were fourteen, you persuaded me to take the fall for your breaking the glass window in the solar, and I spent three days on garlic-shelling duty because of it."

"And I thanked you for that, very effusively." Her eyes danced.

"A few years later, to be sure, but do you remember now, how well and thoroughly you were thanked for that incident?"

A flush stole up his cheeks, and he shuffled back a step to lean his shoulder against the sap-soaked trunk of the tree. "I think," he said, "it would be best if we stick to the matter at hand."

The glow of her face dimmed. "The cloak," she said, her tone formal and aloof once more. "The cloak should allow me to pass into the sídhe, even if I don't have the blood for it."

"'Should?' You aren't certain?"

"It did for the prince – Jack." She shrugged at his blank look. "I read the full story after Mamó and Daideo passed. It was in the solar, in a collection of other texts that they had collected over the years." She met his gaze coolly, unconcernedly. "I was curious to know the truth of the tale."

"And?" Conor prompted after a moment, when she remained silent, lost in thought. "What was the truth of it?"

"I suppose," she said, very quietly, "that it depends on who you ask."

"What does that mean?"

"It's something that Daideo told me once," she said. "That the lord of death is the master of sweet-sounding lies, of deception and manipulation, of making us doubt fact and put our faith in his fictions."

"There's a reason," said Conor, edging closer to where she stood under the rain-sodden branches, "that he's called the dark druid, Ria."

She shrugged. "Well, I have never been very good with staying away from the darkness, from resisting its allure. I suppose it makes sense, because when it comes to him, sometimes I still doubt myself and what I know about him — sometimes am still not sure what to believe, what to think."

"I don't know." Conor sighed, staring out into the falling rain. "You have always had a knack for distinguishing truth from falsehood. You could always tell when I was lying easily enough – anyone, really. It was a talent of yours."

"A familial gift," she said with another rueful smile, and his eyebrows lifted in a silent question. She shook her head. "A joke," she explained. "Daideo's mother. She was a goddess, you know, of fate and truth."

"And war," he said dryly. "And doom, if I remember correctly, so that seems fitting enough."

She laughed, half-hearted and forced, a faint flush rising up her pale throat. "I suppose."

The rain drops on the tips of her long dark eyelashes glistened, then slipped down the pale curve of her cheek, a phantom tear trail threading its way down to the smooth column of her throat. He had moved too close to her, he realized, drawn toward her sadness, her vulnerability, like a half-starved cat toward a spilled puddle of forgotten milk, greedy for even the smallest taste.

He had always been able to resist her brashness, her bonfire-bright boldness, but this – this was his weakness when it came to her, seeing her as she truly was, that uprooted wildflower wilting in its vase on the windowsill, aching for the cool mountain breeze on its petals, the caress of the unfiltered sunlight on its stem, the freedom from captivity and confinement it was born to know —

— and a sorrowful Riona was a dangerous Riona, one who made him forget all too easily why he needed to keep his distance from her.

He cleared his throat. "So you go," he said, retreating away from that rain-streaked face before he did the unthinkable and reached out to cup her cheek in the palm of his hand, caressing her satin-smooth skin with his thumbs, soothe her, reassure her, treasure her like he had done so many times before. "Take the cloak and go to the sídhe and see if it works. It's a day's journey, two atmost. If it doesn't, come back and we'll figure something else out."

"Right." She nodded, her throat hitching slightly. "If it does work –"

She stopped, and for a moment, there was only the sound of the rain dripping through the evergreen branches of the trees, the distant roll of the thunder from far across the green-sloped hills, and he knew what she had left unsaid between them.

If it did work, if she retrieved the sword with the cloak and delivered them, as promised, to her master, then there would be no reason for her to return, no reason for him to lay eyes on her ever again.

"I'll go with you."

He almost spat the words out, a sudden sense of panic clawing at his throat, an overwhelming surge of dread, and her eyes widened. "Conor –"

"Just to be sure." He wiped his clammy palms against his breeches. "It's dangerous, Ráth Crúachan. You might need me."

Her brow lifted, and he winced. An infinitely foolish thing to say to this dark-haired druidess of seemingly limitless power, who could break a man's legs with a few careless words and a snap of her fingers, only to heal them just as effortlessly.

He opened his mouth to say something, he wasn't sure quite what

– a retraction, an apology – but she surprised him, reaching out to rest her hand on his forearm. "Yes," she said, too quietly. "I would like that, very much."

Conor cleared his throat, the tips of his ears burning. "You don't have to lie," he said. "I know that you don't need me. It was a stupid thing to say."

"Conor." She smiled again, wistful and sad. "I have always, no matter how much I have wished otherwise, needed you."

Riona's fingers slipped away from his arm, gently prying the cream-colored cloak free from his grasp. Her words echoed dully in his ears as she moved away, ducking her head under the branches to step out into the driving rain, just as she did on that long ago night nearly ten years ago.

And his heart broke all over again.

Jack was met outside the castle gates by two dozen, stone-faced guards. Their captain stepped forward. 'Bréanainn,' he said to Jack. 'The princess has heard of your approach, and has agreed to hear your suit – you and your friend.' His eyes flickered to the fear-dearg and away. 'She will meet with you in her garden, as she does all her suitors.'

'All?' Jack asked. 'There have been many?'

'Dozens,' the captain said.

Excerpt from 'The Snow, The Crow, & The Blood'

Chapter Thirty-Two
The Vale of Inagh, Éire, 1073

CONOR

Conor stood, still as a stone, a mere stone's throw from the two people he loved most in the world — Haisley and Riona — and knew beyond a shadow of a doubt that he was about to lose them both.

"I have to go," Riona said again, an eerie, haunted expression settling over her face. "I know how to fix this." A slight pause. "I'm sorry."

She turned away.

"Ria, wait –"

She disappeared, and a moment later, Conor heard the faint snick of the door closing shut behind her. He threw a quick glance at the still-sleeping Haisley, then hurried after her, heart pounding with fear, with confusion.

Where was she going? Why was she leaving – leaving Haisley, leaving him, when they most needed to stand as one, to hold fast to the bonds of love and trust that kept them safely moored during the storms of life, to anchor together this bridge of suffering which they must now cross?

He ran out into the rain, calling her name, following her down the steps and out of the courtyard, down to the stables. He shoved open the door which had slammed shut behind her, then froze.

She was saddling her horse.

She was *leaving* him.

"Riona." He took a few cautious steps forward, staring at her, the loose wave of raven-wing hair that fell across her shoulders, the red slash of her lips in her bone-white face, the cold, distant expression in her bluebell eyes. "What are you doing?"

She said nothing, only continued to saddle her horse with quick, feverish movements, and his palms grew clammy at his sides.

Something was very, very wrong.

"Riona," he said, sharpening his voice. "Answer me. What are you doing? We need to go back to Haisley."

She blinked at that, slow and sluggish, as though she were in a deep slumber. "Haisley," she repeated, flat and emotionless.

"Yes, Riona." It came out sharper, more snappish than he intended. "Haisley. Our daughter. She's sick, Ria, and she needs us – she needs you. You can't disappear on her like this." He reached out to her, aching to touch her, to comfort and to be comforted in return, but she continued to stare unseeingly ahead, her fingers splayed out like icy daggers on the dark brown of the leather saddle, and slowly, he dropped his hand.

"Ria," he said again, urgent and loud. "You need to come back inside. You need to go back to Haisley. She needs you."

Be her mother, he wanted to scream, fingers curling into his palms. *Be her mother, and love her.*

He could never understand it, how distant she had always behaved towards their daughter, so aloof and disinterested. She had rarely ever gotten down on the floor to play with her, a few sleepy snuggles at night, content to watch from a chair in the corner as their daughter danced about the room, shrieking and laughing, as he tickled her sides, or as the nursemaid bounced her on her knee.

He knew that Riona loved Haisley, cared for her, but it was as though she had locked that love away in the deepest dungeons of her soul, chained to a wall in the gloomy darkness, too afraid to let it venture out into the light of day lest it cause her pain, leave her vulnerable to the everyday aches and bruises that come with loving another living soul more than life itself.

She certainly had never allowed herself to love him that much, if at all.

He snapped to attention as she started to speak. "I can fix this," she said, hollow and flat, and his brow furrowed.

"What do you mean, you fix it? You can't fix it, Ria, I told you – there's no cure. Just come back inside, just come be with me, please – "

"I can fix it," she said again, a mechanical, soulless repetition, as though she were a mere ghost of her former self, that vibrant, stubborn, vivacious girl he adored with every fiber of his being. "I will go to the lord of death and bargain away my soul, and in return, I will ask that he spare Haisley."

An owl hooted from the rafters above them, echoing in tandem with the faint sound of the rain drumming on the thatched roof. Conor stepped forward, reaching out for Riona's stiff hand. "Ria sweetheart," he whispered. "You're in shock and not thinking clearly. Come on now, come inside and I'll get you some tea. It'll be all right, Ria."

She withdrew her hand from his, slowly, deliberately. "No," she said, not looking at him, head bowed as she stared at the horse before her, saddled and ready, awaiting only its rider. "I will cut my arm and let my blood run into the sídhe, like that day in the mountains, and I will go into the other-realm of Tech Duinn to see

the lord of death, the dark druid, and ask him to spare Haisley's life."
Her face was so cold, so distant, like a dying star falling thousands
of miles from the surface of the earth. "I will fix it."

The memory cut through him like a knife – the faint silver tinge
of her blood as it dripped from her arm, the unnatural eyes of that
thing that crept from the darkness, the piercing, keening wail that
still sent chills down to his bones whenever he remembered it.

It had haunted him on many a night, the thought of it. Riona,
his blue-eyed girl – she had done that, had summoned that monster
from the shadows. What darkness lurked within her, what demons
walked beside her, this woman who he'd loved for so long?

And now she threatened to bring that darkness to the doorstep
of their daughter.

The air ripped from his lungs, and he stepped backward sharply.
"Riona. No. You promised me – you promised. Never again, you
said."

She said nothing, but after a moment of silence, she pulled herself
up, away from him, and into the saddle.

"No," he said, his tongue thick and cold like a sheet of ice frozen
solid over the loch in the late winter months. "No. I won't let you."

That earned him a brief, fleeting glance, her stare distant and
unyielding. "You can't stop me."

The first sparks of anger ignited within him. How could she be so
foolish, so selfish? "It's too dangerous, Ria. For you *and* for Haisley.
Think of the danger you would put her in." Conor found himself
shouting, desperate to shake that horrible, empty expression from
her face, but again, no answer. "Stay, Ria. Stay with me. I know
that you're scared, terrified for Haisley, and so am I, but I promise
you, I will find a way. I will find a way to keep her well. I promise

you, Ria." His voice broke, and he inhaled, slow and deep, fighting against the tears that threatened to overwhelm him. "I love you, Ria," he said, pleading and soft. "I love you, Haisley loves you – stay with us. Stay with me. Trust in me, in us, *please.*"

She said nothing, her only answer a nudging of her heels into her horse's side, and obediently, the mare moved forward, tossing its mane as it trotted toward the door and the rain and the darkness that awaited them.

Something snapped within him, so many years' worth of sleepless nights and bone-weary days, the endless training in the yard, the aches of his muscles and the dust in his eyes, the ceaseless clanking of steel and metal and the shouts of his father and his men, the never-ending ache of the smell of the herbs in the meadows and the taste of the clean, bright air the endless hours of worry for her too, his wildflower girl, watching her vitality and her spirit slowly, slowly shrivel away, day after day, locked away in that damned castle.

Some part of her must be glad to go, he thought suddenly, if she went so willingly to this dark lord of death, if she so clearly longed to be free of him, free of the child born from the love he had thought that they shared.

"You want this." He shouted it at her back, and for a moment, her horse stilled in its tracks, and he stared up at her, his fists clenched at his side. "You do, don't you? You want to leave us. This isn't about Haisley, this is about you – just like when we were younger. This is about how you want to be free of all this, the responsibilities and the duties and –" He stopped, but the unspoken word hung heavy and hurtful in the air between them.

Us. Free of us.

Her shoulders stiffened, but he continued to seethe, chest heaving, because it was true. He knew it was. She was so clearly desperate for any excuse to ride off into the night and never return, to abandon Haisley, to abandon him – him, who had always needed her, against all reason, against all odds of her ever needing him back.

"Riona." She refused to look at him, merely sat straight and stiff-backed in the saddle, staring ahead at the door to freedom that beckoned her, called to her. "If you do this thing – if you leave here tonight, you will *never* see either of us again."

For a few interminable heartbeats, Conor refused to breathe, watching her, waiting, and then her heels dug into the sides of her mare, and they were gone, galloping out the stable door and into the night.

He ran after her, the rain falling in earnest now, heavy and cold, mocking his pain, the bright blinding-hot lash of grief that wrestled with the surge of anger boiling inside him. "Never again, Ria," he yelled after her, his hands shaking and his stomach churning. "You will never see either of our faces again."

And then he was alone, save for the rain that mingled with the tears falling fast and hot down his cheeks, and, just as he had foreseen all those years ago, his inevitably shattered heart.

Ever since that terrible night nearly ten years ago, Conor had regretted it with every fiber of his being — letting Riona vanish into the darkness. He had lain awake so many nights, staring up at the sky stretched out in the cool grass, wishing he had caught her up in his arms and held her close, refused to allow her to leave, forced her to remember that whatever terrible truths were crashing down around them, they were strongest together, that nothing could defeat them, not even death itself, so long as they were hand in hand and heart to heart.

So he hurried after her now, unwilling to watch her vanish again over a rainswept horizon, the need to keep her close, to have her near, propelling him forward into the driving sheets of rain, Oscar grumbling as he loped by his side. "Ria," he called, and she paused, her hands still halfway to her head as she pulled her hood tight around her face. "I'm coming with you."

Her smile, he thought to himself as he fell into step beside her, was the only sun that he would ever need.

The captain led Jack to an oak door
inlaid with iron bars, then placed a key
in the lock. It clicked once, strident and
squealing, and the captain stepped
aside, gesturing for Jack to enter. 'This
is her garden.'

Jack brushed by him without
answering, impatience to at last see his
bride surging within him. His vision
swam for a moment, then settled, and
even as the door slammed shut behind
him and the fear-dearg close at his
heels, the prince sucked in a horrified
breath.

Excerpt from 'The Snow, The Crow, &
The Blood'

Chapter Thirty-Three
Coillte Mach, Éire, 1082

CONOR

"Do you know," Riona said breezily as they ducked underneath the eave of the tumbledown bruiden, shivering with cold and Oscar whining at their feet. "It never rains in the sídhe. So you see, there are a few perks to being the servant of death, after all."

Conor was half-frozen, soaked to the skin, exhausted from hours of walking, and in no mood for her jokes. "The price for never getting your head wet – the eternal damnation for your soul."

"Exactly. Damned I may be, but with fabulous hair," she said, pushing open the door to the hostel, arrowing straight for the small fire burning cheerfully in the red-brick hearth. Conor stomped after her, his boots squelching on the floor while Oscar trotted at his side, tail drooping, evoking a fresh pang of guilt. He should have left the dog with Haisley, with Kayleigh and Páidí, warm and well-fed in their snug little home, not dragged him along on this insane adventure that surely could only end in death for at least one of them.

The host, a red-cheeked, black-bearded fellow, hurried forward to greet them. "Travelers," he said. "It's a nasty night for walking, don't you know. What'll you have?"

"Supper," Riona said, just as Conor said, "A room, with two beds." He shot her a narrowed glance, and she smiled, guileless, the orange-and-red flames illuminating the pale curves of her face. "The supper first," she said. "And for the gods' sake, best make sure there are two beds in that room. My delicate virtue couldn't stand otherwise."

The host shifted on his feet, his brow furrowed, and Conor cleared his throat. "Excuse my sister. She becomes a bit impudent when she's hungry."

"And I am absolutely ravenous right now, so you've been warned," Riona added brightly, and the host frowned.

"We have shepherd's pie," he said. "Fresh from the stove, and bread."

"Delightful." Riona edged closer to the hearth, and Oscar moved with her, shaking out his wet fur. Her nose wrinkled. "A plate of bones for the dog as well, I suppose, and some hot cider for the humans." Riona tugged off her gloves with her teeth, flapping her soggy skirts in front of the fire. "I know that I could certainly use a drink." She turned, still graceful and smooth despite her sopping clothes, the wet hair plastered against her face and sank down on a smooth wooden bench by a table, stretching out her legs with a sigh and wriggling her stockinged toes free of her water-logged slippers. "Join me, won't you, *brother* mine?"

Conor shot an apologetic look toward the host, whose lips were twisted in a decidedly disapproving expression. "If you please," he said, easing down on the bench across from where Riona reclined so regally. "Whenever you get the chance."

Riona eyed the half-dozen other patrons sitting clustered at the other tables in the smoky hall. "He is hardly swamped with customers," she said after the host had scuttled away, huffing to himself under his breath. "And we do intend to pay him, after all.

The least he could do is hurry it up."

"Pay him? With what, exactly, Ria?" Conor drummed his fingers on the table. "Or do you have several pocketfuls of gold tucked away under your gown?"

"Have you been thinking about it then – what's tucked away, as you say, underneath my skirts?" Her eyebrow arched. "Interesting."

"I only have a few copper coins. I was hardly expecting to trek across the realm when I left home this morning."

"Don't be so dramatic. It's a three-day journey, there and back, at most. 'Trek' is a bit much."

"I can't afford to pay the man for both supper and a room."

"Was your plan to starve me then? A few days with no food, that should do her in, was that what you were thinking?"

"Now who is being ridiculous. I told you, I've plenty of dried lamb and fruit in my bag."

"That's a yes, then, to the starving. I'll not be forgetting this, cabbage."

He rolled his eyes even as he fought the urge to smile. "I'm serious, Ria. I can't afford the price of a meal, much less two."

"I'll have to pay for my supper some other way then."

Conor winced as the host bobbled two frothy tankards of mead by them, his eyes round and wide in his bearded face. "She's only having a joke," he said, and the host hesitated with their drinks in his hands, eying him doubtfully.

Riona leaned forward with a too-sweet smile. "I'm really not," she said. "How would you like to see a bit of magic?"

I t hardly took a full hour before they were practically fawning at her feet, the whole damn bruiden, host and hostess, patrons and passerbys alike. Word had spread throughout the village about the black-haired witch performing magic in the local tavern, and even the continued downpour of rain and ominous roll of thunder did not keep them away. The little hall was packed to the brim with spectators, wide-eyed with awe – and a little bit with fear – of her guttural growl, of the sight of the red and green apples dancing along the ceiling beams of the bruiden, of the harp in the corner coming to life on its own to play a lively tune, strum by a pair of clever, invisible hands.

Conor was enthralled himself, watching her while his forgotten plate of shepherd's pie grew cold on the table before him, so entranced was he with the sight of her keen, pointy-chin face glowing with excitement, her fingers flying through the air as she conjured visions of deep purple petals and red roaring dragons and silver-blue horses swirling through the smoky air. He had never before seen her like this, so bright and unfettered and brimming with life.

When had she lost this, he wondered, this blazing vitality, so luminous and bright that it quite literally lit up this dank little room? He watched as she raised her hand, almost idly, carelessly, and flicked her wrist with a few low-voiced commands, and a storm of a thousand golden sparks showered down upon her rapt audience, roaring in amazement, in awe.

She did not belong in the darkness, this girl with her sun-bright smile.

A shadow of worry fell across him, dimming his thrill of seeing her so lighthearted and glowing. He picked at the congealed meat in front of him with his fork, jaw tight. As if sensing his dissatisfaction, the host materialized at Conor's side, wringing his calloused hands anxiously, keeping an entranced eye all the while on Riona in the center of the hall. "Is everything to your liking? Some cider, perhaps? Or tea cake? Sweet bread? Ginger snaps?"

"She wouldn't say no to the cake," he said, nodding at Riona, who caught him looking and waved merrily, causing a shower of golden stars to streak towards the corner of the hall where he sat hunched over the table. Heads swiveled in his direction, then whirled back to gaze up at Riona with wide-eyed fascination.

The host nodded, licking eagerly at his lips. "She's a marvel," he said. "I've never seen such a crowd. My wife cannot pour their drinks fast enough, don't you know. I must have her back again."

"We're only passing through."

"It's no illusion, what she conjures. It's real – real magic." The host shivered a little as Riona cupped her hands and whispered something inaudible into her palms, and out sprang a dark crimson fountain. Conor tensed for one terrified moment, then relaxed against the edge of the table. Wine, he realized, listening as the roar of the crowd increased tenfold, chairs scraping as they scrambled forward, waving their flagons delightedly, and Riona dropped her hands to her sides, watching with satisfaction. The host shook his head in wonder, unperturbed, apparently, that she had conjured away the rest of his drink orders for the evening. "I thought that I'd never see it, the day that magic returned to Éire."

"There will always be magic in the land of Éire," Conor said absently, rubbing at his chin, remembering Mamó smiling down at him as they tramped through the woods, the low hum of her voice as she murmured to him about fairy thimbles and honeysuckle and the magic found within the juices of a rowan tree. "You only have to know where to look for it."

The host clucked his tongue, moving away from where Conor sat, back toward the explosion of light and color and sound that Riona had conjured for them in the middle of the little hall. "Tonight," he said, "I do not have to look very far."

It was well past midnight when at last Conor managed to tear her away from the wondrous crowd, tugging her up the stairs by her sleeve as she licked happily at her sugary fingertips. "Those tea cakes were to die for," she said, smothering a yawn, and even Oscar yipped once, a wordless agreement, his tail wagging contentedly as he trotted into their room.

"I wouldn't know," he said, tossing his leather satchel on the chair by the door. "I was too afraid that I might do exactly that if I tried to take one from your plate."

She made a face, pausing by the door to face him. "It was much easier here, somehow," she said. "The spells, the conjurings. It was so difficult, in the sídhe, so arduous, but here – here it was as natural as breathing."

"I would have thought it would have been the other way around."

"I know." She shrugged. "Perhaps because this is where it was meant to be used. Druidecht is mortal-made magic, after all." She peeked her head around the doorframe, studying the room. "How surprising."

He glanced inside, confused. "What?"

"There are two beds."

"I know." He strode further into the room, stretching out on the one closest to the door, folding his arms behind his bed as he toed off his boots. "I asked for two. I'm a bit old to be sleeping on the floor two nights running."

"Yes, but it's just – well, I suppose for some reason, I expected there to only be one bed, for no other reason than that you specifically requested two."

"That makes no sense."

She laughed, flopping down on her stomach across the other bed on the far side of the room. "Never mind," she said. "It was just a thought. Clearly I was wrong."

A twinge of nervousness pricked behind his closed eyelids. He shot a wary glance in her direction, her prone shape barely visible in the darkened room, the glow from the low-burning fire in the hearth soft and dim. "Were you hoping that there would only be one bed?"

Her answer was muffled, her face buried in the pillow. "Don't flatter yourself."

He grinned into the darkness. "Wouldn't be much of a stretch to think so," he said. "If I'm remembering it right."

There was a long pause, then the bedsprings creaked slightly as she rolled over on her back, her posture a mirror to his own, ankles crossed and arms tucked behind her head. "Conor," she said. "How much of that cider did you drink?"

"A couple tankards." He shrugged. "Maybe three. No – four, actually. Brecken refilled my mug once before I was quite finished."

"Brecken?"

"Our host."

"Oh." A log in the fire popped, sending a faint shower of sparks against the red sandstone wall of the hearth. "I didn't know his name."

"You didn't ask." He yawned, nestling deeper into the straw-filled mattress. "You never do."

"What is that supposed to mean?"

"Nothing." He glanced over in her direction. "Why did you ask me, how much cider I'd had?"

"It seemed," she said, a touch frostily, "like you were flirting with me, and I remember too well how amorous you can get after you have…overindulged in drink."

He gave a gruff laugh, even though the memory of that long ago night flooded through him, a white-hot firebrand of soft skin and hungry touches exploring uncharted territories of voluptuous curves and unimaginable delights for the very first time. "Yes," he said, sounding far hoarser, hungrier, than he'd intended. "I remember too. Very well."

A brief pause. "Conor." He half-winced at her tone, infinitely gentle and preemptively explanatory. "No."

"No to what? I didn't even suggest anything."

She sighed. "Oh cabbage. We both know that we lost whatever chance at happiness we might have had together a long time ago."

"I know." He inhaled deeply, trying in vain to catch the woodsy scent of her, silverweed and fresh-picked clover, among the faint tinge of cedarwood smoke that wafted through the room. "I can't help it though – the remembering. The missing you."

She sighed, heavy and deep. "Don't, Conor."

"Don't what?"

"You know what."

He shifted restlessly on the bed. "I can't help it," he said again after a moment. "It's still there, you know, in spite of everything."

"Everything? That's putting it lightly enough. I tortured you. I broke both your legs, Conor, your fingers."

"You put them back together easily enough."

He could feel her wariness, her guardedness, even shrouded in the dark as she was, emanating all the way across the room. "I broke your heart too."

"You could fix that too, maybe."

The silence that followed this tentative query was torturous, almost too painful to bear, and he closed his eyes, silently cursing himself. On the other side of the room, the mattress shifted, and he peeked over to see her roll over onto her side, propped up on her elbow, serious and solemn in the dim light of the fire. "You were right," she said. "What you told me, before. I cannot come home, back to the vale, once all this is over."

He forced himself to look away, to stare at the crisscrossing wooden beams above them, studying them with determined intensity. "I shouldn't have said that. Forget it."

"Listen to me, Conor. It isn't that I don't want to, you know. I do, more than anything. But –" Her voice cracked a little, and he kept his gaze fixed on the ceiling, unwilling to risk seeing a hint of a tear on her cheeks. It would break whatever parts of him were still whole, still salvageable within him if he did. "But I don't know how to become one of the living again, Conor, after spending so long among the dead. I am a lost soul, just as much as any of them, you know. The things that I have seen, that I have done – I can never come home, not like before."

He was quiet for a moment, watching the soft orange-and-red glow of the hearth-fire playing along the sand-colored beams above him. "Then don't go home," he said at last. "But don't go back to him, Ria. Don't go back to that place of darkness, of despair.

We could find you a new home, somewhere far away from here, high within the mountains on the other side of the vale, close to your cousins' home, where you could be happy – be set free, finally, of all the things that have tried so long to keep you locked away in the shadows. Not just the sídhe, but your mother, the vale, all of it." He swallowed, daring to risk a glance in her direction, her cheek resting in her hand, bright-eyed and intent in the gloom. "You could be who you were always meant to be, a wildflower on the side of the mountain, free to grow, to blossom."

"I will never understand," she said, "how you have always been able to look at me and see something good. How you still can, after everything that I have done to you, is utterly baffling."

He shifted uncomfortably. "You were scared," he said. "Angry. It wasn't right, but I understand it."

"You are *such* a cabbage."

"I know that, too."

A brief pause, and then there was a rustle of sheets and skirts, and she was coming toward him, her pale face shining in the firelight. He sat up swiftly, crossing his arms across the tops of his knees, and she sank down on the end of his bed, studying him, head cocked to the side. "You haven't mentioned your father at all."

"Right." He cleared his throat, keeping his gaze fixed on his hands dangling between his bent legs. "He died a few years ago. His heart gave out, the castle healer thought."

"I see." She was quiet for a moment, watching him through the darkness, searching and grave. "Were you sad?"

"He was my father, wasn't he? Of course I mourned him."

"Yes," she said. "But were you sad?"

His throat felt impossibly tight, too constricted. "No," he managed to whisper. "I wasn't particularly sad," and she leaned forward then, her fingertips brushing through the curls of his hair.

"Oh Conor." Her voice was soft as silk, her hands impossibly gentle as she stroked the sides of his face. "I'm so sorry. I'm so very sorry."

"It's all right." He swallowed thickly. "We were never close, he and I. I had always been a disappointing son to him."

"It was not you who did the disappointing, Conor." She slid closer until she was nestled beside him, their shoulders pressed together as they leaned back against the headrest. She laid her sleek black head against his shoulder, and for a moment, he allowed himself to breathe it in, that dearly loved smell of silverweed and clover. "He was too harsh – too blind to see that you were perfect just the way that you were."

"Still." He rested his cheek on the top of her head, his eyes fluttering shut as she snuggled in closer, tucking herself in tight against his chest. "I should have grieved him more. He was my da." He drew in a shaky breath, another unwilling memory resurfacing, forcing its way into his sleepy consciousness. "My da."

Jack was surrounded by rose bushes, blooming and thriving even in the midwinter air, exploding with blossoms of soft pink petals, and side by side with their velvety, sweet-scented beauty, the severed head of a young man adorning each flowering bush, eyes wide and unseeing in pale, horrorstruck faces, slack mouths ajar with a silent scream.

Excerpt from "The Snow, The Crow, & The Blood"

Chapter Thirty-Four
Maigh Eo, Éire, 1076

CONOR

It was a late morning in early spring, and Conor had been standing outside in the cool sunlight for a very long time, gathering his courage, strengthening his resolve, before he finally rapped lightly on the door of the thatched hut before him.

"It's open," a soft voice called, and he pushed the door inward, stepping inside. "Kayleigh," he said, nodding to where the woman to whom he had entrusted his daughter, sitting by the fire. She looked up from her knitting, and smiled in response, welcoming and warm as always.

"Hello, Conor." She gestured to the back door of the cottage. "She's just outside, getting a bit of sun. She is tired of being cooped up indoors."

"Been especially rainy," he said, his gaze straying toward the window, where he could glimpse a head full of copper-red curls glinting in the sunlight. "It's good to see the sun for a change," and Kayleigh smiled again.

"Go on now," she said, resuming her knitting. "She'll be so happy to see you."

Conor slipped out the door and stopped, watching from a few feet away.

She was so pretty, this little girl of his, his hazelnut, with her tangled mop of curls and pale rosebud mouth. How Riona would love to see her – Mamó's eyes, bright and happy and unclouded by grief and loss, staring back at them out of their daughter's face.

He squatted down by the table where she sat, the nub of a well-worn pencil clutched in her tiny hand, the tip of her pink tongue poking out from the corner of her mouth. "A chnó coill," he said, and Haisley's curly red head popped up, her face breaking into a smile. "How's she cutting?"

"Uncail Con," she shrieked, throwing her arms around his neck, and for the briefest moment, he closed his eyes and breathed her in, smelling of blackberry jam and lavender. "I've missed you."

"Och, me too, little one." He pulled back, studying her face. "You've grown. Look how tall you've gotten."

"Mamaí says I need new dresses."

"Well," Conor said, settling down cross-legged on the grass, and she crawled into his lap, snuggling into his chest. "That sounds a bit like you need to be taken into the village to the dressmaker, now."

She bounced up excitedly, and he winced as the top of her head smacked into his chin. "And a new doll, too! Please, Uncail Con, please!"

Da, he ached to say, the word burning on the tip of his tongue. You used to call me Da, when you were not much more than a babe.

He smiled instead, ruffling her curls. "Let's ask Mamaí first, and if she says yes, I might be convinced to buy a doll or two for my favorite girl."

"And apple cake. It's my favorite."

Conor ignored the white-hot pang in his heart, the sudden memory washing over him in a wave of fresh pain – Riona, grinning at him in the candlelight, sitting among the tousled sheets of her bed clad only in his shirt, feeding him bites of sweet-spiced apple cake between long, lingering kisses. "Mine too." He tugged on a loose curl of her hair. "Go wash up a bit before we go, a chnó coill. I need to speak to Mamaí for a minute."

She skipped away, arms swinging at her sides, and that ever-present coil of worry and fear eased at the sight of her, radiant and glowing with health and blossoming with happiness.

He had made the right call, hiding her away. He knew it in his bones, even though his heart ached for what might have been, for all the years that he had lost, the hundreds of bedtime stories and secret smiles and shrieks of laughter and tiny milestones that he had missed and could never gain back. He had kept her safe, his precious girl, and that was all that mattered.

Conor ducked his head as he went back inside to where Kayleigh stood in the tiny kitchen, stirring at a pot boiling on the cast-iron stove. "Apparently," he said, "someone needs new dresses, and new dolls, and a bit of apple cake. She's quite mistreated here, clearly."

"Clearly," Kayleigh smiled, wiping her hands on her apron. "She's grown like a weed these past few months. A couple new gowns wouldn't hurt."

"I'll see to it." He crossed his arms and leaned against the wall. "How's Páidí?"

"Good, good. He'll be sorry to have missed you."

"Tell him I said hello, and – well, thank you, again. Thank you always."

Kayleigh shook her head. "None of that. We love her like our own, Conor, you know that. She's a sweet-natured child, just like her da."

Conor cleared his throat. "How is she doing? Any sickness?"

"A touch of cold a fortnight ago." Kayleigh turned to face him. "She was a bit high for a few days, but nothing too alarming." His expression must have shown his worry, his fear, because Kayleigh reached out to pat his hand with hers reassuringly. "She's fine, Conor," she said quietly. "You needn't worry so much."

He shook his head. "That's like telling the rain not to fall, don't you know." Conor closed his eyes. "But I'm glad – glad that she's here, with you. It's better this way," and for a moment, he almost believed it.

The sound of running footsteps thundered down the hall, and he stepped away toward the front door. "I'll have her back by supper," he said, then smiled. "We'll bring back the apple cake for dessert."

"Will you stay?" Haisley slipped her hand into Conor's, peering up at him with a beseeching gaze. "For supper?"

Conor imagined it for a moment, a fourth chair pulled up their small square table, Haisley giggling in the firelight, chattering about the egregious amount of purchases he would no doubt soon be buying her. He imagined Páidí, with his kind, weathered face and easy smile, patting her head as she beamed up at him when he returned home from his work in the fields.

Da, she would say to someone who was not him.

"I'm afraid I can't," he said lightly. "I'll have to get back and see to Oscar, poor wee doggie. He'll be lonely without me if I stay away too long."

Haisley's lip drooped for a brief second. "All right," she said, then brightened immediately. "We should go see the butcher and get him a bone. Then he won't be sad."

"There's an idea." Conor wrapped his fingers around her tiny ones and avoided Kayleigh's gaze, soft with sympathy as it was.

"Tell Mamaí goodbye. We'll be back in a bit."

He held tight to her hand as she skipped along beside him, prattling away with buoyant cheeriness, and tried to convince himself that this – her health and her happiness and this occasional affection she showered upon him – it was enough for him.

It would have to be.

'What is this?' Jack gasped to the fear-dearg, staring at the severed head of a beardless young boy, a spiderweb of black-and-blue veins meandering their way up his bluish cheek.

Excerpt from 'The Snow, The Crow, & The Blood'

Chapter Thirty-Five
Coillte Mach, Éire, 1082

CONOR

Conor awoke with a start from his memory-dream, Riona's head still cradled against his chest. Between Oscar's short, staccato barks of alarm, he could hear someone knocking on their door, soft, urgent knocks, and his arm tightened instinctively around Riona's shoulders. "Ria." He nudged her with the tip of his nose, pulling away gently as he slid off the bed. "Ria, wake up."

Her eyes blinked open, bleary and sleepy. "What's wrong?"

"Someone's — Oscar, be *quiet* — someone's at the door."

She sat up, rubbing at her face with the back of her hand. "Who is it?"

"Stay there. Let me take a look." Before he could say anything else, the knocking resumed, a little louder, more insistent, and Oscar's barks became a howl of outrage.

"Please." The muffled voice of the host bled through the door. "I don't mean to disturb, but there's something you need to be seeing."

Conor glanced back at Riona, who shrugged and climbed off the bed, yawning and scooping up the yowling dog in her arms before stumbling over to him. "Might as well open up," she said, then poked his shoulder when he hesitated. "I think that I can handle myself if he means us harm, cabbage, don't you?" She plopped Oscar into his arms and reached past him to undo the latch, pulling the door open. The light from the hallway torches spilled in the room, and Conor watched as Riona's sleepy expression froze into something like horror.

He stepped forward, yanking the door all the way open. "Ria –"

His voice died away, and he stood next to Riona in the threshold, his heart frozen in his chest.

There next to the host, soaked to the bone and with petulant eyes and sullen lips, stood Haisley.

For a moment, Conor simply stared at his daughter, dimly wondering if somehow he had imbibed some of Riona's magic and conjured her here merely by dreaming of her, this sullen-eyed girl with her arms wrapped tightly around her shoulders, chin raised high in defiance.

It was Riona who spoke first, brushing by Conor to reach out and press her palm against Haisley's wet cheek. "Haisley," she said. "What on earth are you doing here?"

Haisley said nothing, her lips pressed in a stubborn line, her gaze fixed on the floor, and the host eased forward a step, his hands raised helplessly in the air. "My wife and I had just settled into bed," he said with a nervous glance at Riona, "when there was a knocking at the door. I opened it up to find her standing there, shivering in the rain. She said that she knew you."

Conor shook himself free of his shock, his rising horror, and set Oscar down carefully on the floor. Haisley, here, so far from home. "She's my niece," he said, and his chest tightened at the look that Haisley shot him from beneath her lowered eyelashes, speculative and scornful.

She knows, he thought. Somehow, she knows the truth.

The host heaved a sigh, clearly relieved. "Well then," he said, clapping his hands together and backing away. "I'll let you rest then."

"She needs dry clothes." He froze in place as Riona skewered him with her cool stare. "And something to eat, some hot tea to warm her."

Brecken's fingers twisted nervously. "My wife is in bed."

"Are you incapable," Riona asked, far too gently to be polite, "of boiling a bit of water and putting biscuits on a plate?"

His shoulders hunched. "I'll see to it." He risked another glance at where Haisley stood, a puddle forming at her feet as the rainwater dripped off her clothes. "My wife's clothes will be a bit large for her."

"It will do for tonight," Riona said, dismissing him with a wave of her hand. "Her own clothes will dry by the morning. Hurry along, man, before she catches a chill. Tea and biscuits, if you please."

He jerked his head silently and hurried away, and Riona reached out and snagged Haisley's elbow, dragging her into the room. "What were you thinking?" She hissed, pulling her toward the fire. "You might have died, you foolish girl."

Haisley jerked her arm free, whirling to glare at Conor, ignoring Oscar's happy pawing at her legs. "You lied to me."

Conor took a nervous step back. "A chnó coill –"

"Don't you dare." Haisley jabbed a furious finger at him, and it was so familiar, the indignant gesture, that Conor's gaze flickered involuntarily to where Riona stood, silent and watchful. "How could you lie to me, all these years? I heard Mamaí and Da talking. I heard them. You aren't my uncle at all."

Riona and Conor exchanged a quick glance. "What did you hear?"

Haisley crossed her arms, stomping her wet boot impatiently on the floor. "That you're my father, obviously – my *real* one."

Conor rubbed at his still-drowsy eyes. "Haisley. This is not – this is not a conversation that we should be having right now, without your mamaí and da here."

"And certainly not on an empty stomach and no sleep." Riona's voice was soft and low, and Conor risked a glance in her direction. Her face was expressionless, empty, her true thoughts carefully hidden away behind high stone walls. "You are angry, Haisley, and you have every right to be, but the best thing for everyone right now would be a bite of food and then bed. We can discuss this in the morning."

"And you." Haisley whirled to face Riona. "Who, exactly, are you? Why should I listen to you?"

Riona smiled, cool and distant. "As fate would have it," she said. "I am your mother, and you'll listen to me because I said so." She turned to Conor, grinning, but he could see the uncertainty hovering beneath the bravado in her expression. "I have been waiting to say that for almost twelve years, don't you know," and Conor watched helplessly as Haisley's whole world fell apart right before his eyes.

After Riona's pronouncement, Haisley simply stared in shock, mouth ajar. Riona clasped her fingers together in front of her and smirked, clearly pleased by the effect of her revelation. Conor licked his lips, nervous, but a soft knock at the door had interrupted any further conversation. "Thank the gods," he muttered, yanking it open to accept the dry gown and tray of bread and a steaming cup of lavender tea from Brecken, who peered into the room with intense curiosity. "Will there be anything else?"

"This is grand, many thanks," Conor said, easing the door shut. He leaned against it, loosing a long sigh. "Haisley," he said quietly. "Let's talk about it in the morning, all right? Just – stall it, for tonight, and get a bit of rest for now."

Haisley did not move from her spot by the fire, hands clenched at her sides, gaze locked on Riona's coolly amused face. "My mother," she said, in a flat voice, and Conor moved forward, easing the tray of food down on the table by the hearth. He put his hands on Haisley's shoulders, and reluctantly, she turned her gaze to his, her green eyes brimming with resentment. "A chnó coill," he said, pleading and soft. "I will tell you everything tomorrow, I swear. But it will do us no good to get tangled in the mess of this now. All right?"

Her expression flickered, and underneath his hands, her shoulders sagged slightly. "All right," she whispered, and he pulled her into his chest, hugging her tight, the rain from her hair and her clothes soaking into his shirt. "I need to check my blood," she said, and he pulled back to brush her wet hair off her forehead. "I feel off."

"Let's do that then," he said. She gave him a tight, forced smile, and it broke something inside of him to see it, his girl, so distant and stand-offish from him.

Nothing more was said between them as Haisley changed quickly behind the curtain in the room, nor as she sat by the fire and pricked the tip of her finger, her tongue peeking out of the corner of her mouth as she splashed the tiny drop of crimson on the dull green rock that hung around her neck, Conor and Riona watching in silence as it glowed silver as the blood seeped into its pores. He said nothing as she drank her tea and ate her bread in stony silence, ignoring them both, then stood, wiping at her mouth with the back of her hand, and without a word, climbed into the bed in the corner, pulling the blankets up over her shoulder and turning on her side, her back to both of them, Oscar nestled into her side.

It had not taken long before her breathing grew deep and even, and soon she rolled over onto her back, one arm flung across her face, fast asleep. Conor sank down on the edge of the other bed, and after a moment, Riona joined him, sitting in silence for a long time, watching their daughter sleep.

"Well," Riona said at last. "One bed after all. Imagine that."

Conor half-laughed, half-sobbed, dropping his weary face into his hands.

"What are we going to tell her, Ria?" He asked, his face buried in his hands.

Her hand rubbed soothingly, lightly on his back. "The truth," she said gently. "She's right, you know. She deserves that much." Her touch fell away. "I told you – she's not a child any longer. She's half-grown, a little woman now."

"She's not even twelve," he protested again, weakly this time, and she nudged him with her elbow.

"Do you remember us at eleven, cabbage? The mischief we made, the trouble we caused?"

"*You* caused most of it, as I recall."

"So I did, and I was rather clever about it too. Is it so surprising that she would be the same?"

He dropped his hands, turning his head to stare at her ruefully. "Kayleigh said that she's been going through a bit of a rebellious stage. I suppose I should have known that something like this was coming." He sighed. "They must be frantic, Kayleigh and Páidí. We'll have to take her home, come the dawn."

"No." Riona shifted to face him, her fingers latching onto his wrist. "We can't, Conor. We've come this far –"

"It's a day's journey, Ria. We'll take her home and come right back. It'll barely cost us any time at all."

"For what purpose? She'll only follow us again. She's come after us for a reason because she's curious, and rightly so, about what all this means."

"Riona." He forced what little steel his father had passed down to him into his voice. "We will not be taking our daughter to that place. We agreed on that."

"That was before." She shifted closer to him, urgent and pleading. "She's here now already. I can protect her, truly. Just let her come, let her see us, know us – let me know *her*, before I'm gone again."

"It's too dangerous," he said again. "We're taking her home in the morning."

"You know it won't do any good," she said. "She's run off once, and she'll do it again. It would be far more dangerous for her to stumble upon the sídhe by herself, without me there to guide her." Her brows lifted even as her lips tightened into a fierce, white line. "You do remember what I did the first time I saw it, don't you?"

"Ria –"

"We need her." Her eyes were a luminous, too-bright blue, sharp and brittle with longing. "I cannot guarantee that the cloak will work, Conor. It'll be good that she's there, just in case." The faint orange-red flames of the dying hearth-fire danced across the curves of her face. "Please, cabbage."

"Kayleigh and Páidí will be frantic with worry."

"We can send them a message in the morning." Her lips trembled. "Tell them that she's safe with you. They'll understand."

"We agreed that this was a bad idea, that we needed to keep Haisley out of this, at all costs."

"That was before. She's already in the thick of it now, Conor. Surely you must see that."

He was weakening, relenting, as he always had, helpless to resist the power of those sad, shattered eyes, those pleading lips, the yearning so clearly etched on every feature of her face.

"Promise me that Haisley will not go anywhere near that place."

Her nails dug into his skin. "She won't," she said. "I swear. I won't let anything happen to her. You must know that. I would never – I would *die* for her, Conor."

"And if at any point," he continued determinedly, "I'm not comfortable with the situation, if I think for a second that she is in jeopardy, it ends right then, Riona, and I take her home – alone – no questions, no arguments."

"I won't –"

Conor cut her off, pressing his finger against her lips. "Promise me right now, Riona."

"I promise," she whispered, and he pulled his hand away from her mouth, rubbing at his aching forehead.

"I am trying," he said softly, "to trust you again, Ria. I believe that you meant well, all those years ago. I believe that you mean well now, but that is not always enough."

"I know." She smiled, strained and tremulous. "It is enough for me that you are willing to try."

He tried to ignore the brush of her fingers against his as she settled closer to him on the mattress. "For Haisley's sake," he said. "That's the only reason I'm willing to allow this. She deserves to know the truth, about who she is – and to know you."

In unison, they looked over at Haisley. "I wish they could have seen her, Mamó and Daideo," Riona said after a moment, and Conor shook his head.

"Ria." His tone was rueful, almost tender even, as he watched their daughter sleeping in her bed, the blanket tangled around her. "She's the very image of you, but with your grandmother's eyes, both of his best girls, all rolled into one. Daideo would have turned her into a right little monster with his spoiling, and you know it."

"I do, and I would have loved to see it."

For a moment, they smiled at one another, only inches apart, and the cavernous void that had stretched so awful and empty for so many years between them vanished, as that long lost thrum of steady, familiar love began singing in his ears once again.

Such a simple, quiet thing, that unsung melody, the tune he had heard humming within him for nearly all his life.

Conor looked away quickly, clearing his throat. Some things, he reminded himself, were better left lost, no matter how soft and pretty and lonely they looked, bathed in the firelight's glow.

He pushed to his feet. "I'll sleep on the floor."

"You don't have to." How could she, with her unscalable walls and impenetrable heart, sound so tentative, so unsure? "There is room for both of us."

"I'll sleep on the floor," he repeated, ignoring the answering sag of her shoulders, and reached behind her to snag a pillow. "But I am stealing this."

He stretched out by the fire, his back to where Riona remained upright on the side of the bed, forcing himself to lie unmoving and still, save for the steady rise and fall of his chest, until at last he heard the mattress creak and the blankets rustle as she laid down to sleep for the last few hours of the night, and he allowed himself to relax into the thin pillow.

There would always be magic to be found in Éire, in enchantments and elves, in the whispering wind, but he had never cared to look for it.

For him, she had always been magic enough.

Jack's horrified gaze left the headless boy to slowly travel over to where a lady stood, her hands clasped neatly in front of her, watching him with a smile on her blood-red lips, her raven-wing hair neatly pinned back from her smooth white face with a bright golden comb.

Excerpt from 'The Snow, The Crow, & The Blood'

Chapter Thirty-Six
The Vale of Inagh, Éire, 1071

CONOR

Conor lay on his back in the moonlight, Riona's head on his chest, and knew that this moment could very well be the happiest he'd ever been, or ever would be again, in his life.

He didn't blame her, but Riona tended to swing back and forth, to blow hot and cold, in her affection for him. Some days, she would be loving and devoted, and the next, without warning, distant and cold, staring at him with the icy blue eyes of a complete stranger. It was hard to navigate the dips and surges of her love for him, but Conor didn't care – whatever scraps of love Riona chose to give him, no matter how fleeting, he would accept unconditionally.

Even if he knew that there was a very real possibility that the next time she decided to love him again could be the last.

But right now, in this moment, she loved him, and he loved her, and it was a beautiful autumn night, both of them sleepy and warm and well-sated with the taste and touch of the other, and she was lying quiet and content and softly, uncharacteristically playful in his arms.

"Would you still love me," she asked, "if I had the snout of a pig?"

"Undoubtedly," Conor said. "I loved you last week when you had that awful cold. Sure now, your nose was as red and swollen as a pig's then."

She thumped his ear. "You arse," she said. "You're supposed to think I'm beautiful, always, even when I'm sick, or when I'm old and gray."

Conor laughed, nuzzling his nose into the silken sheen of her black hair, savoring the scent of her. "I never said I didn't think you were beautiful. Obviously, you still were and would be the prettiest girl in the world, no matter what nose you had."

"So you'll still love me when I'm as old and wrinkled as Mamó was?"

"Of course," Conor said staunchly. "As long as you're as beautiful as Mamó was when you're that old."

She bit him then, light and teasing but with enough zest to provoke a laughing yelp, and they wrestled together in the cool grass like the barely-grown children they were, giggling and panting as they tussled back and forth, until their touches became hungrier, more urgent, sliding up skirts and into hair, pulling each other close instead of pushing away, lips and tongues and arms intertwined so closely that there ceased to be two, and only became one.

Later, the two of them sprawled out on their stomachs, side by side, staring into each other's sleepy eyes, the blue and the gray, the dark and the light. "I will, you know," Conor whispered. "Love you, even when we're both old."

"I know," she whispered back. "You're a very predictable cabbage."

"I can't wait, actually," he confessed. "To grow old with you."

She laughed, a single, silver, tinkling bell echoing through the night. "Why on earth would you want to grow old? It sounds awful."

"To grow old with *you*," he said, nuzzling his nose against hers.

"To see how you change, and how you stay the same."

Riona's brow furrowed. "What do you mean?"

Conor sidled closer, letting his fingers trace the smooth contours of her cheeks, her jaw, her moon-pale face. "I've been watching you for so long," he told her. "Studying you, learning you, like I'd learn the way a sapling bends and shifts in the wind, how it grows steady and tall as time goes, different but still the same. I know how you drink your tea and how you look when you eat your cake, the sound of your voice when you're angry but pretending not to be –"

"So any time I talk to my mother, you mean."

He smiled a little at that, but continued on, still staring intently into her eyes. "I know so many things about you, Ria – sometimes I think I know everything about you, but it doesn't worry me. I know that there are an infinite number of yous that I've yet to know, that don't even exist yet, and I will love every single version of you that may come, no matter what."

Something sad and quiet flickered over her face. "Even if, perhaps, it's not a good version?"

"What do you mean?"

Riona was quiet, letting her fingers play idly with the ends of his copper-colored curls. "I'm not a very good person," she said at last. "Not like you are, or like Mamó and Maeve were." Her voice cracked slightly on the name of her long lost friend, whom Conor knew she grieved still, even deeper and fiercer than she did her grandparents, as much from the unfairness of such a loss as from her own inescapable guilt. "I can be…unlikable, and unkind. Selfish, and I worry that one day, you –"

He kissed her, gentle and sweet, in rhythm with the song of the crickets and the dance of the river in the darkness. "Even your very *worst* version," he said, drawing back ever so slightly, so that his lips brushed against hers as he whispered this most profound truth of him, an unbreakable oath, "it will still be you, and I will love you."

"You might change your mind."

"Never," Conor said, and Riona smiled, the saddest and loveliest sight he'd ever seen, and his heart sank in his chest.

Tomorrow, he thought. Tomorrow, she would stop loving him again. He could always tell.

The only thing to do was to savor her affection and her love while it belonged to him, and to hope that the next day, the next month, the next year, she'd come back to him again.

"Never," he said again, fiercer this time, as though if he protested enough, he could make her believe him — could make her keep loving him, forever, as he knew that he would love her, as surely as he knew that the sun would rise tomorrow. "I'll never change my mind. It's you and I, until the end of our days."

She leaned forward and kissed him again, her beautiful bluebell eyes shimmering with unshed tears. "Oh my sweet cabbage," she whispered. "Never say never."

You asked me to take you to the bride of Death,' the fear-dearg said. 'Behold — here she is.'

Excerpt from 'The Snow, The Crow, & The Blood'

Chapter Thirty-Seven
Lios Lachna, Éire, 1082

CONOR

Conor jolted awake after what felt like only an hour or two of restless sleep, the toe of Haisley's boot nudging him insistently in his ribs. He opened his bleary eyes to find his daughter looming over him, her hands on her hips and a scowl on her lips. "It's morning," she said curtly. "So explain."

"Haisley." Conor twisted around to see Riona standing in the dimly lit doorway, her cloak draped over her shoulders, her silk gloves pulled tight over her still-bandaged hands. "Give the man a minute to wake up."

"He said in the morning, *mother*, and now it's morning, so –"

"Haisley," Riona said again, this time in a quiet tone that brooked no further argument, and Haisley clamped her lips shut in sullen agreement. Riona's gaze flickered to Conor. "Get dressed. Breakfast is ready, and we should be getting on our way."

She jerked her chin at Haisley, who followed her begrudgingly, with a final glare in Conor's direction. As soon as the door snicked shut behind them, he sat up, scratching at his scruffy jaw.

He had no idea what to say to her. To either of them, really.

He came down the stairs a few minutes later to find them sitting across from one another in frosty silence at the table, two matching bowls of porridge loaded with raisins, two squat brown mugs smelling faintly of honey, two thin tendrils of steam rising from each, entwining in the air between them. He stood for a moment beside the table, fumbling for words, when Riona silenced him with a look.

"We've agreed to talk after breakfast," she said, sipping at her tea. "Once we've gotten on the road." She raised an eyebrow and gave an imperceptible nod toward the door to the kitchen, deliberately ajar, and Conor understood.

"All right," he said, sitting on the bench next to Haisley, who wrapped her hands around her mug and her bowl and slid away from him a few inches without a single word. He winced. "Any porridge left for me, Ria?"

"Ask Brecken," she said. "He's earwigging just behind the door over there."

There was a slight cough, and Brecken peeked his head out from the kitchen, his cheeks bright red. "Be right out," he said shamefacedly, then ducked back inside.

Conor pinched the bridge of his nose, a tension headache building in the front of his skull. "Have you figured out how we are to pay for all this, Ria?"

"It's all settled." She set her empty cup down on the table with a hollow rattle. "I've agreed to bless his wife in return for food and lodging."

"Bless her?" Conor eyed her suspiciously. "Why?"

Riona blinked at him, doe-eyed and innocent. "She has a recurring cough, going on for nearly two years now. Nasty thing, apparently. Sets her back for weeks whenever it crops up."

"Then she needs hot milk with honey, and peppermint, not a blessing."

"Funnily enough," Riona said idly, tracing the foggy imprint left by her cup on the smooth wooden table. "The local healer prescribed precisely that. Doesn't seem to have helped much." She smiled, catlike and sly. "Time to invoke a higher power than the all-holy weeds, cabbage."

Conor clenched his jaw. Maddening, insufferable woman. "And that's sufficient? A blessing, and all's square?"

"Well, I did increase his revenue considerably last night with my little performance, you know. Triple, I believe, what he usually does on such a night. And then of course, there's your part."

"My part?" Conor looked up sharply as Brecken bustled back out of the kitchen, mug and bowl in hand. "What's my part?"

"A paltry sum, really." Riona nibbled at the edge of a stray raisin. "He expects you to send it along within the week once you've returned home. Five silver marks."

"Are you mad? For two meals and an hour spent tossing and turning on the man's floor?" He glared at Brecken, who had the sense to drop the food and tea on the table unceremoniously and flee without another word. "It's bloody extortion."

"There was also the matter of those three – or was it four –flagons of cider you drank last night. Costly stuff, apparently."

He opened his mouth to argue hotly when he saw it – that flash of a smirk curving along Haisley's stubborn lips, even with her head bent low over her nearly empty bowl. Riona lifted her brows meaningfully, and he understood.

Clever girl, always so cunning, so sly, coaxing a smile, however unwilling, out of their determinedly angry daughter.

He took a hearty swallow of his too-hot tea, coughing slightly as he swallowed it down. "I'll pay not a coin more than three silver marks," he grumbled, and a little of the tension in his shoulders eased when Haisley's lips again twitched in amusement at his tone.

Somehow, they would be all right, he and Haisley and Riona. He just knew it.

Thankfully, Riona stayed quiet for the first part of the morning as they walked down the muddy road, and Conor fumbled his way through a very condensed version of their past and how it was currently affecting their present. He tried to answer her eager questions simply, concisely – yes, Riona truly was the queen of the vale; yes, she, Haisley, was meant to one day be queen; no, he had no regrets about the choices that he had made – but nothing satisfied her. Each answer he gave only seemed to inspire more questions, each one more complex and confusing than the last, until he eventually threw Riona a desperate, pleading look.

"Haisley," Riona interrupted gently as Haisley launched into another long-winded, convoluted musing, this one spent pondering how, exactly, she could be descended from the gods when she could not even fly, although, you know, it did feel like she might sometimes, when she was running so fast and so swift through the fields, like she might sprout wings at any moment and soar into the sky, and was that a gift handed down to her from the gods themselves. "Let's try and focus on the matter at hand."

"You mean the sídhe." Conor could tell that Haisley was striving very hard to remain aloof and distant, but her eyes, gleaming with fascination, with eagerness, betrayed her. "Because we are going to the sídhe, aren't we? To get the sword?"

"You," said Riona coolly even as Conor winced, cursing himself internally for telling her that particular part of the story, "are doing no such thing."

"But I have the silver blood, like you used to, and I can use it."

"*No*, Haisley." Riona's voice cut through the dewy morning air like the lash of whip, savage and biting, and Haisley shrunk away towards Conor at the sound of it. "You must never use it," Riona said again, more gently this time, and Conor slipped his hand into Haisley's, steadying her. "It is dangerous, far more than you could ever know. I wish by all the gods, Haisley, that I had not....well. Just know that it has cost me –" Her voice broke. "Everything."

Haisley glanced tentatively up at Conor, and he squeezed her hand softly in reassurance. "Do not make the same mistake that I once did," Riona continued, "to believe that it is a blessing, this thread of divinity that runs in your veins. I assure you that it is not."

Conor's throat tightened. "Nothing is a curse or a blessing in itself," he said. "Isn't that what you yourself said yesterday, about druidecht? It is how it's used."

"I haven't used it very well," she said dryly, "have I?"

"You saved me."

Riona halted in her tracks at Haisley's soft voice. Haisley pulled her fingers free of his, reaching out to lay her small hand on the back of Riona's where it hung by her side. "If what Uncail Con says is true," Haisley continued, searching Riona's impassive face, "then you went to the lord of death and offered yourself for me. Did you do that?"

Her throat jumped once as she swallowed. "Yes."

"Could you have done that," Haisley asked, "without the folaíocht?"

"No." Riona kept her gaze fixed determinedly on the sun-dappled horizon, away from Haisley. "But he would not have come for you in the first place, if I had not been born with it."

"That is hardly your fault, Ria," Conor found himself saying, then clamped his mouth shut as Haisley frowned in his direction.

His daughter stepped closer to Riona, her fingers entwining with Riona's limp ones. "Like Uncail Con said, like *you* said, it was what it is used for that matters, and you used it to save me."

Riona's lips trembled. "Always," she whispered. "I will always save you," and in answer, Haisley's arms slipped around her waist, pressing her face into the soft silk of Riona's gown while Conor watched as for the first time in nearly ten years, Riona hugged her daughter tight against her chest.

Then too soon, Haisley was pulling away, and Riona was wiping at the corners of her eyes, a tremulous, timid smile playing at the corners of her mouth. "So now you know," she said a bit unsteadily, and Haisley nodded, serious-eyed.

"I've wondered for a while," she said, looking almost nervously over at Conor. "I'm nothing like them, Mamaí and Da, and once, Bry, a boy in the village, he said something that made me think that I was not…that they were not –"

Before Conor could interject, Riona stepped forward, placing her gloved palm on Haisley's cheek. "Listen to me," she said. "Yes, Conor is your father and I am your mother, but so are Kayleigh and Páidí – very much so. You are just as much their daughter as ours, and always will be, you understand?" Haisley nodded, and Riona let her hand drop away. "So. Do you have any other questions for me?"

"Yes." Haisley pointed at Conor. "Why do you call him 'cabbage'?"

For a moment, their gazes collided, and something honey-warm and bright flared in his chest as Riona's expression softened like butter melting in a flame-warmed cast iron skillet. "I'm not sure," she said. "It's just what I've always called him, ever since we first met, when I was a little girl."

"Because she thought that I was daft in the head," Conor said dryly, and Haisley's brow furrowed.

"It's a bit mean," she ventured, and that softness on Riona's face flickered once, then hardened again, those old familiar walls reasserting themselves. "Mamaí says not to call people names."

Riona laughed, too airily, turning to wander away down the road. "She is quite right," she said with her back to both of them. "It's a lesson *my* mamaí never taught me, and that I subsequently failed to learn."

Conor's heart twisted in his chest, but Haisley tugged at his hand, pulling him along after Riona, firing off questions as Oscar loped along by his side, her earlier resentment forgotten, and Conor pushed it aside, that nagging ache, because here it was, the dream that he had kept cuddled close to his heart for so many years, the three of them, hand in hand, all the hurts that they had endured, for this one brief moment, finally healed.

They wandered off-course, ambling along the side of the stream instead of keeping to the road, savoring the rain-scented air whispering of rebirth and springtime flowers, but Riona said nothing about their wayward path, and Conor couldn't bring himself to care. They were here, together, and it was as though time had slowed to a halt here in the wild green beauty of the countryside, with nary another soul to be seen, only him and his dog and his girls, a few stolen hours of joy in an unending march of years that had brought nothing but sorrows for so long. He wanted to seize it with both hands, this moment of peace, dip it in wax to seal its sweetness, perfectly preserved, untouched by time, so that when he at last grew old and gray and life-weary, he could pluck it from the branches of his memory to find it still whole and ripe and beautiful.

They ate strips of dried lamb and ripe red apples under the midafternoon sky, listening to the clear water of the stream gurgling beside them, the deep green grass cool and damp beneath them, and Haisley talked and talked, arms waving and hands gesticulating, telling them stories of her friends in the village, of her favorite books, about her love of cauliflower but her dislike of kale, of the time when she was eight when she broke her wrist playing iomáint, and even though they both laughed and listened with smiles on their faces, Conor knew that he and Riona were both drinking it in all in with deep, greedy gulps, savoring every word, every grin, because it was all too brief, this stolen interlude here underneath the springtime sun, a temporary reunion that was already ending even before it had truly begun.

He remembered the wooden ball tucked away in his satchel as they finished eating, and he had laid down in the grass to watch them, Riona and their daughter, coaxing and cajoling the delighted Oscar as they threw the ball over and over for him to retrieve.

"How," Conor asked in exasperation, "are you so terrible at something so simple?"

"I would hardly call it simple." Riona put her hands on her hips and scowled. "The little monster won't listen to us."

"He never listens to anyone," Haisley confided, her lips pursed as they stood side by side, studying Oscar as he zipped about in tight circles, tail wagging furiously as he barked in joy at the sight of the wooden ball in Haisley's hand. "He's practically feral. Uncail Con spoils him so."

"Not true," Conor said from where he reclined underneath the tree, arms folded behind his head. "Be firm about it. Show him you're the boss now. He'll mind you well enough."

Haisley straightened her shoulders and held out the ball, and Oscar bounced wildly, whining with eagerness. "Oscar," she said, lowering her voice to exaggerated depths. "Sit! I command you to sit!"

The terrier threw back his head in a howl, then leapt up on her legs, clawing at her frantically, tail whipping through the air.

"Oh for the gods' sake." Riona rolled her eyes. "This is exactly why I prefer cats."

"Silly Oscar." Haisley relented and tossed the ball, and he bounded after it, practically shaking with glee. "But he's a good boyo."

Then into the stream they waded, soaking the hem of Riona's gown and the legs of Haisley's breeches, and when Conor scolded them, laughing, Haisley merely scrunched up her nose in his direction and stuck out her tongue. "We're hot," she said. "Sweaty from chasing your fool of a dog across the countryside all afternoon," and Riona simply smiled, happiness radiating from every curve of her flushed face.

Eventually, they climbed out, dripping wet and grinning, the droplets of water in their black-and-red hair glinting in the later afternoon sun, and the next few hours flew by as they meandered their way back toward the abandoned road that would lead them to Ráth Crúachan. At Haisley's insistence, they stopped in a small village along the way, a few miles south of their destination, and bought thick slices of well-salted ham and fresh-baked apple cake for supper, munching as they walked along under the darkening twilight sky. "No bruiden available tonight," Conor said as they left the village behind them. "Will you be all right camping it for the night, Haisley?"

"An adventure," she mumbled through bites of bread, then shot him a wary look. "There aren't bears around, are there?"

"As if any beast were brave enough to face the wrath of Oscar," Conor said with a wink, and Haisley rolled her eyes, then slipped her hand into his, that old familiar gesture, and Conor drank it in, that overwhelming flood of peace that rolled through him.

They stopped for the night a little while later, building a small fire and a soft bed of leaves for Haisley, and Riona unfastened her fur-lined cloak and laid it over her as she snuggled in by the fire, yawning widely. "No bears," she whispered with a smile. "I'll see to it myself."

"Magic," Haisley whispered back, and Riona tapped her lightly on the nose.

"Not magic," she said. "A skill, a craft, that I have earned the right to wield." She stood, brushing her hands against her gown. "Now go to sleep. It's been a long couple of days."

The fire crackled, a murmured agreement, and Haisley snuggled a little further underneath the warmth of the cloak. "I don't think I can go to sleep," she said. "I'm too excited."

"Try," Conor said from his side of the fire, leaning back against a tree. "I have faith in you. I remember hearing your mamaí telling me how she tries and fails to drag you out of bed for lessons most mornings."

"I can't sleep," she insisted. "I need a story." She peeked at Riona, smiling wryly down at her. "Tell me one of the stories that he told you, your grandfather, the god."

"Och." Riona wandered a few steps away, settling down into the grass just outside the flickering light of the fire. "I'm not much of a storyteller, don't you know. Your da –" A brief pause. "Your uncle, he is much better at the telling of them than I."

Conor raised his eyebrows. "Daideo," he said dryly, "did not share his stories as freely with me as he did with you."

"You listened, nonetheless." He could see the faint curve of her smile in the shadows. "You were always listening."

That warm sensation in his chest unfurled, spreading down through his arms to tingle at the ends of his fingers. "True enough," he said, settling back on his elbows, staring up at the starless sky. "I didn't realize that you were paying attention." With that, he began, telling of Bricriu, a bárd of lilting rhymes and clever verses, the god-appointed brugaid to the great kings of old, and an infamous rabble-rouser who delighted in setting the tempers of the lords and ladies under his roof against one another. Once, Conor said as the crescent moon rose higher in the velvet-black sky, Bricriu entertained even Cúchulainn himself, the most famed warrior in the history of Éire, and with him the kings and chieftains of Ulaid, promising to each of them the curadmír – the champion's portion of the feast – if they completed the challenges set forth by him. The heroes traveled across the realm – to Connacht, under the watchful eye of Queen Medb herself, set to judge the warriors' worth, and to Munster, too, the kingdom of the legendary Cú Roí – and each time, Cúchulainn prevailed, defeating great catlike beasts and monstrous giants, and returned to the bruiden of Bricriu, triumphant, the other disgruntled lords and chiefs following close behind.

"But Bricriu," Conor said, eying the way that Haisley blinked, heavy and slow, "was not through with his trickery, his games, and he presented one final challenge to the kings who stood in his hall, decorated with twelve lush couches, one for each of the great clans of Ulaid, its white marble pillars shimmering with the light of a thousand sapphire stones imbedded in their sides."

"Sapphires look a bit like stars," Haisley said drowsily.

"Daideo said that they were forged from the stars themselves, by the smithies of the gods," Riona said from the shadows, and Conor smiled up at the night sky.

"The final challenge," he said, "that Bricriu saddled the heroes with was no small feat – to cut off the head of black-bearded churl, and then to agree to allow him to return the favor, and take their own heads as his own the following night. One by one, the heroes took their turns, slicing the head of the churl from his shoulders with one smooth stroke, but upon seeing the supernatural man rise from the floor, headless and blind, and retrieve his own head before placing it back on his own bloody shoulders, one by one, the heroes lost their nerve and fled, abandoning their oath."

"I don't blame them." Haisley's voice was sluggish and slurred, half-asleep nestled under Riona's cloak. "No prize could be worth dying for. What was this champion's portion, anyway?"

"Usually, it's the best cut of meat from the table."

"That's silly." Haisley sighed, snuggling her head down into the grass and the leaves, and Conor and Riona exchanged an amused glance.

"But Cúchulainn – he was stalwart and brave, bold beyond the daring of any other man, and he did not flee." Conor lowered his voice as Haisley's eyelashes fluttered down onto her cheeks, Oscar already snoring softly beside her. "He chopped off the churl's head, and then immediately knelt down there in the middle of the hall and presented his neck to the churl, who – I can't remember the rest."

"She's asleep anyway." Riona stretched out on her side, her cheek propped in her hand. "How could you forget the ending of the story?"

"It was a very long time ago, and my father called me away right before Daideo finished."

"Ah. Well, Cúchulainn does indeed win the champion's portion, because the churl reveals himself to be none other than Cú Roí himself, who spares his life on account of his bravery, and so he wins the prize."

"Lamb or beef?"

Riona laughed, that half-forgotten sound, like a silver-chimed bell. "Something far more valuable, I would imagine, if Cúchulainn were willing to risk losing his head for the chance to wield it."

"Did Bricriu hand it over, whatever it was?"

"I imagine so." An owl hooted softly in the trees, and Conor drank it in, the faint outline of her profile as she turned her head in its direction. He closed his tired eyes, focusing on the smell of the smoke, the reedy scent of the needles in the grass. "Conor," she said after a moment. "Would you like for me to stop calling you 'cabbage'?"

He frowned into the darkness. "Over twenty years," he said. "And an eleven-year-old girl is the one to convince you that it's not nice to call people names?"

"I'm serious." The tension vibrated in the air between them, and he sat up, brushing the leaves from his hair. "Should I stop?"

There was a strange formality in her tone, stiff and unsure, and he flinched a little to hear it. "I don't understand."

"It's simple enough." He peered into the gloom, searching for any clue that might be found her expression hidden away in the shadows, but she kept her face turned determinedly away from him. "Would you prefer it, if I stopped calling you 'cabbage'?"

No, he thought. *Call me 'cabbage' forever, in that lilting, teasing tone, so that I might close my eyes and imagine a world in which I have not grown old without you.*

He said nothing of the sort, of course, but merely shrugged. "You've been calling me that for over half of my life. Another day or two won't hurt." She said nothing, but even unspoken, he heard it, her regret, her guilt, and he couldn't bear it any longer, these stubborn, needless walls between them.

It had finally happened, her coming back to him, after years of bitter fantasies, of fruitless longing, in this strange, dreamlike existence where time had ceased and grief had run dry, and he would be damned himself if he let even a single moment of this fleeting second chance at happiness escape him.

He pushed himself to his feet, half-stumbling toward her on shaking legs, and her eyes flew open wide as he sank to his knees by her side, his hands cupping her face, his fingers sliding through her hair. "Conor –"

"Just this once," he said, and then his lips were on hers, insistent, urgent, a drowning man gasping for breath between tidal waves of longing. For a heartbeat or two, she was stiff and unmoving beneath his caresses, and he started to panic, half-pulling away, but then her lips parted, the smooth sweep of her tongue against his, her gloved fingers threading through the curls of his hair with practiced, familiar strokes.

They tumbled together, his palm cupped behind her head as she thudded backward into the dirt, cradling her, protecting her, and she purred into his mouth, a soft, hungry sound that he had never before heard her make, setting all the already sparking parts of him ablaze with the need for more.

"Cabbage." It came out as a breathless gasp, her fingers digging through the fabric of his shirt into his shoulders. "We can't – Haisley is right there, she'll wake up –"

"She won't." He kissed his way down the porcelain-smooth column of her throat, lingering on the ridge of her collarbone, relishing the way she arched her hips into his in unspoken approval. "She's utterly knackered, and a heavy sleeper anyway. We'll be fine."

"But–"

He jack-knifed up and caught her feeble protest with another kiss, deep and hot and urgent, the faint taste of cinnamon-spiced apple settling on his tongue. "Take your gloves off," he whispered against her mouth. "I want to feel you touch me."

She whimpered, but raised her arms slightly, fumbling with her gloves while he explored the too-familiar curves of her lips with his, savoring the hot sweetness of her mouth, the feel of her tongue, far richer than anything he had ever before tasted or ever would again. Then her cool fingers were sliding under his shirt, gentle and light save for the scratch of the linen bandages still wrapped around her poor palms, teasing and touching him along his ribs, dancing their way up to brush across his chest, drifting down his biceps, and back up again, stroking, coaxing him into a wild brushfire fever of need.

"Gods, I've missed you." He let his hands slide down from her from they had been entwined in her hair, groaning at the supple warmth of her curves, the press of her body against his. "There's no one else. There will never be anyone else, only you, forever –"

It was instantaneous, the change in her posture, a limpid-eyed fawn frozen with terror, pinned in by the hungry gaze of a sharp-fanged wildcat.

"Conor. Stop." She shoved at his shoulders, and he jerked away from her, heart pounding.

"I'm sorry, I thought –"

"No." She buried her face in her hands, chest heaving. "I want to, I do, but Conor. I can't let you. I can't let you love me again. I can't."

"I never stopped, not for a minute. You know that."

"Listen to me, Conor. It can't happen, this, between us. It's not fair to you, not like this."

"Ria, I know that you're not staying." He swallowed shakily, aching to touch her cheek, to lace his fingers through hers, to pull her against him and never let go. "I don't care. I only want this one night, you and me, to remember."

"No," she said again, so weary, and dropped her hands away from her white, strained face. "You don't understand."

"Then explain it." He dared to slide forward an inch, closer to where she sat, staring at her bandaged hands clasped in her lap. "Explain it, and we'll find a way. We always do, you and me."

"Not this time." She looked up then, those bluebell eyes, sad and empty. "I lied to you."

His fingers, inching toward her in the grass, stilled. "About what?"

"All of it."

He stared at her, his mouth going dry. "Riona."

"I'm sorry," she said with the mouth still swollen and ripe from his kisses. "But I need to tell you the truth about Jack."

Conor shook his head slightly, the haze of lust and confusion and hurt still muddling his brain. "Jack? The high prince of Éire, from that old story about the dead crow?"

"Yes," she said. "It's him, Conor. The one whom I serve, the dark druid who will kill Haisley if I do not obey his every whim – " She drew in a deep, shaky voice. "The lord of death *is* Jack."

Chapter Thirty-Eight
Tír Soghain, Éire, 524

JACK

She was even lovelier than he had imagined, the bride of death — regal and tall, with sleek ebony locks and sensuous curves hidden beneath the silk of her gown. "So," she said, and he shivered to hear it, the cold death-knell chime of her voice. "You have come to win my hand, I hear."

Jack nodded, heart pounding.

"Very well. To win me," she said, standing there in her garden of blood and bone, surrounded by snow-white roses and swarms of hungry black flies, "you must steal from me the gold which I wear entwined in my hair –" her finger ran along the gilded comb nestled deep within her raven-black locks – " and the silver I wear on my hand –" her silver ring on her finger flashed in the sunlight – "this very night, from the place where I take my rest."

And I, Jack thought, *have slain three giants. To me belong the treasures of the gods. I have felt the kiss of death on my lips, and I have survived.*

So he flashed her his most winning, his most charming smile, the smile of the handsome high prince for whom all women swooned. "Easy enough tasks, I think you shall find, my lady fair, for one as capable and as determined as I."

"Do you think so? Surely, then, you shall not mind, if I were to add another task for you to accomplish for me, in order to win my hand as you so desire."

"My lady, I welcome the challenge."

"Very well." Her black eyes gleamed, obsidian diamonds glistening in the snow-white landscape of her face. "Then along with my ring and my comb, the silver and the gold, I demand that you also bring to me the lips which I shall kiss this very night, in the place where I take my rest, which is neither of the earth or below it." Jack started at this, his stomach twisting at the thought of those blood-red lips being claimed by any other than he. "Should you fail," she continued, "then I assure you of this: – your head shall I claim your head as my prize."

Jack studied the winter-cold beauty of the princess' face, the unparalleled loveliness of her person. "I will not fail, a stór," he said. "Because I assure you of this – after this night, *you* shall be my greatest treasure."

The night fell, and Jack, the High Prince of Éire, sat on the front steps of his lady's castle, all alone in the snow and the darkness.

""Neither of the earth nor below it," he murmured now, the cloak wrapped snug around his shoulders, the sword and purse stowed safely by his side. ""That is where I must find my lady this night, if I am to win her hand.""

The sídhe, of course. An average man would be terrified, no doubt, at the idea of following her into the other-realm of gods and monsters, but not he. It was not his first venture into such a place — and he had shed blood and bone to prove his worth there, and now he had the weapons he needed to conquer all the world to prove it.

This proud, murderous princess would be no match for him, nor whatever — whomever — it was she planned on kissing tonight.

He shivered, hugging the thin folds of the cloak tighter around him. Winter had arrived in full force here in Connacht, the icy bite of the wind slicing right through him, and again, he longed for the flat, sweet-grassed plains of home, the roaring hearth-fires of his father's castle. He would wed his bride, he decided, then take her home immediately, away from these gods-forsaken mountains, that loomed so grim and sinister above him, and the thought of it all – her snow-white curves stretched out beneath him, the rich scent of the loamy soil of home, the scratch of the rough stone of the Lia Fáil beneath his hand as he claimed the kingship as his own, with his rightful queen by his side – warmed him thoroughly.

A movement to his right roused him from his reverie, and there she was, gliding down the stairs a few feet away from where he sat hidden underneath the folds of his cloak, hurrying towards the snow-kissed tree line of fir and elm at the base of the mountain. Jack leapt to his feet, heart in his throat. His bride, his queen, slipping away into the shadows of the night, into the heart of those very mountains he had eyed so warily only a few moments before. A voice deep within him hissed in warning, not to follow, not to enter those fog-shrouded hills, but to run, to flee, to escape whatever doom beckoned to him even now from whatever devilry evil lay waiting among the stony peaks of these western mountains.

He had the purse, the cloak, the sword of starlight itself, for the gods' sakes. It was more than enough to ensure his destiny as the greatest king ever to trod the earth of Éire, to conquer the world with the might of his rule.

But he could not shake the memory of her face, white and black and red, the incarnation of death itself, and he swallowed once, then followed her into the woods.

For hours, it seemed, they walked, slipping through the snow-dusted trees, past a thousand pairs of silent watching eyes hidden deep within the shadows, until at last she paused before a ring of whitethorn trees, clustered tight around a giant slab of a gray-faced boulder. He watched as she leaned forward and pressed her blood-red lips against the surface of the rock, a long, lingering kiss.

He watched in awe as the rock shuddered once, then split in two, and the princess stepped unhesitatingly into the gaping crevice, and as soon as her long skirt vanished into the hollowed-out doorway, the opening closed up once more, smooth and silent. The sídhe, he thought. Just as before, when the fear-dearg had led him to the fairy-realm of Oweynagat. Jack gathered his cloak tight around him and approached the dark gray rock, and paused, uncertain of how to proceed, when suddenly the boulder moaned, then splintered down the middle, an identical gaping mouth of a hole to the one which his princess had walked through only seconds before. Jack licked nervously at his lips, gripping the sword of starlight a little tighter in his hand, the purse clasped in the other, and walked through the doorway into the otherworld.

He blinked, and a warm rush of air washed over him, smelling faintly of salt-water and briny seaweed, and he found himself standing on a sandy beach surrounded by craggy, dark brown cliffs speckled with bright green sprays of sea-grass and reeds. It was strangely familiar, he thought, as he surveyed the rocky bluff, listening to the caw of the gulls and the distant bark of the seals, and then he realized – Baoi Bhéarra, the infamous island where the sons of Mil Éspaine had battled to the death against the gods of Éire, in search of vengeance for their slain father. He remembered being a child, his father's hand resting on his shoulder as he pointed out to him the great landmarks of old that marked the passing of gods and men, the reverential hush in his father's voice as he told Jackhim the story of how mortals came to Éire in a tidal wave of blood and tears.

It was in Baoi Bhéarra that the gods had divided the world in twain, between the living and the dead. It was here that the lord of death had died, and had been reborn, pulled forth from the waves and an obsidian crown set upon his head, ruler of the shadow-realm of Tech Duinn.

Jack spun around on his heel, supremely grateful for the conceal-ing folds of his cloak of darkness, his fingers trailing over the ebony hilt of the sword of starlight, then froze.

There, walking barefoot through the sand, his arms out-stretched, stood Donn, golden-eyed and smiling, and Jack watched his bride press her blood-red lips to those of the lord of death himself. There, walking barefoot through the sand, his arms out-stretched, stood Donn, the golden-eyed lord of death in the flesh, smiling at the black-haired princess, and Jack watched his bride press her blood-red lips to his.

He watched and watched, his fury rising all the while, his pulse pounding wildly at his temples. His queen, his destiny, wrapped in the arms of another, that snow-white skin stroked and stained by another's greedy fingers, that black-silk hair caught up in another's eager grasp, that crimson mouth parting with a hungry sigh for the taste of another's lips.

It should be his lips to which hers should surrender, his and his alone. How dare he, this thief of souls, to steal from him what was meant to be his.

Underneath his outraged fingers, the hilt of the sword hummed in wordless accord, an unspoken confirmation to act, to take back what was his by right.

Even as the lord of death took the princess by the hand, leading her a little ways up the beach, Jack stalked forward, the cloak of darkness wrapped close around him, shrouding him from view, the sword gripped tight in his furious hand. His bride. His. This so-called lord of death had stolen his bride.

The words echoed through him, a monotoned chant of momentous doom, calling him down a path of vengeance and retribution he had no choice but to walk.

He would show him, this impostor, who the true master of death was.

Concealed safely underneath the cloak, Jack hurried silently past where the lord of death meandered down the beach, hand in hand with his princess, and waited by the threshold of the wide open doorway of the red-walled bruiden, sword in hand, heart thudding with jealous anger – righteous, he corrected himself, it was righteous anger, for the girl was meant to be his – and as soon as they stepped towards him, out of the sun and into the shadow of the hall, the lord of death reached up to cup the soft white cheek of the princess in his hand, and at the exact same moment that they smiled adoringly into one another's eyes, Jack whipped off the cloak in one furious motion.

The princess' blood-red lips fell open in a scream at the sight of him looming before them, the sterling blade of the sword of starlight gleaming in the warm light of the sun. The lord of death whirled around, his golden-fire eyes bright, hands upraised, but it was too late. I – in a flash of silver, the unbeatable blade, the god-slayer, arced down, a single, savage stroke, and the lord of death shrieked through an explosion of crimson-dark blood, clawing at his mouth with wild, frantic hands.

The princess screamed and screamed as down into the sun-warmed sand tumbled a pair of blood-smeared lips, her lover sinking to his knees as he bellowed in agony, and Jack stared down with immense satisfaction at the ruined face of the lord of death. He twirled the sword in his hand, and smirked. "Not so terrible now, are you," he said, pressing the tip of the blade to the soft flesh just underneath the immortal lord's quivering chin. "So much for the lord of death.,"

And planting the heel of his boot against his heaving chest, Jack drove the sword deep into Donn's throat.

A cacophony of low-throated, keening wails broke through the air all around him, and he looked up to see hundreds of pairs of shadowy eyes staring out at him from the rocky crevices of the cliffs —, and for a moment, he caught a glimpse of a familiar, squat shape with a rat-thin tail and a dirty red cap watching him, gleaming dark eyes wide with shock and terror. He blinked, and it was gone, and there was only the weeping princess and the lord of death lying flat on his back, staring up at him with glowing golden eyes as he twitched in the death-throes of his agony on the blood-soaked beach, as the ocean waves continued to crashing and to rolling in the distance.

"No," the princess sobbed, crawling on her hands and knees through the sand to reach for her lover, whose convulsions grew fainter and softer. "No, no –"

"Quiet," Jack snarled, and she looked up, the porcelain-pure complexion of her skin corpse-white and stretched thin with grief over the bones of her face.

"You will pay for this," she said, her black eyes shimmering with rage and tears. "You will pay with your life, with everything, for this."

Jack grabbed a fistful of her midnight black hair, twisting savagely, and she screamed again, reaching up to claw wildly at his wrists, but he dragged her away through the sand, away from the lord of death who lay dying himself in the sand, his golden eyes bleary and dull, but watching – watching Jack with something akin to resignation in his eyes. "I doubt it," he said as the princess sobbed, scratching at his bare arms with her sharp nails. "I have everything that I need – the sword, the purse, the cloak. I have you too, you foolish girl." He threw her down into the sand, and she scrambled away from him, her black hair falling loose and wild from her elaborate braid. "I have this –" He reached out and ripped the golden comb from her hair, and she yelped as the long strands of black hair tore out from the roots by the force of his grip. "And this, too." He dropped the blood-stained sword in the sand, pinning both her hands to the ground with one of his, even as she struggled beneath him, screaming and spitting, and wrestled the silver ring from her finger, waving it before her tear-stained face. "And the lips of your lord – that was your last requirement, was it not?" He threw back his head and laughed, a feral, triumphant sound, pinioning her chin with her fingers as he forced her to turn her head, to look at the bleeding body of her lover there in the sand. "Would you still like to kiss them now, a stór?"

A low, keening sound was her only response, her eyes squeezed shut tight against the sight of her slain lord.

Jack grinned. "I thought not. I am, after all, the much more preferable option, even before I cut up that face of his. You – you were just too much of a fool to realize it." He released his grip on her chin with a rough, contemptuous shove. "But it matters not, because you are mine now. Mine and mine alone. That was your word, was it not? I take these objects from you – your ring, your comb, his damned lips – and you become mine."

"Never," she gasped through her sobs. "Never will I belong to you."

"I thought you might say that." He again seized her chin in his hand, holding her thrashing head still as he stared into her red-rimmed eyes. "But I know exactly who you are, and that is mine." His fingernails dug into her skin, and her blood, dark red and wet, bloomed against the pale porcelain of her skin. "Because, here I am, both of your treasures in my hand, the lips of your lord bleeding out on the ground from the slash of my sword, tasks you swore no mortal could ever accomplish, and yet so I have, and so you are mine now, my lady and mine alone." His hands slid down to wrap around her throat, squeezing on the tenderest part of her flesh as he straddled her, staring down at her face with a vicious kind of triumph. She choked, sputtering and gagging as she fought to breathe, and he smiled, slow and cruel. "Now I ask you, princess – who is the master of death now? Who?"

A sudden blast of artic-cold air suddenly enveloped him, the heat from the sun-warmed beaches vanishing in an instant, and the princess froze, rigid and still, beneath him.

"You are."

Jack spun around at the sound of the midwinter voice behind him, grabbing for the ebony hilt of the sword of starlight, but his fingers scrambled uselessly in the sand, gone oddly cold and icy to the touch. Gone, how could it be gone –

He froze, seeing for the first time who it was who stood before him, clad in dark gray robes, her hair falling loose over her shoulders, her fathomless stare fixed directly on him.

The Mórrígan.

"You should not have touched her." She nodded in the direction of the princess he kept pinned against the ground, gone quiet and still underneath him. "Thrice now, you have killed a gift that did not belong to you."

Jack stared at the winter-cold face of the goddess of fate standing before him in the sand that felt suddenly like new-fallen snow underneath the palms of his hands. "Mo bhanríon," he said. "It is … it is an honor to meet you."

Her expression remained remote, impassive. "Few mortals have ever looked upon my face, and fewer still have lived to speak of it."

He pushed up on his knees, away from the motionless body of the princess, who stared up at him with a vacant, broken gaze. "Mo bhanríon," he said again. "I was merely attempting to free her – to save her from the curse that the dark lord had so obviously placed upon her soul."

"Liar." He opened his mouth to protest, retreating immediately when she pinned him with her deathless stare. "Or a fool. Did you not once consider how a mere mortal girl was so easily allowed to enter and exit the realm of the sídhe, of Tech Duinn itself?"

Fear, wild and white-lipped, nibbled along his spine. "I – I assumed that the lord of death allowed her to –"

"There is no lord of death." The Mórrígan's attention wandered over to the motionless body that lay in the blood-soaked sand behind them, and Jack watched as her hand came up, and in a flurry of feathers, down from the sun-bright sky descended a raven, landing on her wrist with fluid ease. Her lips moved swiftly in a silent incantation, and the labored breaths of the lord of death fell immediately still. "For centuries, he has studied the art of death at my knee, learned the secrets of both the mortal and immortal worlds from my hand – and by him, under my tutelage, balance was established and maintained." Her bottomless gaze slid back to his face, and Jack fell backwards in the sand, his lungs frozen in terror. "That balance is lost now."

"Mo bhanríon –"

"I gave him this girl, this lady whom he loved and who loved him in return, as a gift for his service to me. Their souls were bound together, their fates eternally intertwined, and you – you slew them both." Uncontrollable, bone-shaking shudders were rushing up and down Jack's spine, caught in the throes of a fear he had never before dreamed possible as he stared up into the face of the nightmare goddess. "But they are not the first of my disciples whom you have killed. Do you remember the first of them, that lay dead in the snow by your hands?"

The image flashed in his mind – the dark red blood, mingling with the soft black feathers of the blank-eyed raven, sprawled out in the early winter snow. "I did not – I did not know –"

"Liar," she said again in her midwinter voice, her other hand reaching up to stroke the sleek back of the bird perched on her wrist, and Jack trembled anew as shards of ice crawled along the length of the sand, slithering and snapping their way towards him. "You cannot deceive me, child. I know what was in your heart that day, when you shot him from the sky."

"It was only a bird," Jack pleaded desperately, and the Mórrígan raised a long white finger. Overhead, the bright summer sky split in two with a thunderous crack, and Jack watched in horror as the very air turned to ice around him, the sunlight growing wan and dark, a thousand snow-white stars peeking out from the newborn gloom.

"Do you know," she asked as the darkness crept in all around them, shrouding the once sun-kissed cliffs in shadows, the sound of the ocean waves growing distant and muted, drowning in the velvet-black softness of the winter night. "Do you know how it was done, all those centuries ago, when it fell to me to balance the workings between life and death?" Jack could not bring himself to answer, his teeth chattering too fiercely to speak, and the goddess stepped closer. "The earth-mother – my sister – loved him, this Donn who sailed to our land from far across the dark sea. But the sea took him, drowning his u body under the unforgiving weight of a thousand salt-water waves. My sister mourned him still, and wept rivers of tears for his loss, begging me to restore him to her, as I and I alone could." Her fathomless eyes narrowed ever so slightly. "And so I pulled him out of the waves, water-logged and brine-soaked, and so he was reborn by the power of my eternal fire, and placed him here." She gestured towards the shadows of the sídhe, and Jack jerked to see trees, gray-trunked and ice-licked, sprouting from the once-sandy beach. "Tech Duinn," she said. "The realm of lost souls, of fallen gods, of monsters, both mortal and undying, neither of this earth nor below it – as you well know."

"What," said Jack through fear-whitened lips, scuttling backwards on his hands as he stared at the fast-shifting landscape all around him, the snow drowning out the sunlight, the warmth of the sea-breeze even now growing brittle and cold all around him. "What are you doing?"

"You wished to know the workings of death," she said. "Deep within the cave of cats, I saw the birthing of the world, the origin of all life, and with my own hands, I brought forth Death, its balance." Her gaze drifted across the frost-covered world. "Do you recognize it? It is the place of your death as well – your rebirth."

"Mo bhanríon," Jack whispered once more, his voice cracking painfully, but she continued, unperturbed and serene, distant as one of the far-off stars that gleamed so bright and cold against the midnight sky.

"My sister pitied those mortal-born weaklings that had arrived on our shores," she said, resuming her story. "For them, she sacrificed it, my lovely sister, that fertile being of hers, from whose breath the earth itself was born, the trees and the vines from the flowing locks of her hair, and from whose tears the rivers and the lochs sprang into being, and her creation-art with it." A shadow of something like sadness passed over the Mórrígan's face, there and gone in the briefest of moments. "All for naught. This world will die too, one day, once the last, lingering touch of her evergreen fingers, coaxing new life from its depths, has vanished." She paused, tilting her head back to gaze up at the new-awakening stars far above them. "I have seen it. I have watched it fall into ruin, and all that once thrived upon its richness with it."

Jack's hand crept into his doublet, searching for the rough leather of the purse.

Vanished, just like the sword.

"She is nothing more than a spirit now, my sister." He glanced back up at where the goddess stood, her head tilted back to observe the newborn stars emerging from the velvet blanket of the eternal night that unfurled across the once bright sky, his heart thudding with dread. His treasures, he thought frantically. His precious, beloved treasures, the key to his greatness – gone. "My sister is doomed to drift forever upon the winds of Éire, voiceless and ethereal as the sky itself."

Abandoning all attempts at subtlety, he plunged his hand into his other pocket, his panic rising to uncontrollable heights, fumbling for the airy folds of the cloak, and found nothing but a handful of silver coins and a few shreds of lint.

"But," the Mórrígan continued, almost dreamily, either oblivious or indifferent to his frantic searching. "Her purpose was served, and another world was created, one that will endure, one that will last beyond the impermanence of this life you mortals cling to so fiercely – a place of joy for the only undying parts of those mortals whom she loved so briefly but so well. Magh Meall, far beyond the western sea. They must journey there, at the end of their days, the spirits traveling across the bridge she built for them with the last strengths of her breath." She sighed, and her gaze returned to Jack, boring into him with coldblooded intensity. "And there must be someone to serve as an anchor for that bridge, to provide them rest, and solace, and guidance along their way, so that my sister's sacrifice would not be in vain."

He slid away from her, the soft-falling snow brushing against his feverish cheeks, fingers trembling. Where had they gone, his stolen treasures, his only hope of salvation from this undying creature who stood so immovable and stone-faced in front of him.

"So I chose him – Donn, the one who started it all." The Mórrígan folded her hands across her waist, her fingers laced together. "He was not pleased, at first, with my selection, but he grew fond of it, this place and this work. And so I gave him gifts. The command of the beasts of the sídhe, a beautiful and devoted lover … and the most dangerous gift of all – I gave him hope."

"Hope," Jack whispered faintly, and her face glowed with an ice-bright fire.

"Indeed. I told him, that I had looked into the cobwebbed strands of the cosmos, read the writings of a hand not yet born, and had seen his salvation – a young man, a prince, who would one day be reborn by the power of the gods, who would set him free from his bonds and release him from his damnation here in this realm of lost souls."

"Where is my sword?" It burst out of him, a quaking, terrified gasp. "My cloak, my purse – where are they – I need them –"

"He thought," the Mórrígan said, "that I meant that you would release him from the confines of the sídhe, that he would be free to once more walk among the land of the living, as was his destiny." If it had been any other being who stood before him, he would have thought it was a smile that curved along the edges of her mouth, but there was nothing of kindness, of humor, etched into the unfeeling stone of the goddess' features. "But I am the goddess of fate, and I alone know the truth, boy. There is no such thing, save that for the fates we all make for ourselves, mortal and immortal alike."

He was crying, weeping wild, desperate tears. "You doomed

me," he managed to say. "You doomed me to this."

"Fools," the goddess said, dangerously soft. "All of you mortals." Jack flinched away from the vicious crack of that final word. "You doomed yourself, as he did, as did this girl here, when first she kissed the lord of death." She motioned towards the unmoving body of the princess, her shallow breaths the only sign of life present in her unnaturally still form, the corpse of the erstwhile lord of death lying a little way behind them. The raven rustled its sleek black feathers, and again the lips of the Mórrígan moved, wordless and fast, and a long, slow sigh drifted from the limp body of the princess in the sand.

"I saw it all, you know," she said as Jack watched the princess become utterly still and unmoving before him. "From the moment you shot my raven out of the sky, insolent imp that you are, I saw how it would unfold, the bleakness of your eternity." She beckoned towards the waiting woods, a silent signaling for something, someone, to approach, and from the shadows emerged the fear-dearg, his head bowed, his fingers clasped in front of him.

"You damned fairy," Jack gasped, his fingers biting into the ice-hard dirt beneath him, aching with cold. "He did this to me."

"No." The Mórrígan gestured towards the fairy. "You could have chosen otherwise at any point, could you not? But you could not resist, and you have no one to blame but yourself."

"Why?" It burst out of Jack's heaving chest, his tears evaporating in the white-hot rage that suddenly coursed through him. "Why would you do this to me, you little gobshite? Why?"

The fear-dearg said nothing, merely stared at Jack with his beady black eyes, and then the goddess raised her hand. The air before Jack shimmered once, and a bright orb of pure golden light materialized before him, drifting towards him. The Mórrígan reached out to touch it gently with the tip of her finger, and it shivered in answer before floating towards him, a slow, inexorable procession of otherworldly light. "There," she said. The glinting orb nudged gently against his lips, and they parted involuntarily, transfixed as he was by the allure, the beauty of its pull. "Now you will become the king you so desired to be."

His eyes fluttered shut and he inhaled deeply, and an inferno of heat and fire exploded within him, roaring its way through his veins, thrumming through his temples, a volcanic rush of power and peerless strength. His vision blurred, and he sank to one knee, head bowed, chest heaving, as a strange new fire took root deep within him. He looked down at his hands, flexing his fingers to savor the surge of this new power coursing through him, then his gaze darted up to meet the implacable gaze of the Mórrígan as she stood before him.

"You asked to be the master of death," she said, "and so you are," and Jack's stomach twisted in horrified understanding.

"No," he managed to gasp through the surge of shudders racing through him, endless and uncontrollable waves of nauseating power and bone-deep fear. "No, please, don't –"

"You killed the lord of death. You wielded the sword of starlight against him, and he is gone, and balance must be restored – the bridge between worlds must be restored." She did smile now, cold and unforgiving as the ice that even now crept over the green buds of the trees, draining them of their brilliance, their dewiness, their vitality. "And that, boy, is now your fate."

Jack's chest splintered, despair coursing through him. The "But I don't want to be the lord of death – I want to live –"

"And you shall," she said, "forever." Jack choked, a wordless protest, but she remained unmoving and implacable in the fast-falling snow. "Now," she continued, "you serve me, Jack of Cnoc na Teamhrach, king of the sídhe and lord of Tech Duinn – and of death."

He hissed through his teeth, a new, furious maelstrom of hatred overpowering the pain and terror that surged within him. "I will never serve you," he snarled. "You nightmarish bitch."

Her fathomless eyes flashed, black ice and silver snow. "Fool," she said softly. "I offer to show you all the secrets of the undying lands, to unveil for you the mysteries of the cosmos – and you spit it back in my face?"

"I don't need your wisdom," Jack said, shoulders heaving with rage and despair. "I am no miserable, whining weakling like he –" He jerked his chin towards the ruined body of Donn, the lord of death – the former lord of death, he realized with a savage, sickening jolt. "I will not grovel at your feet for your poor mercies, will not beg you for hollow favors and foolish boons." He stumbled to his feet, head still spinning with this strange, sickening power churning through his body. "I will escape this hellhole," he said, snarling. "I will break your curse, and when I am free at last, I will become the king as I was promised – the king of all Éire, and anyone who dares to question me, everyone who has ever wronged me, will suffer my wrath." He spat on the ground. "I swear it."

The Morrígan stared at him, dispassionate and cold, then raised a single finger. The snowflakes froze in midair, then collapsed back down on the earth, hardening and crystallizing into a smooth veneer of pristine white frost. Slowly, she knelt down in the snow, lifting a handful of glimmering white crystals in the palm of her hand. She blew gently upon them, and Jack's eyes widened as they swirled around her, a panoramic wonder of diamond-like brightness and light. "Black of hair," she said, rising to her feet. "White of skin. Red of lip."

Jack frowned, glancing down at the princess lying motionless at his feet. "What about her?"

"Not her," the goddess said. ""I have seen it written in the webbing of the world, your freedom. It lies with another – like, but not like, she who will be the freeing of you from the realm of eternal night."

He drew in a deep breath of the impenetrably cold winter air. "Yes," he whispered. "I knew it, even then, that day – what I saw in the snow. My destiny."

The Mórrígan stared at him for a long moment, the only sound the hush of the falling snow, then slowly, turned away. "The creatures of the sídhe are yours to command," the goddess said, waving her hand. "Keep the balance between this world and the next, and the bridge my sister built that binds them together – if you can."

"Wait." Jack staggered forward, as the wet, glistening flakes fell thicker, faster all around him, shrouding the blank staring eyes of the princess and her lord in a thin white pall of eternal snow. "Who? Who is she? Give me a name – give me guidance."

"You have rejected my guidance," she said without turning around to face him. "I will leave you now, lord of death. I shall not see you again."

Without another word, the Mórrígan vanished into the shadows, and Jack stumbled after her, half-blind with panic, with fear, pushing aside the ice-slick branches of the new-grown trees, slipping on the frost-slick stones covering the ground. Just ahead, barely illuminated by the faint glow of the shining silver stars far above him, the white crescent moon peeking out from behind the thick dark clouds that covered the midnight sky, lay the banks of a fast-churning river. He dropped to his knees beside the murky water, leaning over to peer into the coursing waves.

It was not his familiar black eyes that he saw, framed within the narrow, clean-cut lines of his once handsome face, but two golden orbs burning against the darkness, alight with an immortal blaze, staring back at him.

PART III

Chapter Thirty-Nine
Lios Lachna, Éire, 1082

CONOR

For a moment, the only sound was the crackling of the fire, the distant call of the owls in the trees, as Conor stared at Riona, nervously fiddling with the blades of grass between her now-bare fingers.

"Riona," he said as calmly as he was able. "Jack, the high prince from a children's fable, is the lord of death who is threatening to kill Haisley. *Your* lord of death."

She flinched a little at the deliberate inflection, but he didn't care. That honey-warm feeling was fading now, growing cold and congealed in the pit of his stomach, as the weight of reality resettled onto his shoulders, the stark truth of what they had become. He had been dreaming, and now he was awake, bitter and clear-eyed once more. "That explains it," he said flatly. "The tasks he wants you to complete, the objects you must retrieve – they were all his once, weren't they? From the story? The cloak and the purse and –" He hissed softly. "And the sword."

Her lips tightened, and her features grew distant, frozen, aloof once more, and they were fathoms apart again, even though he could but raise his hand and touch the loose strands of her hair. "Yes."

"So you lied to me," he said. "Again."

She twisted around to snatch up her gloves where they lay

crumpled on the ground, tugging them curtly over her bandaged hands. "I did not lie, Conor. But…I do think that I have been lied *to*."

Conor stiffened. "What do you mean?"

"I told you," she said, "that once I retrieved them for him, our bargain would be complete and I would be free, and Haisley – she would be safe." Riona rubbed her palms together, the only sign of her anxiety. "That was the agreement that Jack and I made, but – I k*now* that he is lying. There is something far greater, far more sinister than a few magical objects, no matter how powerful they may be." She shook her head. "They're not what he truly wants – at least, they're not all he wants from me, but I don't know what else he might be after."

"So this is all for nothing, then." Conor swore softly. "What are we *doing* here, Riona, running around the countryside like dogs chasing our tails? Why put Haisley in danger so unnecessarily?" He began to pace, back and forth. "Gods, Riona. This is *Maeve*, all over again."

It was the wrong thing to say. Something dark and unreadable guttered in her expression, but before he could speak, she cleared her throat and continued. "Regardless. He does want the sword, very much, and the purse and the cloak. I know that much is true. He wants to use them, as he once did, when he was a mortal prince and he first won them with the help of the fear-dearg." His brow furrowed as that same shadowy expression drifted across her face. "They are extremely powerful objects, destined to bring unimagined greatness to whomever wields them, and greatness is the one thing that Jack has always craved, in his mortal and immortal lives alike."

"How did he become the lord of death? I don't understand – he was a prince, a human, and Donn was made the lord of Tech Duinn centuries ago."

"Don't you remember the story?" Riona's lips twisted. "How Jack came to seek the girl with black hair and white skin and red lips in the first place?"

"The raven," he said slowly. "The raven, dead in the snow."

"Not just any raven." She raised her eyebrows at him. "The Mórrígan's."

Even the night around them seemed to shiver at the sound of her name, and involuntarily, Conor found himself shifting closer to the fire, to the comforting warmth of the sparks that bedazzled the midnight black air.

"She was the one who placed Donn as the ruler of Tech Duinn," Riona said, "and she was the one who appointed Jack as his replacement, as vengeance for the death of her raven as much for Jack killing Don. An éraic, a blood-debt owed, for which he paid very dearly." Absently, Riona ran the tip of her finger over her forearm, tracing the scars that mutilated her skin, hidden beneath the silk sleeve of her gown. "*Her* blood, that once ran in my veins, and that runs in Haisley's now."

A trickle of fear ran down his spine. "She shouldn't be here," he said, glancing nervously at where Haisley still slept, peaceful and deep, curled up by the fire. "She's too close to all of this madness."

"She is only a pawn to him, Conor, the means to get what he truly wants from me. She'll be safe enough, as long as I do what he wants."

"I don't understand." Conor rubbed at his forehead wearily. "What does he want from you, Ria? If he's not Donn – if he's really

Jack, the high prince of Éire, then what does he want with you?"

"What they all want, all of the sídhe locked away in the other-realms, neither of the earth or below. I have met so many of them – the púca and Fiadh and the blackthorn queen. All of them, every last creature that I have met over these last ten years, they all want the same thing from me. To be set free – to go home."

"Éire," said Conor slowly. "*Our* Éire, outside of the sídhe."

"Yes. And Jack is no different. He too wants to be free."

"That's impossible." Conor jerked his hand away to scrub furiously at the scruff of his jaw. "Even if he has all three of these treasures that he has ordered you to find for him, then he cannot escape the sídhe. That's not how it works. You yourself said it – the Morrígan bound him to the land of the dead. Even with these treasures, he couldn't break that curse." He paused. "Could he?"

"I don't know." She paused, her head tilted back to gaze unseeingly at the starless sky. "With the cloak? Perhaps." She paused again as she stared into the fire, the breeze wafting loose strands of raven black hair across her snow-white cheeks, a stark contrast, and Conor shivered at the strangely spectral look the shadows cast over her face.

"But *why*? What is it, exactly, that you think he wants from you?"

"He wants what was promised to him," she said softly. "What he believes is his destiny. To be High King of Éire, to lay his palm against the rock of the Lia Fail and hear it roar out his name, to have the sea-waves rise up and acknowledge him king. He wants," she said, "to rule all of Éire, both the realm that is of the earth and the realm that is not, the mortals and the sídhe alike."

"Ria."

"Think of it – the dark druid himself loose in a realm that has not known magic in hundreds of years," she said again, her fingers twisted in her lap. "He would be the most powerful king our world has ever seen, once he is no longer bound to the sídhe."

Conor shuddered. "Then you can't," he said through the lump in his throat. "You can't give them to him, these treasures. You can't."

"I have to. If I don't do this for him," she said, "Haisley will die."

"If you do," he shot back, "then everyone else will die."

"I don't care."

"Ria –"

"I don't care, Conor," she half-snarled, fists clenched. "I only care about her. You don't know what it's like – standing beside so many biers, mourning so many graves, keeping so many death-watches. They consume me, the memories of those I have lost too soon – consume me whole, leave me broken and lost and *alone*, and I will not add my daughter's number to them, I will *not*."

Her voice shattered, and Conor found himself crawling toward her, wrapping his arms around her trembling shoulders, pulling her close. "It's all right," he whispered against her hair. "It's all right, Ria."

For a long while, the only sound was the crackling of the fire, the muted hoots of the owls from the nearby trees, until at last Riona pulled away, wiping at her eyes. "I don't have any other choice, cabbage," she said quietly. "He needs my help, and I must give it to him. Simple as that. Either Haisley will die, or Éire will burn." She lifted her hand and pushed her wayward hair, a glossy sheath of midnight rain, away from her moonbeam face, and her gaze met his, sad and resigned. "And we both know which of those I will choose."

Chapter Forty
Lios Lachna, Éire, 1082

RIONA

She had dreaded that look on his face for so long, watching the color leech out of his freckled face as the understanding which she had arrived at some time ago dawned on him now for the first time – the understanding of what she would have to do, the monster that she would have to become, if she were to see this through. "We all want to be free, Conor," she said, as gently as she was able. "Jack is no different," she said again, because it was the truth, she knew. There had always been that unspoken affinity between them, a longing for something more than the fate that they had each been given. It had blinded her for too long, the sympathy she felt for him, driven mad by the depths of his despair. She swallowed nervously as Conor remained silent, staring at her with shattered gray eyes. "I am his last hope to be free. His only hope, really."

Conor's pallid face did not even flicker. "That doesn't mean you have to do this."

"Conor." She smiled, small and tight. "Of course I don't have to. I could always refuse." She hesitated, studying him closely, noting how the tension eased ever so slightly at the corners of his mouth. "But if I don't –"

"Don't say it."

"He will kill Haisley." She shook her head. "It's a simple enough bargain, a straightforward trading of souls – mine, for hers."

"It's far more complicated than that, Ria. You will doom all of Éire if you do this."

She ignored him. "Either I accept and set him free, or I refuse, and he kills Haisley out of spite, and I am powerless to stop him. There is no victory here, Conor. I've been racking my brain for so long now, trying to figure out some way to defeat him, but I can't." She closed her eyes, steadying herself for a moment, then looked at him again, memorizing the lines of his face, the soft sheen of his gray eyes. "Tomorrow I will go into the sídhe and fetch his sword, and then go, and I will give him what he has always wanted and then –" Her voice trailed away again, but she knew he understood what she had chosen to leave unspoken, this terrible truth which she would be forced to accept.

Jack would loose centuries' worth of pent-up rage on the hapless mortals of the realm, with no one powerful enough to stop whatever destruction and the desolation he left in his wake.

"And what about the rest of the realm?" Conor demanded. "Would you let them suffer, let them die, with no qualms?"

"Of course I have qualms," she said, still so softly. "I pity them, but —"

But not as much as I love my daughter.

The words, though unspoken, hung heavy and irrefutable in the air between them, an insurmountable, unmovable wall.

"Their blood will be on your hands." He reached out, his fingers gripping her chin, forcing her to look him in the eyes as he spoke. It was almost painful, seeing the clear gray of his eyes so darkened with pain, with anger. "Do you understand that? You will be just as terrible of a monster as he."

"I already am." She pushed at his wrist with the tips of her fingers, and his hand fell away. "And I don't care, as long as *she* is safe."

"You cannot do this, Riona."

"I must." Her lips trembled as she smiled. "Haisley will be safe. I will make very sure of that."

"No." Conor came to life, leaping to his feet as he dragged his hands through his hair. "We can find another way – another way where innocents don't have to suffer to keep our daughter safe."

"I don't think that there is one."

"You keep saying that to me," he snapped. "Every time we face an obstacle, a problem, you have no faith, none, that we can solve it, that we can conquer it, together. You always give up so readily, so easily." He pressed his knuckles against his eyes. "So tell me, Riona – is it me that you do not trust, or the idea of no longer being alone?"

She recoiled. "Don't be cruel."

"Every time." She could see his chest heaving in the soft firelight glow, his hands gripping his hair. "Every time something goes wrong, you run from me. You leave me, sitting by the river or standing in the rain, wondering what I did wrong to drive you away, and it has taken me this long to start to think that it was never anything I did, but rather something that you did not want, something that terrified you far more than any threat we ever faced, that makes you run."

"And what is that?" She asked before she could think better of it, then bit down hard on her lip as he laughed humorlessly, his head tilted back towards the sky, far above where she still sat in the grass, arms curved around her knees.

"You tell me, Riona, because the gods know that I've never been able to figure you out."

On the other side of the fire, Haisley shifted in her sleep, the leaves rustling underneath her as she snuggled deeper into Riona's cloak, and Riona's own lips trembled as she watched the pale features of her daughter's face, faintly illuminated by the orange-red flames. "I don't see why you are so upset," she said. "You will both be happier, safer, this way."

"Except," he said, "for whatever savagery Jack unleashes on my homeland in his quest for the throne."

"He *swore* that Haisley would be safe. He can't break that vow." She shook her head, eyes downcast again, unable to look at his face, twisted with pain and grief. "No one will be coming to hurt either of you any longer."

"*You* hurt us. You hurt me, every time you leave me."

It was the smoke, she told herself, that was blurring her vision, causing the sting of hot tears to prickle in her eyes. "I left you," she said, "because I loved both of you far too much to ever have to lose you."

"Ria." She did look up then, at where he stood, his face half-hidden in the darkness. "I don't know why it has never been easy for us, the loving of each other."

"Just unlucky, I suppose," she said, and after a moment, he sighed, a heavy, resigned sound, and crouched back down next to her, his fingers pressed to his lips. "Cabbage," she whispered. "I'm really scared."

He dropped his hands and looked at her, solemn and sad. "The last time you said that to me, we were about to tell your mother that you were with child. This must be a fearsome thing indeed, if it frightens you as much as that."

A surprised laugh burst out of her, and then his fingers slipped into hers, squeezing them gently. "Very well," she said through the lump in her throat. "Let's figure out a way then. You say that we can, as long as we're together. What do we do then, to keep Haisley safe and not let Jack loose in Éire?'

He sat down heavily next to her, keeping her hand clasped tightly in his. "Have you thought about…you know," he said. "Killing him?"

"Jack? Yes." She leaned her head against his shoulder. "It's not that simple though. I've thought and thought about it, and if I did find a way to kill him, it could create even more problems. There has to *be* a lord of death, someone to tend to the ordering of the world, to rule over the sídhe-realms and tend to the lost souls." She paused. "And besides, even if I somehow managed to kill Jack, it doesn't protect Haisley. The blood-sickness would take her anyway. It's only his magic keeping her well as it is."

Conor frowned. "Except," he said slowly, "I think I might have a way to – well, not cure her, but to treat the disease, to make it more manageable, and not…fatal."

"So Haisley mentioned." Riona paused, brow furrowed. "How would it work, then? This treatment?"

"Well, it's only a theory right now, but after you – " He cleared his throat. "After we discovered that Haisley was ill, I spent most of my nights in Mamó's solar, reading through her books and her notes. It turns out that before you were born, she treated a young boy of about twelve who had the blood-sickness. He was too far gone when he was brought to her, a very sick lad, but she tried and found some measure of success with stabilizing him a bit before he passed. She had a whole sheaf of notes scribbled down, as well as some ancient texts from other lands in the east that she had obtained, and I went from there."

"And?"

"It's not really a disease of the blood, from what I can tell." He shifted a little to face her, that old familiar spark returning to his face, the look she remembered from their youth, whenever he talked about his passion for herbs and flowers and green, growing things. "It's not that the blood itself is sick, but how the body overall fails to process food properly." He hesitated. "I don't know how many of the technical details you want to hear."

"Keep it simple, cabbage."

He smiled, ever so slightly, and on impulse, Riona slid closer to him. "I started experimenting ways to duplicate that process of absorbing food into the bloodstream with an artificial compound. I began with sheep's blood and wormseed, but it wasn't strong enough. It's taken a while – years, actually – but I think, I *think* I've figured out that I need to use cow's blood and fenugreek instead, and theoretically, it would work far better."

"You think," Riona repeated. "How sure are you?"

Conor glanced at her ruefully. "Fairly sure."

"Are we willing to bargain our daughter's life on you being 'fairly sure'?"

"No," he said, "but I am willing to bargain it on you and me being strong enough, smart enough, to figure this out. Together." He paused. "Are you?"

They were quiet for a moment, the fire crackling behind them, the owls hooting in the distance, so like all those nights that they had once spent together in their youth – under the stars by the river or out on the terrace outside their tower room. It felt like centuries had passed, Riona thought, since those long lost days of first love, yet it was still so clear in her remembrances, an evergreen growing thick and wild on by a mountainside stream, its scent ever fresh, ever strong. Ever enduring.

"All right," she said at last. "So you need to make sure this treatment of yours works, and I need to find a way to kill the lord of death and not completely wreck the orderings of the afterlife." She laughed drily. "Simple enough."

"Well, I can't help you with the afterlife issue, but as far as killing the lord of death, if young prince Jack managed it, that utter gobshite, then so can we." He paused. "The other sídhe-creatures," he said slowly. "You mentioned that you befriended some of them – helped them?"

"Yes." She paused, remembering the silver hair, the hungry eyes of the fairy-queen, and shivered. "Although I'd hardly say we're friends."

"How do they feel about him? Jack?"

"He is their lord. They obey him unquestioningly."

"Yes, but *you* are their lady, aren't you?"

"No, I'm merely a servant to the lord of death. I have no power there in the land of the dead that he does not grant me," she said, then hesitated. "Although –"

Conor leaned forward, his eyes clearing suddenly of their darkness, like sunlight breaking through the lingering clouds after a late autumn rain. "Although what?"

"There was one time, when I left the sídhe, when one of them — Fiadh — she came with me. I told her not to harm anyone, and as far as I know, she didn't – not even when I left her for so long, while I was in Emain Ablach, retrieving the spear and the purse.

She obeyed me, even though it went against her nature, almost as though she were bound to do so." Riona pondered this for a moment, the symmetry, the rightness of it warming her chest. The way that they all watched her, with that strange, expectant air, as though they had been waiting, all this time – waiting for her. "Possibly," she said at last. "Possibly, they might follow me. But Fiadh could also just be the exception. She is very attached to me, far more than to him these days."

"Fiadh," he said. "That's the name you gave Kayleigh when I introduced you. Friend of yours?"

Riona smiled. "Of a sort." Her amusement faded away as she stared into the fire. "I didn't realize, not fully, until after I had found the purse, used it as my own but – it was so natural, the impulse to harvest its power, a reaping that was innate as breathing, and I wondered then, if that's why she was so fascinated by me, because I was a link to them, her old masters and the treasures they tasked her with guarding. Then I spoke to the púca and something he said –"

"For the gods' sake, Ria, did you make friends with every demon in the sídhe?"

She pressed her face into his arm, laughing softly. "Oh cabbage, you have no idea." She breathed him in for a moment, sweat and dirt and the richness of the earth. "When I held that purse in my hands," she continued after a moment. "I felt it, the power of the gods vibrating within the soft fabric of its folds, and I – become, something else, something more, a creature spun from cobwebs and shadows, but of unimagined might, and –" She inhaled deeply. "And the thing is, Conor, for a moment there, I understood him. His ambition, his ruthlessness, all of it. I felt it, burning within my heart as well." The scars on her arms seemed to burn as she remembered how easy it had been, to spill a few drops of blood and feel the invisible bond that tethered the monsters to their shadow-lands snap under the weight of her spells, and she shook her head. "It was like they belonged to me – as though they were calling out to me, as long lost friends."

"That makes sense though, Ria." His voice was slow, puzzling his way through the problem in that deliberate, quiet way of his. "You are descended from the gods, and those treasures – the purse and the cloak and the sword – they belonged to the gods, didn't they?"

Riona sat up suddenly, a jolt of inspiration slipping down her spine. "The sword," she whispered. "Conor – I could use the sword to kill Jack. It's the god-slayer, remember? Whoever wields it cannot be defeated by any living soul. It's how Jack himself defeated the lord of death in the fable!"

Conor leaned forward, a wary hope flickering across his face. "Are you sure? It seems like quite a risk for him to take, sending you after the one thing that could defeat him."

"Yes, but he would never dream that I would ever consider using it against him. He thinks that I'm on his side, that he's won me over completely – and even so, he knows that I would never do anything to risk Haisley's life."

"But you said earlier — there always must be a lord of death. What happens to the realm of the dead and the souls who travel there, if he isn't there to oversee it?"

Riona heaved a long sigh and sank back down on the grass, staring up at the starry sky above them. "I don't know," she admitted quietly. "But it's the same principle as before — if I can just keep Haisley safe, then I'll figure out the rest later. That's what matters,

Conor. Nothing else."

He lowered himself down on the ground next to her, facing her so that the tips of their noses brushed against one another's. "I hope you're right."

"I know I am," she whispered, then leaned forward and kissed him, soft and gentle and sweet.

It didn't seem like there was much else to say between them, huddled close together, arms and lips entwined, then later watching the firelight play over their daughter's slumbering face. They had always spoken best when their words were silent, with gentle touches and finger brushes and quick looks, that implicit understanding that was woven between them, almost from the very first day that they had met.

Riona had never been one to believe in destiny, in fate — contrary to whatever divine lineage she might lay claim to — but if she did, Conor Ó Ruairc would certainly have been hers.

Neither of them slept, lying side by side in the cool hillside grass, watching the stars wink out over their heads one by one, as the dawn crept out on shy, tentative paws, a pale purple shadow to the east. Riona sighed, then lifted her head from his shoulder. "I should go," she said. "I still need to find that sword."

"I know."

"So I should go," she said, "before Haisley wakes up."

"I'll tell her that you said goodbye."

Riona nodded, then softly kissed his cheek. "I don't know how long it will be, if it works and the cloak allows me to breach its borders. Time is…different in the sídhe. Sometimes an hour in there can be mere minutes here, and sometimes it can be days, weeks. I'll be as quick as I can but –"

"Ria." His eyes were clearer than she had ever before seen them, moonlight glinting off well-worn river-rocks beneath the tumbling waves. "I'll be waiting."

She nodded once, then climbed to her feet, her knees stiff and aching from the long night. "I will find the sword," she said, pulling out the cream-colored cloak of darkness from the pocket of her gown, "and then I'll come back to you, Conor Ó Ruairc."

"You always do."

It was strange, how a smile could look so much like heartbreak, as the one tugging at the corners of Conor's mouth did. Riona did not trust herself to speak, but simply nodded again, jerky and uneven, then wrapped the cloak around her shoulders in a single, swift motion, and turned away, heading north toward the royal cairn of the first kings of Connacht, the burial mounds of the long dead warriors of Éire, the dread sídhe-realm of the Mórrígan herself.

Ráth Crúachan.

Chapter Forty-One
Neither of the Earth Nor Under It, Not Then Nor Now

RIONA

The magic of the cloak made it laughably easy, breaching the borders of the most dreaded realm in all of Éire. Riona had braced herself to bleed out a dangerous amount of blood on the moss-covered rocks surrounding the ominous mouth of the cave nestled within the towering cairns of stone and mud that stood gathered around the grassy plain of the former home of the Connachta kings, but as soon as she had approached the mouth of the cave, the cloak pulled tight around her shoulders, the air rippled once and she stepped right through, leaving behind the early morning sun and finding herself shrouded in the unrelenting shadows of eternal night once more.

She turned in a slow, wondering circle, pulling the cloak from her head and shoulders as she stared at it with wide eyes.

All that blood she had shed, for all those years — and for what? Truly the might found in the artistry of the gods was a terrible, all-powerful thing.

She glanced around at her surroundings. It was almost the mirror image of the land of the dead, the sídhe-realm of the Mórrígan, with its velvet-soft sky scattered with the faint white lights of a thousand gleaming stars, the frost-bitten branches of tall gray ash trees, the wafer-thin carpet of diamond-white snow that blanketed the forest floor. Almost, but not quite the same. There was something reverential in the air here, solemn and awful in its severity, no invisible humming of hidden monsters prowling within the depths of these woods.

Even monsters were too afraid to wander freely here.

There was a faint rustling above her, and she looked up sharply to see them, dozens of midnight-winged ravens sitting perched in the branches of the trees, watching her intently with their beady, unblinking eyes. The home of the Mórrígan, indeed.

Riona licked at the sweat beading above her upper lip, trying to remember that brief flash of a vision from the revelation spell. She had seen it, the dark yawning mouth of the cave, the star-dappled sky, the falling snow drifting down through the darkness to shroud the red sandstone walls of some unknown castle in a veil of pure white flakes, the ravens sitting quiet and still with watchful bright eyes among the gray barren branches of the trees.

She had seen other things too, giant, soft-pawed felines creatures prowling soundless through the shadows, with great yellow eyes and sharp-tipped ears. The cave of cats, it was called, the birthplace of the cat-sìth herself and her offspring.

Fiadh.

Riona raised a trembling hand to her lips, her heart pounding wildly – for the first time, with hope, rather than fear.

She had been a fool not to think of it before, when she had told Conor of the cat-sìth's loyalty, her affection. Because Fiadh would of course know where the sword was hidden. She thought of all the times that Fiadh would be prowling nearby as she and Jack wandered through the starlit woods of Tech Duinn, of how pointedly Jack would draw her attention to the sleek sídhe-beast, how he would nudge them together, encourage that tenuous bond of friendship between them — because Fiadh would never reveal where it lay hidden to him, not without the blood of the gods running through his veins but, perhaps, to *Riona*, she might.

She remembered how he had suggested, ever so casually, that Fiadh accompany her on that very first quest, her search for the Gáe-Bolg, as though the real test all along had been to see if the cat-sìth would lead her to other, far more precious hidden things.

Just, Riona realized with a shiver, as she had, the purse of plenty lying there so innocently among those heaps of gold and silver and spears in the black and burnt nest of the Ellen Trechend.

He had no doubt kept Fiadh close all these centuries, had ensured that Fiadh be the one who greeted her upon her arrival in the sídhe, with her throaty purr and curious yellow eyes. Riona remembered Fiadh as she had seemed to her when she first arrived in the sídhe, how the cat-sìth had watched her with those bright yellow eyes, so eager, so hungry. Not, she realized, with the hunger of a belly, but of the soul, aching to see even the smallest glimpse of her former masters again.

Fiadh's loyalty had always been hers, not Jack's, and Riona's breath caught in her chest as she wondered if, perhaps, just as Conor had suggested, they all were — all those sídhe-creatures, with their strange, terrible beauty, who had watched her with such unwavering, focused intensity as she roamed throughout the snow-kissed woods of Tech Duinn with Jack at her side. It was not him at whom they had stared.

It was *her*.

A branch snapped above her, and she looked up sharply. The

ravens were gone, vanished in a silent flutter of night-black wings, because something else now prowled among the branches of the trees, here in the cave of cats, as though summoned home by the mere whisper of her thoughts.

"Fiadh."

The frost-kissed limbs above her head creaked once, and then a familiar pair of glowing yellow eyes peeked through the shadows, ears pricked and fangs gleaming faintly underneath the pale light of the stars. "Good girl," Riona said. "Show me where it is hidden, Fifi. Take me to the sword."

The cat-sìth snapped her teeth in answer, then leapt down from the trees, crashing to the ground before her with that same unearthly grace from all those years before, her stubby tail lashing. Riona hesitated for a moment, then removed the purse or plenty from her pocket. Fiadh's eyes snapped to it immediately, a low purr humming in her throat. "You *do* recognize it, don't you?" She stared at the cat-sìth, who stared in turn at the purse, unblinking and intense, and Riona shivered at the idea that it was this that had drawn the cat to her side — that Fiadh had been watching, ever since Riona had retrieved the purse from its hiding place, waiting for her to return to the sìdhe. "Because we need to keep it safe," she said, more to herself than the fairy-cat. "That's what you want, isn't it. For me to help you keep the purse and the cloak safe, to keep them hidden – right, girl?" A wet nose nuzzled against her throat, and she reached to stroke the silky softness of the cat-sìth's sharp-pricked ears, Fiadh's answering purr rumbling deep within her throat. Riona nodded, then knelt down, tucking both the purse and the cloak into the gnarled roots of an ancient yew tree. Then she was off, loping away into the shadows of the trees, with Riona sprinting behind her, her gown caught up in her hands as she ran alongside the yellow-eyed keeper of the treasures of the Tuatha Dé Danann.

It could have been minutes, or it could have been days, as Riona hurried behind Fiadh's graceful form, slipping past the icy branches of the trees to whatever hidden corner of the sídhe the sword of starlight lay secreted away from the rest of the world. Time had once again vanished, here in the other-realm, an insubstantial thing, when eternity stretched out in dark, endless waves at her feet. She was far more at home here, underneath this timeless sky with its never-changing stars, than in the world of the living with its too-bright sun and unending litany of hurts. It steadied the thundering pace of her galloping heart, the frantic pounding at her temples, the familiar sense of home settling over her shoulders like a well-tailored gown, close-fitting and warm.

She had always lived in fear, in that other-world of her past life. That nagging worry had nibbled at her elbow for as long as she could remember – that she was doomed to watch with helpless, grief-wrung hands as death stole away all that she loved, that she would be powerless in the face of its inevitable might, that there would be no ending to her story that did not end in darkness and despair.

Darkness there might be, she thought as she slowed to a halt beside Fiadh, staring up at the red sandstone walls of that vine-covered hall which had appeared out of the starry-eyed mist in front of them, but it was not despair coursing through her, blazing-eyed and powerful, as she stalked towards the ivy-laden doors. It was determination, righteous and all-consuming, the clear-eyed sense of purpose of one who had come to claim a destiny that had always been hers to choose.

For the first time in her life, she was no longer afraid.

Riona flicked her wrist with a guttural growl at the overgrown door, Fiadh hovering close by her side, and with a resounding crack, it flew open, the shattered oak hanging weakly on long-rusted hinges. She stalked through, pushing aside cobwebs and vines, the starlight glinting through the dust-fogged windowpanes, huge sheets of glass that stretched from ceiling to floor. Riona's fingers trailed along the side of a white-marbled pillar studded with dozens of twinkling blue sapphire stones, noting the tables laden with cloudy silver platters and dull copper goblets, the twelve gold-inlaid couches arranged in a wide circle about the hall, and there in the middle of the room, on a dais high above the others, a cushioned throne made from ivory and silk, glinting in the dim light with a thousand blood-red jewels embedded in cushions.

Next to her, Fiadh licked eagerly at her black jowls, and Riona's brow furrowed in recognition. "The bruiden of Bricriu," she murmured, scratching Fiadh's scalp in silent thanks. *Clever Conor.* Always helping her, even when he didn't realize it. Her gaze traveled over the abandoned couches, the empty throne. "Twelve couches for the twelve heroes of Ulster, the greatest warriors in all of Éire, who traveled far and wide to compete –" Her breath caught in her chest. "For the curadmír," she whispered. "Of course. The champion would win the sword of starlight, not the best piece of meat."

"Well," said a sly voice from behind her. "They would win that too."

She whirled around toward the dark-skinned man leaning against a balustrade of a balcony above her, grinning amiably.

"Never underestimate the appeal that a well-cooked steak has on a hungry belly."

"Who are you?"

"The master of the hall." He rubbed idly at the wood railing with his thumb. "I apologize about its current state of disarray. I assumed that I would not be having visitors any time soon, so I felt supremely unmotivated to clean."

"Bricriu," Riona said. "The trickster bárd."

He bowed, low and mocking. "I'm honored," he said. "I'd hardly expected to still be remembered by you lot. Mortal memories are, notoriously, quite short."

"So I've heard. Unfortunately, I don't have a lot of time, so I'll be frank. I need the sword," Riona said, stepping forward, her hands fisted at her sides. "The sword of starlight. I know it is here, and I command you to give it to me."

He eyed her with mild interest. "You *command* me? That's quite a pair of stones you have there, hidden under that gown."

Fiadh's ears flattened against her skull, her lips rippling with a vicious snarl, and Riona laid her hand gently on the cat-sìth's rigid spine. "I am Riona," she said calmly. "The blood of the Mórrígan herself runs in my veins, and I am here to claim the sword of starlight as my own."

"Are you." It was not a question, as Bricriu peered down at her, his fingers tapping speculatively against the wooden railing. "How interesting." His stare latched onto hers, and for the briefest moment, something flickered across his face, a dawning awareness, a sense of awe, of satisfaction, almost, then it was gone, his features rearranging themselves back into their former sly grin. "You don't have much of the look of her."

"Regardless," Riona said, her fingers tightening in Fiadh's fur. "You are bound to tell me where it is. It is mine to claim."

He shrugged. "I am not the one who holds the secret of the sword. For that, you must ask your feline friend there."

"But she brought me here, to you." Fiadh nuzzled against her the palm of her hand, a wordless encouragement. "She would never lie to me, deceive me. You, on the other hand, might."

"Certainly I would." He gave a mocking salute. "I am the most legendary trickster in all of Éire, you know, a bárd, who spun his lies through sweet-sounding songs. When Cúchulainn died at the hands of your ancestor, the Mórrígan, she retrieved the sword her father had fashioned from the waning light of a falling star and hid it away here in my hall, all those centuries ago. Only one other mortal has wielded it since."

"I know. Jack, the lord of death."

"He was not, at that time, the lord of anything but impudence and very bad decision-making."

"On that, we are agreed." Riona stepped forward, peering up at him. "Tell me where the sword is hidden. It is mine by right to wield."

He stared down at her, his face unreadable and strained, as though he were fighting some internal battle of momentous importance, wrestling with a strong-armed demon just beyond her sight, then his shoulders sagged a little. "It's true," he said quietly, half to himself. "I can feel it, the blood of the gods within you, faint as it may be. To you alone I am permitted to reveal this secret."

A rush of relief washed over her. "Where is it?"

He stared down at her, intense and burning. "Where it belongs, as befitting its birth," he said at last. "Among the stars."

She frowned, puzzling over the cryptic response. "I don't understand," she said. "What game are you playing now, trickster? Just give it to me and let me be gone."

He looked away, and his lips flattened into a tight, tense line. "I have told you my secret, one that has not crossed my lips in nearly seven hundred years. Do with it what you will, little queen."

"But I still do not understand –" Riona froze. "How do you know my name?"

He raised his hands in a helpless gesture, backing away from the railing into the shadows behind him, and Fiadh growled once, urgent and low, and Riona's gaze snapped to the far corner of the hall.

"Now see," Jack said from where he leaned against the doorway, his arms folded across his chest. "That wasn't so hard, was it, a stóirín?"

Chapter Forty-Two
Neither of the Earth Nor Under It, Not Then Nor Now

RIONA

Riona's fingers tightened around the sleek strands of Fiadh's fur. "My lord," she said with unnatural calm. "How lovely to see you. So unexpected."

"Well, what can I say." He straightened, tugging at the hem of his doublet. "The missing of you grew too much for me to bear, and I found that I couldn't stand it any longer. I heard a rumor that you were here, wandering about the realm of the Phantom Queen herself – what a brave girl you are – so I thought I'd stop by, see how things were progressing."

"Well enough." Her fingers itched for the cloak, to slip it over her shoulders and disappear, to sneak away from the burning intensity of his golden-fire gaze. "A bit tired from all this scampering about, doing your dirty work for you."

"Yes, I heard about your little run-in with Finnevara." He smiled, slow and cruel and not at all soft. "Clever girl, turning his own serpents on him. Don't worry though – I'm not angry with you. He had it coming, the lecherous bastard. It was a well-pronounced judgment on your part – just as I taught you to do." His golden-fire eyes gleamed. "How do you find that his cloak suits you?"

"I wasn't able to get it," she lied, heart pounding. "The

fairy-queen wouldn't give it to me."

"Oh, my sweet, foolish girl." His expression darkened as he edged closer to her. "I *know* that you have it, little liar."

Riona's hands fisted at her sides. "Yes," she said slowly. "I have it, but not the sword – or the purse."

"Not yet." He smiled again, sharp with that merciless, relentless beauty. "You have become so distracted, meandering about the countryside with your little family, that I thought you might again require motivation, and so I have come to give it to you."

Her throat closed up, tight with dread. "What do you mean?"

"Tell me," he said, reaching into his pocket. "Do you recognize this, a stóirín?"

Entwined in his fingers was a thin silver chain, a tiny green stone, still smeared with dried blood, dangling in the middle.

Riona's knees buckled, the air around her growing heavy and thick with terror. "Haisley," she stuttered. "How? She's not here, she's not in the sídhe, and you can't leave –" She hissed through her teeth. "You used the cloak."

"I used the cloak," he said, smiling. "The cloak which you so kindly found for me, and then so foolishly abandoned. Silly girl, to leave it and my purse so carelessly stuffed into the roots of a tree."

"How did you – there's been no *time* –"

"Oh, Riona." He shook his dark head, lips curling. "A few paltry days and nights in the mortal world and you have forgotten all the secrets that I've so painstakingly taught you. The only thing we have here in plentitude," he said, eyes burning, "is time."

"What have you done, what have you *done* –"

"First things first, a stóirín." He tucked the chain back into his pocket, refolding his arms across his chest, and Riona fought to calm herself, to plot, to plan some way out of this deadly web he had so carefully lured her into. "I believe that we have a bargain to fulfill."

He would not have killed her, she told herself frantically. She was of no value to him dead, a wasted soul, so Haisley was alive, somewhere. She only had to find her.

Conor, on the other hand – Riona slammed the door on that whispered thought, venomous and cruel, and focused her attention on the lord of death standing before her. He raised his eyebrow. "What's the matter?" He asked. "Have I said something that upsets you?"

"You can have the cloak."

"I *already* have it, Riona. We have already discussed what a fool you were to part with them so ill-advisedly. Now *where* is my sword?"

"How would I know? You heard the riddle, same as I. Ask Bricriu what he meant."

"That liar." Jack snorted. "He won't tell me. He was under specific instructions to lead you right to it whenever you finally showed your face here, and look at how he has failed at what I commanded him to do, yet again. Do you know how many times I have questioned him, tortured him, ripped him apart, limb by limb, only to put him back together so I could do it all over again? Never once has he given me so much as a hint, even one as cryptic as the one with which he blessed you, the little gobshite."

"Because it's not yours." Riona took a cautious step backwards. "Bricriu knows that. Fiadh knows that. It does not belong to you."

"It should." Jack's lips curled into a snarl. "I earned it, you know. I let that giant cut off my head all those years ago, just as Cúchulainn did. I met death without flinching. I paid the price. It should be mine, as the cloak and the purse should be." He wagged his finger at her. "I *knew* you had that cloak, Riona. I knew that you found it hidden away inside the cairn of Queen Medb, that you failed to bring it to me, as you swore you would, just as I knew that you would not be able to resist the call of the purse of plenty, buried away in the ash-covered realm of Emain Ablach. I knew that you would see it, and crave it, and take it as your own, that you would try, foolishly, to hide it from me, that you would forget that you can hide nothing from me, the lord with all-seeing eyes." He drew in a deep breath. "And I know that you will find my sword as well, wherever it is tucked away in this gods-forsaken palace, whatever that bastard meant by his maddening little cypher. I have earned it, Riona, and the destiny that accompanies it – earned it with my blood and my tears, with my very soul, I have paid for it. And you – you are the one to find it for me."

"Jack," she said, her desperation climbing. "Just give me Haisley. Please – just give me Haisley, and I will find whatever you want, give you whatever you want."

"Little fool," he said, almost tenderly. "I want so much more from you than a cloak and a sword and a purse."

Riona tensed. "I know. I know what you really want."

His golden-fire eyes flashed. "Do you now."

"I figured it out, a while ago." She took one slow, cautious step forward, keeping her gaze locked on Jack. "You want to be free to return to the mortal world."

"I *am* free to return to the mortal world," he said, far too mildly. "The cloak grants me that freedom, as we have discussed."

"But you can't stay, can you? You are still bound to the sídhe, to

Tech Duinn." Riona's fists clenched at her sides. "What you really want, what you *need*, is for me to let you return free to the mortal world – not just the temporary freedom that the cloak gives you, but for good."

"What a clever girl you are." His nostrils flared. "I knew from the moment you were born that I'd never be stealing your soul. I knew who you were destined to be from the moment you drew your first breath." He smiled, beautiful and terrible as the dawn. "I have waited *so* long for you, a stóirín. Don't you understand," he said, sliding forward, eyes gleaming. "Everything I have done –"

Da, Riona thought. Sean, and Aisling, and Cian and Aaden. Maeve.

" – I did to make you see that death would conquer everyone in the world but you."

Riona fought the urge to scream, to lash out at him with that power that he himself had given her, that hummed along the tips of her fingers, but instead, she spread her arms, a helpless gesture. "Here I am, begging you for my daughter. Give her to me, tell me where she is, and I will give you whatever it is you want."

"Now, now." He merely smiled. "She is right where you left her, with that red-haired lover of yours. I took it from her while she was sleeping – no harm, no foul, only a timely reminder for you that I can claim her as mine own whenever I so choose, because you, Riona, are no match for me." Riona studied him closely, searching his golden-fire gaze for any sign of deception, but he merely stared back at her, mockingly cool, and the iron band around her heart eased a little. "After all," he said, "a bargain is a bargain."

He pointed at her, the connemara stone dangling from his finger, an innocent, glimmering threat of unimaginable violence. "Find my sword," he said, sliding his hands into his pockets. "Ask that black-haired feline of yours where it is. The gods only know why it is that she has refused to show me all these years. Find it, give me the cloak and the blade, and then your red-headed brat can skip back to the arms of that sweet-faced new mamaí of hers whole and unharmed, and you – you can set me free at last." He tucked the stone necklace into his pocket, careless and cruel. "Tell me where it is, hidden 'among the stars' – whatever that means, the gods damn that deceitful little bastard."

A memory blossomed unbidden with her – Haisley, drowsy and dozing by the fire, her eyelids heavy with sleep, murmuring about blue-fire gems that shone as bright as stars.

The sapphire stones in the marble pillar glinted faintly in the dim light of the hall, taunting her, teasing her. "It must be outside somewhere," she said. "With the stars. That's what Bricriu said."

"Bricriu," said Jack, "is a liar, and a trickster. The answer will not be as simple as that. Try again." He stepped forward, a lean-ribbed wolf stalking its doe-eyed prey. "You know, don't you." His nostrils flared. "What he meant by stars."

Riona swallowed the thick lump of fear in her throat. "Hyacinth flowers," she said. "Also known as blue stars, because of their shape. There must be some growing nearby."

Jack stared at her, hard and unflinching. "In the midst of all this snow?"

"Sure now." Riona's fingers twisted into the folds of her skirt. "They're hardy flowers, strong and enduring. Mamó once told me about them. They survive the winter easily enough, to bloom in the spring."

"Well, aren't you the little fool." Jack waved an impatient hand in the air. "There is no spring here in the realm of the Phantom Queen, only this unending gods-damned winter that she has mocked me with all these centuries, nothing but snow and ice and this bloody cold, night after endless night." He hissed through his teeth. "There is no life here, a stóirín, only death – or haven't you noticed?" His fingers dipped back into his pocket, no doubt to play with the sparkly silver chain hidden there.

A savage surge of hatred bubbled anew within her. "It's the sídhe," Riona said as steadily as she could. "It operates outside the laws of nature and time. Haven't *you* noticed?"

His lips curled into a snarl. "It would be unwise to mock me." He jangled the chain in his pocket. "Or should I remind you?"

"There are hyacinths painted on the hearth of the solar down the hall."

Riona looked up sharply to see Bricriu lounging on the wooden railing above them, picking at his nails. "You couldn't have said that earlier?"

"I owe him no answers," he said with a derisive sniff in Jack's direction. "Only you, and it pains me to see such a pretty lady so distraught by this bastard."

Jack's eyes narrowed. "Show me."

"Down the corridor," said Bricriu airily. "Second door on your right. Happy hunting."

Riona could see Jack's fingers twitching impatiently. "If I find that you are lying to me, trickster, yet again –"

"I know." He yawned delicately. "You will flay the skin right off my bones. It was horribly unpleasant the last dozen times, and I am hardly inclined to relive the experience." He smirked. "I was forbidden to betray the secrets of the Phantom Queen to any other than her kin." Bricriu waggled his fingers in Riona's direction. "Behold, her kin. Now go forth and smite whatever you like with that damned sword, for all I care. My duty is fulfilled."

For a moment, Jack hesitated, staring up at Bricriu with suspicious eyes, then slowly, backed away toward the door at the other end of the hall. "Do not move," he snarled in Riona's direction. "Or the only pieces of your daughter that you will ever again see are her bones."

He vanished through the doorway, and Riona turned immediately to the white-marbled pillar, running her hands along the bright twinkling gemstones.

"Sapphires," she said. "The sapphires are the stars."

"You do not have long before he too realizes that." Bricriu leaned his elbows against the railing, watching her. "Best hurry."

"Which one is it?" Riona tugged futilely at the glinting stones, one after another. "There must be hundreds of them."

"That I cannot say." He jerked his chin. "But someone else can."

Riona whirled around. "Fiadh."

The cat-sìth slunk forward from underneath one of the long wooden tables, her yellow eyes glowing like torchlight in the dimly lit hall. She prowled up to the marble pillar, circling it slowly, then heaved herself up on her back legs, scraping the rough underside of her paw against a brilliant blue gemstone in the center of the column. Riona reached up, gripping the jewel in both her hands, and pulled.

From out of the pillar slid an ebony hilt adorned with the glimmering stones, and there followed it a shining silver blade, so bright and keen that suddenly the dark hall was illuminated by the radiance of its sheen. "The sword of starlight," Riona whispered, running her gloved hand along the flat side of the blade. From above her, Bricriu tsked scornfully.

"All this fuss," he said, "over *that*."

"It's beautiful," Riona whispered, and Bricriu made a derisive noise.

"It has ruined so many lives, corrupted so many souls." His mouth flattened into a hard line. "So much suffering, for its sake."

Riona shivered at the viciousness in his tone, sliding the sword into her belt. "I have to leave," she said, looking up at the bárd to see him loping down the curved staircase that led to the balcony. "I have to leave before he sees this – to protect them." *The god-slayer,* she thought. Whomever wielded it could never be defeated, never be overcome by any living soul.

He was no god, though. He would die a thousand times easier than anything divine.

"Will I still be able to leave, without the cloak?"

"The confinement spells forbid mortals to enter, and for the creatures of the sídhe to leave." He shrugged. "I do not think that they have any reason to prevent the opposite from occurring."

"Good." Riona moved toward the door. "He has the purse and the cloak – I can't let him get the sword too. How much time has passed in the mortal realm, since I arrived here?"

Bricriu fell into step beside her, watching her closely with his dark, bright eyes. "Five days."

Guilt pooled in the pit of her stomach, and she turned away, frowning as she considered how best to secure the sword into the belt of her dress. "I need a scabbard," she said crossly. "I'll cut off my leg with this thing."

"You are truly leaving?" Bricriu whistled softly. "Bold, indeed.

He will kill whomever it is that you care for so much if you disobey him. There is no mercy, no kindness in his heart."

"Oh, I know that much to be true," Riona said grimly, heading for the door, the sword still clutched in her hand. "But you're wrong. He won't kill her. Not until he has what he really wants from me." Fear prickled along her spine. "At least, not Haisley. But." She swallowed. "Conor might already –"

Her voice trailed away as her eyes stung with hot tears, and Fiadh mewled unhappily, sensing her distress, her nose sniffing at her skirts. Bricriu cleared his throat. "When you see your kin," he said, "put in a good word for me, would you? Make sure that she knows that it was I that helped you. I would like to be released back into the open air of the land of the living, not locked away here in this dust-coated tomb for the rest of eternity."

"Oh." Riona paused. "You must not know. The gods are gone, vanished from the earth."

Bricriu remained unmoved. "I do know."

"So," Riona said slowly. "She is lost, as are all the rest of them. I have never met her. The Mórrígan."

For a moment, his dark eyes latched onto hers. "Little queen," he said, and the lord of mischief and song seemed unfathomably sad, a terrible kind of pity swirling in his eyes. "You will."

Before she could answer, he stiffened suddenly, holding up a finger as he listened to some whispered warning that only he could hear. "What's wrong?"

"He's gone," Bricriu said tersely. "The lord of death has left."

Riona stumbled backwards, toward the doorway at the far end of the hall. "Left the castle? When?"

"No." Bricriu's lips flattened, his narrow face taut and grim. "He has left the sídhe."

Her heart stuttered in her chest. "Why would he leave? Why would he not come here, to take the sword from me?"

"He cannot." Bricriu's dark gaze fell to the bright shining sword at her side. "Even he cannot withstand the might of such a weapon, were you to wield it against him." He looked at her then, solemn and sad. "He knows," he said, "that he would die – forever, this time." By her side, Fiadh growled once, her tail lashing, and Bricriu shook his head, mouth grim. "Go, little queen. Go quickly."

Riona turned and ran down the length of the hall, her slippers slapping against the stones, the sword of starlight clasped in her hand, the cat-sìth loping at her side.

Fate be damned, she thought as she burst out into the bleak cold of the eternal night sky. If that monster laid so much as a finger on her daughter, she would kill him, even if by doing so, she sealed her own doom.

Whatever the cost, whatever the price, she would make him pay.

Chapter Forty-Three
Ráth Crúachan, Éire, 1082

CONOR

"I can't find my necklace."

Conor looked up from where he crouched by their campfire, banking the still-warm embers. Five nights, he thought with that too-familiar twinge of dread. Five nights had passed since Riona had gone, vanishing into the early morning shadows, arrowing her way north. Four days and five nights he had idled away with Haisley, wandering about the countryside, visiting the small villages along the way, sleeping under the stars.

Waiting.

He had not been able to stand it any longer, and had dared to venture further north, to the edge of Ráth Crúachan itself, camping on the farthest outskirts of that wide, grassy plain, marred only by the dozen or so looming cairns carved from heavy gray stones and rich black mud, the burial mounds of the great rulers of old. He tried to ignore it, the yawning mouth of the cave that burrowed its way underneath the green-grass plain, the single whitethorn tree that grew by its door, fighting the urge to beat his fists against the moss-covered rocks and scream her name until she appeared, safe and smiling, in its doorway.

If he had to wait much longer, he would go mad.

He shook away the heaviness of his thoughts, turning his attention to where Haisley still reclined in her bed of leaves and grass. "Your necklace?" At his knee, Oscar whined once, low and pleading, eyes fixed on the sausages Conor had set to cook in the smoldering embers of the fire. "It's probably caught in your cloak somewhere, or buried in the leaves. I'll help you search for it once I've fixed breakfast." He shot her a quick, assessing look. "Are you feeling all right, a chnó coill?"

"A little hungry." She rubbed at her eyes. "Tired of sleeping on the ground."

"It won't be much longer. The sausages will be done in a moment."

"And the problem of sleeping on the ground?"

Conor forced a smile. "Not too much longer for that neither. She'll be back, soon enough."

Haisley flopped her head back down in the grass, staring at the bright green leaves above her. "Do you think she's all right?"

"Och yes," Conor said with a cheeriness that he did not feel. "There's no one more capable of watching her own back than Riona. She's a wild one, always has been, ever since I first met her."

"How did you meet?" She didn't look at him as she spoke, her gaze fixed determinedly on the slivers of blue sky peeking through the branches.

Something tugged in Conor's chest. "I had just arrived in the vale from Soghain, and I'd slipped away into the woods for a bit. She came galloping down the path, and her horse kicked me in the head and well-nigh killed me."

"Did she feel very guilty?"

"Irritated, more like." The ghost of a smile pulled at the corners of his mouth as he leaned down to prod at the now-sizzling sausages.

"I bled all over her shirt."

Haisley sat up, her fingers picking at the hem of the cloak. "What is it like? The vale?"

A rush of images, memories that he had kept locked away for nearly ten long years, burst into color in his mind – sloping green hills and gray-ivy walls and the murmur of the river rolling nearby, narrow hallways and wise green-gray eyes and the corners of a warm great hall set dancing with the laughter of two young girls. He swallowed thickly. "It's the most beautiful place in the world," he said, ducking his head down to rummage through his satchel. Running low on biscuits and fruit. They'd have to make a trip back to the southern villages and replenish their supplies if Riona was gone much longer.

"Will I really be queen of it one day?"

"Your mother wants you to be." He cleared his throat. "I mean, *Riona* wants you to be. But I suppose it depends, on what you want."

"I don't know that I would be a very good queen."

"In time, you would." He handed the last few biscuits in his satchel to her. "You have a good heart, Haisley, and a clever mind. The most important qualities, I think, in a ruler."

She stared down at the biscuits in her hands, turning them over and over, lips pursed. "What about Mamaí, and Da? Would they come with me, if I went to the vale?"

"Without a doubt." He reached over and tugged at a loose red curl gently, and she peeked over at him, almost shyly. "They would follow you anywhere, don't you know."

"They must be angry with me for running off."

"As they should. It was a foolish thing you did, Haisley. Thoughtless and unkind, to leave them like that."

"I know." Her bottom lip trembled. "I was just so angry."

For a moment, Conor saw her there, heard her in the quivering tones of their daughter's voice. "Well," he said, gentle and teasing. "It's in your blood – on Riona's side, of course. All your less admirable qualities come from her, obviously."

"Obviously," she said with a quaky smile, and he ruffled her curls with his fingers.

"Let's find that necklace, and then we'll eat."

"What," said an inscrutably soft voice from behind them, and the hairs on Conor's arm prickled in sudden, strident warning, "a lovely little moment of familial bliss this is."

Conor whirled around, and there he was – a golden-eyed, dark-haired demon, his shoulder leaning against the trunk of a slim birch tree, his black boots crossed at the ankles. Conor pushed Haisley to the ground behind him, to shield her from *him*, even as fear clawed at his throat. "Riona," he managed to say, more of a prayer than a query, but the golden-eyed man – the lord of death, Conor realized through the pounding in his temples, the lord of death was *here*, in the mortal world, smiling so amiably, so gently at him, at his *daughter* – simply waved his hand, cutting him off.

"She'll be along soon enough, I'm sure." He yawned. "No doubt she is even now rushing to save you, her precious farm-boy and your redheaded scamp of a progeny."

Haisley whimpered, and Conor stepped backward instinctively, to shield her from that golden-fire gaze that lingered on his daughter's face. "Leave her alone. This is between you and Riona, it has nothing to do with her –"

"On the contrary," he said, something serpentine and cruel distorting the clean-cut lines of his face. "This has *everything* to do with her." His gaze latched onto Haisley, cowering behind Conor's back. "I was going to take *you* next, you know, her carrot-headed lover-boy, until she came along. Probably for the best, as far as my interests were concerned." He flicked his fingers dismissively in Conor's direction. "Would she have risked everything for you, as she has for the little brat you forced upon her? She didn't even want you, you know," he said to Haisley, smiling with a soft, teasing kind of cruelty, the most malevolent, the most terrible kind. "She loathed the very idea of you, from almost the first moment she became aware of your existence, another set of iron bars trapping her inside the cage into which she had been born. You have never been anything more than a burden to her, a duty she felt compelled to fulfill."

"Don't listen to him, a chnó coill," Conor said urgently as Haisley whimpered again, keening and small. "He's a liar, don't listen to him. We loved you, both of us, more than you could ever know."

"Now who's the liar." Jack's nostrils flared as he pushed away from the tree, stepping forward into the light. How beautiful he was, Conor thought in spite of himself. No wonder Riona had felt so drawn to him, magnetized by the sheer force of this otherworldly beauty. "She left you both so easily, didn't she, without so much a single backward glance over her shoulder. She *betrayed* you so easily."

"She didn't," Conor managed to protest through white, cold lips, a flurry of unwanted imaginings flashing through him. Riona. His wildflower girl, so beautiful and bright-eyed, wrapping her arms around this soulless monster as softly, as tenderly, as she had once embraced him. "She would never."

"Wouldn't she?" Jack's voice was a soft drawl of serpentine persuasion, and Conor's gut twisted as a myriad of images exploded in his imagination – Riona, her black hair entwined in those long, cool fingers, her red lips parting under death's greedy kiss, her singsong voice sighing out the Jack's name – and he, Conor, merely a forgotten toy that had been discarded in the far corner of the room, dust-ridden and outgrown. "You never could be worthy of her. You tried for so long, didn't you, but you never could quite be the man she deserved. Small wonder, then, that she would seek solace in the arms of another."

He shook his head, trying to break free of the strange fog that had descended on him. "That's not – that's not true." Almost against his will, his arms fell to his sides, staring into the burning golden eyes of the lord of death.

"Isn't it?" Jack's teeth clicked together with a snap as he spoke, edging ever closer to where Haisley cowered in the grass. "If it hadn't been me, it would have been someone else, you know. One of those ever-present princes, a warrior-chief, a strapping young flaith – anyone, really, would have been an improvement over you. Look at you." Conor glanced down involuntarily, sluggish and thick-headed, to stare at his hands, calloused and rough, his nails forever stained with the juices of a thousand different herbs and the rich dark soil of the earth. No amount of scrubbing could ever get them clean, these hardened healer's hands that had once had the audacity, the hubris to aspire to touch the snow-white skin of a wildflower girl, to cradle her porcelain cheeks between his rough and dirty palms.

"Yes, look at you," Jack said again, almost in his ear, a triumphant song. "You, with your mud-stained hands and your dullard ways.

She was meant for far more than you."

"I know," Conor whispered, hazy and far-away. "I know she was."

"Of course you do," the lord of death said, his hand idling forward, a snake half-hidden in the grass, weaving its way toward an unsuspecting mouse snuffling about in the sun. "It has always been so clear, hasn't it, how far she had to stoop, to debase herself, in order to be near to you, clumsy little coward that you were, more content to play in the dirt with weeds than to wield a sword like the man your father meant you to be."

"My da died," Conor said dully, and from behind him, Haisley made a half-choked sound, the start of a scream that was cut off abruptly mid-gulp, and Conor blinked briefly in confusion, staring up at Jack's smiling, golden-eyed face.

"He surely did." Conor dropped his gaze, the lump in his throat grown too painful to bear. "One of my greatest disappointments, seeing how she almost balked at killing him. It was quite the setback, her lingering softness for you."

Conor frowned at that, a faint ray of awareness clawing at the foggy haze that had settled around his shoulders, but before he could speak, he heard Oscar snarl, a vicious, spine-chilling growl that he had never imagined his friendly little dog was capable of uttering, and his head snapped up to see Jack's hands resting on Haisley's shoulders, her green eyes round and glassy in her too-pale face, staring at him in wordless terror.

"Haisley." He staggered to his feet, but Jack held up a finger, and Conor screamed as he watched Haisley's eyes roll back into her skull, sagging against his velvet-clad chest.

"Calm yourself, *cabbage*," Jack said. "That is what she calls you, is it not? No reason to upset me further, you know, or to distract me. I would hate for my concentration to slip, and oops –" His finger crooked, and Conor yelled again, his throat hoarse and dry as Haisley's whole body spasmed before him, hands twitching and legs shaking. Jack straightened his finger and she stilled immediately, going limp and soft under his hands, and Conor forced himself to remain rooted to the spot, his gaze fixed on his daughter's ash-white face.

"Da," she whispered, eyes brimming with tears. "Da, help me," and Conor's chest shattered into a thousand broken glass shards.

Oscar huddled at his feet, snarling and shaking, his wiry body vibrating with rage, and Conor licked the sweat from his upper lip. "Easy, boyo," he said. "Easy now."

"He is no fool," Jack said, his eyes bright with malice. "The little mongrel. Far wiser than you, it turns out. How easily you fell for my charms. If only you had been the one born with the blood of the gods in your veins and not that black-haired princess of yours, things would have been much, much simpler. She was so stubbornly resistant to all my charms."

"I told you once before." Conor's gaze snapped away from Haisley's face, and there she was, her blue eyes blazing with fury as she emerged from the mouth of the cave. "Your charms are not as potent as you think they are."

"Riona," Jack cried, his fingers tightening in Haisley's loose curls. "How lovely of you to join us – and to bring me a gift as well, I hope, for your daughter's sake."

For a moment, Riona stood still as a stone, her eyes fixed unwaveringly on Jack's face, impassive and unfathomably calm. "Let her go," she said. "And it's all yours."

"Liar." He smiled knowingly, nuzzling his nose against the top of Haisley's head, her eyelids squeezing shut, and Conor's vision blurred with rage, with helpless fury, as he watched the smooth column of Haisley's throat jump in terror at his touch. "We both know that you have no intention of handing anything over to me, do you now?"

"It was worth a try," Riona said coolly, and how, by the gods, was she so calm, so unruffled, when their daughter stood wrapped in the arms of death, a mere hair's breadth away from an irreparable doom. "I am assuming," she continued, "that you are too cowardly to fight me, one on one, and leave the two of them out of it."

"The *two* of them?" Jack's eyes gleamed. "So the farm-boy is fair game as well, is he? How good of you to include him."

It was almost imperceptible, the ripple of tension that bled through her shoulders, but Conor saw it for the briefest moment, even as her gaze remained steady and unflinching on the lord of death. "If you had any sense," she said, "you would have gone for him first. I only saved her in the first place because he loved her." She shrugged, dismissive and scornful. "She was merely an inconvenience with which I was saddled, all those years ago, never the one who truly mattered, but you were too blind to see that."

Jack's lips flattened into a furious line, but Conor's breath caught.

His clever girl, to use him as a shield between death and their daughter.

"You *always* preferred him to me," Jack said, his golden-fire eyes turning toward Conor, burning with wrath. "You should have been mine, as all the others were, body and soul, to do with as I pleased."

"What a pity," Riona said lightly, as her fingers wrapped around something hidden within the soft folds of her rose-silk skirts, a silver-sharp gleam with the faintest glint of sapphire-blue. "It is every girl's dream, I'm sure, to be left unsatisfied by the lord of death."

Jack snarled, and Conor braced himself to lunge forward, to throw himself between Haisley and the lord of death by her side, when suddenly Riona froze, her gaze transfixed by something hidden in the branches above them.

Conor followed her white-faced stare to the raven, glossy-winged and bright-eyed, sitting silent and watchful in the tree.

Jack laughed, a malicious sound. "Stupid, *stupid* girl," he said. "Did you think that I would come so unprepared, knowing that you would try and wield the unvanquishable sword against me?" He shook his head, his fingers stroking Haisley's trembling shoulders. "Toss it down on the grass," he ordered, jerking his chin up toward where the raven perched on the overhanging branch. "Or your farm-boy here will watch as we show him what, exactly, you and I did to his father all those years ago, but this time, it won't be a sour-faced, gray-haired man for whom he will mourn."

Something snapped inside Conor, and he roared, throwing himself forward with furious abandon, his fists clenched as he swung toward that smug, beautiful face. Jack's eyes snapped to his, and he smiled once, sharper than any briar's tooth, wicked and cunning, and even as he heard Riona scream his name, Jack's lips moved, and that same terrible, guttural growl that he had heard on Riona's lips that first night she arrived back in his life split through him.

Then he was lying shattered on the ground, broken and bleeding, consumed by a fire-tipped agony which he had never before dreamed possible, blackness creeping in around the edges of his visions. From far-away, he could hear them screaming – Haisley and Riona, his daughter and his wildflower girl – both of them yelling indecipherable, fury-laden words at the lord of death. The very air splintered, an awful, unearthly sundering, the reverberating crack of unnatural storms booming all around him.

He hadn't allowed himself to think of his father in years, but inexplicably, he thought of him now, as he lay broken and bloody in the grass under the pale warmth of the morning sun, that all-but-forgotten voice with its flecks of steel and rust-reddened iron telling him stories of war, how the sound of the drums would roll across the fields like thunder in the deep, drowning out the screams of the wounded and the dying. A battle, he thought almost dreamily. There was a battle raging all around him, otherworldly and vicious, searing the sky and scorching the earth, two beings of unimaginable might, determined to destroy the other.

He hoped that Haisley was safe at last, that she wasn't too scared, wherever she was. He hoped that he was on his way there now, feeling the subtle prod of invisible fingers, prying that essence of himself away from his blood-soaked skin, peeling away his beaten-down soul away from whatever remained of his fragile body.

He would see Mamó again, and his da, and Maeve.

It wouldn't be too bad, leaving behind this world of little joys and many sorrows for the shores of Magh Meall.

He drew in a ragged breath, choked and fluid-filled, but then two cool hands pressed themselves to either side of his face, stroking and soft. "Conor," she said, then a string of jumbled, guttural words, and that same sensation of his bones being re-knitted and his flesh resewn rolled over him, and he opened his eyes to see her staring down at him, those terrified bluebell eyes, her face whiter than he had ever seen it, a bright red gash marring her porcelain-pure cheek.

"Conor," she said again, her voice cracking. "You almost *died*."

"Haisley," he stuttered, and Riona's hands dropped away from his face as she whirled around.

"Stupid," he heard Jack say. "To drop the sword so carelessly – and for what? The life of a mere mortal man?" His tongue clucked. "I am disappointed that even after everything, you are still *such* a soft-hearted little fool, Riona."

Above him, Riona made a strangled sound, and Conor pushed himself up on his trembling elbows, swiveling to see Jack, the sword of starlight in one hand, and his other, wrapped tight around Haisley's throat. "Amergin and I both tried to warn you, if you remember, that it would be your undoing, that tender heart of yours." He grinned, careless and cruel. "Better for you if you'd stuck to that silly childhood vow – to love no one and nothing, because look where it has gotten you, a stóirín. Look at everything it has cost you."

Conor lurched to his knees beside Riona, fists clenched, but she laid her hand on his forearm, her eyes moving to the branches above them.

The raven still sat, perched among the bright green leaves, his gaze fixed unblinkingly on Haisley's pallid face.

"Now," said Jack, his feral, handsome face flushed with victory, backing away slowly toward the yawning mouth of Ráth Crúachan. "It's up to you, what happens next. Our bargain is fulfilled – you've brought me my treasures, and I have spared your daughter's life." He smiled, and Conor hated him, the soft, vicious beauty of his expression. "It won't kill her, you know, being brought back to my realm."

"Da," Haisley choked out, her fingers digging into Jack's arm. "Please – please, Da, please help." Her green-gray eyes flew to Riona's face, widening in a desperate, unspoken plea.

Riona didn't move, but only stared back at their daughter, expressionless and still.

"Be a good girl," Jack said to Riona, and Conor blinked back the sweat and blood oozing down his forehead from new-healed wounds to see the lord of death draw the tip of the starlit sword across Haisley's forearm, sprinkling the ground with a few drops of silver-crimson blood. "Come home, Riona, and do as I ask. Do what it is you were born to do, and sever the confinement spell laid on the sídhe by your ancestors, once and for all."

"Jack." Riona spoke at last, muted and low. "*Please*. Give her back. Please."

He smiled again. "If you want her," Jack said, his fingers reaching up to twist around Haisley's bright copper curls, as he dragged her into the leafy shadows of the whitethorn tree, Haisley's heels kicking at the ground, toward the gloomy darkness of the cave of cats. "Then come home, a stóirín."

There was the barest hint of a ripple in the air at the mouth of the cave, and they were gone, disappearing into the cool night air, and Conor watched as his daughter vanished from his sight.

Chapter Forty-Four
Ráth Crúachan, Éire, 1082

RIONA

H*aisley.*

Distantly, Riona could hear Conor screaming their daughter's name, over and over, raw with terror, but she merely stared at the dark mouth of the cave, taunting her, mocking her.

No cloak. No silver-lined blood. No access.

The lord of death had taken her daughter, stolen her away right underneath her nose, and she had failed to stop him — to save her, as she'd sworn she would.

It was instinct, blind intuition that had her grappling for the sheath strapped to her side, tugging at the hilt of the hunting knife tucked away inside its leather casing. Something furious and feral thrummed at her temples, a terrified scream of urgency, prompting her to press the tip of the razor-sharp blade to the soft skin of her wrist and slice into her flesh, desperately seeking that life-saving flash of silver folaíocht.

Please, she begged whatever gods there were left who might care to listen. Please. Help me, help me now, and I will give you anything, everything, in return.

A cruel swell of scarlet greeted her silent prayers, no silver to be seen, and Riona dug the blade deeper into her forearm, twisting the handle as she drove into her skin. Nothing – still nothing, only an endless surge of deep crimson-red.

"Ria." Conor pulled himself up onto his still-weak legs, struggling to stand. "Ria, stop."

"There must be some left." Riona pressed the back of her hand against her sweat-soaked forehead, the hilt of the knife hot and slick with blood, her breaths ragged and uneven. "I have to find a way – there has to be something –"

"Ria, listen to me. Put the knife down."

"No." Riona stared at the red-stained blade. "I know what I have to do."

"Ria –"

"Whatever the cost," she whispered, and she raised the sharp tip of the knife above her wrist, and with a single, fluid motion, slashed it along the long length of the vein that ran up her arm, deep down to the bone.

From behind her, Conor yelled, and she watched with a strange detachment as the blood spurted forth, a veritable fountain of thick dark crimson, and she sank to her knees, letting it flow and pour out onto the ground beneath her, soaking into the gnarled roots of the trees.

His hands seized her shoulders, a tight, urgent grip. "Ria, for the gods' sake, stop, you'll kill yourself –"

"Where is it?" She whispered, blinking fiercely to peer through the sudden blurriness of her vision, seeing only an endless stream of red in the dirt before her. "Where is the rest of it?"

"Ria, put some pressure on the wound now. Now, do it *now*."

He was pulling at her, pressing the hem of his doublet against her wrist, and without hesitating, she snapped out an incantation, guttural and fierce, and he flew backwards through the air, arms and legs flailing, crashing into the ground by the stream with a muffled groan.

"I can't find the silver," she said dimly, and she fumbled slightly as she switched the knife from her right hand to her left, clutching at it limply with what little feeble strength she still possessed in her ruined wrist, and without another word, drove the tip of the blade deep into her other wrist, slicing upward all the way to the crook of her elbow.

Conor was screaming in earnest now, bellowing her name over and over again, but it was from a very great distance, as she stared at the surge of blood that cascaded down over her once-white hands, seeping into the soft silk of her gown, dripping onto the earth just outside the mouth of the sídhe-cave, seeping into the roots of the single whitethorn tree in the full bloom of spring that stood outside its doorway. So much red, so much so that her hands appeared clad in a pair of vibrant scarlet gloves, shiny and bright, and she flexed her fingers lazily in front of her face, watching the flash and shimmer of the red-and-silver flow pouring from her wrists.

Silver.

She shook her head, and it came back to her in a roar.

Jack. The sídhe.

Haisley.

The stream of silver-crimson blood spooled on the floor, and the trees around her shivered in response. She climbed to her feet unsteadily, head whirling, hands shaking, and looked back at where Conor crawled toward her, his freckled face still smeared with blood. "I'll find her," she said, her voice sounding oddly thick and slurred, even to her own ears. "I'll bring her back to you, Conor. I swear it."

"*Ria*, no –"

Then she was gone, into the yawning mouth of the cave, the familiar blast of the icy night wind skating across her face, and when she opened her eyes, she found herself once again in the silent watching world of the sídhe.

As soon as the star-lit air brushed across her skin, Riona knew that she was healed. That hidden thrum of magic flowed through her, a soothing balm against the savage sting of her many hurts, welcoming her home.

The silence whispered, the wholeness in her arms and in her heart whispered, that this was always meant to be her home.

Far above her, the ravens still sat, watchful and quiet, their bright eyes fixed on her face, the dark-winged familiars of death, waiting for her to summon a soul for them to harvest as their own.

She forced herself not to shudder. "Is she here?" Her voice echoed faintly among the barren, ice-coated trees. "My daughter. Have you seen her? Please – please help me."

She was greeted with preternatural silence, the ravens hunched unmoving together among the trees, and frustration rushed through her.

"Take me to my daughter," she said, her fingers flexing at her sides. "I am the child of the Mórrígan, and I command you to take me to her this instance."

"They do not obey you."

Riona whirled around, knowing already what – who – she would find in this snowy, tomblike land, her face as distant and cold as a bleak winter morn, sitting on her marbled throne.

"You look nothing like him." The goddess' depthless black eyes roved over her face. "Who he once was, not that mortal form which he was cursed to endure."

"That's strange." Riona wiped her palms feverishly against the silk of her skirts. "All my life, I have heard, over and over again, how much I do look like him, and here you are, the one who has known him the longest, telling me the truth."

Her long white fingers stilled on the armrest of her throne. "That is, after all, my gift. I see the true nature of things, little queen. There is no lie that can deceive me."

It was, without question, a warning, a hoar-frosted warning of doom should she so much as try and speak an untruth to the all-seeing Phantom Queen. Riona swallowed. "Please," she said. "Please help me. I only want my daughter back. He has taken her, he has stolen her, into the sídhe, and I –"

"Stop." The Mórrígan rose from her throne, her black-and-gray skirts cascading around her on the ice-kissed ground. "You do not understand what it is that you ask."

"I do." Riona's eyes burned with the sting of desperate tears. "I do understand, and I will do anything – anything, whatever it takes, to save her."

"Many say such things," said the goddess. "Few truly mean it."

"I mean it." Riona stretched out her trembling hands to the marble-faced goddess, pleading. "You know truth, don't you? Look at me now – hear me now. I will pay whatever cost, no matter how high."

"You do not even know her," the goddess countered, as ruthless and cold as the bitterest winter night, "nor she you. What has she done, to earn this devotion from you?"

Riona closed her eyes, her breaths coming hard and fast as she cried. "A mother needs no other reason to love," she cried, "than existence. And I do love her – I do. I will…I will do *anything* for her."

"It will take everything."

"Then take it." Riona fell to her knees, a decades-worth of pent-up tears pouring down her cheeks. "Take it – whatever it is, whatever you require, take it. There is nothing too precious."

The Mórrígan was silent for a moment, her piercing black gaze boring into Riona's. "Do you know," she said at last, "why I do not often concern myself with the affairs of this world, both mortal and immortal alike?"

Riona shook her head, fighting back the whimper that threatened to escape through her quivering lips. She would refuse her, this implacable, stony-souled goddess. She would refuse to help, and all would be lost.

"So many have pleaded for my intercession over the years." The Mórrígan wandered away from her ash-and-marble throne, her gown trailing soundlessly behind her, and the ravens perched high in the trees followed her every movement with their bright eyes. "Humans, yes – kings and queens, war-lords and druidesses, peasants and paupers alike, but my own immortal kin as well. My husband himself, the king of the gods, who kneels to no one, threw himself at my feet, a dozen times over, prostrate and weeping in the mud, to implore my aid, just as my father did before him. Rarely do I grant it, however. Rarely do I interfere, even when the power to prevent the sorrows of tens of thousands of souls lies in the palm of my hand."

"Why?" Riona whispered. "Why would you not, why would you refuse to help, to spare them so much pain?"

"Because I have looked into the cobwebbing of the cosmos itself, and I have seen how it all ends." Her hand drifted up to pluck a snow-laden blossom from the branch of a tree, a tiny red flower frozen forever in a crystallized blanket of frost and snow. "I have watched the world die, consumed by storms of ice, awash in waves of fire. The earth-mother herself has long since gone, turning her back on all that which she has created, walking away without a backward glance to drown herself in the depths of the mouth of the sea." The Mórrígan snapped the delicate flower in half with a twist of her long white fingers, and Riona shivered at the sound of the ice breaking, the ruthless ruining of something so beautiful. "It all ends, you know – life. Only the wisest know this, and the millions of fools who do not call me cruel, unnatural, but it is the truth which they cannot bring themselves to face, the meaninglessness of it all. Mortal or immortal, it matters not. I have watched them all die, a hundred times, and so I simply cannot bring myself to care about any of them."

"I care." Riona was crying in earnest now, a flood of furious tears trickling down her cheeks. "I care."

"Only because you, like all the rest, are too foolish to know better."

"Please. *Please* – let me save my child."

The Mórrígan looked up at that, black-eyed and steady. "I have just told you that the world will one day burn, crumbling in upon itself like a weak-kneed stallion at the end of its life, bleary-eyed and wheezing."

"I don't care about the rest of the world." The words ripped out of her, a scream of desperation and fear. "I don't care – let it burn. Let it all burn to ash. I only care about her."

"She is insignificant."

"She is significant," sobbed Riona, "to me."

"That," the goddess said coldly, "is very short-sighted."

"I know." Riona could barely speak over the sobs racking her body, clawing at her hair with wild, frantic fingers. "I know, I know. It is selfish and horrible and cruel, but I don't *care*. I don't care. Please – please –"

There was a long, heavy silence, and Riona wept harder, keening over at the waist, rocking back and forth as her sobs tore through her, a feral, bestial wailing, born from that most primal, unbearable pain.

Haisley, she thought. *My Haisley.*

A light touch on the side of her flushed, tear-soaked cheek, and Riona jerked her head up, gasping at the sight of the Mórrígan's fathomless eyes staring down into her own. "Once," she said, and the ice in her voice was gone, something feather-soft and quiet threading its way through her almost inaudible whisper. "I felt this too. Once, for a brief moment, as I walked by the river, my hands on my stomach, I felt him kick within me, a strong, insistent thrumming of his feet against the palms of my hands, and I thought – perhaps, perhaps this is the meaning for which I have been searching for so many hundreds of years." Riona shivered as the Mórrígan straightened, her cool fingers sliding away from where they had touched her wet cheek. "It was not, I soon learned, enough." She paused, and Riona watched as the goddess' ice-white lips softened imperceptibly, a relenting of her iron-like will. "But it was something, an all-too-fleeting moment of hope, of a taste of what might have been happiness, in this existence I have been doomed to, the knowing of all things. Truth is not a gift, little queen, but a heavy curse indeed."

Riona staggered to her feet, shaking uncontrollably. "I will bear it," she managed to stutter through her stiff lips. "I will bear it, the truth. I can do it."

"I know." The goddess lifted her hand, and Riona watched as an orb of pure golden light materialized in the palm of the Mórrígan – an apple, like none other that she had ever before seen. "It was written in the webbing of the world, long ago, for you to eat of this fruit. Take it now, child of my child."

It was gorgeous, a silent song of unimagined beauty with no melody, and Riona found herself aching to hear it, yearning to let its soft golden notes wash over her in a cataract of light and sound. "What is it?"

"Death." Riona's lips parted in shock, and the golden fruit vibrated once in the palm of the Mórrígan, idling through the air toward where she still stood, rooted to the ground. "If you wish to defeat death, then you must become it, to feel its kiss upon your skin, its taste upon your tongue."

"I don't…I don't understand what it is that you want me to do."

The Mórrígan merely looked at her, implacable and uncaring, a goddess crafted from stone and iron and the deeply buried roots of the earth untouched by the warmth of the sun, and Riona saw it — the terrible truth which the Mórrígan had long known.

She recoiled, and the golden apple shivered again, impatient and eager. "No."

"Then leave," she said. "Let her die, and be gone back into the world of the living, but know that he will never rest, never relent, in his quest for you, what he believes to be his salvation."

The luminous fruit shimmered, wheedling, cajoling, a silent pleading. "No," Riona said again, but it was an empty protest, a defeated sigh. "I can't. It would kill him — it would break his heart forever, if I did this."

Their eyes met, the blue and the black, and for a moment, Riona saw him there, echoes of her grandfather, in the Phantom Queen's ghostly smile.

"For every light," said the goddess, "there must be a shadow. You must become the shadow, or the lost souls of your world, my sister's children, will never again know the light."

"I —"

"Whatever the cost." The depthless black eyes met hers again, unforgiving and cold once more. "Whatever it takes. I know that you meant it, because I have *seen* you. I have seen you alight with the undying fire of death itself burning in your eyes." She stroked the shimmering edge of the golden thread with the tip of her finger. "It is the closest thing to destiny that exists, this path that you must now walk."

Riona stared as the bright golden apple came to a halt in front of her, waiting for her touch. She reached out with a tremulous finger, the incandescent sphere sliding over her skin with a whisper of white-hot warmth.

"Little queen." Riona tore her eyes away from the glowing circles of light swirling about her. "Do not forget," the Mórrígan said, "the balance that must be kept between this world and the next, and the bridge that binds them."

There was a hint of gentleness, of something akin to a thousand-year-old sorrow threading through the goddess' icy voice, but before Riona could question her, express her confusion, the Phantom Queen turned away, curt and dismissive.

"Go," the Mórrígan said, and the incandescent fruit thrummed more insistently at the sound of the goddess' voice, "and do what you must." Those terrible black eyes flared for a moment with an unearthly light. "Do you understand?"

"Yes," Riona whispered, and the Mórrígan wandered away, back toward her white-and-gray throne.

"Then take it," she said without another glance, "and eat."

Riona closed her eyes, her fingers wrapping around the scorching heat of the glowing golden apple, a hint of something bitter-tasting and ash-like wafting toward her as she drew it to her lips and did as the Mórrígan commanded.

Chapter Forty-Five
Neither of the Earth Nor Under It, Not Then Nor Now

RIONA

Riona hurried through the shadows of Ráth Crúachan, the aftermath of that golden fire thundering in her pulse.

Destiny, the Mórrígan had said, and Riona ignored the pang in her heart at all the lost lives – of Da and Cian and Aaden, of Aisling and Sean, of Maeve, who had been snatched away so that she would be grief-stricken enough, to choose to walk a path that no one else would.

They tumbled through her as she ran, flashes of incoherent, fragmented memories –stories of blood-debts and shadows and lights and the need for balance, of unending feasts and healed hurts and rebirths, of ravens lying dead in the snow, of stolen treasures and black-haired brides, tangling together in a screaming mess of disjointed remembrances. An icy branch lashed across her face, and she wiped at the sting with the back of her hand, grateful for the clarifying lash of pain on her cheek.

For a moment, she could almost see her, that girl she used to be, on that long ago day in the vale, twisting around in her saddle to grin at Conor, his skinny arms wrapped around her waist.

Cabbage.

Her steps slowed, her sobs coming too fast for her to breathe.

As she gasped, reeling under the pain and weight of this newly-donned mantle which she had agreed to wear, she looked down at her bare hands, the linen bandages tattered and rust-stained, the kaleidoscope of scars from so many years of sacrifice. She was not a goddess, not a child of Tuatha Dé Danann, like Daideo had been, but something new entirely: a mortal-born girl with silver blood running through her veins, a druid well-versed in the arts of light and dark, straddling the division between the realms of the living and the dead, not divine but not wholly mortal neither.

A bridge, she thought hazily. The Mórrígan had said something about a bridge. It had resonated, a dusty bronze bell stirring awake in the far corners of her mind, but she could not remember what it was.

Her hands clenched at her sides as she tilted her head back, staring up at the star-studded sky, the soft-falling snow wafting against her face in a soothing caress. She was so close – so close to a life-shattering epiphany, one that would rip up the very foundations of eternity and alter them forever. It was there, just beyond her reach, hidden somewhere in the dusty recesses of some half-forgotten memory, but she could not wrap her searching fingers around it and bring it into the light.

Something brushed against her leg, and she looked down to see Fiadh, her lithe body tense, watching her with those glowing yellow eyes. She nudged Riona's fingers with her nose, a silent urging, and Riona ran her palm down her sleek-furred spine. "Soon," she said. "Only a little while longer."

"So I keep telling her as well."

Riona whirled around. He was standing across the snow-covered clearing, idly admiring the glint of the starry silver sword under the pale light of the moon. "Where is Haisley?"

He pointed the blade in her direction. "Do you have any idea," he said, "of how sick I am of the sound of that little brat's name? It's all anyone cares to talk to me about these days. Not 'Jack, how's it cutting?' or 'Jack, tell me, why would you *not* relish being the king of nothing but shadows and dull-witted beasts?' No. Only Haisley this and Haisley that." He sighed. "My first act," he said, "as the High King of Éire will be to pass an edict that no one shall ever again speak the name of Haisley in my presence."

Her fingernails dug into her palms. "You are still so sure of that. That your plan will work."

"And what do you know of my plan, a stóirín?"

"I know that you mean for me to break the confinement spells of the sídhe and the bond which compels you to remain in Tech Duinn. I know that you mean to use the treasures of the gods to compel the Lia Fáil, the king-maker, to roar for you – for you to be named High King of all Éire, of all its realms, the mortal and immortal alike, and to rule forever with the powers of the purse and the sword and the cloak combined."

"My apologies," he said with a smile. "It seems that you *do* know quite a bit about my plan. Perhaps you are not such a fool as I had thought."

She shook her head. "I won't do it though. I won't help you."

"Oh well then. Perhaps you *are* such a fool as I had thought. Of course you will help me, because we both know what will happen if you do not."

"I can't though," she said. "I've used up all my folaíocht in my veins."

"Little liar. You are here, are you not? Here in the sídhe where you thought you were no longer allowed to go." His eyes gleamed. "You had to cut rather deep, I see, to make it happen. You won't last long once you return to the mortal world, no matter how hard your bumbling healer tries to save you."

"That bumbling healer," she said, "is worth a hundred of you and I."

"Speak for yourself," Jack said, lifting the sword to admire its sheen in the starlight. "I myself am rather pleased with what my cold, hard heart has gained me." He smiled, and she bit back a snarl at the sight of it, so gentle and so cruel. "But it has all righted itself in the end. Your heart, such as it is, never truly belonged to him, anyway, did it? Only with her."

Riona flattened her clammy palms against the soft silk of her gown. "Where is she?"

"Oh, she's fine. A bit hysterical, but who isn't, these days." Riona hissed through her teeth, and he laughed, low and dark. "Oh, very well." He reached out with his free hand and tugged at the nothingness of the air. The brittle folds of the cream-colored cloak appeared, followed by a flash of copper-red hair and glassy green eyes.

Riona lunged forward, a wordless scream of panic roaring in her ears, but Jack raised the sword of starlight to Haisley's throat. "Careful," he said. "Remember who holds the purse of plenty, with its power of rebirth. Without it, there is nothing and no one, no power in this world or any other, that can bring back your daughter if I slit her pretty little neck wide open with this particular sword." He grinned. "I should know."

She forced herself to remain still, her gaze fixed on her daughter's ash-white face. "Haisley," she said. "Are you all right?"

Her daughter made a muffled sound, eyes wheeling with terror even as her lips never moved, and Jack's smile widened. "A simple silencing spell. We need to have a little chat, you and I, with no interruptions."

Riona's fingers trembled with the urge to strike, to lash out with whatever fire burned within her, but kept quiet. *Remember*, the voice of the Mórrígan still echoed in her memory.

Remember the balance between the worlds, and the bridge that binds them.

"Riona," Jack said softly, toying with the frayed ends of Haisley's curls, and Riona's attention snapped back to the present. "Come now. Is it really worth it, all this bickering between us? What do you care for the rest of the realm? I thought we'd reached a mutual understanding, during our non-time together in the sídhe. Whatever changed your mind, a stóirín?"

"I promised to serve you, to complete your tasks." Riona forced herself to focus only on Jack. If she looked again at Haisley, she would break, shatter into a thousand pieces, unable to bear the sight of her daughter's too-white face. "I did not promise you an eternity."

"And I was promised a kingdom undying, with power beyond my wildest dreams, and see what that got me."

"I'd say that you got exactly what you deserved."

"Well, try to understand it from my perspective, won't you? For so long, I have been locked away, doomed never to die, but never truly allowed to live, denied the birthright that was given to me so long ago – to rule all of Éire as its gods-chosen High King, because of one silly, foolish, hotheaded mistake in my boyhood." Riona swallowed, her gaze drifting back to Haisley, standing so unnaturally still and silent by Jack's side. Her darling little girl. "All I want is the chance to live the life that I was promised, the life that I was owed. And you – this is what you were born to do." He edged forward, and her gaze snapped back to his face, so handsome and so hungry, those golden eyes glowing with an insatiable fire. "You could join me, you know," he said, and she flinched to hear that velvet-purr creep back into his voice, coaxing and assuasive. "You could rule by my side, a little queen no longer, but one far more magnificent and greater than any the world has ever known, and I your adoring king – as we were always meant to be." Another slow, sinuous step forward. "It was you I saw, all those centuries ago, there in the snow – not that little lovestruck fool of a princess. It was *you*." Riona sucked in a breath as Jack's grip on the sword relaxed ever so slightly. "I knew it the moment you called forth the bean-sí that day in the mountains," he continued. "It was in your eyes as you stroked the ears of the dread cat-sìth with such wondrous tenderness, as you admired the moon and the stars and the soft winter snow of the eternal night sky here in this realm." He laid his hand with unutterable gentleness on the top of Haisley's head, and Riona shuddered before she raised her head to stare unblinkingly into his black-and-gold eyes. "The blood of the Mórrígan herself runs in your veins. Your place, my lady, has always been by my side – not mine, not yours, but *our* rightful throne."

It was a too-familiar echo of the Mórrígan's own words, but she ignored it, focusing instead on the ragged rise and fall of Haisley's chest. "It won't work on me any longer, Jack – your lies, your manipulations. I know them for what they are now. You no longer have any power over me."

He smiled, and Riona's desperation soared to unimaginable heights, because she *had* to kill him, this lord of death, but there was something – something that she must remember first. "And what makes you think that it is a lie? Do you doubt how much I want you still, even after you have seen what lengths I have gone to in order to win you as my own?"

Her heart pounded more furiously in her chest. Now – now was the time to strike, to unleash this newfound golden power, but she groped about with blind, searching fingers, her grasp on that power tenuous and unwieldy. "Never," she managed to say. "You will never win me. I told you that, when I first came to you. And I meant it."

"So you did." He tsked softly. "But I came so very close, didn't I? Yet you never quite crossed that bridge, unfortunately – only a few tentative steps here and there, before you scampered back to safety on the other side."

The bridge, Riona thought distantly. Something about the bridge between worlds, into Magh Meall, which she now would never be allowed to cross.

"Oh well," Jack continued. "As much as I would enjoy your…companionship as my queen." His teeth gleamed in the starlight. "It's hardly a requirement. I'll take what is rightfully mine with or without you by my side, and you cannot stop me." She shook her head, and he smiled again. "You will find, I think, that the paltry bit of magic which Amergin has taught you pales in comparison to the power of the *real* gods. You are nothing but a shadow compared to them."

Shadow, Riona thought distantly through the roaring in her ears. Shadow, and light, the need for balance.

"And yet," Jack continued, his golden-fire eyes burning more maniacally than ever before. "A shadow is enough for my purposes. So go on now – cut deep and cut true, Riona, and find those last few remaining drops of folaíocht in your veins and set me free. You'll die, it's true, but –" his smile curved along his lips like a pale-skinned snake coiling to strike "– the fact that I won't slit your daughter's throat and be done with it should be motivation enough, I think."

"She's so afraid," Riona whispered, almost to herself, and Jack grinned in triumph.

He stroked his fingers along Haisley's ash-white face, her green eyes glassy. "Don't be afraid," he murmured, mocking and cruel. "Mamaí is here now. Don't you know, Mamaí will do anything that I ask, anything to save her precious baby girl. Won't you, Mamaí?"

"Let her go, Jack."

"'Let her go, Jack'," he mimicked, lips curling. "Such weakness. I taught you to be *strong*, to take what you want without asking and damn the consequences."

"That hasn't worked out well for you."

"Hasn't it?" His teeth bared in a snarl. "I've got you right where I want you, Riona. We both know that you are stalling, only moments away from giving me what I want, what I deserve, because if you don't –" His fingers dug into Haisley's hair, jerking her head back to expose her daughter's throat, and a wave of insurmountable panic clawed at Riona's own. What was it, that faded scrap of truth, that secret that she could not remember, that she was not even sure how she had come to know? "If you don't, you will watch as your little hazelnut – that's what he calls her, is it not? – bleeds out and dies right here before your very eyes, and you will be powerless to stop it."

Hazelnut.

And suddenly, Riona remembered, as clear and bright as though it were not then but now, an ever-present thing, unbound by space and time.

The bridge between worlds.

Chapter Forty-Six
The Vale of Inagh, Éire, 1071

RIONA

It had been a difficult labor, filled with uncertainty and fear. For over thirty hours, the midwives had worked on her, coaxing and commanding her, their practiced hands pushing and stroking her fevered skin as she sweat and moaned, walking about the room with her hand pressed to her back, lying in the bed, kneeling by the window to let the cool autumn breeze waft against her too-hot face.

"Breathe, Ria," Conor had said, too many times for her to count, and she wanted to scream at him, because of course she knew to breathe, the stupid cabbage, what else could she do but keep breathing, drawing breath after painful breath as the waves of pain rolled through her, and yet nothing. Fecking. Happened.

Then finally, *finally*, Clia looked up from where she crouched next to Riona as she sprawled on the sweat-soaked sheets, and nodded. "It's time," she said, and Riona groaned, not from pain but from a bone-deep relief, because thank the gods, it would soon be over.

Then she was screaming, her fingertips digging into Conor's forearms as she struggled to bring their child into the world, gasping and wheezing between each too-sharp, agonizing undulation. "Breathe, Ria," he said again, and she snarled.

"Cabbage, I swear by the *gods themselves –*"

"I see the head," Clia called, and Riona gritted her teeth, pushing as hard as she could, and then collapsed backward onto the mattress as Conor stumbled his way to the foot of the bed.

"Let me catch it," she heard him say. "Let me be the one," and even in the midst of all this unimaginable, gods-damned pain, she felt a twinge of remorse, of affection for her freckled-faced boy.

He would be, she knew, the very best of fathers.

Then the pain rolled over her in unbearable waves, and she screamed again, long and shrill, and then there were two screams piercing the cool evening air, the second weak and thin. Riona pushed up on her elbows to see Conor, eyes bright and shiny with tears, holding a squalling, wrinkled thing to his chest.

Gods, it was ugly, this blood-stained, pinched-face goblin-child that she had fought so hard to bring into the world.

"Ria," Conor said, tears trickling down his cheeks. He reached out with one shaky finger toward the screeching infant, and Riona watched as a tiny, red-wrinkled hand wrapped itself around Conor's finger, clinging to him, his face melting in wonder. "Look at our daughter, Ria," he said. "She's the most beautiful creature in the whole world," and Riona laughed, hoarse and exhausted, because it most certainly was *not*, this scrunched-up, flaky-cheeked thing, then sank back down on the bed, eyes closed, covered in sweat.

It was Conor who swaddled the baby in soft linen, who wiped her eyes and her nose with a warm cloth, who snuggled her close against his chest while the midwives cleaned Riona after her labor, who walked the tiny bundle about the room, a soothing bounce in his step. "That's your mamaí," he whispered against the top of the baby's head. "Say hello to your mamaí, she did such a good job, kept you so safe."

Riona smiled weakly. "Come here," she said, and then the mid-wives crept out the room, closing the door behind them, and it was only the three of them, Riona and Conor and their sleeping babe, curled up on the bed between them as they lay on their sides, facing each other.

"You did so good, Ria," he murmured, reaching out to brush away a damp lock of her hair from her face, and she smiled again.

"I know," she said, and he looked so unbelievably happy, so heartbreakingly young, her cabbage with his copper-red curls and freckled nose and beautiful gray eyes.

Then the long hours of no sleep and endless worry caught up with him, and she watched as his eyelids drooped, drifting off to sleep next to the baby in their bed, their chests rising and falling in unison together, and Riona at last looked down at her daughter.

It really was an ugly little thing. Its face was mottled purple and wrinkled with a short stub nose, its fingers curved like claws at its side. It was almost hairless, with only the thinnest swatch of dark hair. Riona reached out to touch it, fingering the downy softness of the texture, wondering when it would come, that maternal devotion that she had read so much about and known so little of in her life.

Riona shifted restlessly, wincing at the soreness in her muscles. Maybe she should feed it. She pursed her lips as she looked down at the sleeping infant, its tiny mouth slightly ajar. She was reluctant to wake it. What if it started squalling again, with that shrill, mewling cry? Better to let it keep quiet while it was willing to do so. The midwife had said that that first feeding could wait an hour or two, and Riona was dreading it, cringing at the idea of its gummy mouth gnawing at her, drooling on her.

It was a bit revolting so far – motherhood. She was not sure this wrinkled, ugly creature that had been rumbling around in her womb for so many months was worth all this.

As if she had spoken aloud, the baby stirred, then opened its watery eyes and stared at Riona, unblinking and quiet, and for the first time in her life, Riona fell instantly and irrevocably in love.

It was nothing like she had ever known before, this bottomless well of love, so deep that it ached in her bones like the bitterest winter cold, pervading every inch of her being. It was the roar of a black bear high on the mountain cliffside, awakening from her months-long slumber in the darkness, the howl of the wolf under the midsummer moon, the thundering of the river, its banks swollen and full of depthless power after long winter weeks of unrelenting storms.

It could uproot mountains, could halt the ocean-tides in their course, could conquer the world and all its realms, this kind of love, so pure and all-prevailing as it was.

Riona stared into those milky-blue eyes, and the very foundations of her world shifted underneath her, rearranging themselves into some new, unknowable realm, fraught with danger and worry and so much joy.

She reached out a trembling finger, tracing the curve of her daughter's soft nose. "Look at you," she'd whispered. "Look at how beautiful you are."

Beside her, Conor shifted on the bed. "She is lovely, isn't she," he murmured. "Just like her mamaí."

Riona cleared her throat, irrationally embarrassed. "She's wrinkly. Like a hazelnut."

Conor laughed. "Our little chnó coil."

"Let's call her that, then. Haisley."

"Haisley," he repeated sleepily. "I like it."

"Conor," she said, that strange new sense of worry seizing her heart. "We're not married."

"That's hardly my fault. I've been asking for months, but you said –"

"She's not legitimate. I know that we've talked about this, and I said it wasn't a concern, but – but I'm worried now. What if she's mocked because of it, sneered at? What if when the time comes, she won't be acknowledged as queen? What if –"

"Ria." He reached up to cup her cheek with his palm, running his thumb gently along the curves of her face. "We'll cross that bridge when it's time, all right?"

"But –"

"We'll cross that bridge," he said again, more firmly, his sleepy gray eyes steady on hers, "together, like we always have. All right?"

She nodded, throat thick with emotion.

"All right," Conor said again, tossing his arm across his eyes, and Riona kept a silent vigil as the only two souls she had left to love in this world drifted away into dreams beside her.

She wished Daideo could see her, this beautiful light that she had brought into the world, and Mamó, and Maeve. She wished her da could have cradled her baby in his arms and blessed her with a name, in the same way that Daideo had blessed her all those years ago. She wished, very much, that they were here, to give her strength and solace in the coming storms, to stand with her and Conor as they set out on this new path of life, filled with thorns and roses alike.

And there would be many bridges, she thought, which they would need to cross together. Many battles to fight, many wars to wage in the coming months and years, but right now, in this soft moment of bittersweet gladness, they all seemed very far away, as she cradled them in her arms, her child and her lover, remembering those she had lost.

All of her griefs and all her joys, together.

Like a bridge, Riona thought sleepily. A bridge that spanned space and time, that joined past sorrows, with this new, bright joy – an unbreakable bridge binding them together, the loves she had lost and the ones she now found, for all eternity, in life and in death. They would always be connected, her griefs and her joys, because without those griefs, her joy would not shine so bright, the bitterness dulled, leaving only the light.

Daideo had told her, long ago, of a bridge, one which the world's first mother had formed from her own blood and bones, a final act of sacrifice.

Triumphant, even in death.

Riona looked into her daughter's face – the green-gray eyes of her grandmother, the copper-colored curls of Conor, the pointed chin of her brothers long lost to her — and at last understood what it was she meant to do.

Chapter Forty-Seven
Neither of the Earth Nor Under It, Not Then Nor Now

RIONA

You are the bridge, Daideo had told her. *We all are,* and she understood that now, what had once confused her – that it was a living thing, this bridge, not one of iron and wood, nor of blood and bone, but of the threads of hope that bound the souls across the bright blue waters with the ones they left behind.

Not then nor now, but always. Neither of the earth nor under it, but everywhere, in every place, hidden from view.

She was a creature born of both shadow and light, and she was not alone.

Riona looked at her daughter, white-faced and glassy-eyed, the amalgamation of so many lives and so much love.

The cure is in the poison.

She stretched out her hand to where Haisley stood, locked in the grip of the dark lord of death, and whispered, guttural and deep, the spell of soul-stealing.

From the ice-laden trees above, a raven cawed, hoarse and humming with power, and Haisley shivered once, then blinked in Riona's direction, those lovely gray-green eyes growing heavy and bleary underneath the weight of her mother's whispered command.

Mamó's eyes. She would never see her grandmother again now,

in the realm of Magh Meall.

But Haisley would, and Conor. She would make sure of it.

"Haisley," she said as her daughter's eyelashes fluttered down to rest on her too-pale cheeks. "I love you always. Never forget – I love you, I have loved you, will love you, forever."

There was only a long, slow sigh in answer, and then Haisley slumped against Jack's chest, head drooping, arms hanging limply at her sides.

Far above in the snow-shrouded trees, the raven squawked again, harsh and triumphant, and something shapeless and gray drifted across the snow to rest at Riona's feet.

Jack's eyes widened in shock, stumbling backward from Haisley's lifeless form as her body fell forward into the snow. "You killed her," he said in a blank voice. "You killed her. I can't believe it –"

"Believe it." Riona glided forward, her gown swishing through the snow, an avenging goddess hell-bent on exacting her vengeance. "You have no leverage over me now, Jack, and I can do whatever I like to you."

His gaze snapped up to hers, and Riona relished it, the faint shadow of genuine fear that flickered there in his eyes – pure black, drained of their unearthly fire, as he stared at her. "Idiot," he snarled. "You've given her right into my hands. She's lost to you forever now."

"The only thing that's lost," Riona said, cold as the snow shimmering in the trees all around them, "is you."

A faint shadow of understanding flickered across his face, and he took a single step back. "It's not possible."

"We're in the land of the sídhe, Jack," she said with a smile, as gentle and cruel as any he had ever bestowed on her. "Someone once told me, long ago, that here, anything is possible." She whistled once, high and piercing, and Fiadh leapt down from the snow-covered branches above them, crashing to the ground with a menacing growl, stalking forward on her catlike paws, tail lashing with an unmistakably savage hunger.

Jack stumbled backward, eyes wheeling as all around them the monstrous sídhe-beasts he had once commanded emerged from the shadows, in answer to Riona's call – the fear-gorta, skeletal and emaciated, followed by the sleek-furred dobhar-chú, slathering and hissing as it lumbered through the snow, and the Enbarr, an ice-blue shadow flitting among the trees as it cantered toward them, the unmistakable evidence of their allegiance to the new-crowned queen of the sídhe.

Riona raised her arms high in the air, and as one, they advanced on him, drawn by the irresistible call of her silver-tinted blood, of the golden fire that now burned in her veins and not his. *Hers*, she thought as she looked at them as they circled Jack's pale-faced form in the snow. United and whole again, at long last, the last of the descendants of the Tuatha Dé Danann.

"Stop this," Jack screamed, spittle flying from his lips. "You cannot do this – I am the king of the sídhe, I am the lord of *death* –"

"You were," Riona agreed, "but no longer."

Fiadh roared, then leapt, bone-white claws flashing in the starlight. Jack shrieked, his blood spraying across the pure white snow as he staggered away from the snarling cat-sìth, clutching at his ruined face.

"How ironic," Riona said as she prowled closer to him, relishing the snap and spark in her blood as that newfound power rolled through her veins. "You destroyed the face of the first lord of death, and here I have done the very same to you. There's a symmetry there, if you care to look for it."

Jack wiped savagely at his ruined face, his lips curled in a snarl, unsheathing the sword of starlight with a vicious flourish. "Go on," he snarled, and at her side, Fiadh pressed her pointy-ears flat against her skull and snarled right back, fangs glistening in the moonlight. "Send that monster of yours after me again, and you'll watch as I carve her up like a lamb for the Imbolc supper." He laughed, a desperate man's last bid for survival. "Even she is no match for the sword forged in the smithy of the gods, and you – fool that you are – handed it right over to me."

"I am many things, Jack," Riona said, and lifted her finger, a silent call to her most dreadful subject, "but a fool is not one of them."

The snowflakes drifting down through the moonlit sky halted abruptly as an unnatural stillness crept over the clearing. Fiadh shivered, her ears drooping and her yellow eyes slitted as she stared into the shadows of the trees.

"Keep that foul beast away from me." Jack scrambled to his feet, his hands clutched tight around the ebony-blue hilt of the blade, waving it toward where the cat-sìth crouched in the snow. "Remember that I have the sword. The sword of starlight, mind you, and whomever wields it cannot be defeated by any living soul, neither man nor god."

"I know," Riona said, as slowly, slowly, a trail of ghostly footprints appeared in the snow before them. "But you can be defeated – by one who is neither living nor a soul." She gave a curt nod, and the frigid air shimmered once. Then he was there, standing in the snow, a dark-haired boy with deep-set eyes, blacker than the coldest midwinter night, handsome and tall with a cruel, pale mouth. Poor lad, she thought with a sudden, inexplicable pang, that long-lost prince who dreamed too greedily of a greatness never meant to be his.

Jack's face paled, the golden-fire of his eyes flickering out, a dying candle caught in the crosswind of a midsummer storm. "You think you can summon the fetch," he screamed through blood-stained lips. "It answers to me and me alone, its *master*."

"You are that no longer." Riona felt it burning within her gaze, that preternatural golden-fire, and Jack hissed at the sight of what once was his power sizzling in another's eyes. "This is what you wanted, wasn't it? To be free? What was it you told me, about the true meaning of freedom? You said that was what death really was – being freed from our cages of blood and bone, yes? So." She raised her hand, and the other-Jack tilted his head and smiled an eerie, toothless smile. "Enjoy your freedom."

"Stop!" Jack screamed, his face bloodless, his black eyes stark against the white marble of his face as he stared at the fetch leering before him. "I command you to stop! She is not your master, *I* am your master, you stupid beast!"

"Let's find out if that's true, shall we?" Riona asked, then smiled – a cruel, wicked smile. "But before I do– tell me, am I still too soft-hearted for your liking now?"

"You *bitch* –"

Riona dropped her hand, and the fetch opened the mouth of the other-Jack, whispering something inaudible and soft as it inhaled the wintry air with a long, greedy hiss.

The sword landed in the snow, the cloak slipping from Jack's slack hand, as he stumbled forward onto his knees, his eyes turned milk-white in their sockets, his skin growing waxen and translucent against his skull. He crashed face-down in the snow and was still, and as suddenly as it had come, the fetch vanished, the only lingering sign of his presence the fast-disappearing footprints in the snow.

Riona stumbled forward, rolling Jack's limp body over onto his back to stare down into his sightless eyes. Gone. The boy who had become the lord of death had not died, but was gone, a soul not lost but expunged entirely, and there was only one who could take his place.

Even as she thought it, the sídhe-beasts retreated into the shadows, their heads bowed low and their eyes downcast. The wintry air hardened behind her, and she swiveled in the snow to face the Mórrígan.

"So be it," she said, remote and cold as ever, and Riona shivered, edging closer to where Haisley lay sprawled out in the snow, her arm thrown over her eyes. "Now do as I bid you. Return to the land of the living, so that you may be reborn, as a queen undying."

Riona's eyes fell on Jack's ruined body. "The purse," she whispered, and the Mórrígan's fathomless black eyes flashed.

"They are yours to command now," she said. "Keep them safe. Use them well."

"I will." Riona returned her gaze to Haisley's lifeless face, lost in a deathless dreaming. "Once I leave here –"

"Only one who defeats death can become a master of it."

Riona sank into the snow beside her daughter, her finger tracing the soft curve of Haisley's cheek. "I understand." She exhaled, soft and slow. "I have accepted it for what it is, my fate, and that is enough."

"Our fates," said the Mórrígan, "are of our own choosing. Never forget that, when they arrive in your realm, the souls seeking the peace of Magh Meall."

"But I don't know how to help them."

"You will learn," she said, "as he never cared to learn. You will master many things which he thought beneath him. There are matters of far greater depths, boundless truths, which he never sought to decipher. I will teach you the truth of things, as he never allowed me to do."

"But not the whole truth," said Riona, and the Mórrígan, impossibly, smiled.

"Little queen," she said, "there is no such thing." From the trees, the ravens rustled their wings and cawed, low and crooning, a mournful echo of their mistress' words. Riona shivered – not, she realized in dread, but in unison with the unearthly beauty of their song.

The goddess tilted her head. "You, I think, will be more curious than he, more willing to delve into the very foundations of the cosmos, to study its workings, to know it, as a sister-soul, the creations of the earth-mother herself. After all –" The goddess turned away, drifting toward the trees. "It is in your blood."

She disappeared, and Riona was alone with the watchful eyes of the sídhe-creatures, and Haisley's gray-shadow soul curled next to her still-warm body, cocooned in the protective arms of death under the pale crescent moon, there in the snow.

She took the purse and the cloak from Jack's ruined body but left the sword lying where it had fallen from his hand. The cloak she cast aside before hurrying back to where Haisley still lay, her face white and her eyes sealed shut, and knelt back in the snow by her side, purse in hand. She inhaled once, steady and deep, letting the silent siren-call of the purse's power flow through her, and then dipped her fingers inside before running them over her daughter's lips. "Breathe," she whispered. "Come back to me, my darling."

For a terrifying moment, nothing happened, then the gray shadow still entwined catlike about her ankles slipped over her daughter's skin, seeping into its pores. A puff of warm air, and Haisley's green eyes fluttered open and latched onto hers, cloudy and confused.

Riona allowed herself one long look, drinking in the sight of her, then laid her palm against her cheek. "Sleep," she whispered, and as quickly as they had opened, Haisley's eyelids fluttered shut again, a slight stain of pink flooding into her pale cheeks, her chest rising and falling in slow, deep heaves as she breathed in her slumber.

She remained still for a moment, then looked up to see Fiadh crouched nearby, watching her intently. "It's better this way," she said. "I don't want to have to say goodbye."

Fiadh, unsurprisingly, said nothing, but the warmth in her eyes spoke volumes.

"I can't believe," said Riona, "that I ever was so silly as to think you actually wanted to eat me."

Fiadh let out a huffy purr that sounded for all the world like a scornful laugh, and Riona laughed too, weak and tired, then bent over to rest her forehead against her sleeping daughter's. She heaved Haisley up in her arms, staggering under her weight, dragging her toward the entrance to the sídhe-realm of Ráth Crúachan. "By all means," she grunted as Fiadh prowled along next to her, stubby tail lashing, mewling anxiously. "Keep yowling at me. That's very helpful."

Fiadh pinned her ears back against her skull and dug in her paws, her irritation palpable.

"I know my duty," Riona assured her, stumbling over a gnarled root as she dragged Haisley's limp form toward the faintly illuminated mouth of the cave. "I'll come back with you. But not until I take her back to the otherworld. The gods only know how much time has passed." A twinge of misgiving prickled along the back of her neck as she considered this – had it been days, a month, years even, since she had left Conor there, surrounded by those gray-stoned cairns, ominous and foreboding?

It didn't matter. He would be there, whenever they came out. He would wait, she knew, until he was old and gray, waiting for his girls.

Riona ignored the agony slicing through her, the knowing of how soon she would again have to break his heart. Focusing all her energy, her attention on Haisley, her arms wrapped underneath her daughter's limp body, her curly red head resting on her chest, Riona pulled her toward the cave, toward the world of sunsets and springtime and the living.

A world in which she no longer belonged.

The enormity of what she had done, the fate that she had accepted, settled over her, and a sob escaped her, bone-rackingly deep, like she had never before known. She would never reach the shores of Magh Meall, beyond the star-studded sea, never again see Daideo and Mamó, never see her da or her brothers or Aisling, to say to them all the things she had never been given the chance to say before they were snatched away from her, robbed of their joys and hopes and dreams, all because of her.

She would never see Maeve, the sister of her heart, the apology that lay scalding-hot on the tip of her tongue would never be spoken, never to be heard by her dearest friend, not only in this brief existence here in this land, but in whatever life she now lived in the far-off world beyond the star-studded sea.

She would never be forgiven for all her sins, all her failings, the unwitting crimes that she had foisted on everyone she had ever loved, condemned to the shadows of unrelenting night, unloved and guilt-ridden, a stain that could never be washed clean.

Riona wept as she walked, blinded by tears, stumbling across the snow-crusted ground, Haisley clutched in her arms. Alone. She was alone, forever, with no one and nothing to love. She had lost everything and everyone.

Irrevocably alone.

A low purr rumbled at her elbow, and she looked down, half-blinded by the sting of her tears. Fiadh, her nose nuzzling against the side of her gown, her yellow eyes soft and limpid with emotion. She yowled once, pressing her sleek-furred body close to Riona ribs, a wordless show of affection, of sympathy.

Riona swallowed her tears. "Thank you," she managed to say. "Not alone. Never alone. I remember." Daideo's voice, soothing and warm, was whispering to her, somehow, in the cat's purr, reaching across the vastness between worlds, a reminder that some things were too precious, too permanent to ever be truly lost. "Good girl." She paused, chest heaving, gathering her composure, her courage, then looked down to the cat-sìth waiting patiently by her side. "Help me get her home," she whispered. "And then we will go back to ours."

Forever.

Fiadh rumbled deep in her throat, then eased her glossy black shoulder underneath Haisley's drooping legs, and together with the sídhe-beast, Riona carried her daughter, for the last time, back out into the sunlight.

Chapter Forty-Eight
Ráth Crúachan, Éire, 1082

CONOR

It seemed to Conor like no time at all had passed, a few heart-rending seconds, between when the echoes of his scream dying away to when they stumbled back out of the shadowy mouth of the cave, Haisley sagging against Riona as she half-dragged, half-carried their daughter along. His heart hitched in his chest, and he shoved to his feet, staggering toward them with outstretched, shaking hands. "Haisley," he said, and Riona eased their child down onto the ground, brushing her hair back from her pallid face.

Then his face was buried in her sweat-soaked curls, clutching her limp body to his chest, dry sobs rolling through his chest as he rocked her back and forth. "She's all right," he heard Riona say. "She's only sleeping," and he made a wordless choking sound, the thrum of her heart faint and sluggish beneath his hands.

She was alive, he thought dazedly. They both were alive, they had escaped –

A whimper, and he looked up to see Riona slumped on the ground, her wrists blossoming with dark red streams of blood, too-deadly roses unfurling across her snow-white skin. "Ria."

"I need the purse," she managed to say, fingers fluttering. "Please, Conor – help me."

As gently as he could, Conor lowered Haisley's unconscious form to the ground, crawling toward where Riona wheezed, blood gushing from the wounds on her wrists. "Where is it," he gasped, reaching out to touch her too-pale face. "Ria, where is it? Let me help –"

"Pocket," she said, through ragged breaths. "In my pocket. Took it from him, right after."

Conor's fingers trembled as he searched her pockets, ignoring the crimson lakes untouched by silver spooling around him, seeping through his shirtsleeves, his breeches, deep into the ground. "Right after what, sweetheart?"

She opened her eyes, bleary and dull. "After I killed him."

"Good. He was a monster."

"Maybe." Her eyes fluttered shut again. "Me too, though."

"No." His hand closed around something small and leathery to the touch, tucked away in the pocket of her gown. "I should never have said that, Ria. I was wrong, I was so very wrong, I'm so sorry –"

"The purse," she said, barely a whisper. "Need it."

He pulled it from the soft folds of her cloak – a faded brown purse with three golden boars embossed on its side, against a canopy of pale blue and silver. "Here." He pressed it into the blood-soaked palm of her hand. "You'll be all right now. I found it. You'll be all right."

She let out a heavy sigh, her fingers slipping inside the purse. For an interminable moment, Conor was frozen in terror, watching as her breathing, then stilled, her body going limp and lifeless in his arms, and even as fresh sobs tore from his throat, a preternatural hush fell over the clearing.

A treacherous hope bloomed in his chest. "Ria."

Her eyes opened, and he knew something terrible, something

unnamable had happened in those fleeting moments where she had hovered there on the threshold between the worlds of the living and the dead. They were wrong, those beautiful bluebell eyes, no trace of their usual light, so clever and sly and full of laughter as they once were. "Ria," he said again, but she pushed herself upright with her elbows, and Conor's gaze fell to her wrists.

They were bloodstained yet clean, untouched by time or pain – no wounds, no scars from those long years of sacrificing and siphoning away her own lifeblood in exchange for their daughter's health and her happiness.

She was healed – from every hurt, every scar that had formerly marred her skin, and fear sank its icy bite deep down to his bones.

He knew before she spoke what she intended to say, because she had said it to him once before, with that same blank expression on her face.

"I have to go."

Conor staggered to his feet as she rose in a fluid motion, her gaze fixed on the ground. "Riona," he said unsteadily. "What happened?"

"I made another bargain." She moved away from him, closer to the entrance of the cave. "And now I must honor it."

"No." He leapt forward, seizing her wrists in his hands. "No. We had a plan –"

"The plan changed," she said simply, and he had never known desolation like this, bone-deep and throbbing through the core of his very being.

"Ria," he said again, because he understood now, the full weight of what she had sacrificed for the sake of their daughter – an eternity of darkness and shadow, a renunciation of all the joys that had once awaited her far across the star-studded sea. "You said there must always be a lord of death."

"No lord," she said. "Not any longer." A pause, deliberate yet brief. "But there *is* a lady, Conor."

"Please," he said, voice cracking with despair. "Please, no."

"There must be a balance," she said, gentler now. "One who must act as a bridge between the worlds, and I – I am the anchor for that bridge now."

He had not thought it possible for his heart to break within his chest again, not after she had shattered it so many years ago, but something in his chest splintered nonetheless at the set expression on her pale face, the tightness of her blood-red lips. "We lost you once before, Ria — Haisley and I, we won't do it again. *I* won't do it again, do you hear me?"

She looked at him then, the blue of her eyes fading, seeping down into the black of her pupils, and from far below their depths, he saw it – the faintest glimmer of a bright golden flame. "I'm sorry, Conor," she said simply, pulling herself free of his grip, grown slack with shock as he watched. "There was no other way."

"There is *always* another way."

"You said that to me before." She took a step backward. "You were wrong then too."

"Don't do this." He could not move, rooted to the ground, watching the girl whom he had loved for nearly all his life fading away in front of him. "This is not who you are. This is not who you were meant to be, this thing of darkness."

"It doesn't matter," she said, and it broke his heart all over again, the gentle certainty in her sing-song voice. "This is who I am now. I am the lady of death. You and I both know it."

"No."

"It's true. I have learned so much these last ten years. You were right, about balance, the scales between life and death, between light and shadow, between our world and theirs." The blue of her eyes flickered again, slowly, inexorably draining away. "And I am that balance now. It is my duty to serve as the bridge between the worlds, to stave off the devastation, the ruin that would occur if the doors between them were left unguarded." Riona let out a long sigh. "I cannot let that happen, Conor. I cannot."

"I don't care. I don't care about any of that." He cupped her face in his hands, urgent and trembling. "I only care about you." The last drops of blue vanished from her eyes, an incandescent mass of swirling shadows and fractured light. "We're a team," he said, almost savagely. "You promised me – we would do this *together*."

"We will – we already have, Conor. All this time, we have been working together, you and I, on our own paths, in our own ways – apart but not separate." She made a motion as though to reach out to him with her hand, then stopped, fingers curling in on themselves. "I understand that now, what I didn't before – we won't ever be apart, not truly. The sídhe is neither above nor below the earth, neither here nor there, only hidden from view – a bridge between the worlds." She smiled, and he could still see echoes of his Riona in that smile, the sad, soft-hearted girl she kept secreted away from everyone in the world but him. "We have been working together," she said again. "And look –" A gesture toward where Haisley slept, chest rising and falling in a peaceful rhythm. "Look at what a fine job we have done. There she is, safe and sound." Her smile slipped away. "But for every light, there must be a shadow. For every victory, there must be a loss – for every joy, there must be a sorrow."

"Don't." The word shattered as he spoke it, hanging in the air between them. "Don't leave me."

"I could never, not truly." A brief pause. "But it calls to me now, incessant and shrill, the binding of the sídhe, as it bound him for all those centuries. I have to go."

"But I only just found you again," he said, and for the briefest moment, she wavered, her face growing tender with wonder, with affection.

But then she shook her head, lips tight, and he bit back the desperate plea aching to be said. "This is my chance to set right all my wrongs," she whispered. "I have done so much wrong. Let me do this one thing right. Let me be who I was born to be."

"It's not right." He grew frantic, anguish clawing at his sorely beaten heart. "Nothing about this is right."

"It is," she said, as she pulled away, retreating toward the dark mouth of the cave. "That's why it hurts so much."

"I'll come after you." He almost spat out the words, fighting back the tears that were screaming to be set loose, to throw himself at her feet and wrap his arms around her knees, holding on for hours, for years, for all eternity, for however long it took for her to yield and finally, finally, at last stay with him. "I will find a way into Tech Duinn, and I will come after you, Ria."

"No, you won't. There is only one way in, and you will never risk her, Conor. We both know that." He swore silently, glancing at where Haisley slept on, unaware that her mother had sacrificed every last part of herself for her, again – again and again, in an unending cycle born to repeat itself until the end of time. "I left the sword and the cloak inside," she said, her back to him, head bowed. "I knew that you would try to use them, and well – it's better, that they not remain in the realm of mortals. Too dangerous, mixing divinity and humanity. Just look at the result." She gestured vaguely at herself.

"You have left me so many times." She stopped at that, her shoulders stiff underneath her cloak. "Sometimes for an hour, sometimes for weeks, sometimes for years, but I always waited for you, had faith that you would come back, and you have never once failed me." He paused. "Promise me that you will come back again, Ria. Promise me that you will find a way."

He waited during the silence that followed, the taste of hope bitter on his tongue, tea steeped for far too long with far too little honey, and when the rejection came, he almost keeled over from the weight of the blow.

"She will wake after you kiss her." Riona turned back to look at where Haisley lay, unconscious and dreaming, in the cool green grass, and he watched helplessly as that faintly burning flame buried deep within her eyes flared golden, shifting and changing and glowing unnaturally bright. "A kiss for life, instead of for death. It seemed fitting." She appeared to be drinking it in, the sight of Haisley's peaceful face, a dying soul desperate for one last drink from a cool mountain spring. "It's only a sleeping spell. I did not want to have to say –" Her voice broke off, and that unutterable tenderness overtook her face again, brief and poignant. It vanished, almost as quickly as it had come, and she returned her now-blazing gaze to him. "You told me that you had found a way to stave off her sickness. Make good on that promise for me, Conor. I will do what I can on my end, but I cannot interfere, if her harvest comes."

"Ria –"

"Take care of our daughter, Conor." She paused. "Although that goes without saying, I suppose. You are the most wonderful father.

I always knew you would be." She paused, and then it was gone, that brilliant blue of her eyes, only pure golden fire now, unearthly and luminous. "Oh Conor," she said softly. "Are you crying?"

He reached up, his fingertips brushing against wet cheeks. "I –I am."

She shook her head with a rueful smile as she backed into the mouth of the cave, the branches of the whitethorn tree slowly swallowing her whole. "I swear," she said, her fingers trailing along the bright green leaves of the nearby tree, a wordless farewell to the life she would never be allowed to live. "You really are *such* a cabbage."

Then she was gone, disappearing into a world into which he could never follow, and Conor was alone in the woods with his still-sleeping daughter, weeping for the girl he had loved and lost all over again.

This time, he knew, forever.

Epilogue

Shannagirah,
Éire, 1124

Conor stumbled over the gnarled root of a fir tree as he slowly climbed up the mountain side. No matter how old he became, he thought ruefully as the toe of his boot caught on the stiff wood of the tree root, he could not outgrow his clumsiness. He tripped forward, but before he fell, a hand caught him underneath his elbow.

"Easy, Da," Haisley said, pulling him to his feet. "There's no rush."

Conor smiled at his daughter, bright-eyed and straight-backed, healthy and blooming in the flowering of her womanhood. "I'm in no hurry, a chnó coill. I'm only old – feeble and short-sighted. We old men are clumsy by nature, don't you know."

"Don't blame it on your years. You've always been a bit of klutz."

He laughed softly. "True enough." He looked up the steep slope of the mountainside, inhaling the warm summer air. "Almost there."

"Da." Haisley slipped her hand into his, fingers squeezing gently, that old familiar gesture. "Are you certain about this?"

"I'm sure." Her grip tightened around his, and he turned his head to smile at her reassuringly. "It's time."

She nodded, and they climbed the rest of the way in silence, side by side, father and daughter, her copper-red curls mingling in the breeze with the thick white strands of his hair. It was a gorgeous day, golden sunlight in a cloudless blue sky, the hum of the wildlife rustling all around them as they made their way up the mountain, pausing only when they could see that slight swelling in the ground, the tight-knit circle of slender whitethorn trees, full and bright and bursting with their summer foliage.

Haisley glanced sideways at him, and he inclined his head in the direction of the moss-covered boulder outside the copse of trees, half-hidden beneath the shade of the thick branches looming overhead. "There."

She stood utterly still for a moment, and when he looked down at her, he saw a single tear slide down her cheek. "Och, a chnó coill," he said, reaching out to brush it away with the tip of his thumb. "Don't cry. You'll be all right. You have your mamaí and da to see to in their aging years, and Mac – as good of a man as I could have wished for you to find, that one is – and Kieran and Roisin, and all her littles –" Conor tapped her nose gently. "And there's the vale as well, yours to care for and to tend. You'll hardly even notice I'm gone."

"Da." She leaned her head against his shoulder, and she shuddered as more tears fell from her eyes, dripping down onto his time-weathered hand. "There won't be an hour I spend here in this life that I don't miss you."

Conor pressed his lips to the top of her head. "You're a good girl," he murmured. "The best girl." He tilted her chin up to face him with his forefinger. "Take care of yourself, now, do you hear? Check your blood often, and eat your greens, no matter how much you have a dislike for them. And enjoy your apple cake, as often as you like, but be smart about it now, and –"

"I know, Da."

"And the extract, the siliú – if ever something happens, if you run out and cannot make more, you come back here, all right, and call for me, and I'll –"

"Da." Haisley pressed her fingers against his lips, and he fell silent. "You've spent the years training two dozen apothecaries on how to make the siliú just so. They've been grilled on the subject relentlessly until all they do is dream of cow's blood and fenugreek." She smiled, wobbly but determined. "I can't come back here, Da. I won't."

He nodded through the thick lump that had risen in his throat. "I know." He swallowed, his eyes drifting to the waiting copse of trees. "I'm your father, though. It's my job to worry."

"You've worried enough." She stood on her tiptoes and pressed a kiss to his paper-thin cheek. "Go. Be happy, Da." She reached down and withdrew a small knife from her boot, then walked toward the looming gray boulder. She drew a deep breath, then pressed the blade into the middle of her palm.

A well of crimson, then there, swirling in the middle of a pool of red, three shining silver drops, and Haisley bent down and pressed her palm flat against the rock.

The boulder shivered once, then splintered down the middle, and a rush of night-cold air poured forth from the hidden realm of Tech Duinn.

Haisley stepped back, lips trembling, and Conor watched as his daughter smiled one last time at him. "I love you, Da," she said, her voice cracking.

"Haisley." He touched his fingertips to his lips and blew her a silent kiss. "You were the greatest joy of my life, from the moment you were born into my arms. I have no regrets."

She nodded, then looked down at her hands, wringing them together. "Tell her…tell her that I say thank you, for saving me." Her throat jumped. "Both times."

"I will."

She exhaled shakily, then turned and walked a little way down the mountain. Conor rested his back against the trunk of white birch, and waited.

She did not keep him waiting long.

Conor knew when she arrived, that half-forgotten prickling of awareness tingling at the back of his neck, the faint scent of cinnamon and silverweed wafting toward him. "Conor, you fool," he heard that singsong voice scold from the hidden depths of the other-realm. "What, in the name of the sídhe, are you doing?"

"I thought I'd try and be a step ahead of you, just this once," he said, stepping forward to the dark yawning void. "I'm dying."

There was a beat of silence, and then there she was, pulling the cloak of darkness from her shoulders as she came forward, clad in pink-rose silk and satin slippers, raven-wing hair and blood-red lips and lily-white skin. His heart seized in his chest. She was still the most beautiful thing he'd ever seen, even now with the golden-fire blaze of her eyes that latched onto him with an expression of unmistakable annoyance.

"Nonsense," she said, hands on her hips. "You've got at least another year or two in you. I should know. I check on you often enough."

"And here I was worrying you'd forgotten all about me."

"I cannot even forget about a troublesome pebble in my shoe, much less something as irritating as you." She looked him up and down, her brow furrowing. "Though I hardly recognize you, cabbage. For the gods' sakes, can none of your precious weeds be used as tonics? Look at all those wrinkles."

"You now," he said, edging closer toward her. "You still look divine, Ria."

"You told me that I looked like a wildflower."

"That was my second impression." He took another slow step. "My first thought was that you were a goddess come down from the sky to whisk me away to the land of undying youth."

She gestured behind her, toward the waiting darkness of the other-realm. "And you see now that you could not have been more wrong about that."

"Ria." He was so close now that he could see the slight flare of his nostrils when he whispered her name. "I was so very wrong about so many things. We both know that."

The golden light in her eyes dimmed for a moment, and he could almost see it, that deep-buried hue of bluebells in the spring. Then she glanced away from him, over his shoulder, and froze. "Conor."

"She's there." Conor watched the myriad of emotions flashing across her face. "She brought me here, used her blood to call you forth."

She was trembling, pale-faced and scared, the dread queen of Tech Duinn, the lady of death. "Is she – is she happy?"

"Have you not looked in on her at all, Ria? All this time?"

Riona was silent for a long moment, staring at him. "I was too afraid," she said at last. "I have made my peace with my choice, but it is a fragile one – too fragile, to be able to see her and not allow regret to break what little is left of my unbroken heart."

It was a searing ache within him, that longing to thread his fingers through her own, to pull her close and feel the steady beat of her heart in time with his own, but he knew that even if he did, there would be nothing there, only the thundering silence of a pulse long gone cold within her withered veins. "She is very happy, Ria," he said instead, and Riona's eyes darted back to his face, and he smiled, encouraging and gentle. "She married a good man with a good heart, has children and grandchildren of her own, that Kayleigh, Páidí and I have made it our mission in our final years to spoil as thoroughly as possible." She smiled at that, tremulous and soft, and the ache in his chest eased at the sight of it. "A happy life, Ria. A very happy life you have gifted her."

"A long life," Riona countered. "That is what you gifted her – how clever of you, Conor."

"Well, I had help, don't you know." He paused. "She is the queen of the vale, Riona, every bit as regal and good-hearted as her mother before her."

Her gaze dropped away from his. "I was never very good at matters of the heart."

"I disagree."

Her blood-red lips twitched. "Well," she said. "What do you know, you thick-headed cabbage."

Something soft and sweet, a pale purple blossom of hope, unfurled in his chest. "Ria," he said. "I was hoping that you would do what you always used to do, when we were young, and be a rebel, a rule-breaker again, and steal an ill-begotten soul for me."

She looked up, her eyes narrowing. "What do you mean?"

"I'd like to come home, Ria." He rubbed his chin, his nerves suddenly on edge as he prepared to say what he had come here to ask. "I'd like to come home to you now."

Riona was perfectly still, watching him, as though even the summer breeze dared not caress the strands of her midnight-black hair without her consent. "This is not your home, Conor," she said at last. "You were meant for more than this."

"So were you." He shrugged. "And yet here we are." The wind hummed all around him, warm gusts of air swirling through the bright green leaves, nipping at the hem of her long silk skirt. "I know what I am asking, Ria. I've thought about it for a long time, and this is what I want. I have missed you," he said, stuttering a little as he spoke, and it was surely there now, that glimmer of blue shining underneath all those layers of golden flames. "I have missed you every day for over fifty years, since that first night you left me standing in the rain, to save our daughter. I have longed for you ever since, staring out into the endless dark of the night sky, wondering if you were somewhere standing beneath it too, looking up at those very same stars, aching with the missing of me as I was for you." She looked away from him, the muscles in her throat jumping erratically, and he knew he had his answer. "I know now that it was not the same, the sky and the stars that I lived under for all those years and the ones you walk underneath, but I want them to be, Ria. I cannot bear to spend another hour in any other world than the one in which you exist, no matter how dark it may be."

"You would give up Magh Meall?" She asked, her fingers stroking the rose-pink silk of her skirt absently. "You would sacrifice all its delights, the joys of eternal youth in the realm of undying bliss, for the evils that prowl within my woods?"

He was quiet for a moment, studying the stiff line of her shoulders, the nervous movements of her fingers. "Ria," he said in a soft voice. "Do you remember that day in the mountains, the day that we saw the bean-sí?"

"I could hardly forget it."

"Do you remember what you asked me, about the wild hemlock that grows in the forests?"

Her golden eyes cut to his. "The balance, between life and death."

"That's right." He moved a step closer. "Even as a young boy, I knew that death is as natural a part of life as anything else. It is not a fearful thing, not when it provides that much-needed balance."

"For every light," she said. "There must be a shadow."

"Exactly." He shrugged ruefully. "But I am old now, Ria. I do not fear the darkness that waits inside your realm, because I know that the opposite is true as well. Where there is darkness, there must be light, and I think that you are that light, Ria, and I am willing to spend all of eternity basking in your glow, if you'll let me."

There was a distinctly blue sheen lurking within the fiery gold of her eyes now. "I don't know that I can make you young again," she said at last, and his hands fisted in excitement at his side.

"Then I shall stay old forever."

"That's quite a risk, Conor."

"Well," he said. "You have been telling me for years not to be such a cabbage, and here I am, trying to be brave, for you, Ria."

She almost smiled at that. "There is so much pain there, within my woods. It is not a place of bliss, Conor."

"Neither of us ever knew much happiness in our mortal lives. Why start now?"

"You are very persistent."

"Ria." He reached out to brush her fingers with his own. "I have already spent a lifetime apart from you. Do not force me to spend an eternity away from you as well."

Her palm slid against his. "If you annoy me," she said, "know that I will feed you to Fiadh."

"I still do not know who that is, but I shall hazard a guess that she is quite fearsome." There it was, a full-fledged smile, and he rested his forehead against hers. "Ria," he whispered. "Please. I want to go home."

She closed her eyes for a moment, and when they opened again, he was drowning in a sea of blue-golden waves. "Come on then," she said, and pressed her hand against his chest, murmuring something low and muffled underneath her breath.

Then he was gone, flying through the cloud-swept sky, a rush of gray and pale blue smoke searing his eyes, lightheaded as he soared across the vast expanse of a bottomless world. Darkness exploded around him, a thousand silver stars embedded like frozen dew-drops in the midnight sky. He stumbled forward onto his knees, his fingers sinking into the ice-crusted soil of a winter-frosted earth.

He raised his hands, strong and free of wrinkles, up to his head, to feel the forgotten spring of thick, wild curls.

"Cabbage."

He turned and there she was, pale face illuminated against the silver glow of the endless night sky, smiling at him with rose-red lips, the girl he had loved, the woman he had lost, the goddess she had become.

"Welcome home."

THE END

Author's Note

Dear Reader,

Almost nine years ago, I sat sleepless through the worst night of my life. It's not a night that I choose to relive very often: my then one-year-old daughter was diagnosed with Type 1 diabetes, a disease in which, for reasons that are still unclear, the pancreas stops producing insulin, and in turn the body goes into DKA (diabetic ketoacidosis). She was so little when she was diagnosed that it was hard to recognize the signs of her body shutting down – increased thirst and urination, lethargy, weight loss, etc. When we finally realized how very sick she was and rushed her to the hospital, her blood sugar was dangerously high.

We almost lost her.

I remember sitting by her bed throughout that long, dark night, beside myself with fear and grief and so much guilt – I'm her mother, I kept thinking, I should have known, I should have stopped this, I should have saved her – silently begging someone, anyone to help my girl, be it god, devil or both, I didn't care. Very Faustian, I know, but I was ready to pay whatever price asked of me to keep her safe.

I was thinking about it again, years later, driving home from soccer practice as she chattered away in the back seat. I thought about how happy she was playing with her friends, with me, how each day she finds joy in the littlest things in life, how bright and funny and kind of a person she is becoming, how this lifelong burden that the universe has put on her little shoulders could have turned her bitter and resentful, and instead made her generous and wise beyond her years. Her pancreas might be broken, but there's not a damn thing wrong with her heart, and if a mysterious figure ever does appear on my doorstep, demanding my soul to make good on that bargain, I'll hand it over without a qualm. It was worth it.

That's when it occurred to me – the idea for this book, or at least the fundamental query of it. How far, exactly, would a mother be willing to go for her child? Would she doom herself? Would she watch cities burn and kingdoms fall without batting an eye, so long as her child was kept safe and warm? What monsters would we become, as mothers, in defense of these beautiful, bright creations which we have born from our bodies?

Yes, I thought. We would – a thousand times yes, we would, even if it meant our own damnation.

And so Riona was born, a woman far more like me than I like to admit – not a terrible person, but not a wholly good one either, too selfish and stubborn to be truly virtuous. She is a reluctant mother, as I was, most of that reticence springing from a secret, nagging voice in our heads always whispering that we will never be good enough, that we will inevitably fail this, the greatest challenge which we will ever undertake. The rest of it unfurled more spontaneously – I'd always loved the Irish fable of the young prince who killed a crow and then inexplicably looked at the carnage lying there in the snow and thought to himself, 'Well wouldn't that make a lovely wife.' I wove the threads of that tale into much of the convoluted and oftentimes contradictory mythology of the character known as Donn, the lord of death, in Irish mythology, as well as much of the fascinating lore the ancient Celts believed about the nature of the afterlife and the other-realms of the sídhe, and an entirely new story was born – one of shadow-monsters and blood-magic (inspired by the unceasing routine of 'taking' my daughter's blood in order to ensure her health) and the uncertain line between legend and truth, as well as, most significantly, the unmeasurable depth of parental love.

Also important to note — there are many references to the existence of T1D in ancient times; the Egyptians reference it, describing it as a disease marked by excessive urination and weight-loss, and prescribed a whole grain diet to reduce symptoms; the Greeks also mention it, and correctly name the pancreas as the culprit, the failure of which organ is directly related to the onset of the disease; most notably, scholars in ancient China and India also have written about the disease, with doctors in India actually learning to have ants test the sweetness in a suspected diabetic's urine in order to evaluate their condition. Scholars in China and India both learned enough to distinguish between T1D and T2D. There have been a variety of treatments prescribed by doctors and scholars across many different cultures – dietary restrictions, frequent horseback riding, rancid animal meat, and mixtures of herbs, such as fenugreek and wormseed.

However, a diagnosis of T1D was a death sentence for any afflicted, usually with a 1-2 year life expectancy, until 1922, when Dr. Frederick Banting and Charles Best, along with J.B. Collip and John Macleod, building on the research done by German researchers Oskar Minkowski and Joseph von Mering and British scientist Sir Edward Albert Sharpey-Shafer, successfully injected a dying fourteen-year-old boy – Leonard Thompson – with an extract developed from cow's blood.

Within twenty-four hours, the boy's sky-high glucose levels had returned to nearly normal ranges, and from that day on, millions of lives that otherwise would have been lost — including my own daughter's — were saved.

I have combined several elements of all of these brilliant scholars and scientists in developing Conor's explanation of his "discovery" of siliú, but it by no means undermines the extraordinary, real-life achievements that were made by all of these thinkers and researchers, from 1552 BCE to 1922AD, and even to this day, as we still continue to study and learn more about this dangerous disease in order to one day find a complete and total cure.

At times, this book was an incredibly hard story to write, deeply personal and filled with painful memories, but nevertheless one that I was determined to tell in the hopes that this story might one day bring solace to other parents, especially mothers, knowing that their sacrifices, their ceaseless labor, no matter how invisible and alone that they might feel, is not in vain, and never unseen.

Best,

Christy

Acknowledgments

I have so many people to thank here, and it feels impossible for my words to do justice to the gratitude and love that I feel for everyone who has supported me on this journey.

First, thank you to my incredible and talented cover designer, Marta Dec, who designed the most beautiful and thoughtful cover for this book that is so personal and close to my heart. Thank you also to my wonderful editor, Danai Christopoulou, for all her enthusiasm and insight for this book — I am forever grateful for your wisdom and hard work!

Thank you to my amazing fellow authors who have supported and encouraged me in this journey — especially Jill Tew and Eliza Chan — and for my incredible beta-readers who gave me their invaluable insights when this book was in its very early stages — Nicole , Hannah, Cara, Morgan, and one more, my dear friend Eliza. I appreciate and love all of you so much! And of course, a very special shout-out to my beloved friends and writers, Sarah and Serene, who have been my unwavering and most loyal cheerleaders, critique partners, does-this-look-okay-sounding-boards, and ride-or-die-writing-besties for so many years now. I adore you and our wildly hilarious and unhinged group thread more than you'll ever know.

All my love and thanks to my dear friends and mom-village who keep me afloat and smiling even in our shared madness of soccer practices, stomach bugs, work deadlines, and all the other chaos that comes with being a parent in the twenty-first century — Lauren and Sarah and Sydney, Melissa and Anna and Wilson, and my aspirational-communal-living, meet-for-drinks-in-ten-minutes, gossipers-in-crime, Briana and Courtney — I love and value all of you to the moon and back, and can't imagine doing any of this without you.

To Tessie, my best friend and the sister of my heart — I'll never be able to express enough how much your friendship means to me. You are the best person I've ever known, and I would burn the world down for you in a heartbeat if you ever needed it, because if you said it must be done, I trust your judgment implicitly. You are kind, generous, and incredibly empathetic to everyone around you, and every day, I wake up and strive to be more like you. I love you dearly.

To my family — my mom, my dad, and especially my brothers, the built-in best friends that I've loved my whole life — thanks for always cheering me on and supporting me, both when I was just a kid, scribbling stories with my notepad and pencil, dreaming of the day that I'd be a real author, and now, when that dream has finally come true. I love you all so much, and am forever grateful that the universe decided to combine all of our chaos and craziness into one beautiful, sometime messy, but always beloved family.

Joey, there are so many things to thank you for — our beautiful home and our crazy, wild, wonderful life, how you always make me laugh and have always loved me unconditionally and unwaveringly, even in my very worst moments, for being my friend and my lover and the rock on which I lean when everything feels as though it's spinning out of control — but for this book, it seems appropriate to thank you especially for being the most amazing and loving father to our children. Parenting is the hardest challenge we've ever undertaken, but I am forever grateful that I have you on my team to balance out my bad days when I feel like I'm failing at that task, and to show our children every day what a good and kind man looks like. Thank you for being the kind of dad I always knew I wanted my kids to have. I love you so so much.

To my children, I dedicate this book to you, so that you always know how deeply, profoundly, unshakably I love you — and have loved you, ever since I first felt the faintest flickers of your existence. Then I loved the idea of you — what you might look like and who you might be — but now that I know you, I love you for YOU, your smiles and your quirks and your big, beautiful personalities. I hope that one day when you are grown and look back at your childhoods, you remember these days, so bright and carefree and fleeting, and that you know that they were the best days of my life, even when I was exhausted or grumpy or stressed. The four of you will always be my very best things, and I love you endlessly and always, no matter what.

Lastly, to my readers — thank you thank you for loving my books. This has truly been a lifelong dream of mine, and to know that there are people in the world whom I have never met and likely will never meet who my writing has brought some measure of the happiness which I have been gifted from books for so many years is such a mind-blowing and humbling concept. I am so grateful for your support and your kind words — none of this happens without you. So thank you, dear reader!

Pronunciation Guide

The pronunciation of Irish words often depends on the region/mood/intention of the speaker. This is my best rendering of the terms used in the text, but there will be differentiations among Irish speakers according to the factors listed above. Also, some of the words are used in their archaic forms, and that can affect pronunciation as well. So please consider this merely a helpful starting point and remember the most important thing is to enjoy the tale.

Names:
Riona – REE-uh-nah
Connacht – KAH-nuhkt
Ó Conchúir – OH KON-coo-err
Ó Ruairc – OH ROH-reek
Fiadh – FEE-ah
Mamó – MAH-moh
Aisling – AHSH-leeng
Mamaí – MAH-mee
Daideo – DA-doh
Maeve – MAY-uvh
Amergin – ah-MERH-jin
Eabha – EH-vah

Ellén Trechend – ill-AIN trekh-end

Áine – OH-nyah
  Niamh – NEE-vuh
  Ériu – AIR-u
  Finnevara – fin-YEE-ver-uh
  Bricriu — BRY-crow
  Páidí – PAW-dee
  Cú Roí – coo-ROO-ee
  Aillén – AY-lin
  Dagda – DAHG-duh
  Cúchulainn – KOO-koo-lane
  Fomorian – FOH-moh-ree-an
  Lugh – LOOG
  Mórrígan– MOR-i-gin
  Nuada – NOO-ah-duh
  Midir – MEE-deer
  Étaín – EH-teen
  Fúamnach – FOO-ah-mah-nah
  Aodh – AH-yuh
  Goibinu – GO-ree-new
  Manannán mac Lir – Mahn-ah-nahn mahk LEER

  Places:
  Éire – AY-ruh
  Inagh – EYE-nuh
  Tír Sogháin – TEAR sah-in
  Tech Duinn –Tach-DOON
  Ráth Crúachan – RAH-crow-AN

Leinster – LEN-stir
Grafadh Mór – Graffa MOR

Emain Ablach – EE-vawn AH-blahnk

Tír na mBan – TEER-nah-vhan
  Tír na nÓg – TEER-nah-nohg
  Tír na mBeo – TEER-nah-mee-VUH
  Mil Espaine – meel-ISH-pain
  Cnoc na Teamhrach – knuck-NAH-tah-RAWk
  Cnoc Meadh – knuck-MEH-uv
  Maigh Eo – MAY-oh

Terms:
Tuatha Dé Danann – TOO-ah DAYDAH-non
a stóirín – UHN-stor-EEN

folaíocht– FOH-ley-oh-sat
  cat-sìth —KAT-shee
  fear-dearg – FAY-er DARE-ig
  a chnó coill – UHN-noh-KILL
  mo bhanríon – MOH BAHN-ree-on
  curadmír – KUH-reh-dree
  connemara – CON-eh-MAH-rah
   druidecht – DREE-druh
  claíomh solais – klee-UVH soh-LUHSUH
  féth fíada – feh-FEE ah-DEH
  Gáe-Bolg – GUY-bohl-guh
  Aithníonn ciaróg, ciaróg eile – AH-tin-yown KEE-roh-geh,

KEE-roh-geh eh-LAY
   iomáint – um-AW-nick
   brèagha –BREE-yah
   fidchell – FI-key-ell
   púca – POO-kah
   bean-sí – BAN-shee
   sídhe – SHEE
   dobhar-chú – DOOR-who
   sluag – SLOO-ah

Helpful Links / Resources:

https://www3.smo.uhi.ac.uk/gaeilge/donncha/focal/features/irishs
p.html
https://www.scoilgaeilge.org/lessons/fuaimniu.htm
https://www.teanglann.ie/en/

About the Author

Christy Healy is the author of the adult fantasy novels, *Unbound* and *Unseen,* and their upcoming companion novel, *Undying* (2026). She has been a lifelong reader and writer, weaving stories of her own into the myths and tales of the Celtic, Indo-European, and Greco-Roman worlds that she has loved for so long. She lives in North Carolina with her children, her dog, and her husband.

Follow me on Instagram @christyhealywrites for more updates, or check out my website: christyhealy.com

Also by

www.ingramcontent.com/pod-product-compliance
Lightning Source LLC
Chambersburg PA
CBHW071727110726
47908CB00006B/1529